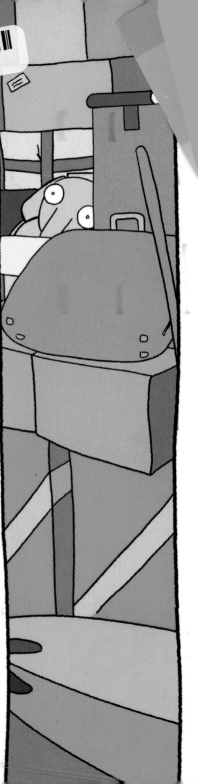

THE ODDS

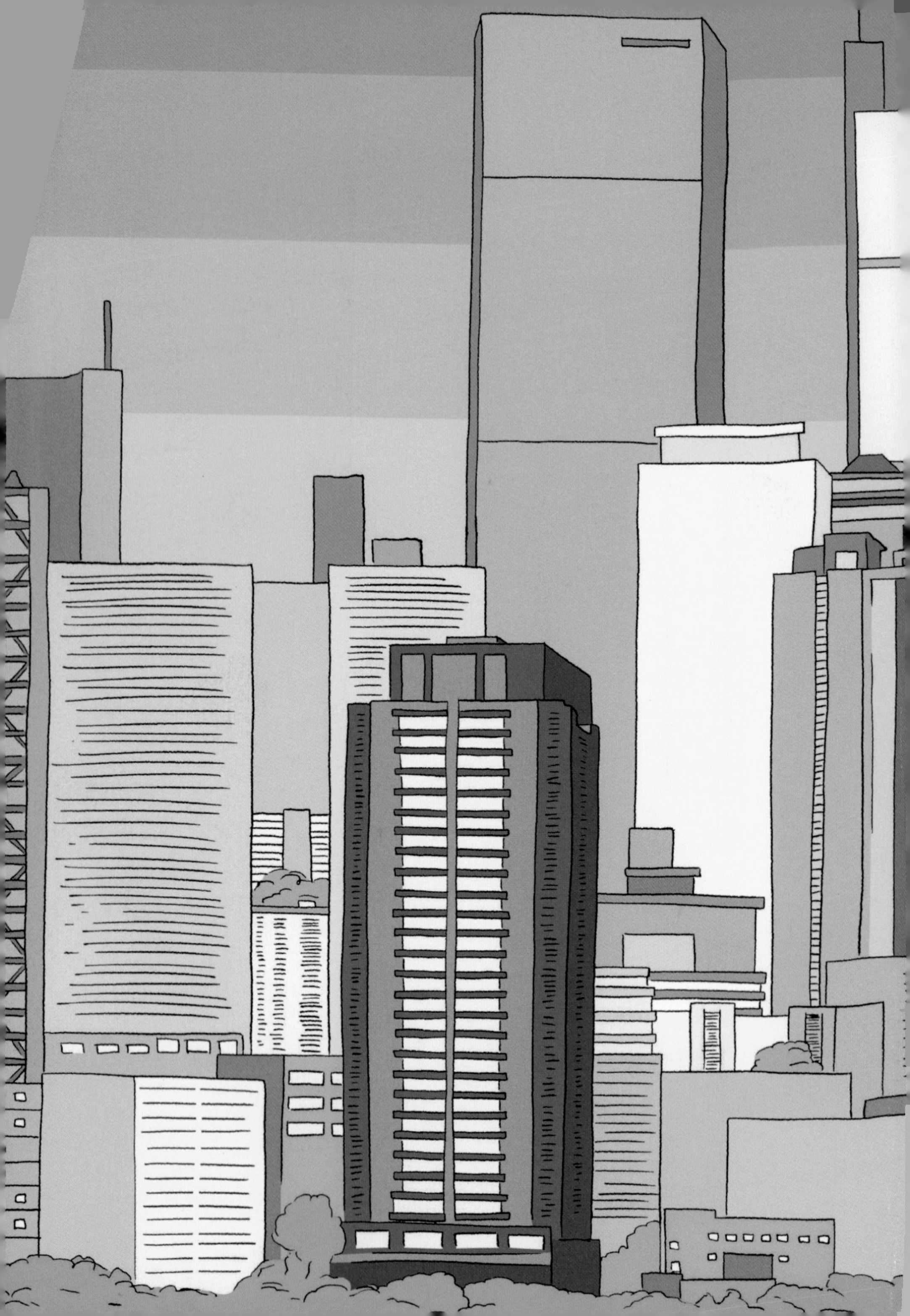

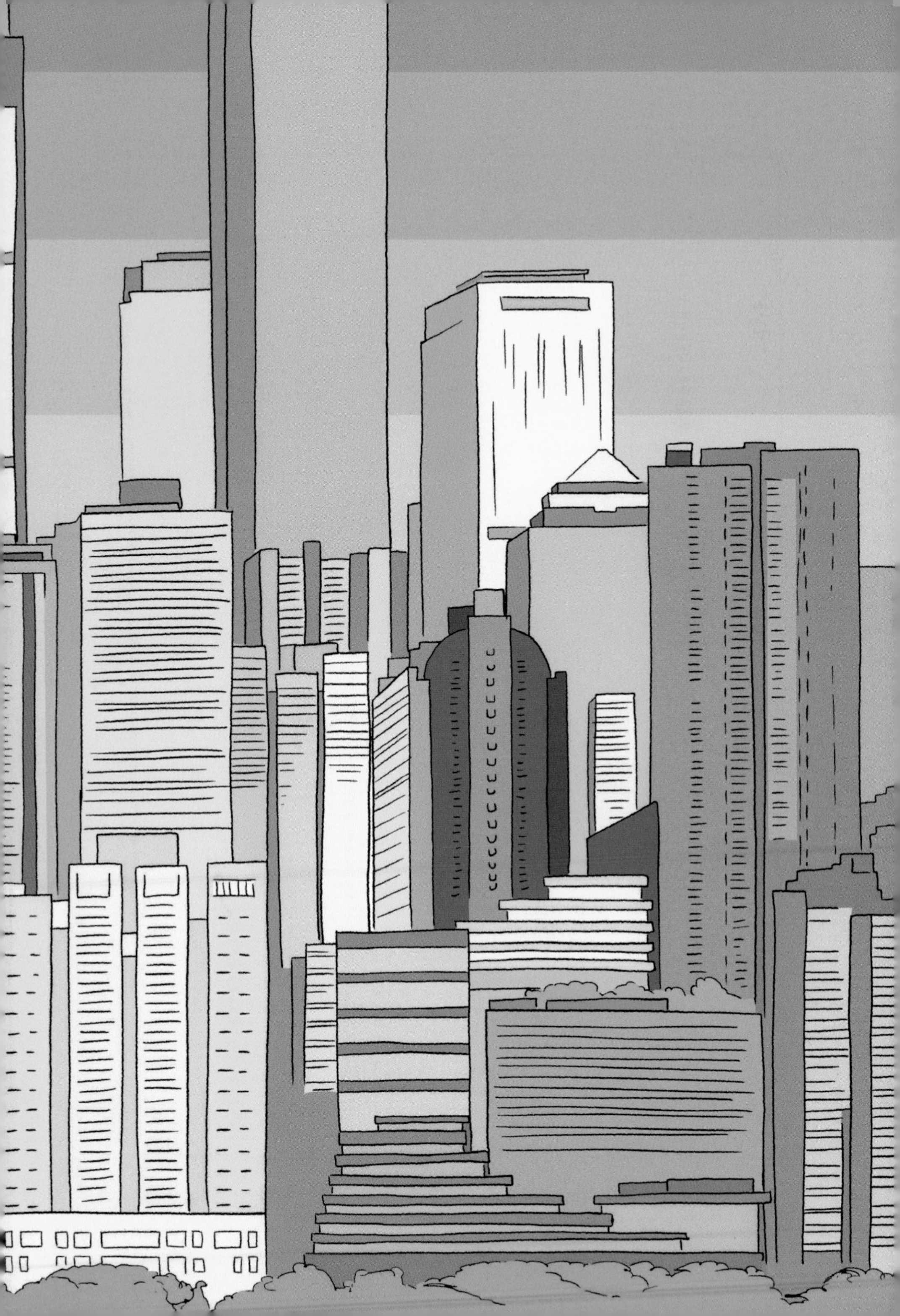

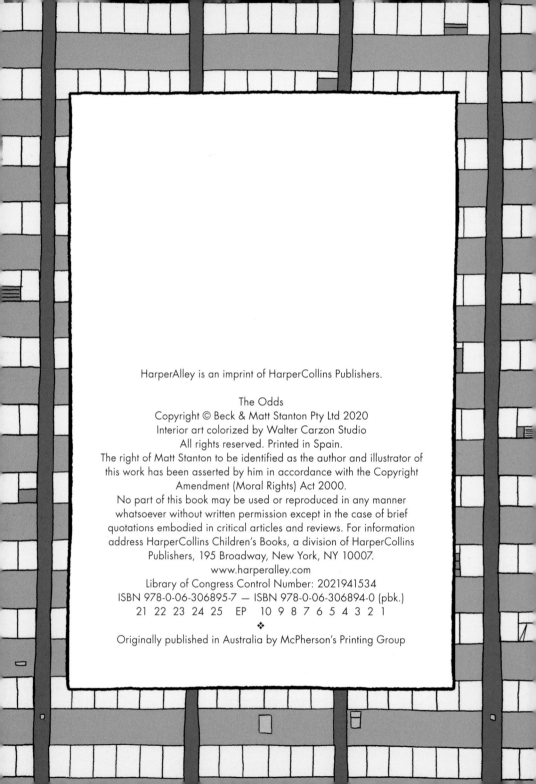

HarperAlley is an imprint of HarperCollins Publishers.

The Odds
Copyright © Beck & Matt Stanton Pty Ltd 2020
Interior art colorized by Walter Carzon Studio
All rights reserved. Printed in Spain.
The right of Matt Stanton to be identified as the author and illustrator of
this work has been asserted by him in accordance with the Copyright
Amendment (Moral Rights) Act 2000.
No part of this book may be used or reproduced in any manner
whatsoever without written permission except in the case of brief
quotations embodied in critical articles and reviews. For information
address HarperCollins Children's Books, a division of HarperCollins
Publishers, 195 Broadway, New York, NY 10007.
www.harperalley.com
Library of Congress Control Number: 2021941534
ISBN 978-0-06-306895-7 — ISBN 978-0-06-306894-0 (pbk.)
21 22 23 24 25   EP   10 9 8 7 6 5 4 3 2 1
❖
Originally published in Australia by McPherson's Printing Group

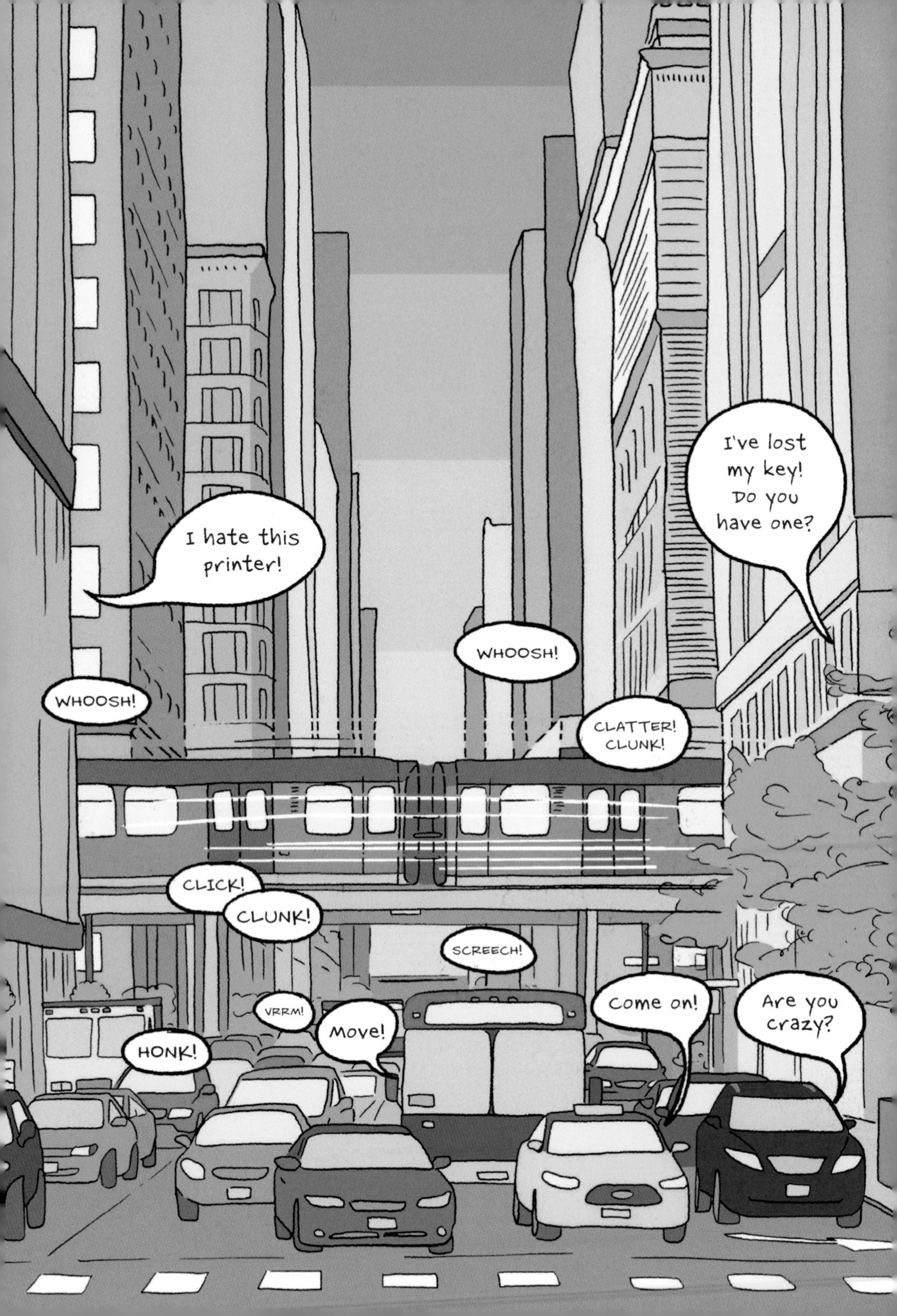
I hate this printer!
I've lost my key! Do you have one?
WHOOSH!
WHOOSH!
CLATTER! CLUNK!
CLICK!
CLUNK!
SCREECH!
VRRM!
HONK!
Move!
Come on!
Are you crazy?

For Beck

Thank you for seeing me, knowing me, and loving me.

Dreaming with you is my favorite place.

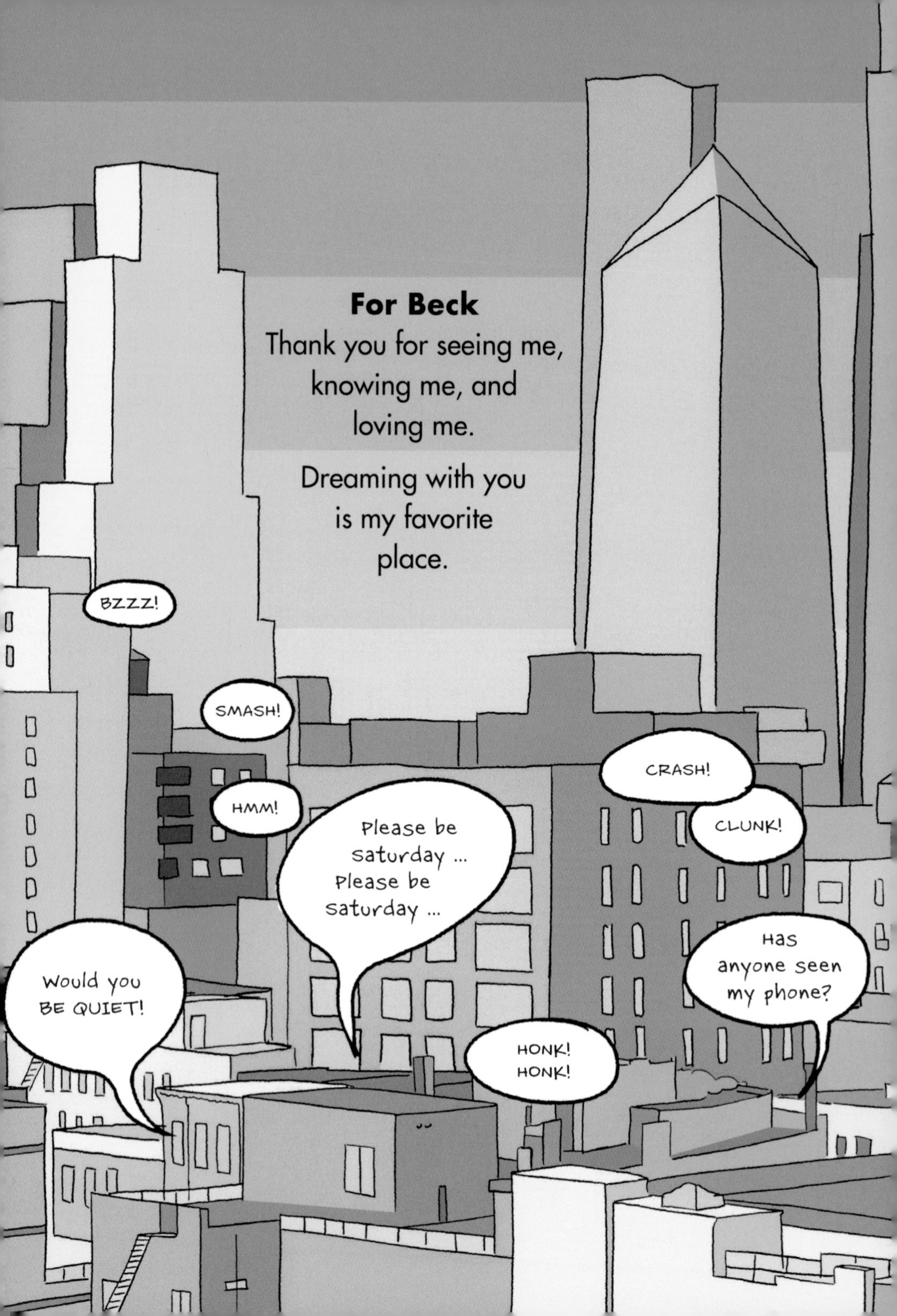
BZZZ!
SMASH!
HMM!
CRASH!
CLUNK!
Please be saturday ... Please be saturday ...
Would you BE QUIET!
Has anyone seen my phone?
HONK! HONK!

THE ODDS

words and pictures by

Matt Stanton

An Imprint of HarperCollinsPublishers

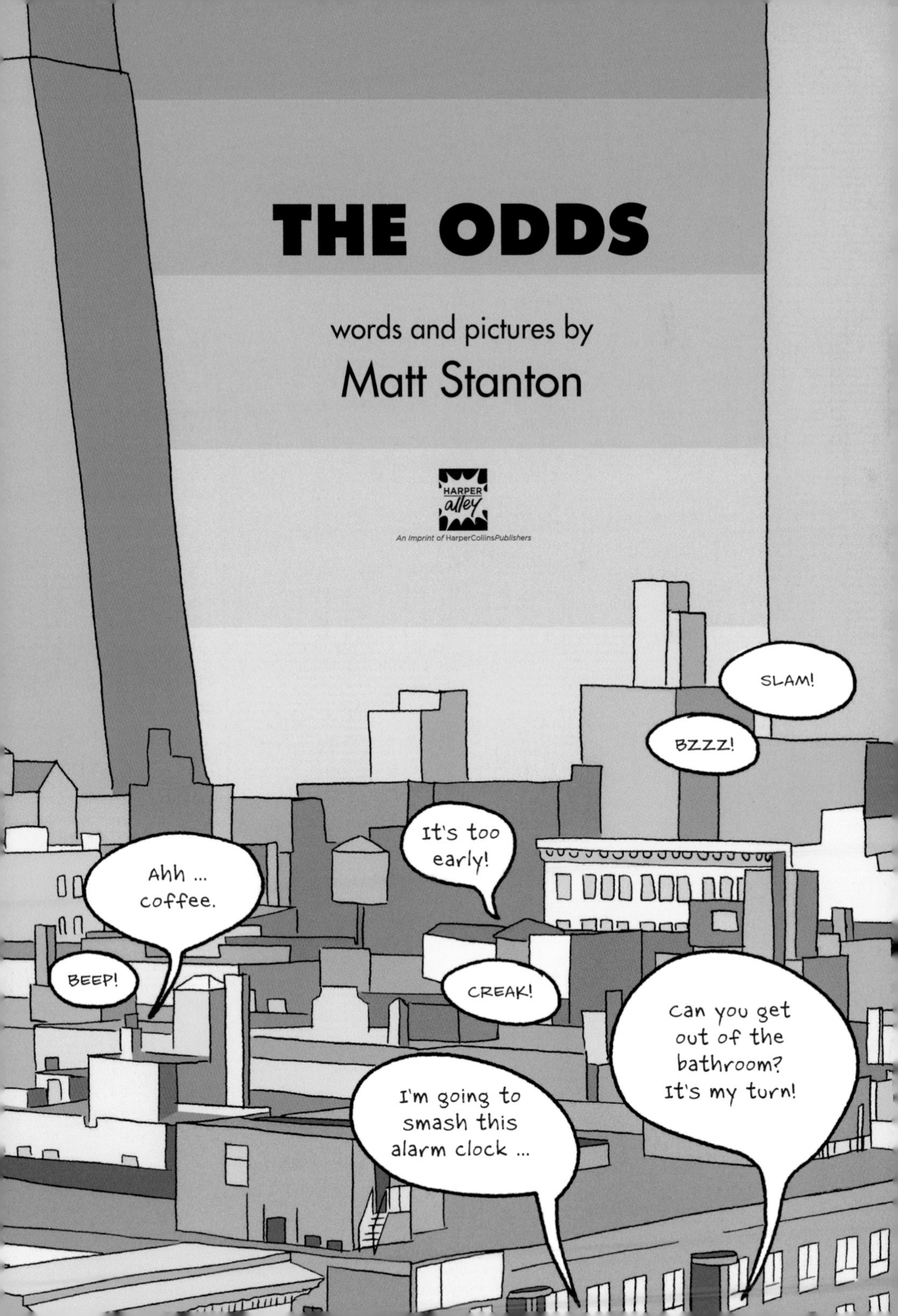
SLAM!
BZZZ!
It's too early!
Ahh ... coffee.
BEEP!
CREAK!
Can you get out of the bathroom? It's my turn!
I'm going to smash this alarm clock ...

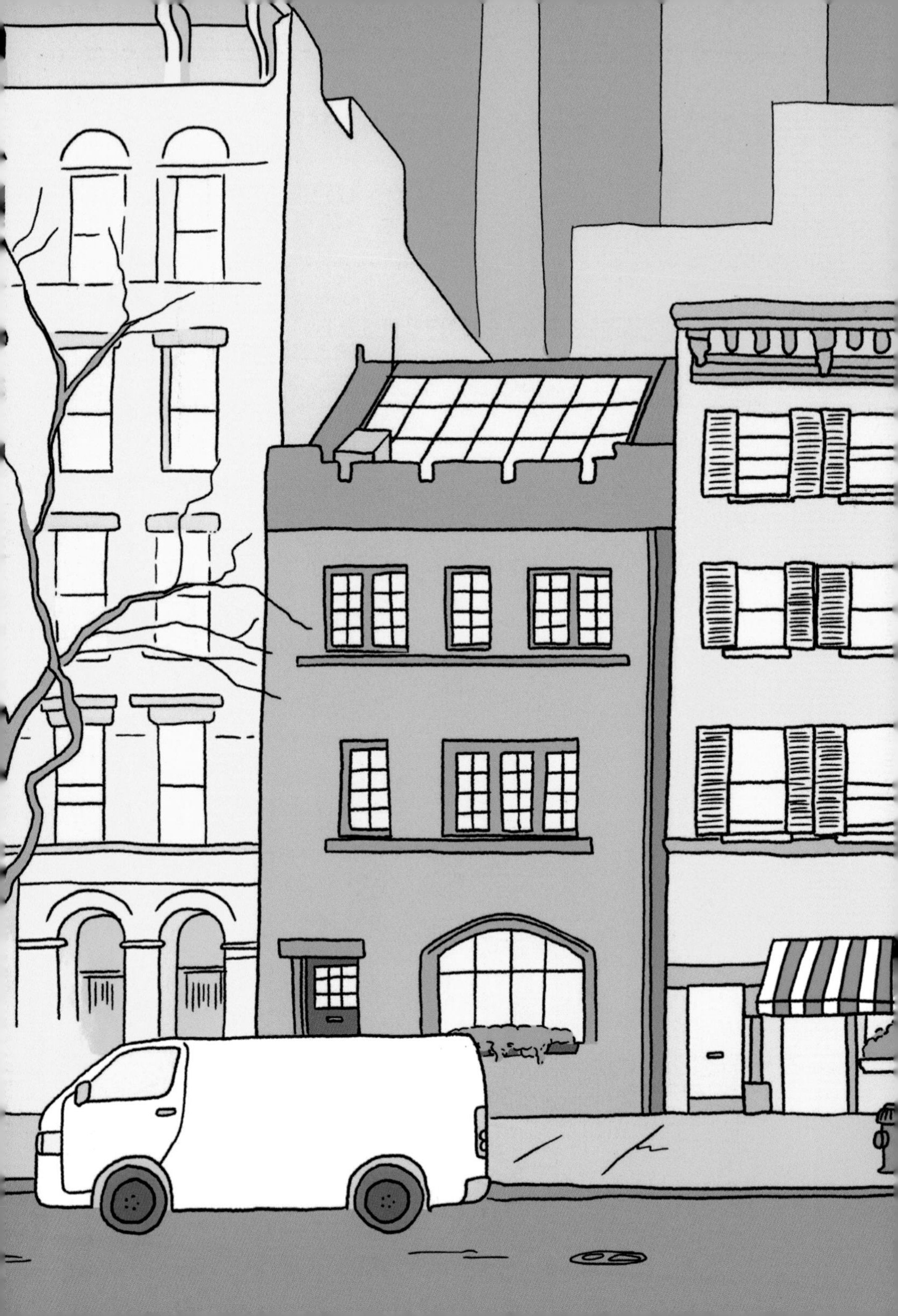

CHAPTER ONE
The Odds arrive uninvited

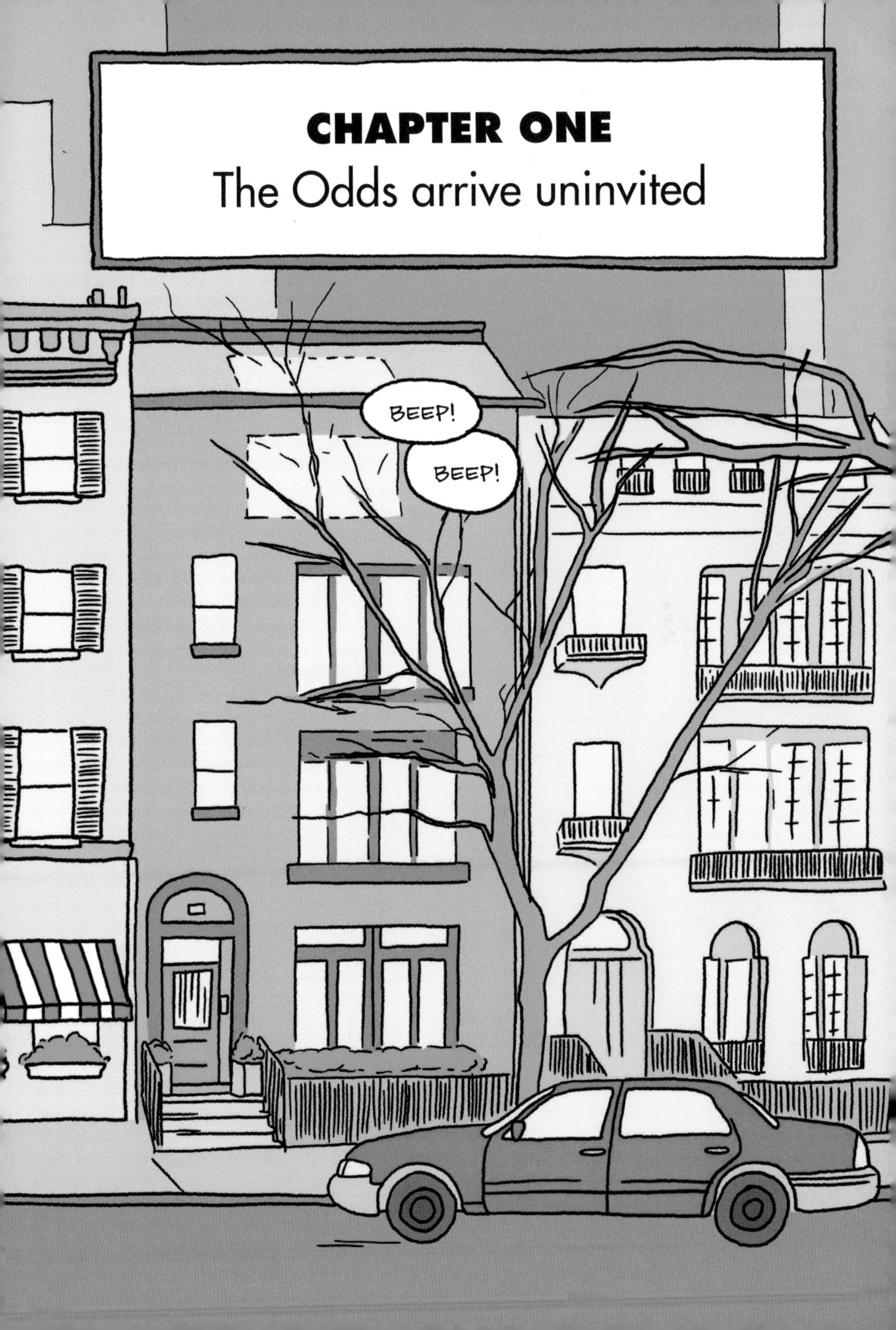
BEEP!
BEEP!

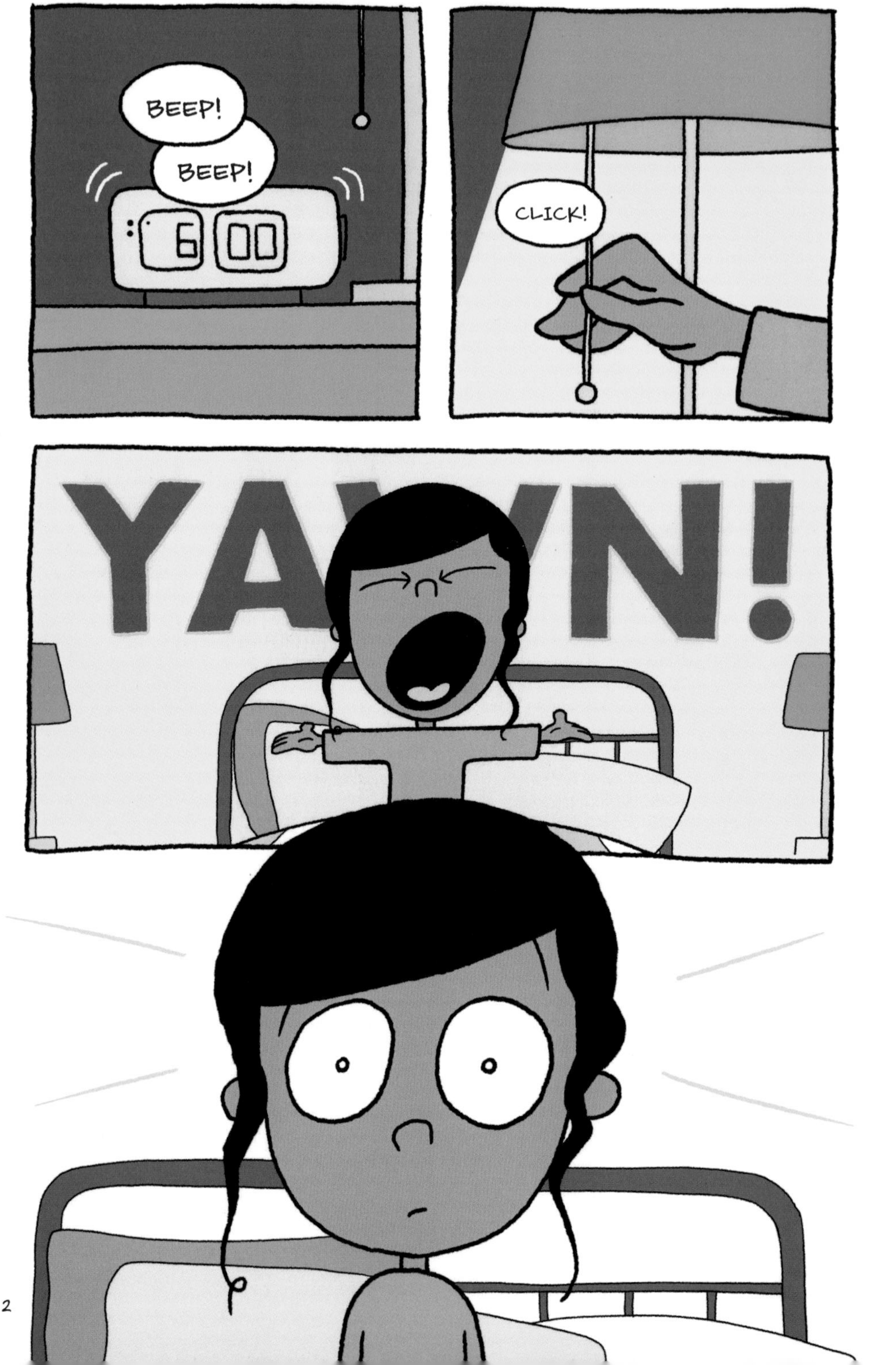
BEEP!
BEEP!
6:00
CLICK!
YAWN!

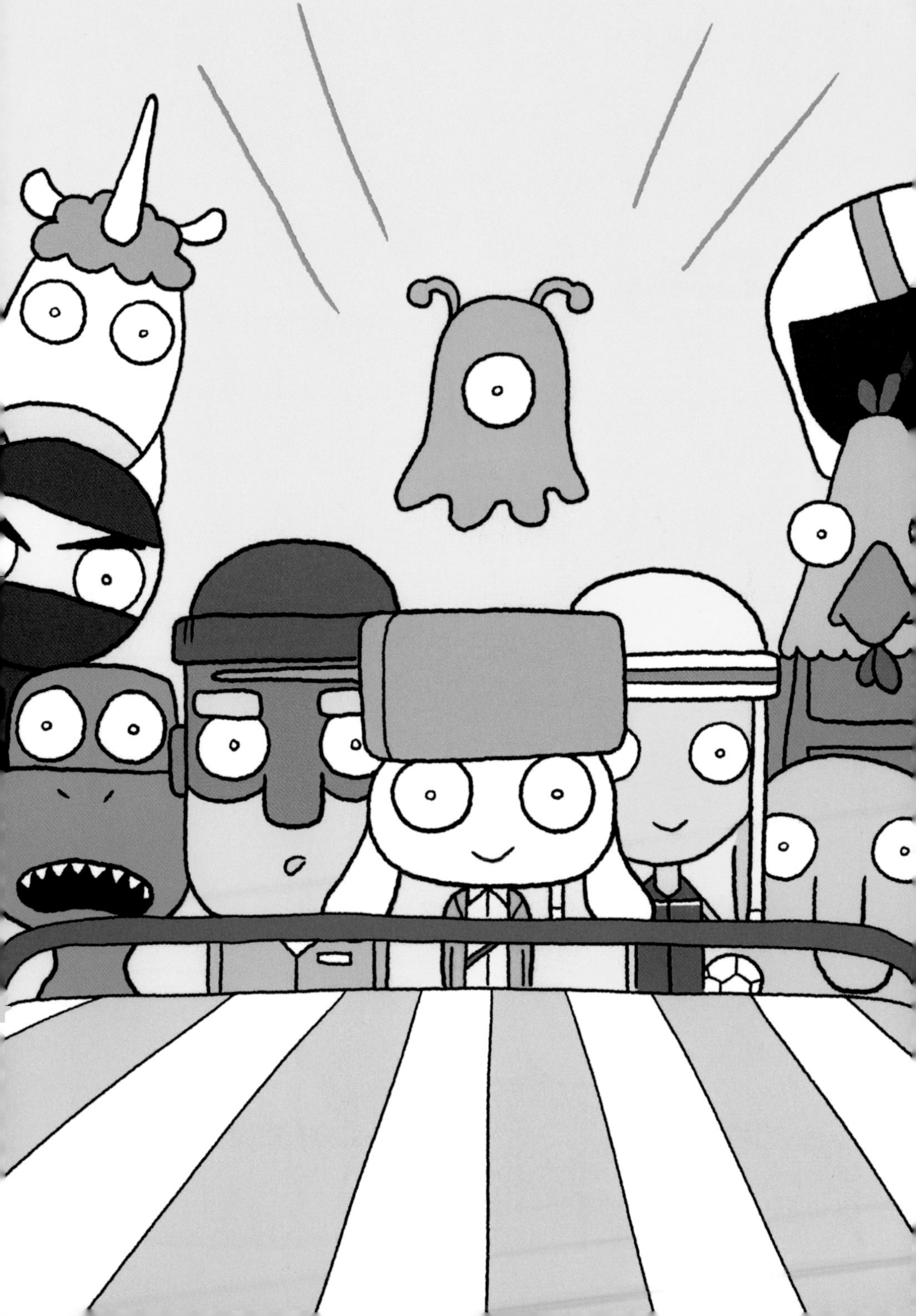

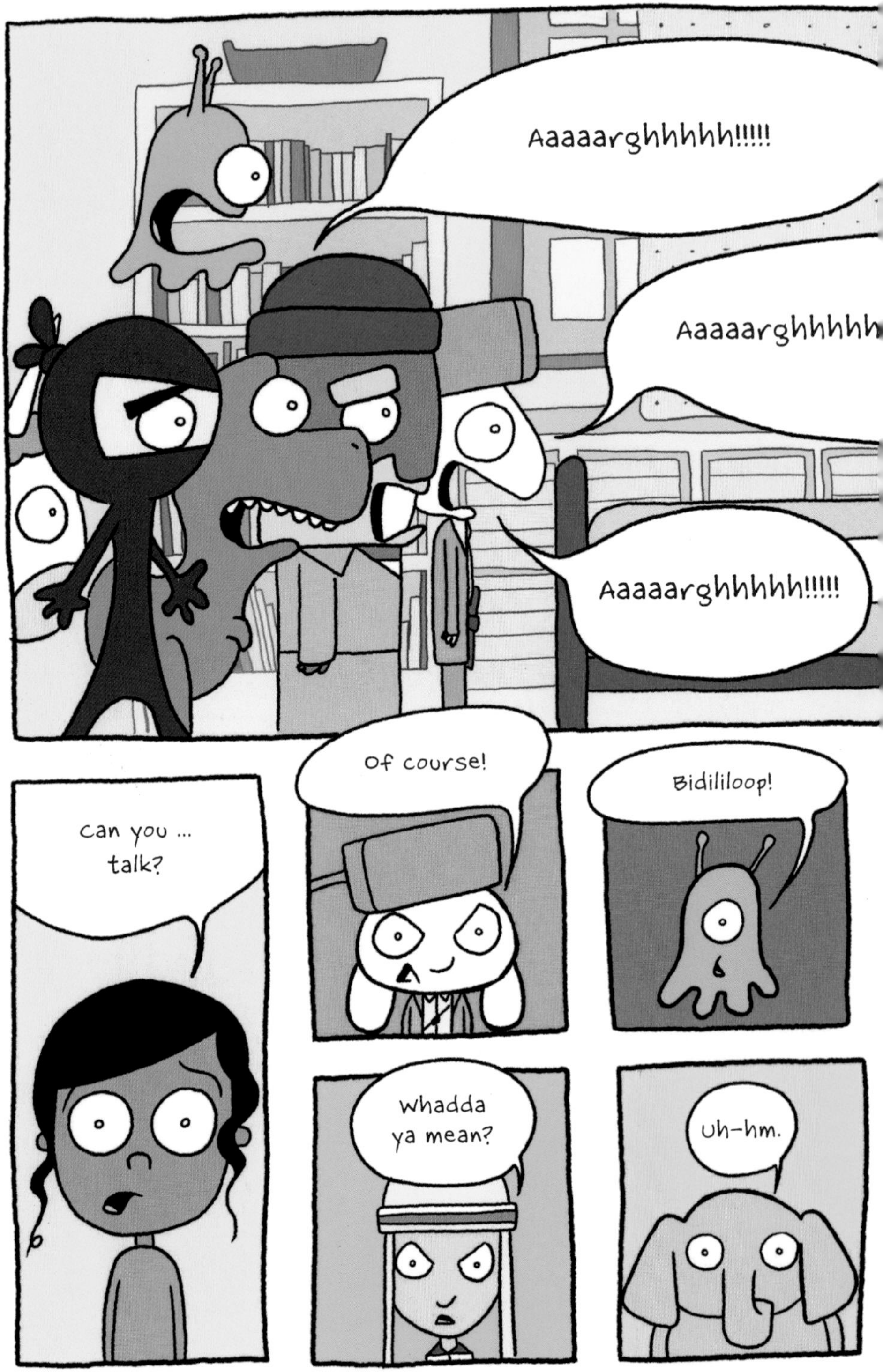
Aaaaarghhhhh!!!!!
Aaaaarghhhhh
Aaaaarghhhhh!!!!!
can you ...
talk?
Of course!
Bidililoop!
Whadda
ya mean?
Uh-hm.

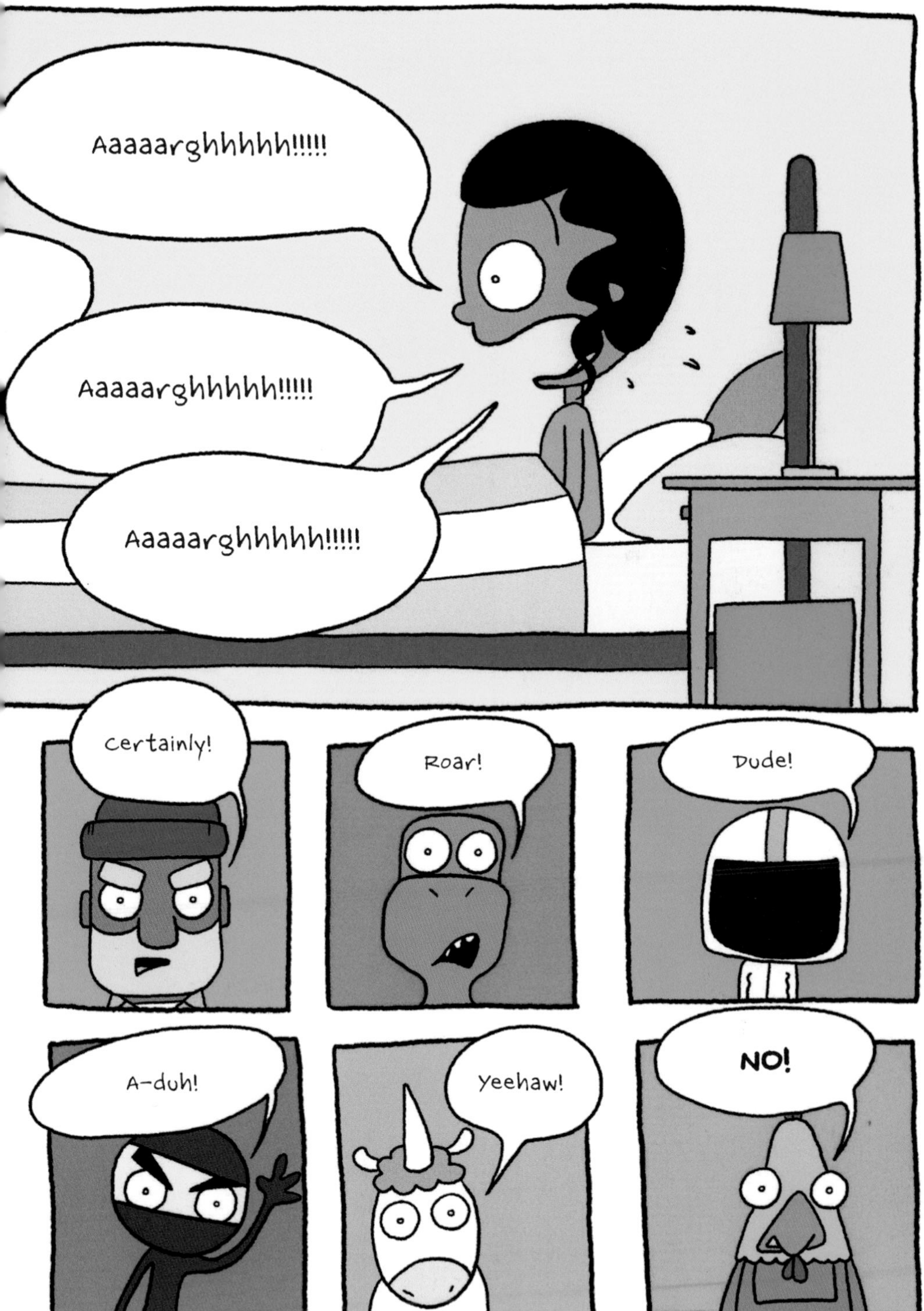

Aaaaarghhhhh!!!!!
Aaaaarghhhhh!!!!!
Aaaaarghhhhh!!!!!
Certainly!
Roar!
Dude!
A-duh!
Yeehaw!
NO!

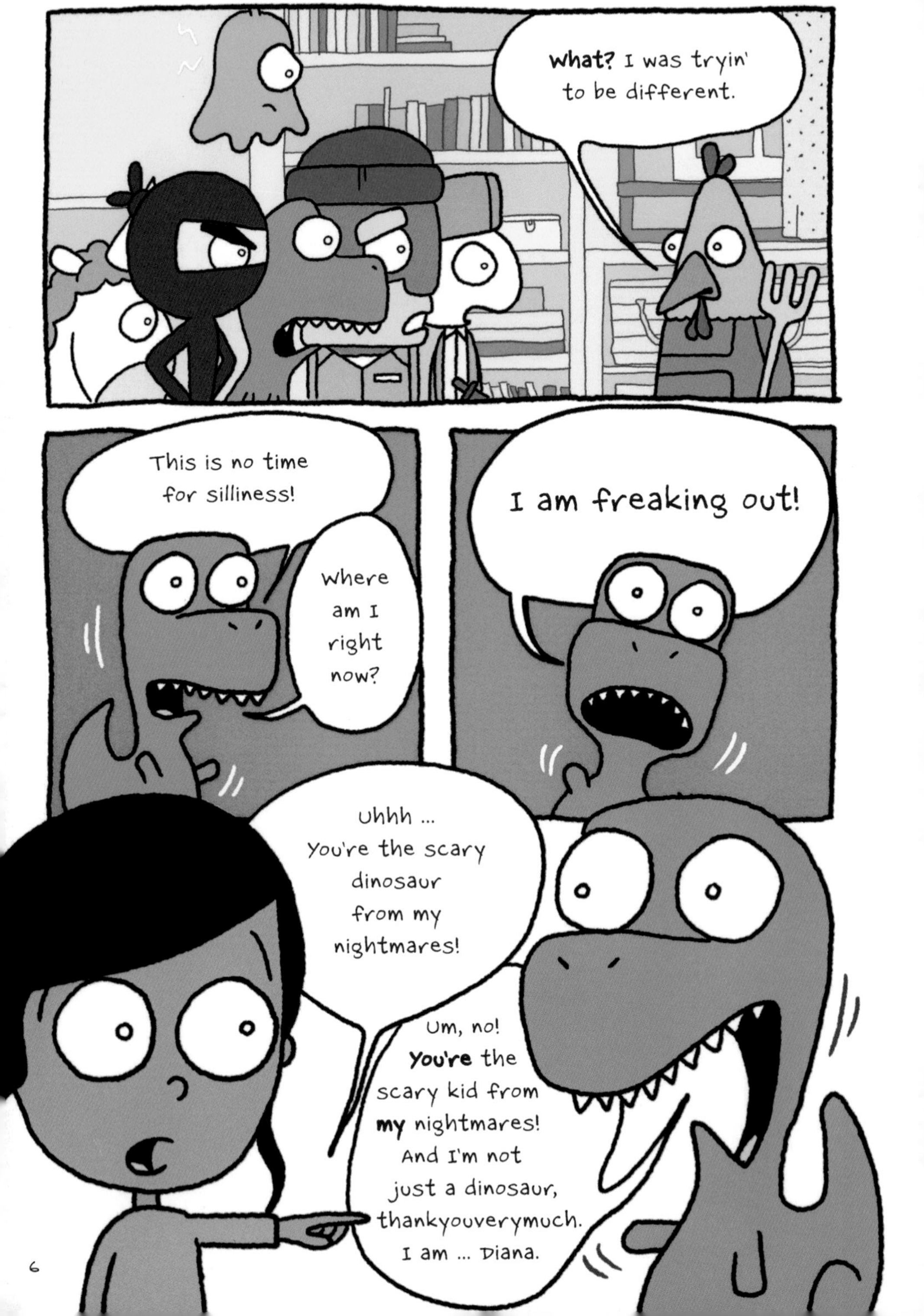
What? I was tryin' to be different.
This is no time for silliness!
Where am I right now?
I am freaking out!
Uhhh ... You're the scary dinosaur from my nightmares!
Um, no! You're the scary kid from my nightmares! And I'm not just a dinosaur, thankyouverymuch. I am ... Diana.

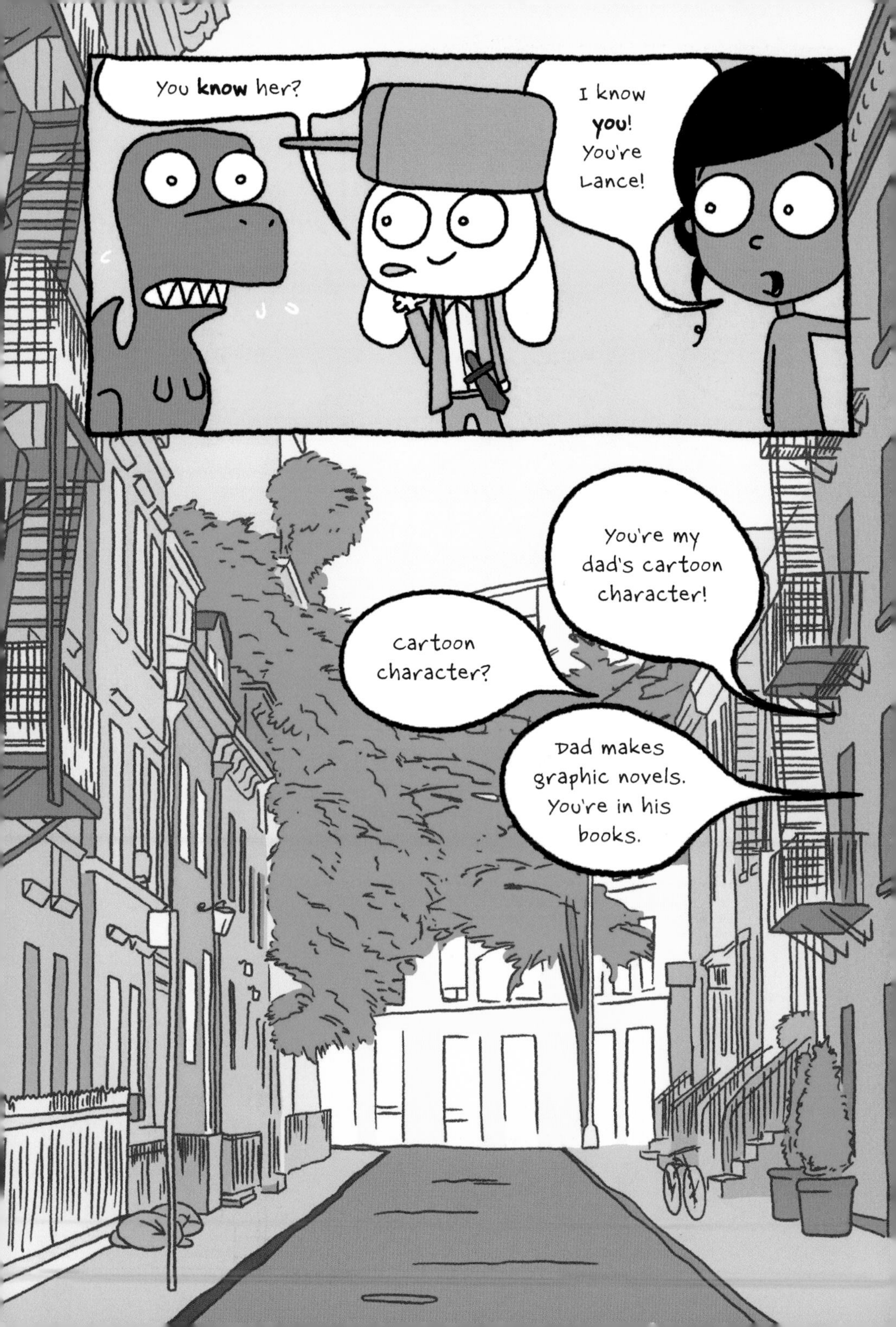
You **know** her?
I know **you**! You're Lance!
You're my dad's cartoon character!
cartoon character?
Dad makes graphic novels. You're in his books.

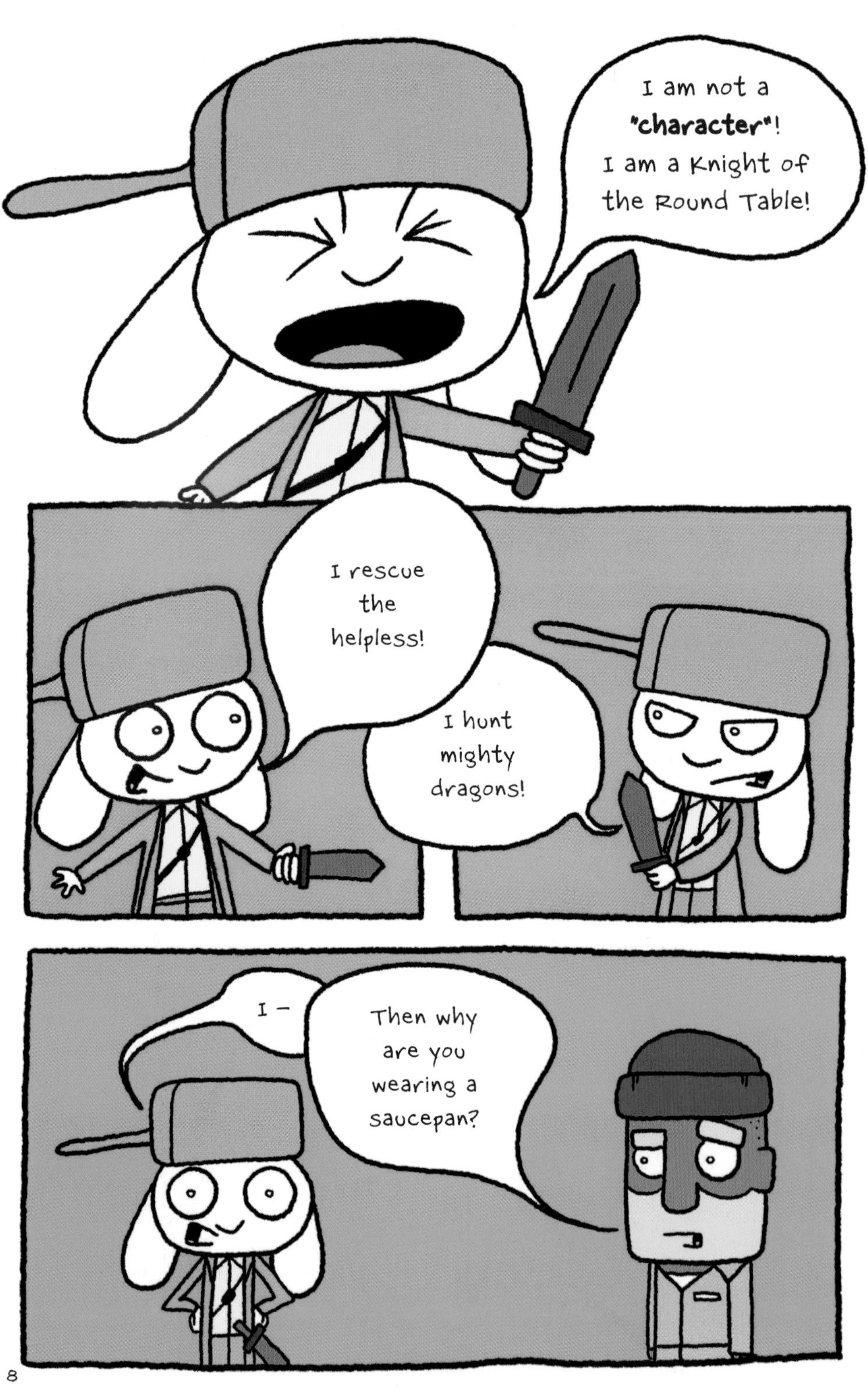
I am not a **"character"**! I am a Knight of the Round Table!
I rescue the helpless!
I hunt mighty dragons!
I —
Then why are you wearing a saucepan?

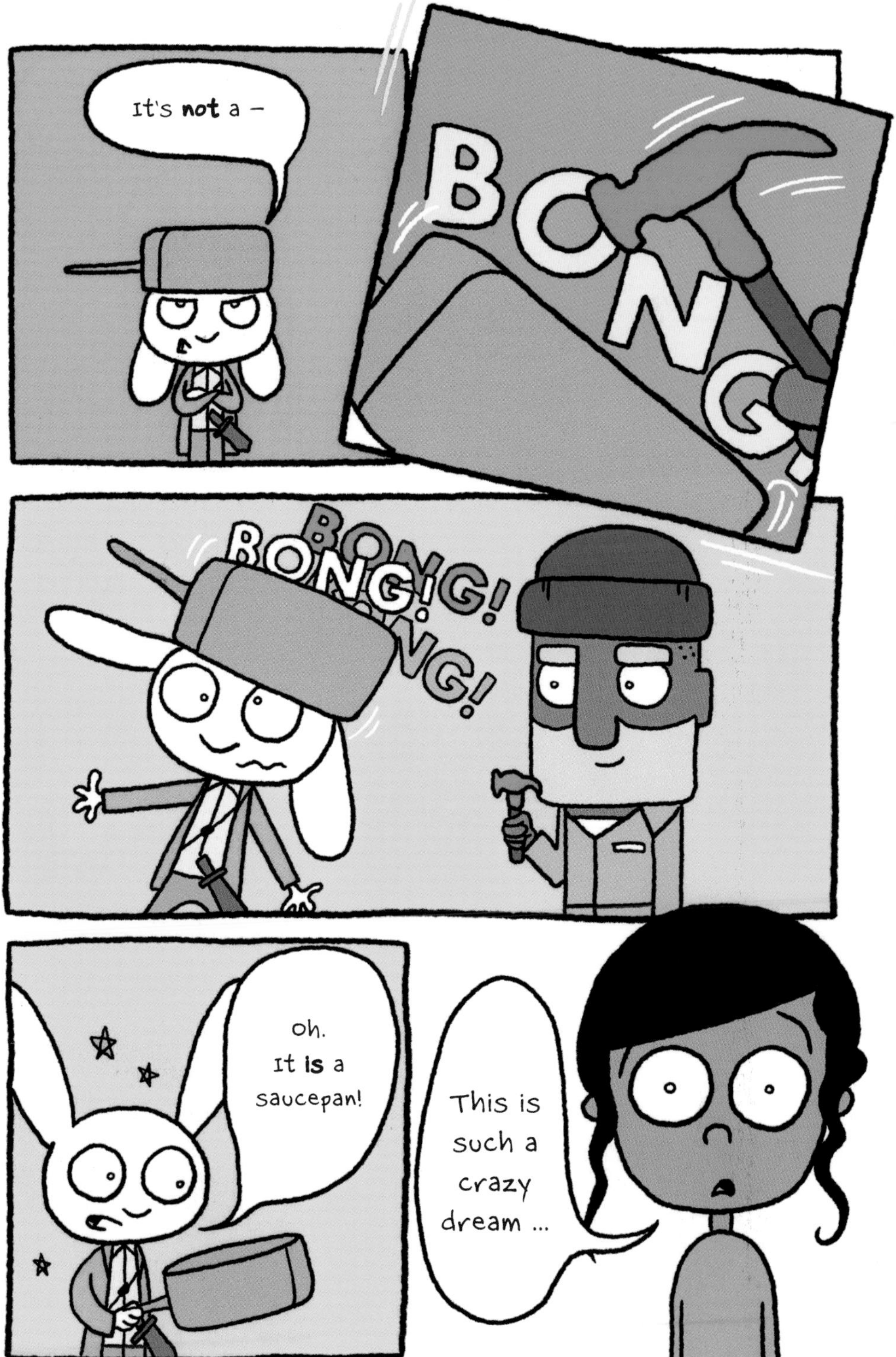

It's **not** a –
BONG!
BONG!
BONG!
BONG!
Oh.
It **is** a
saucepan!
This is
such a
crazy
dream ...

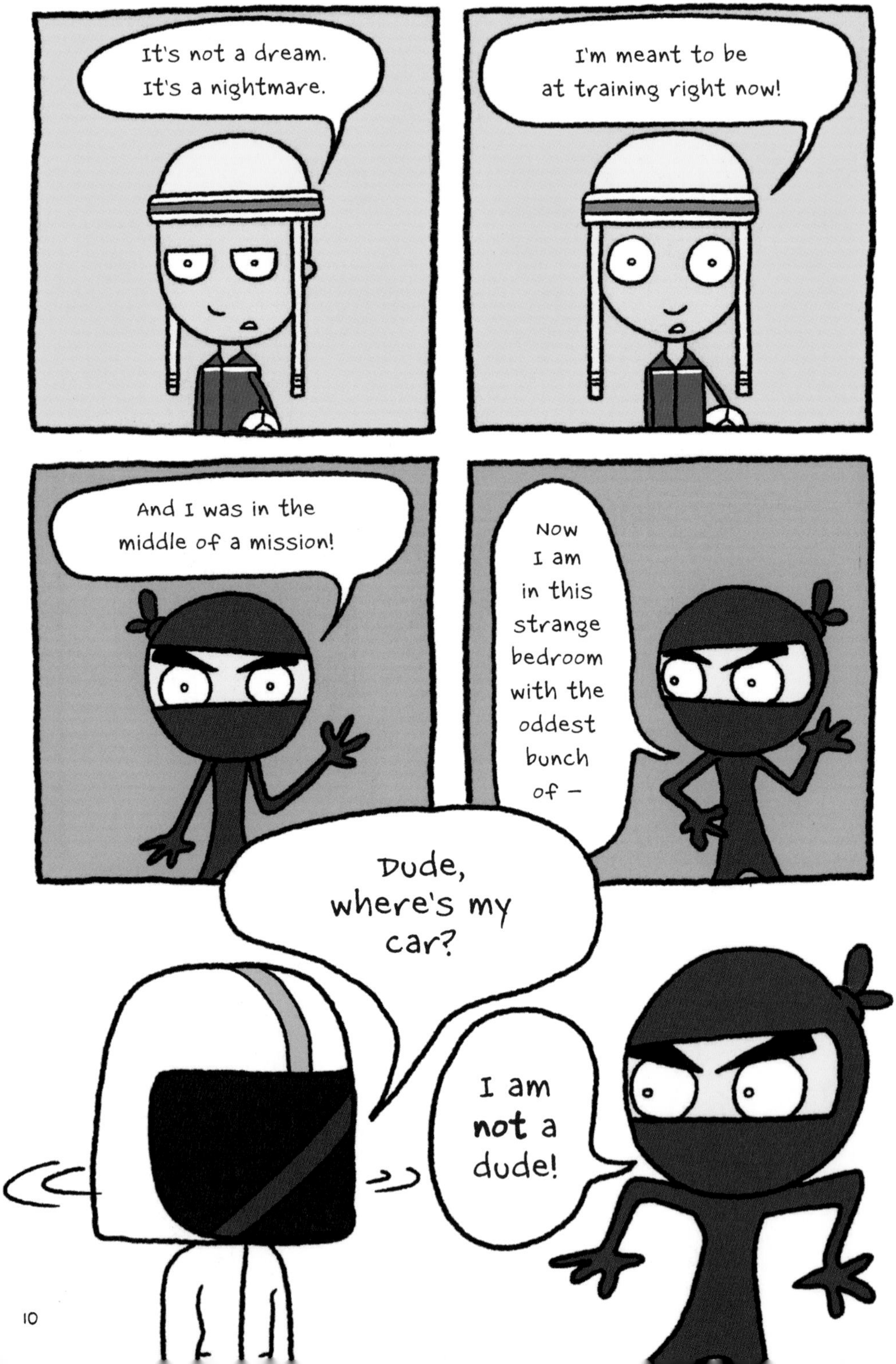
It's not a dream. It's a nightmare.
I'm meant to be at training right now!
And I was in the middle of a mission!
Now I am in this strange bedroom with the oddest bunch of –
Dude, where's my car?
I am **not** a dude!

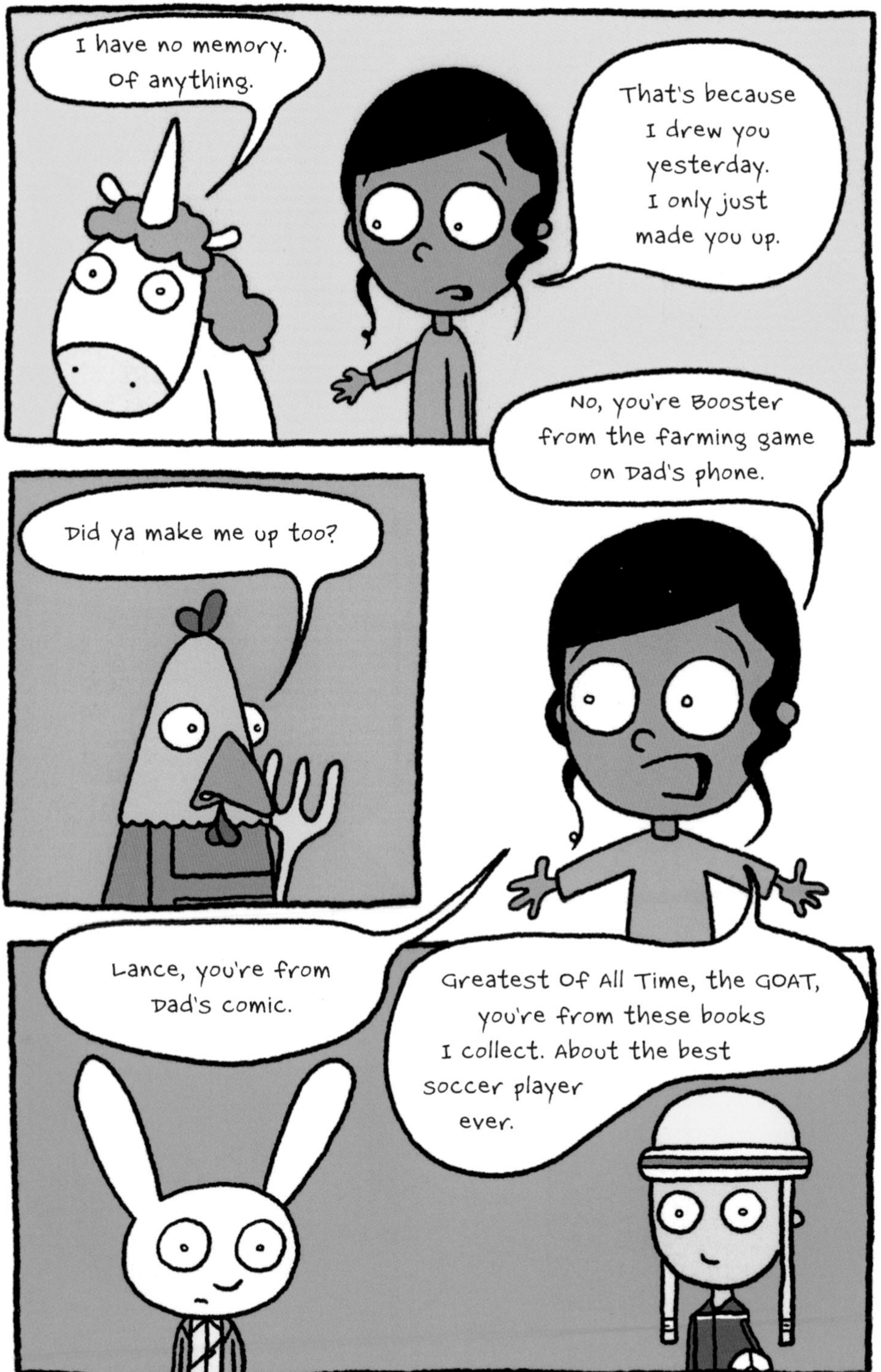
I have no memory. Of anything.
That's because I drew you yesterday. I only just made you up.
Did ya make me up too?
No, you're Booster from the farming game on Dad's phone.
Lance, you're from Dad's comic.
Greatest Of All Time, the GOAT, you're from these books I collect. About the best soccer player ever.

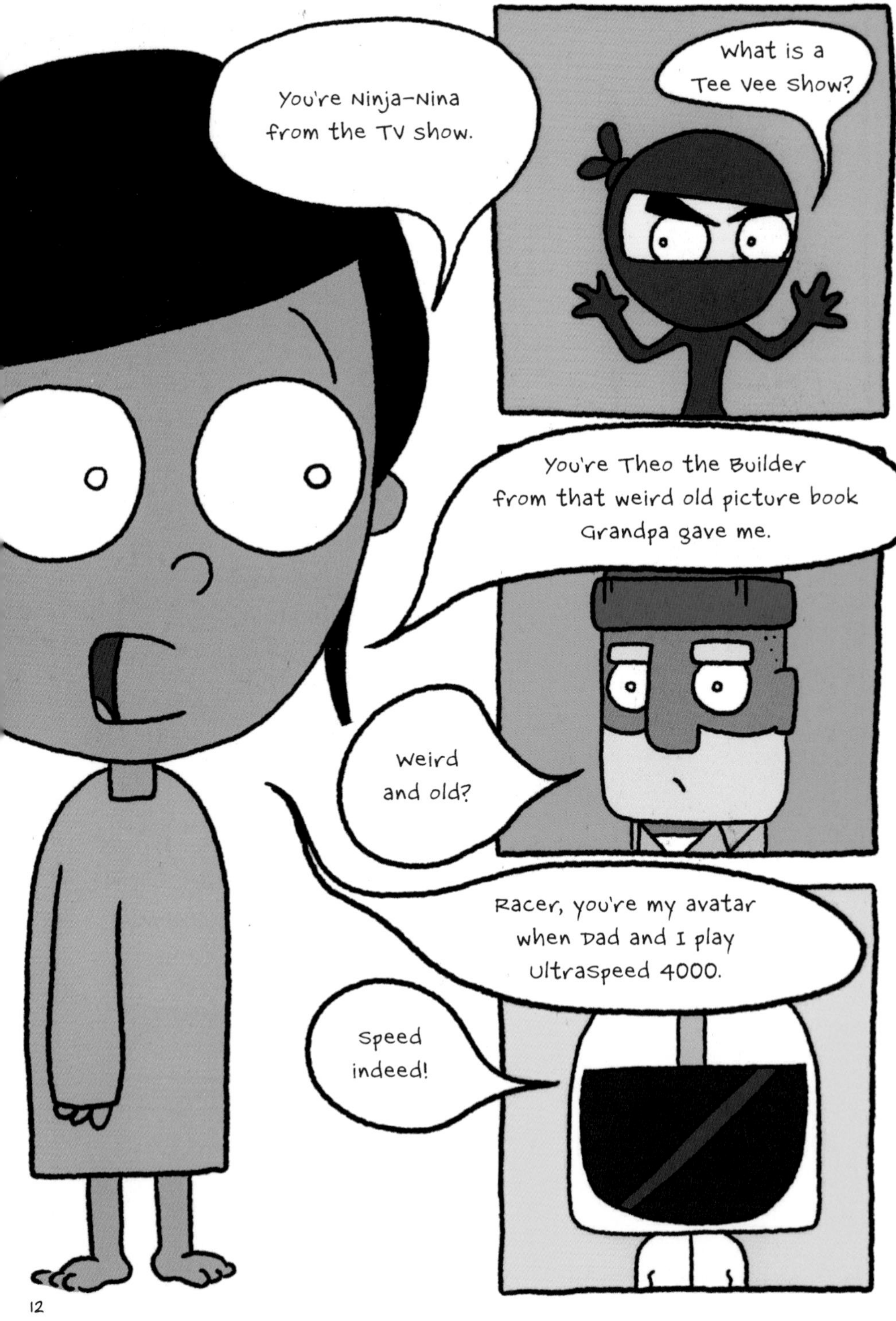
You're Ninja-Nina from the TV show.
What is a Tee Vee show?
You're Theo the Builder from that weird old picture book Grandpa gave me.
Weird and old?
Racer, you're my avatar when Dad and I play Ultraspeed 4000.
Speed indeed!

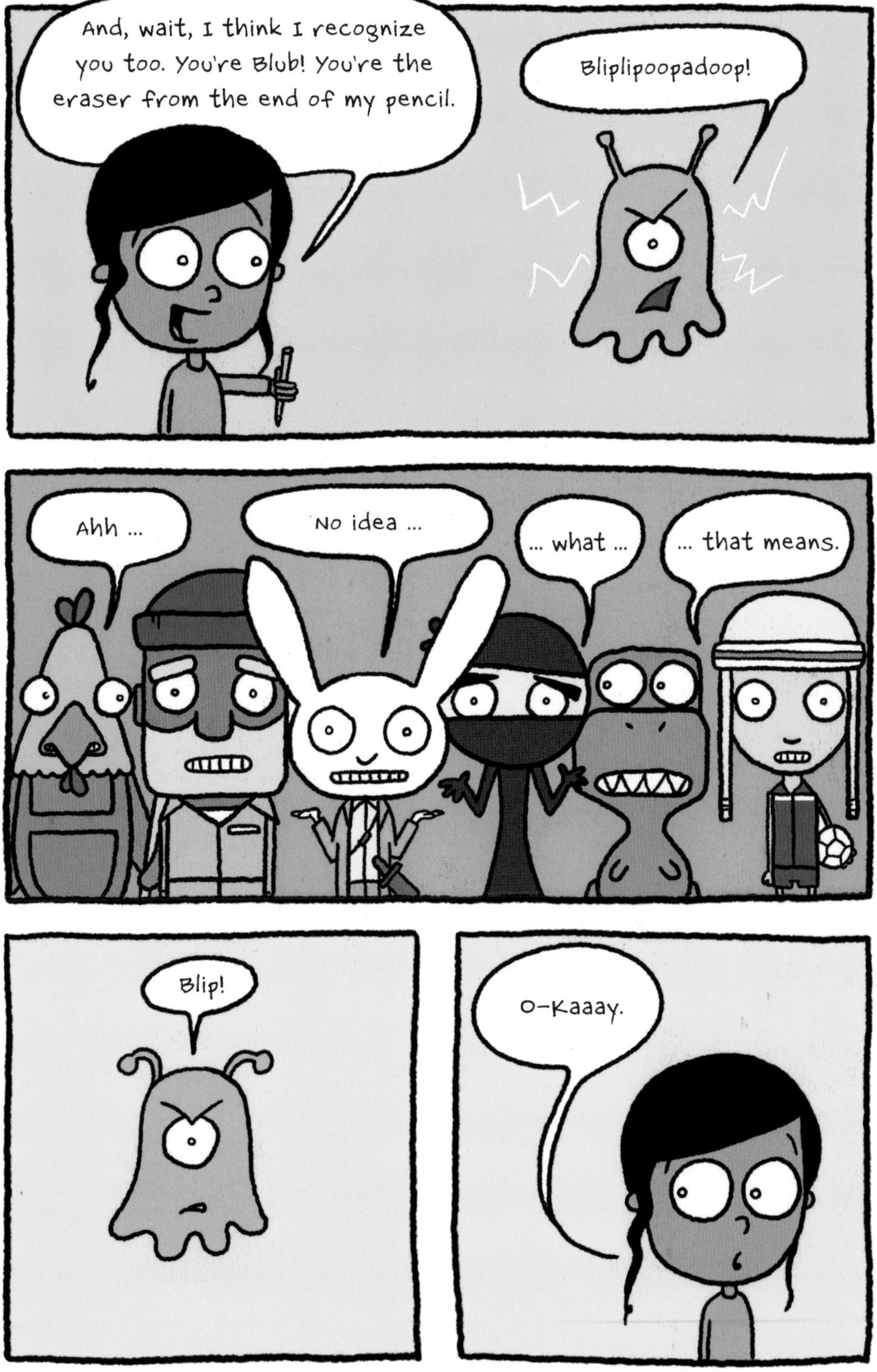
And, wait, I think I recognize you too. You're Blub! You're the eraser from the end of my pencil.
Bliplipoopadoop!
Ahh ...
No idea ...
... what ...
... that means.
Blip!
O-Kaaay.

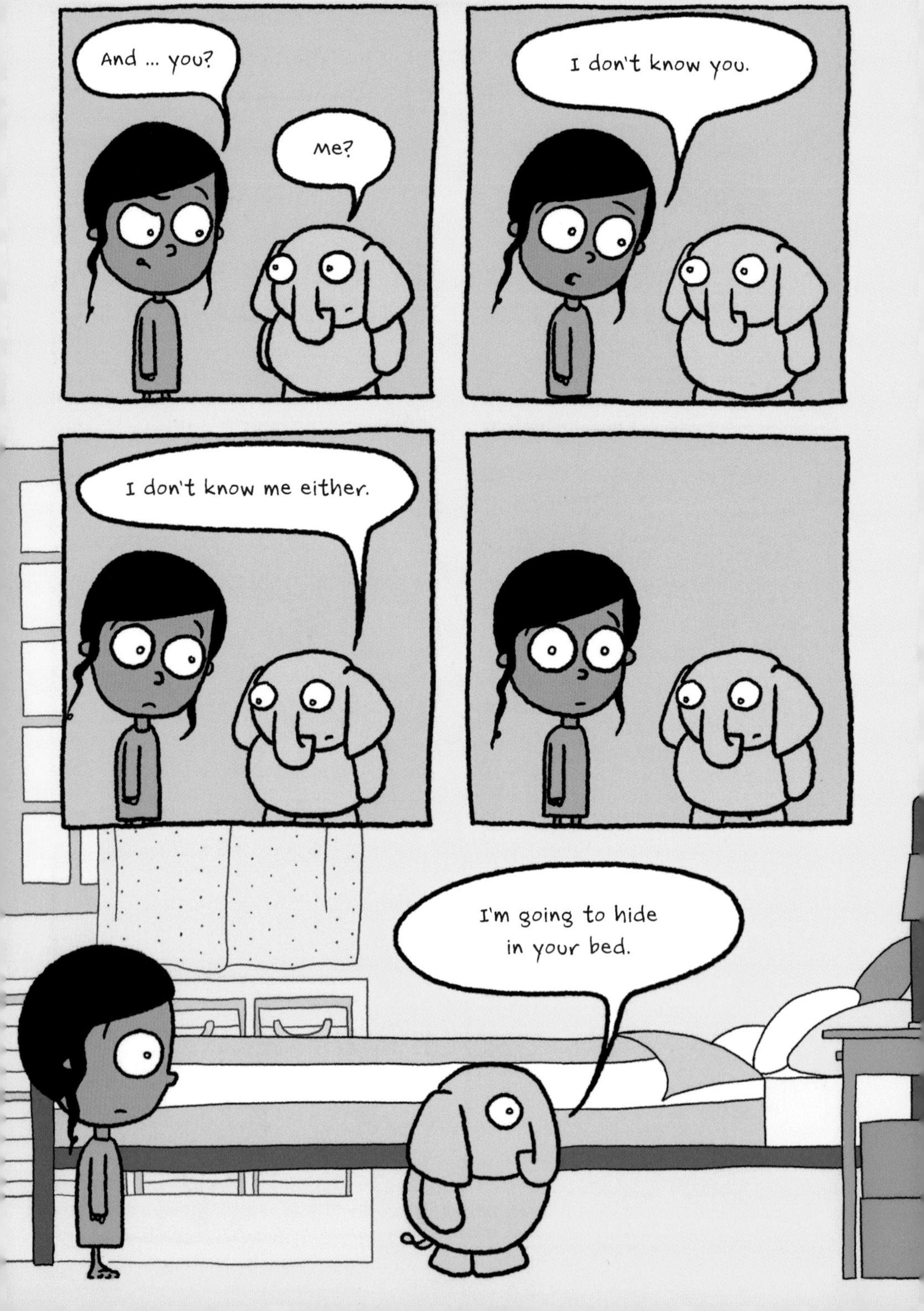
And ... you?
Me?
I don't know you.
I don't know me either.
I'm going to hide in your bed.

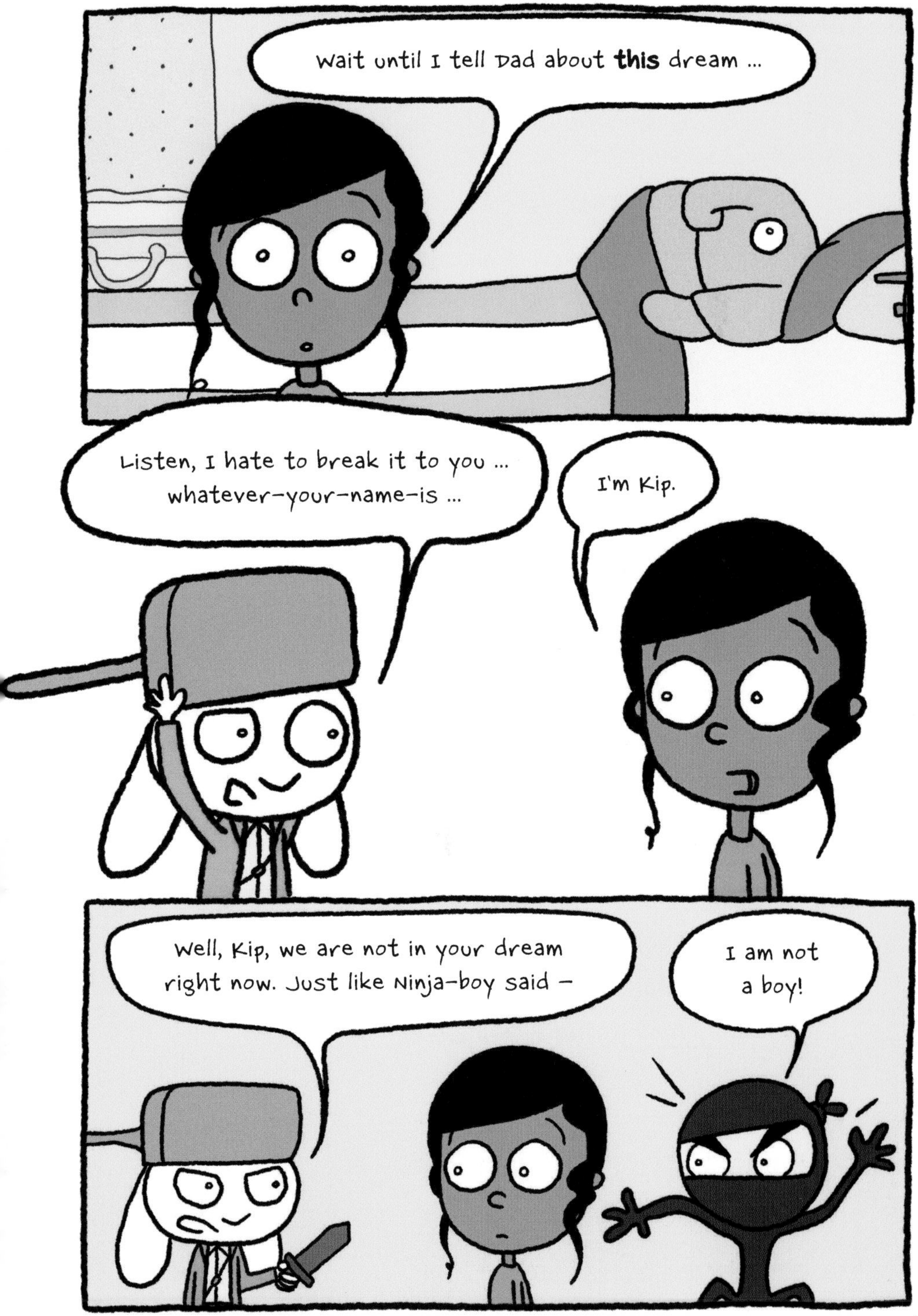
Wait until I tell Dad about **this** dream ...
Listen, I hate to break it to you ... whatever-your-name-is ...
I'm Kip.
Well, Kip, we are not in your dream right now. Just like Ninja-boy said –
I am not a boy!

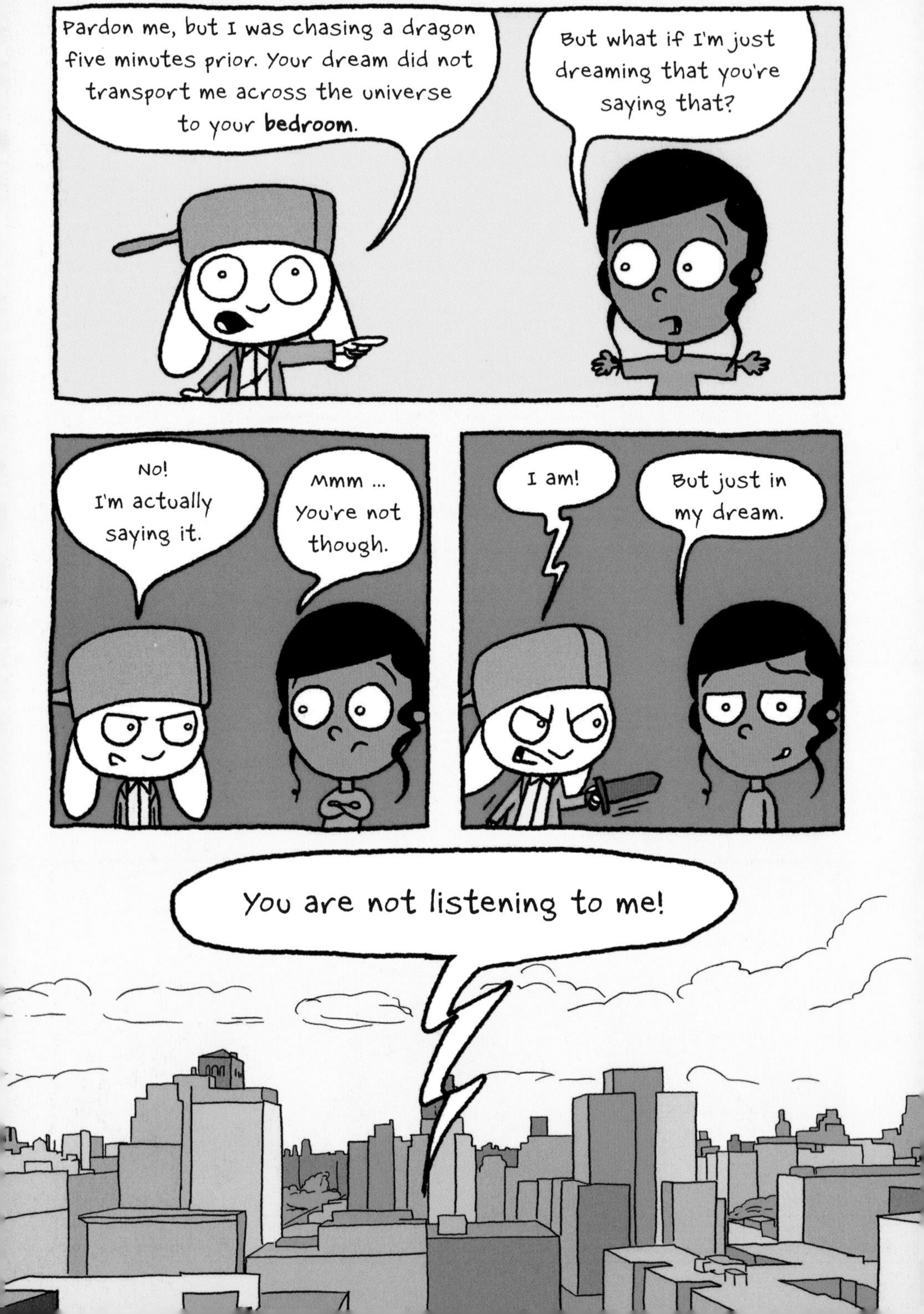
Pardon me, but I was chasing a dragon five minutes prior. Your dream did not transport me across the universe to your **bedroom**.
But what if I'm just dreaming that you're saying that?
No! I'm actually saying it.
Mmm ... You're not though.
I am!
But just in my dream.
You are not listening to me!

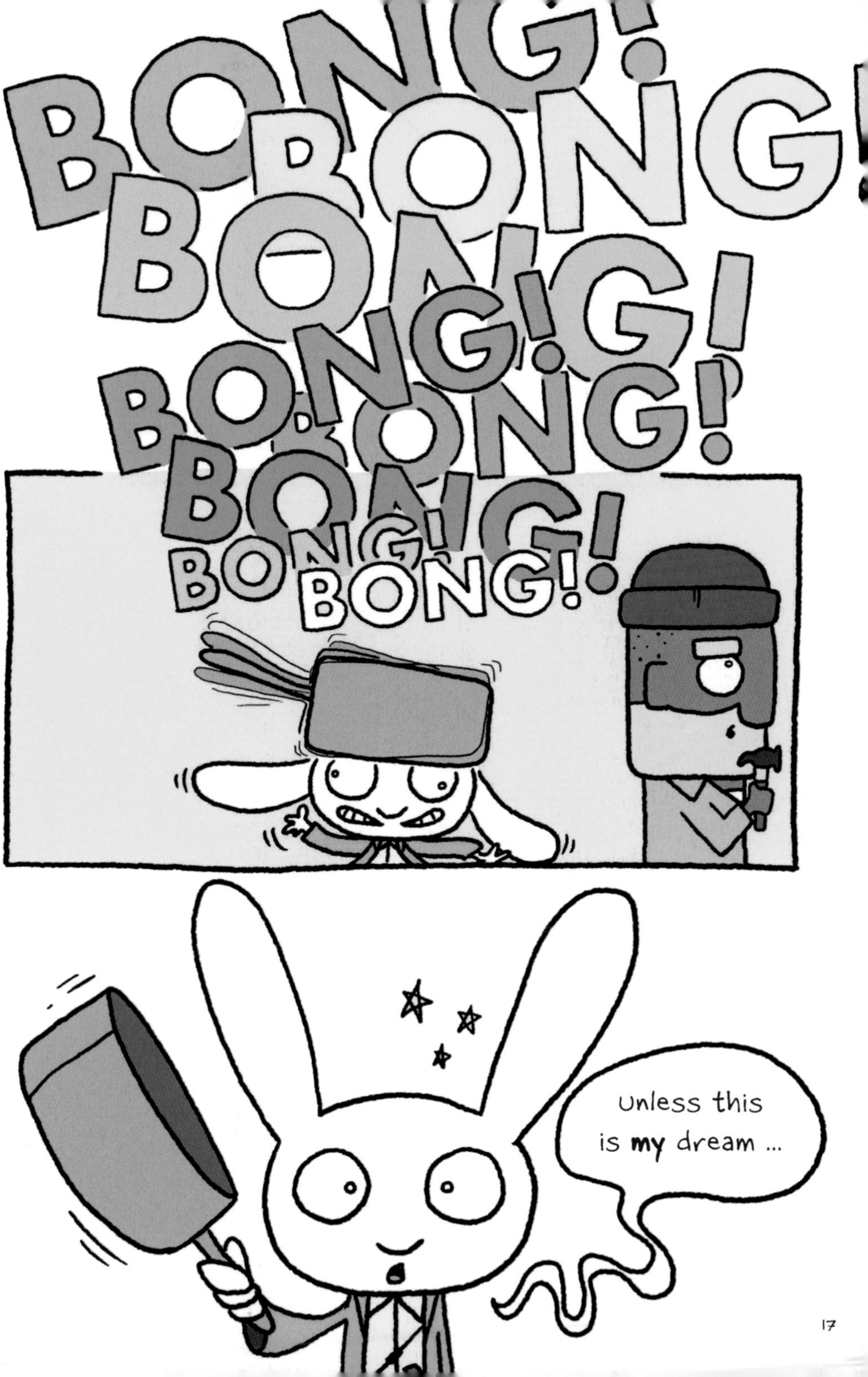
BONG! BONG! BONG! BONG! BONG! BONG! BONG! BONG!
Unless this is my dream ...

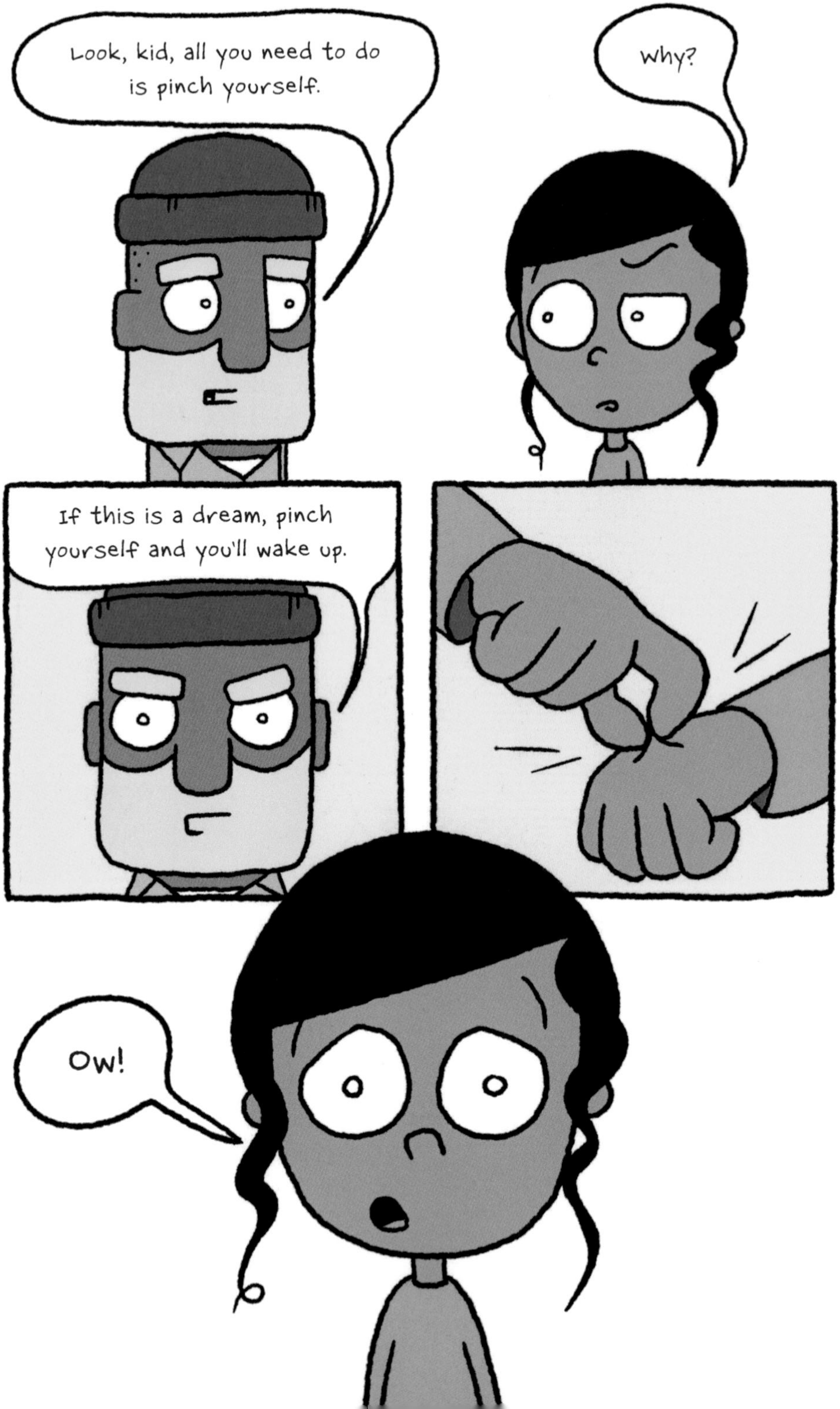
Look, kid, all you need to do is pinch yourself.
Why?
If this is a dream, pinch yourself and you'll wake up.
Ow!

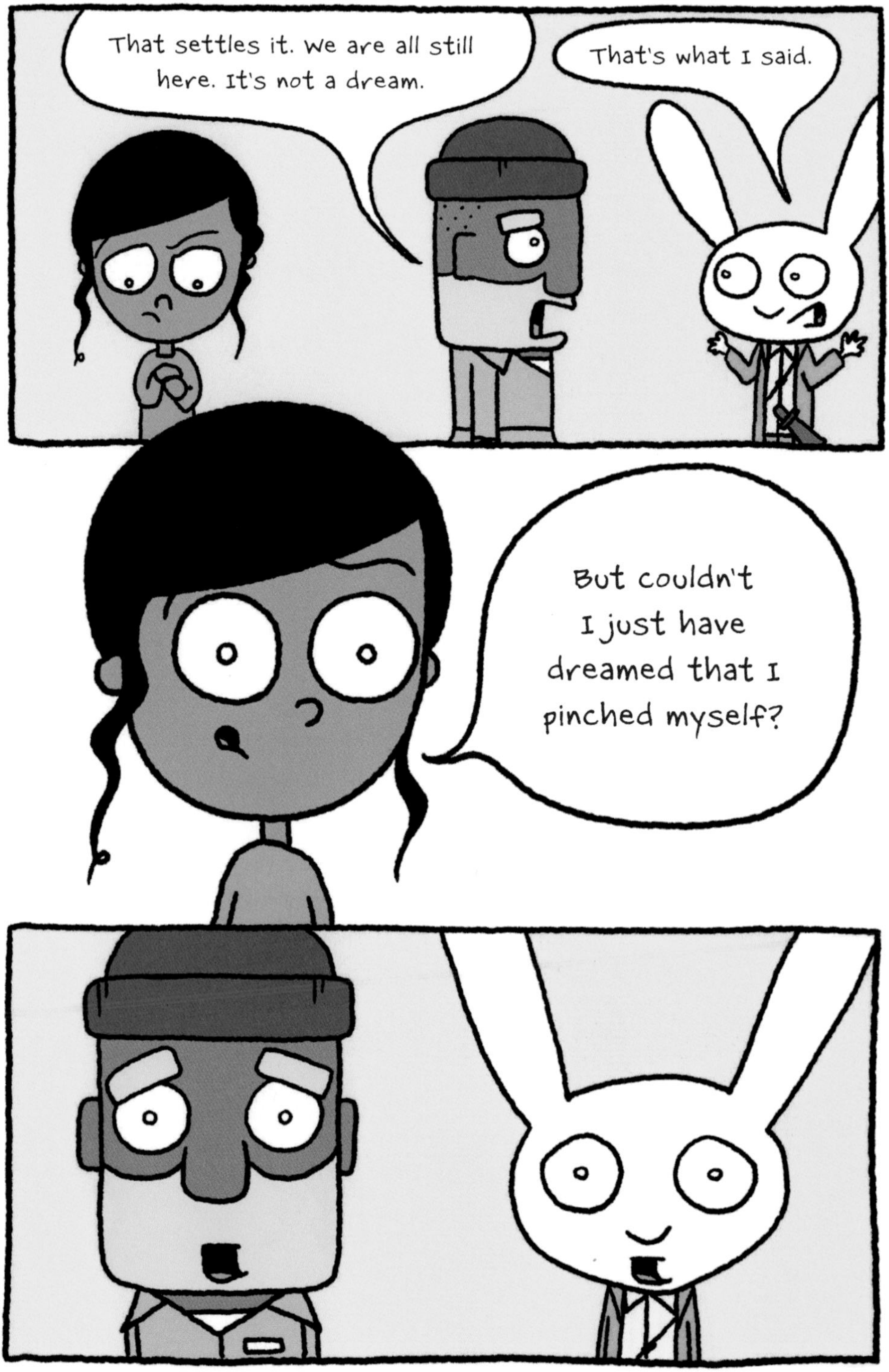
That settles it. We are all still here. It's not a dream.
That's what I said.
But couldn't I just have dreamed that I pinched myself?

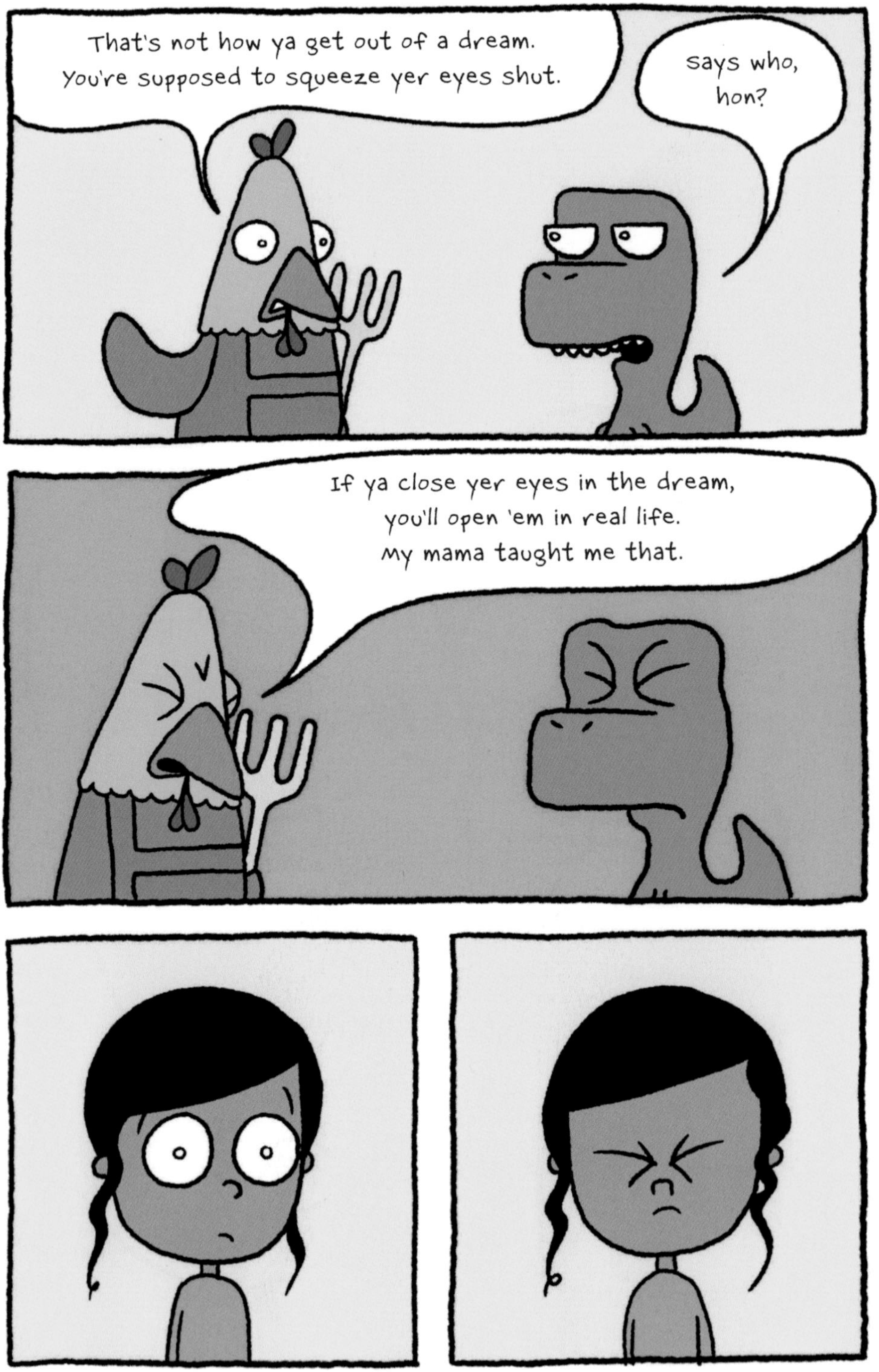
That's not how ya get out of a dream. You're supposed to squeeze yer eyes shut.
says who, hon?
If ya close yer eyes in the dream, you'll open 'em in real life. My mama taught me that.

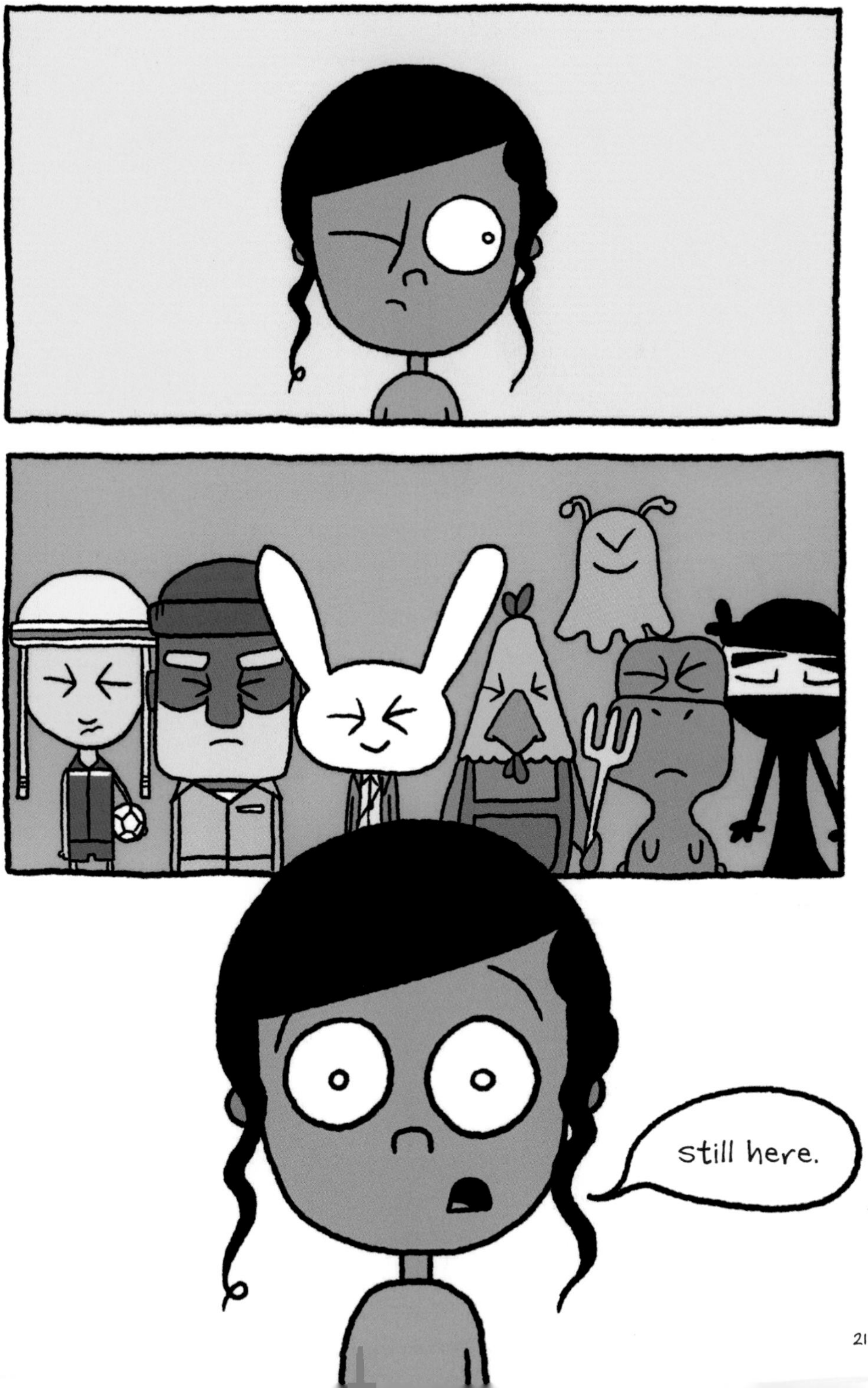
still here.

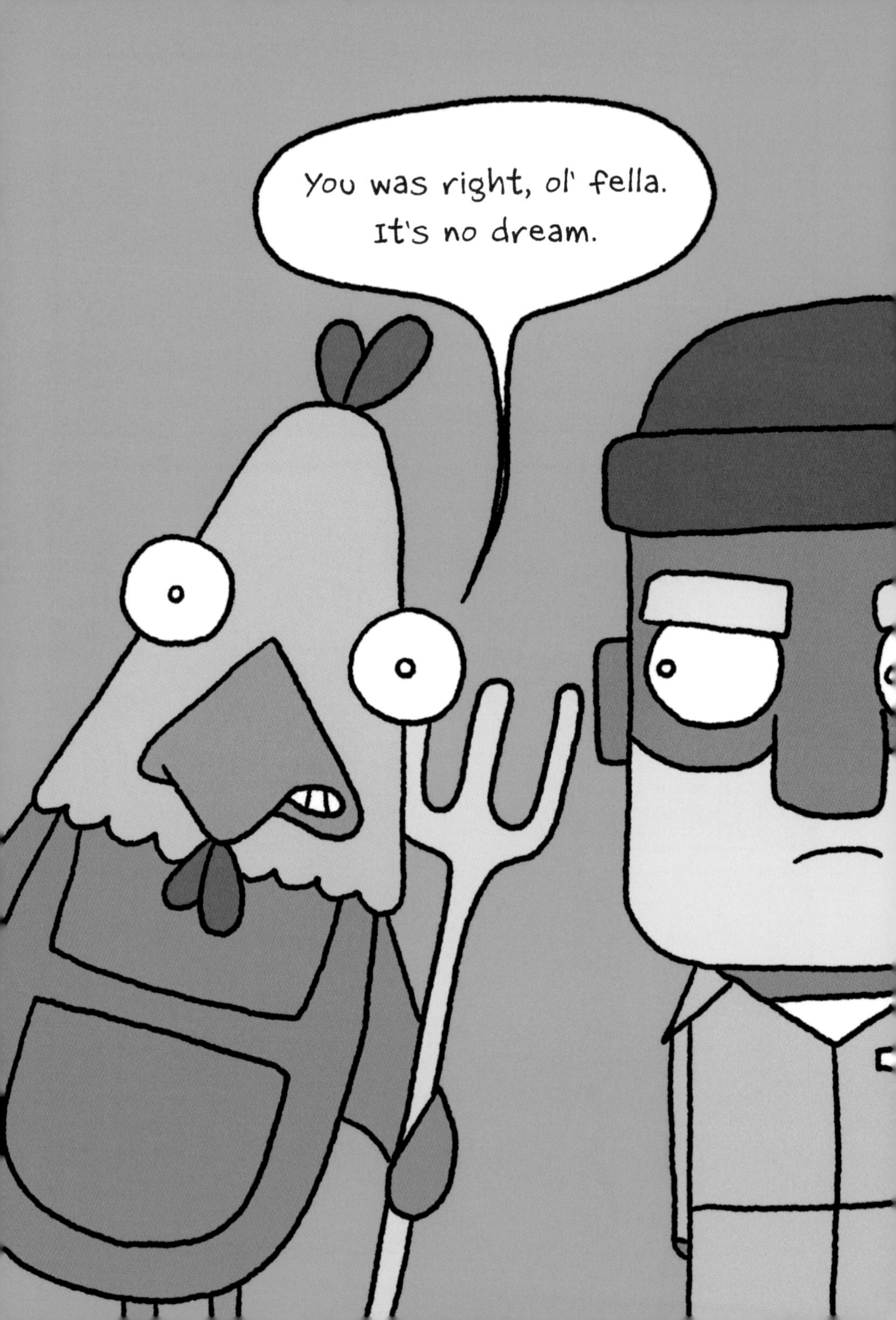
You was right, ol' fella. It's no dream.

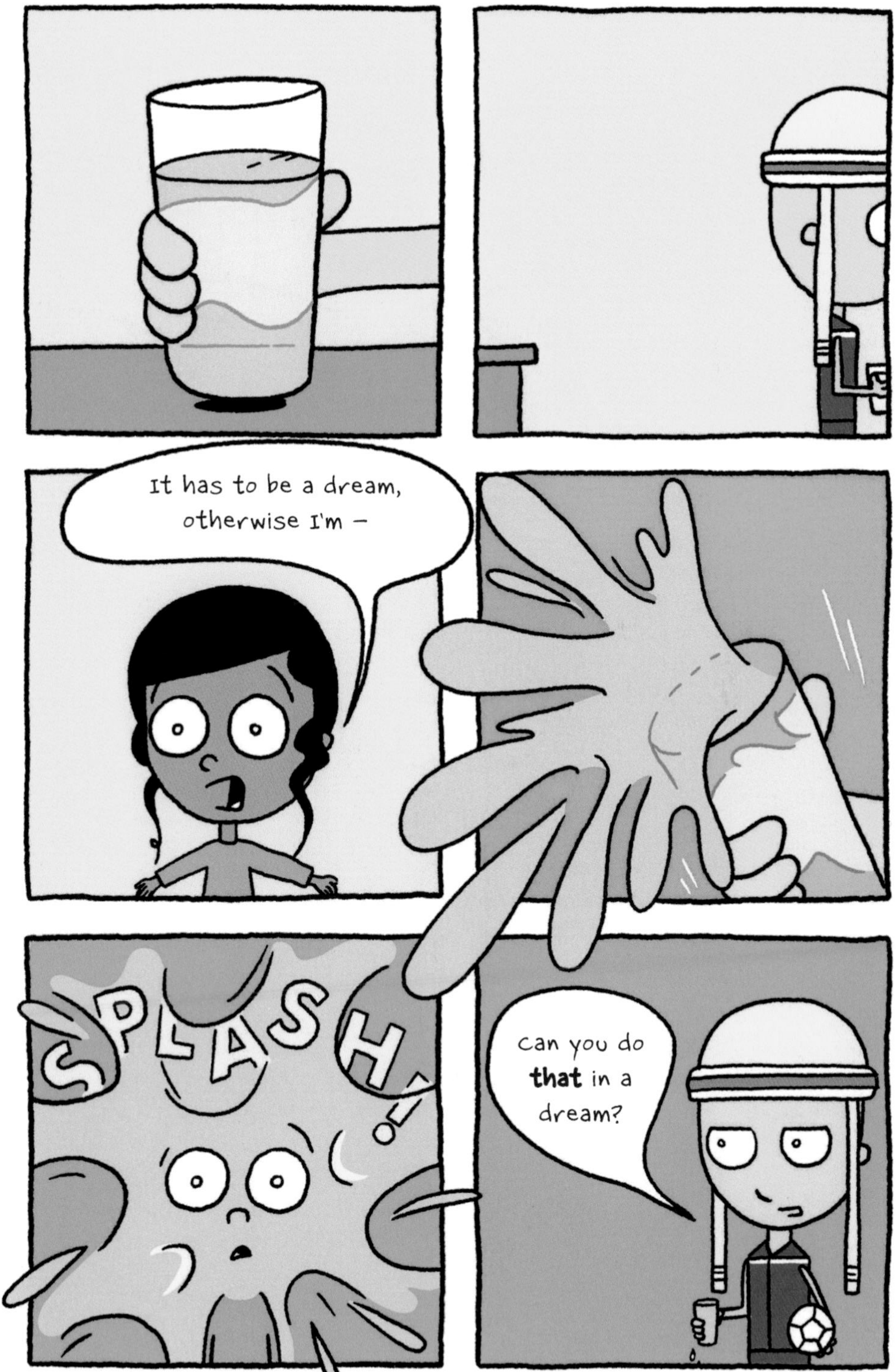

It has to be a dream, otherwise I'm –
SPLASH!
can you do **that** in a dream?

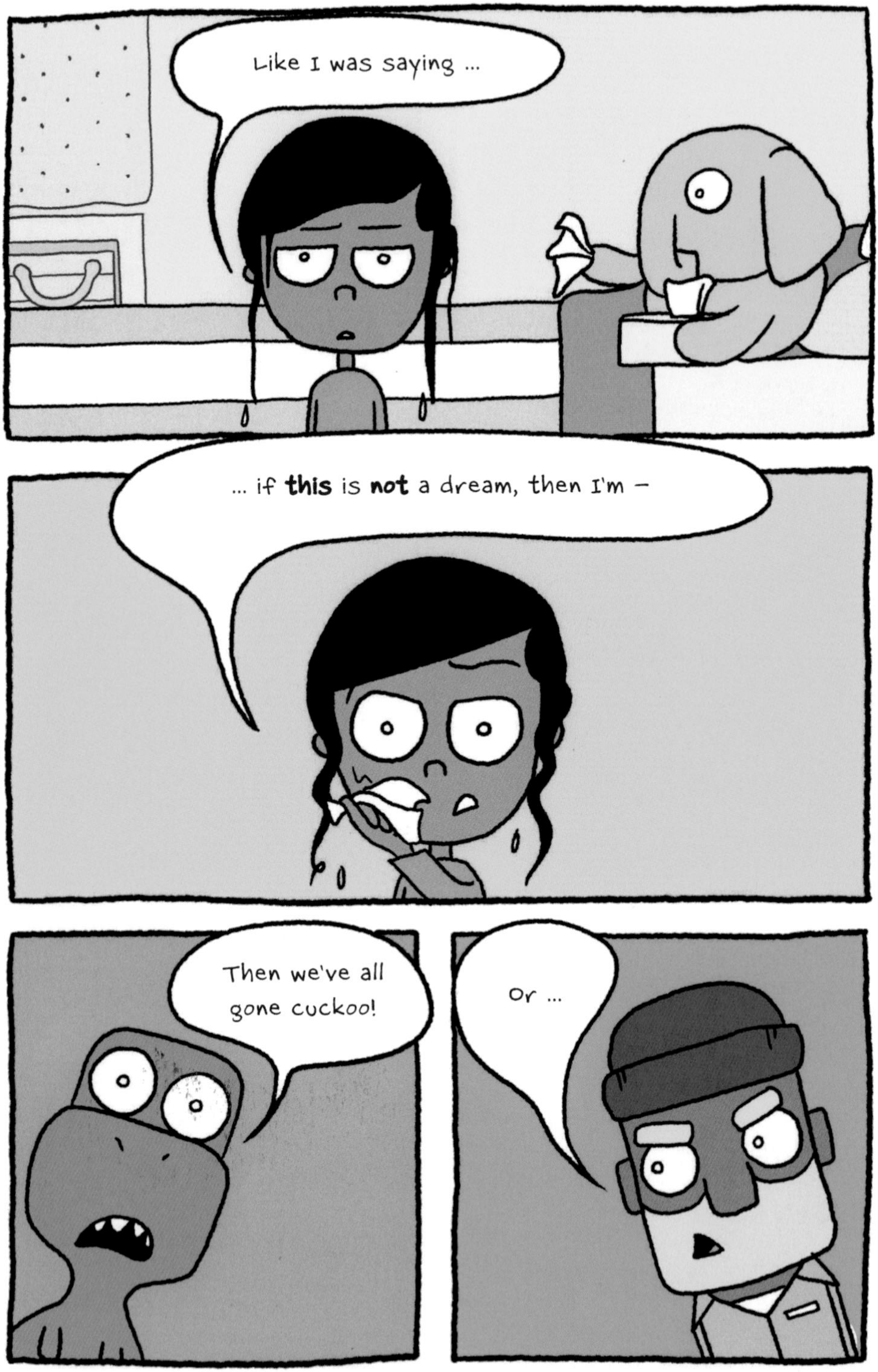
Like I was saying ...
... if **this** is **not** a dream, then I'm –
Then we've all gone cuckoo!
Or ...

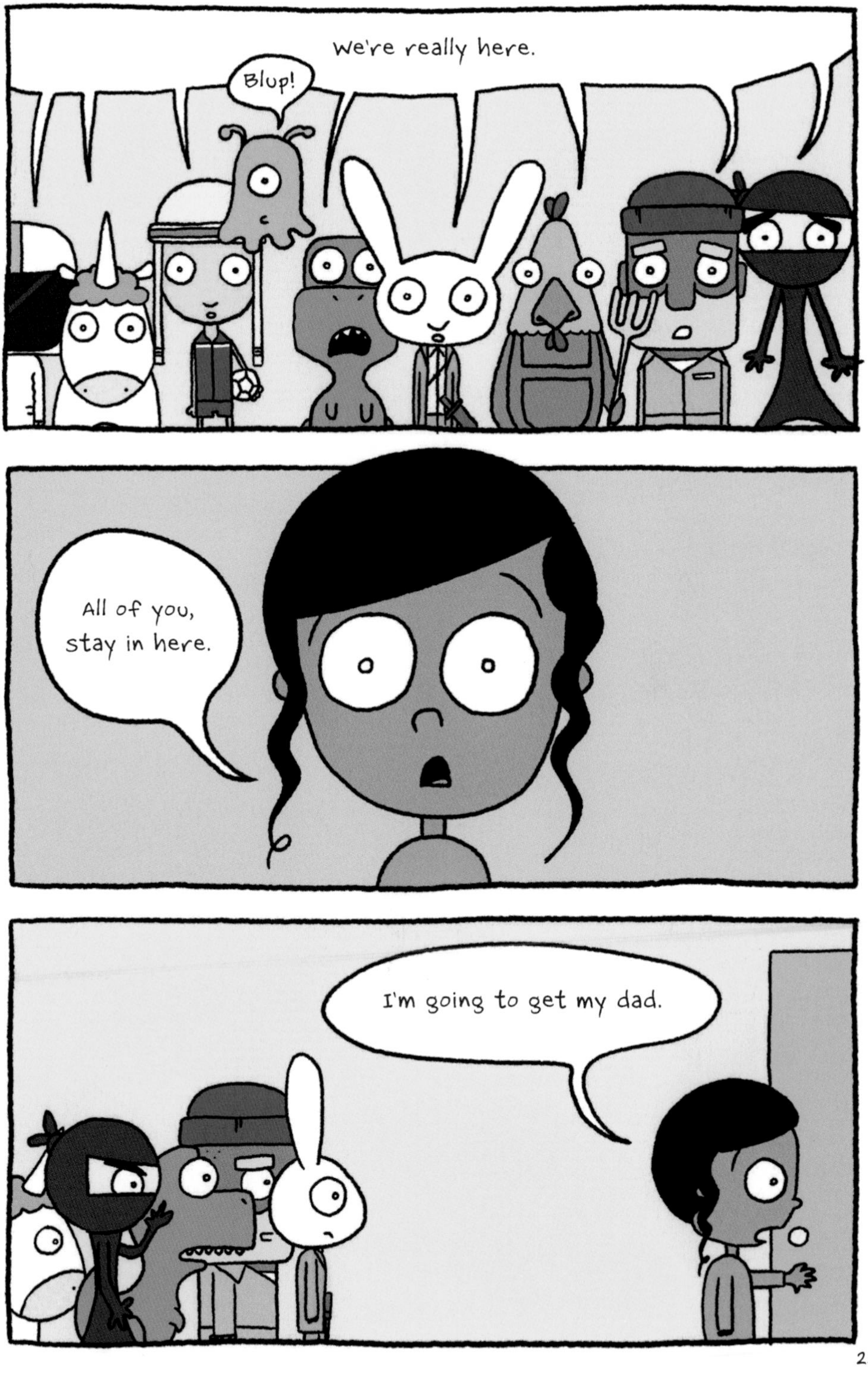
We're really here.
Blup!
All of you, stay in here.
I'm going to get my dad.

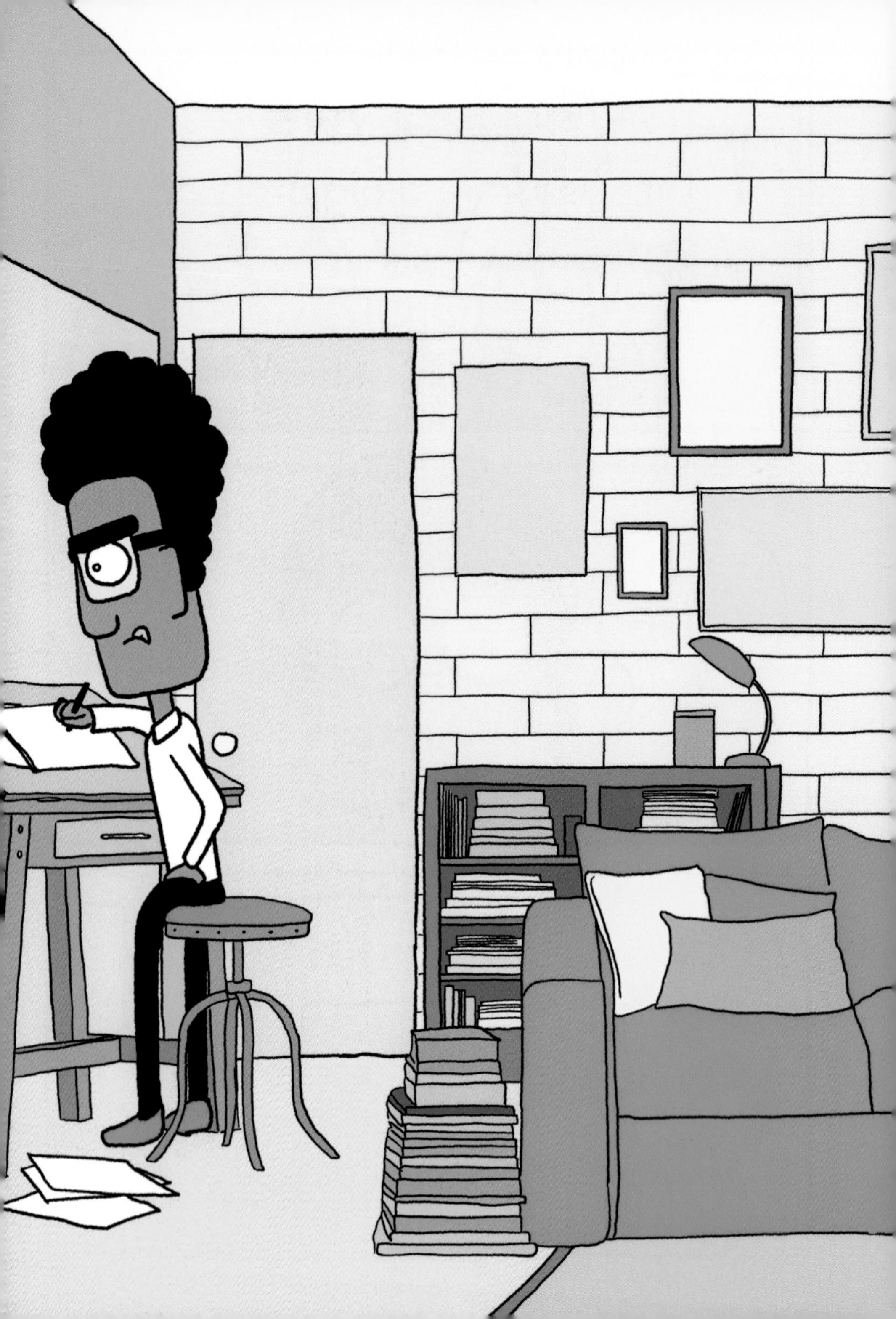

CHAPTER TWO
The Odds are a big problem

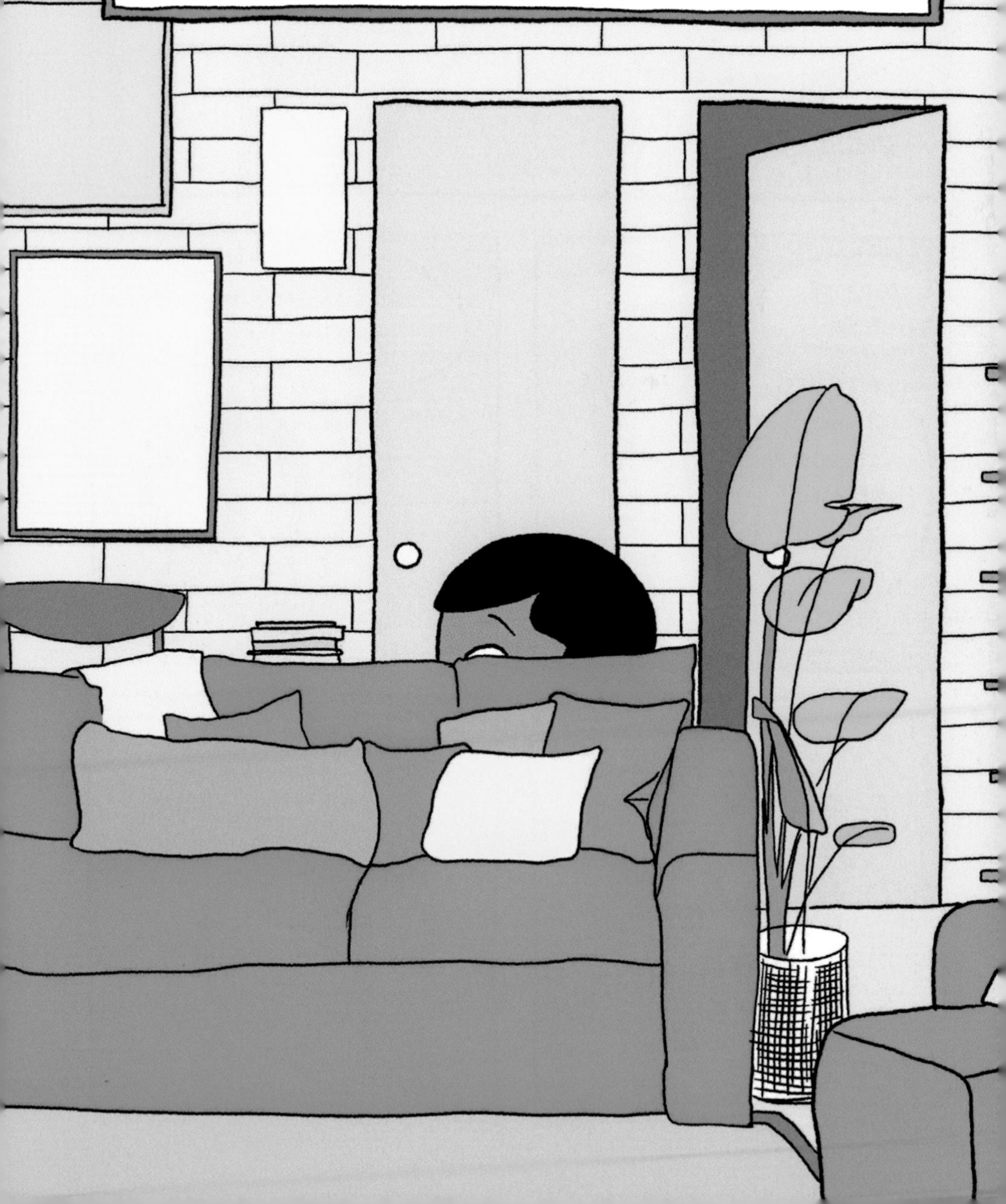

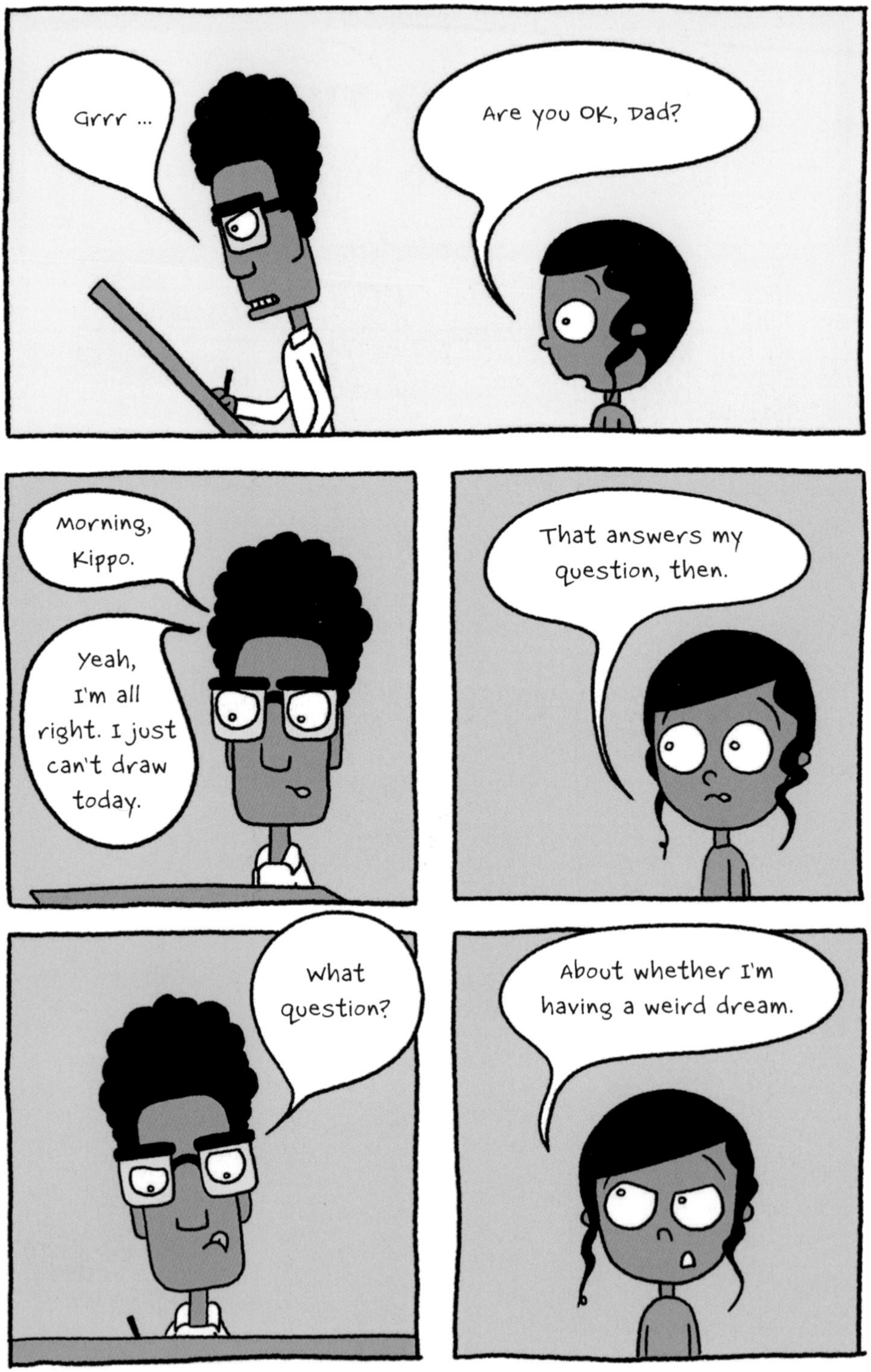
Grrr ...
Are you OK, Dad?
Morning, Kippo.
Yeah, I'm all right. I just can't draw today.
That answers my question, then.
What question?
About whether I'm having a weird dream.

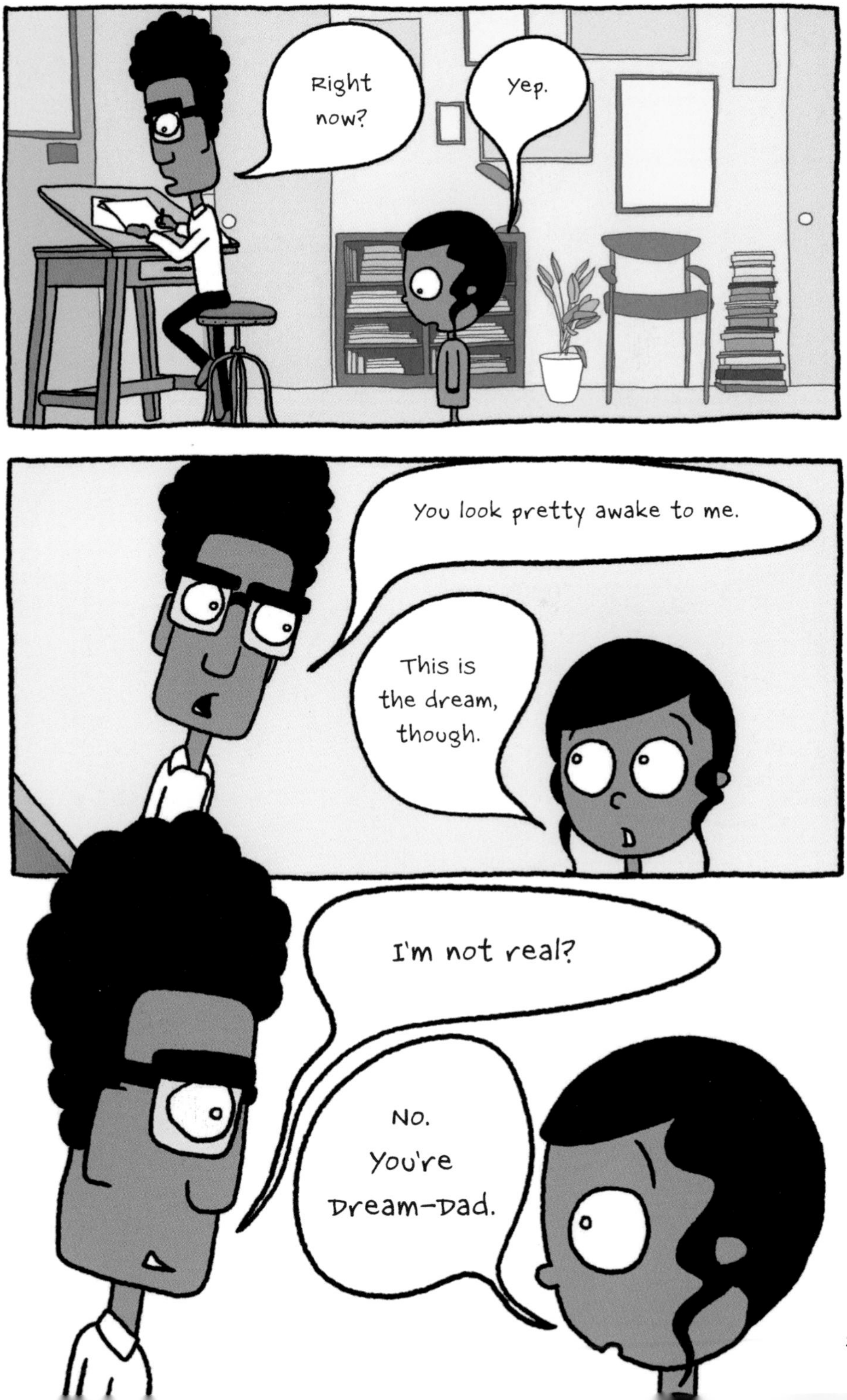
Right now?
Yep.
You look pretty awake to me.
This is the dream, though.
I'm not real?
No. You're Dream-Dad.

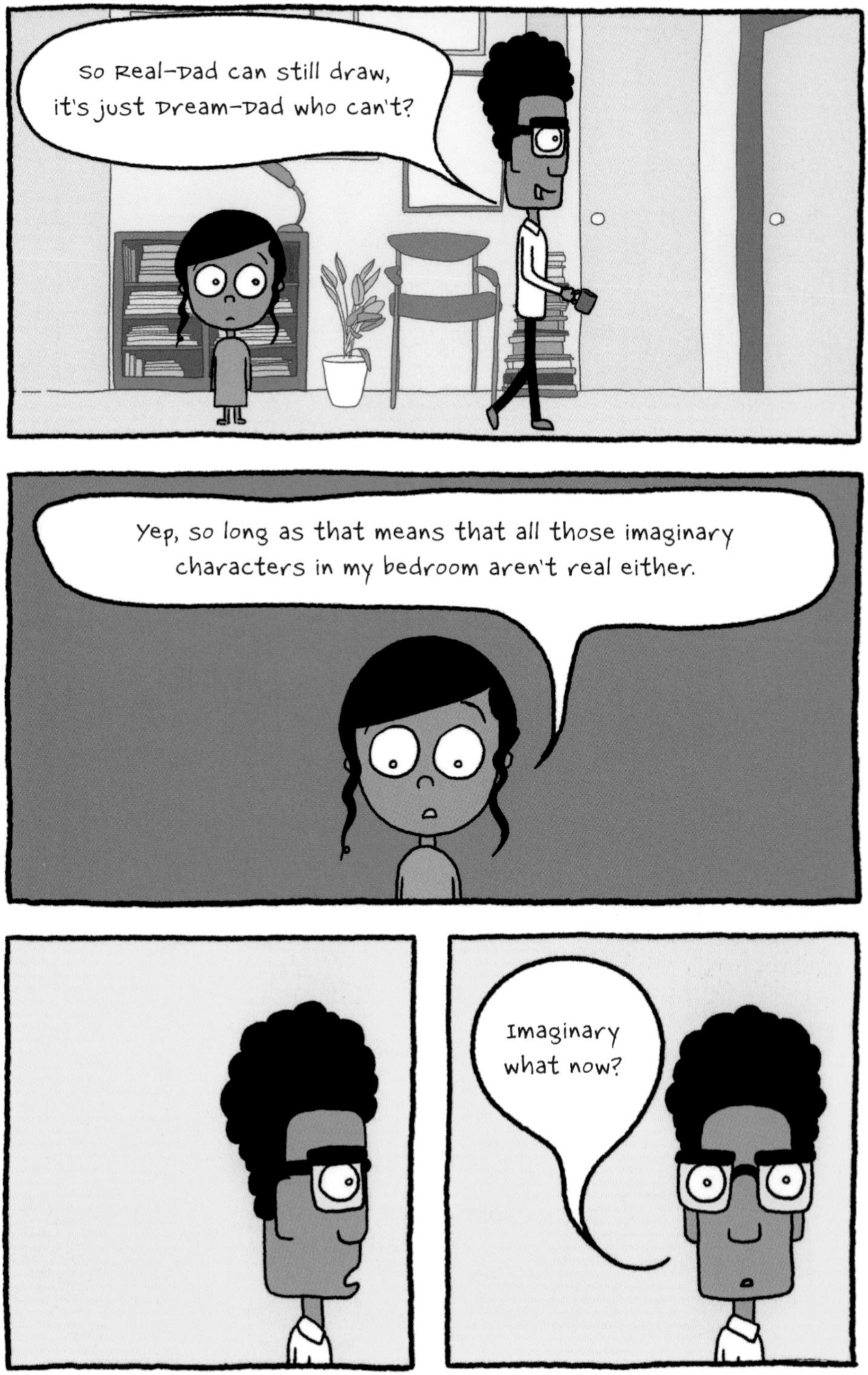
So Real-Dad can still draw, it's just Dream-Dad who can't?
Yep, so long as that means that all those imaginary characters in my bedroom aren't real either.
Imaginary what now?

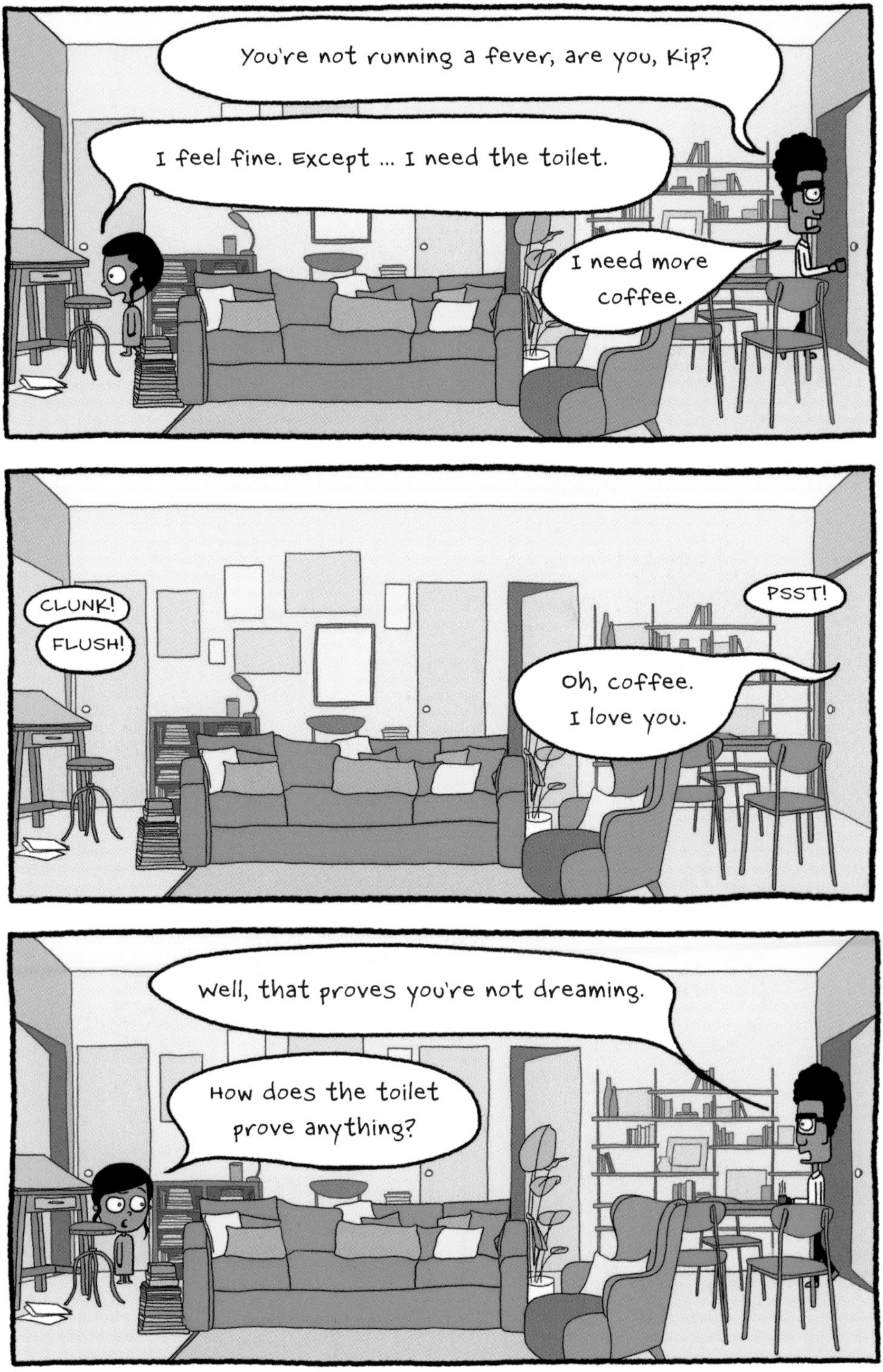
You're not running a fever, are you, Kip?
I feel fine. Except ... I need the toilet.
I need more coffee.
CLUNK!
FLUSH!
PSST!
Oh, coffee. I love you.
Well, that proves you're not dreaming.
How does the toilet prove anything?

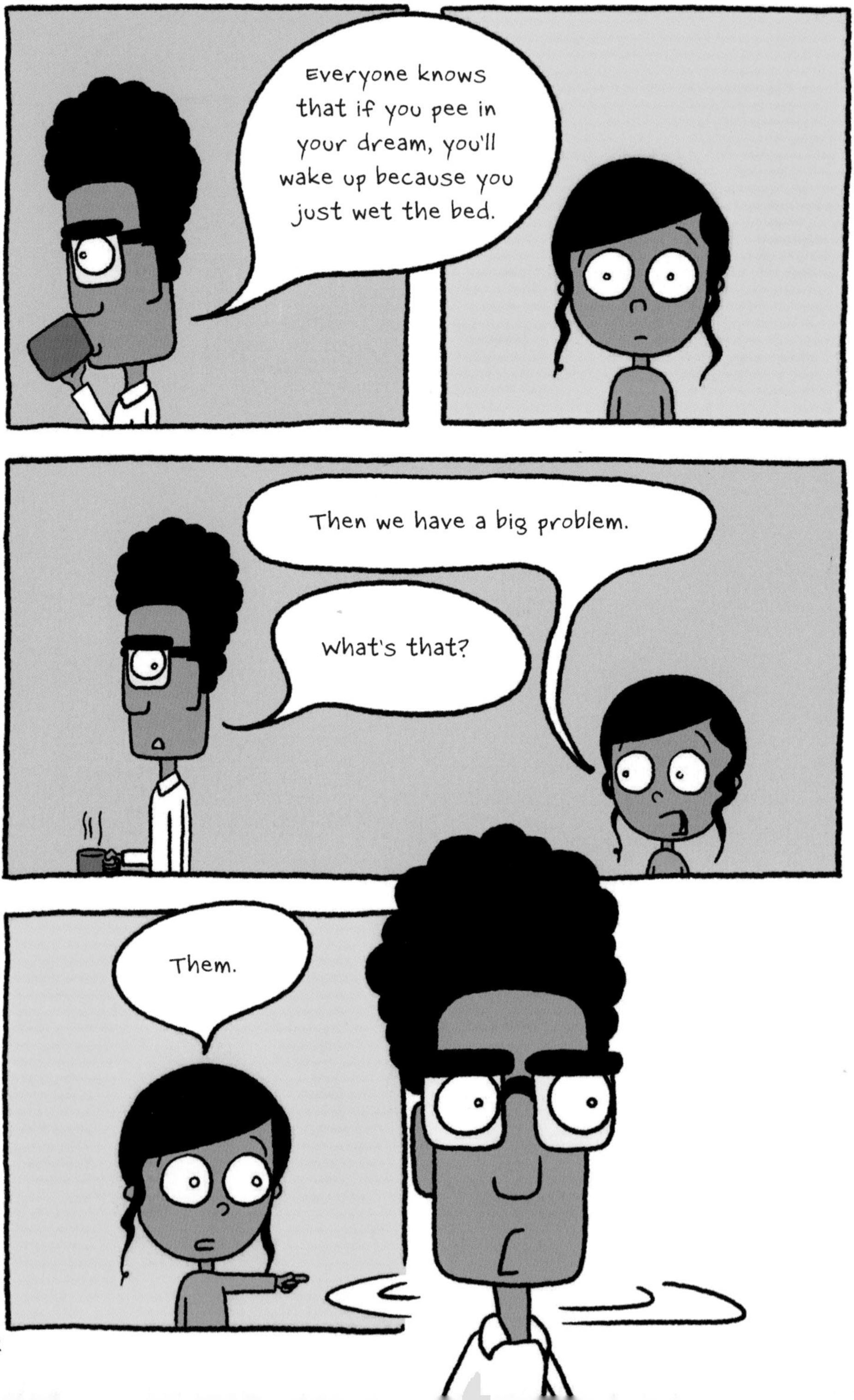
Everyone knows that if you pee in your dream, you'll wake up because you just wet the bed.
Then we have a big problem.
What's that?
Them.

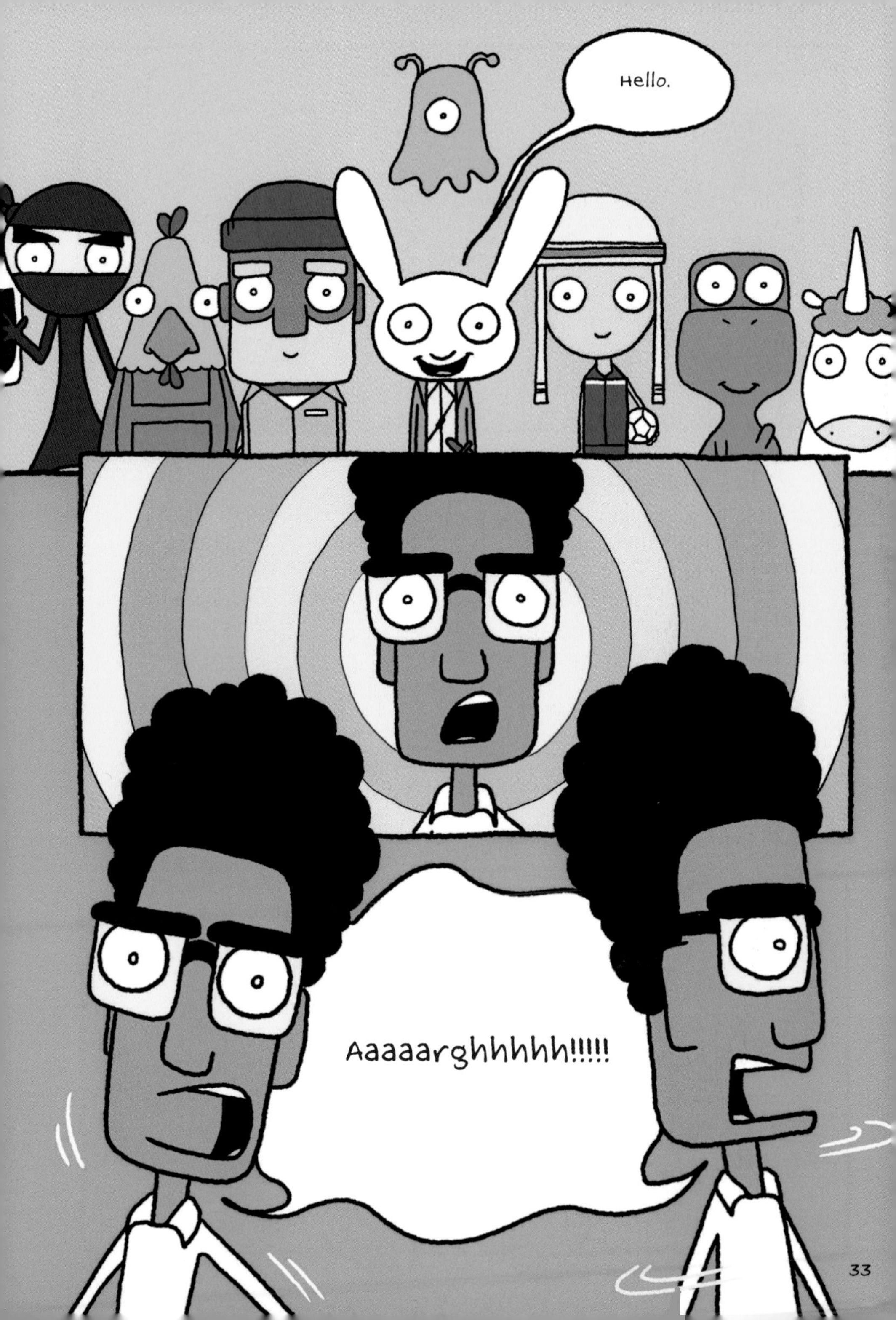
Hello.
Aaaaarghhhhh!!!!!

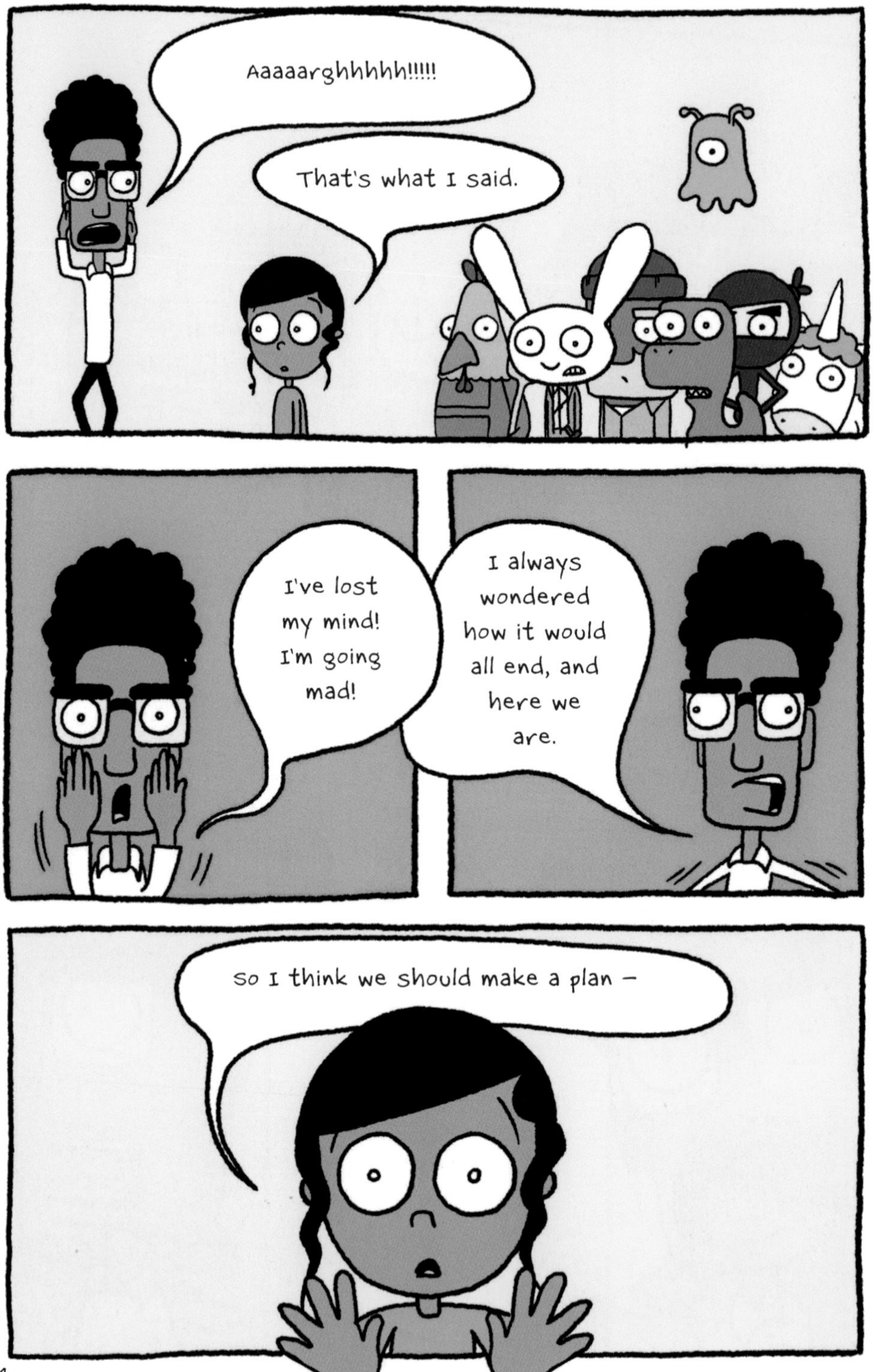
Aaaaarghhhhh!!!!!
That's what I said.
I've lost my mind! I'm going mad!
I always wondered how it would all end, and here we are.
So I think we should make a plan –

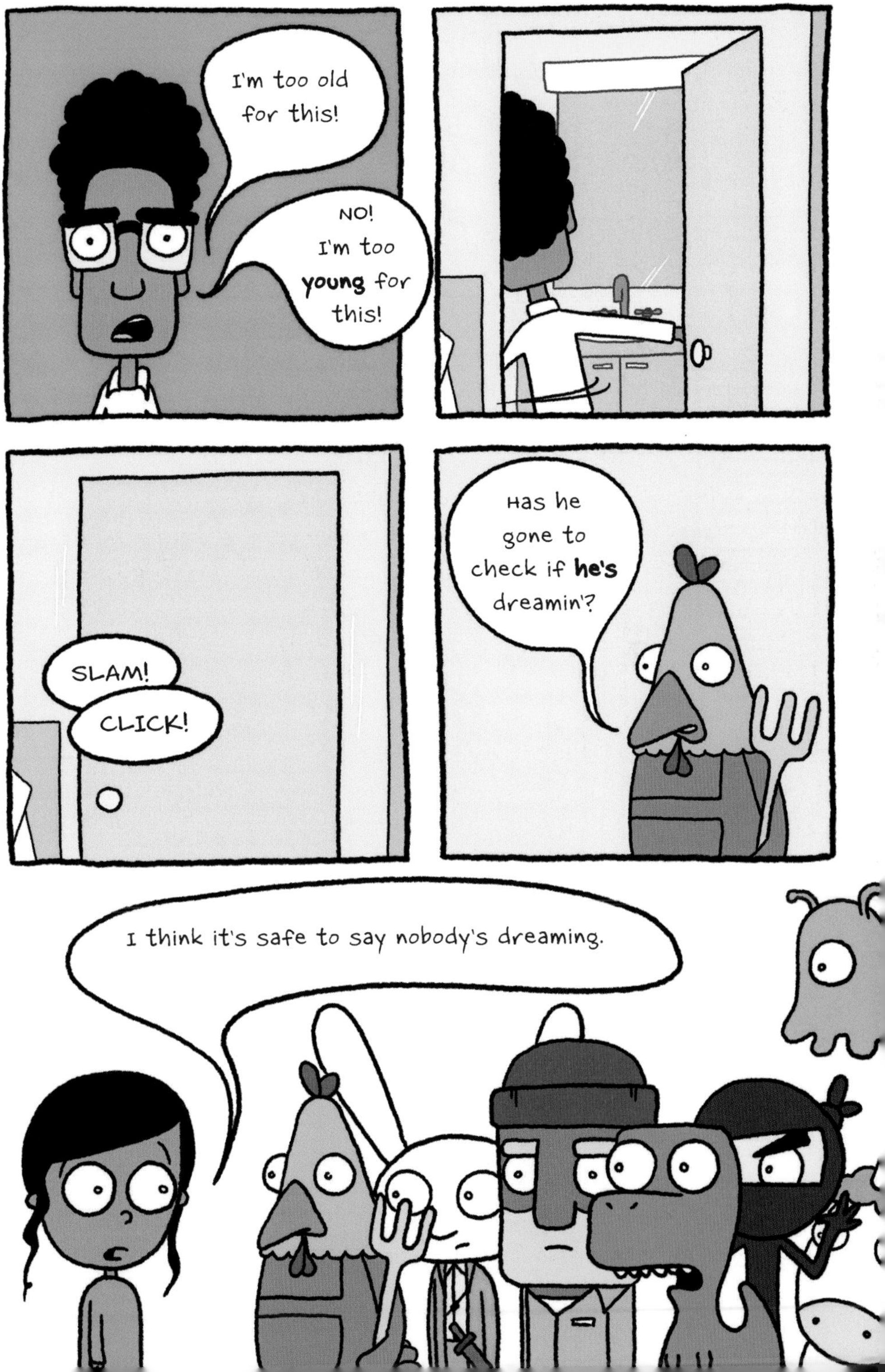
I'm too old for this!
NO! I'm too **young** for this!
SLAM!
CLICK!
Has he gone to check if **he's** dreamin'?
I think it's safe to say nobody's dreaming.

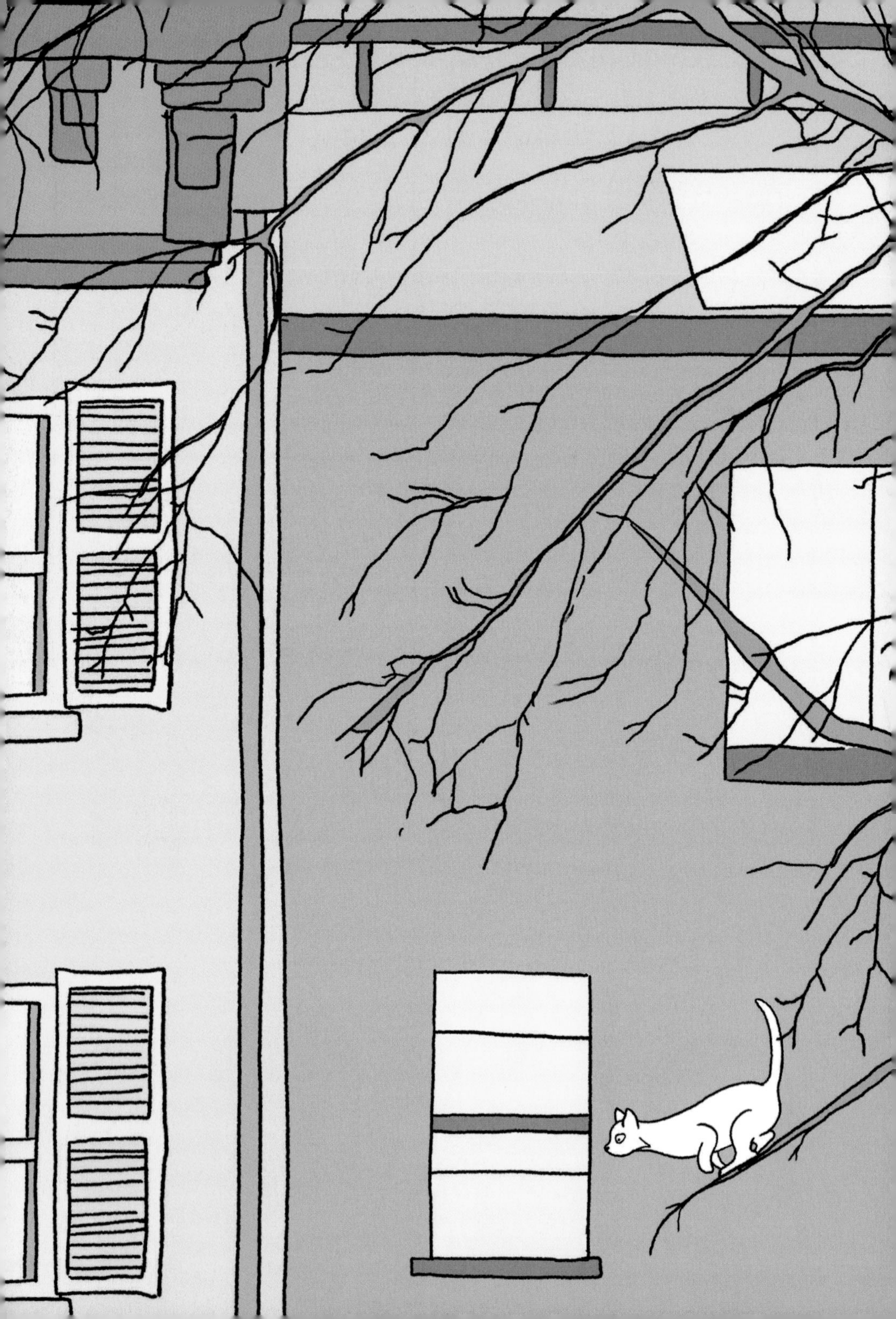

CHAPTER THREE
The Odds make themselves at home

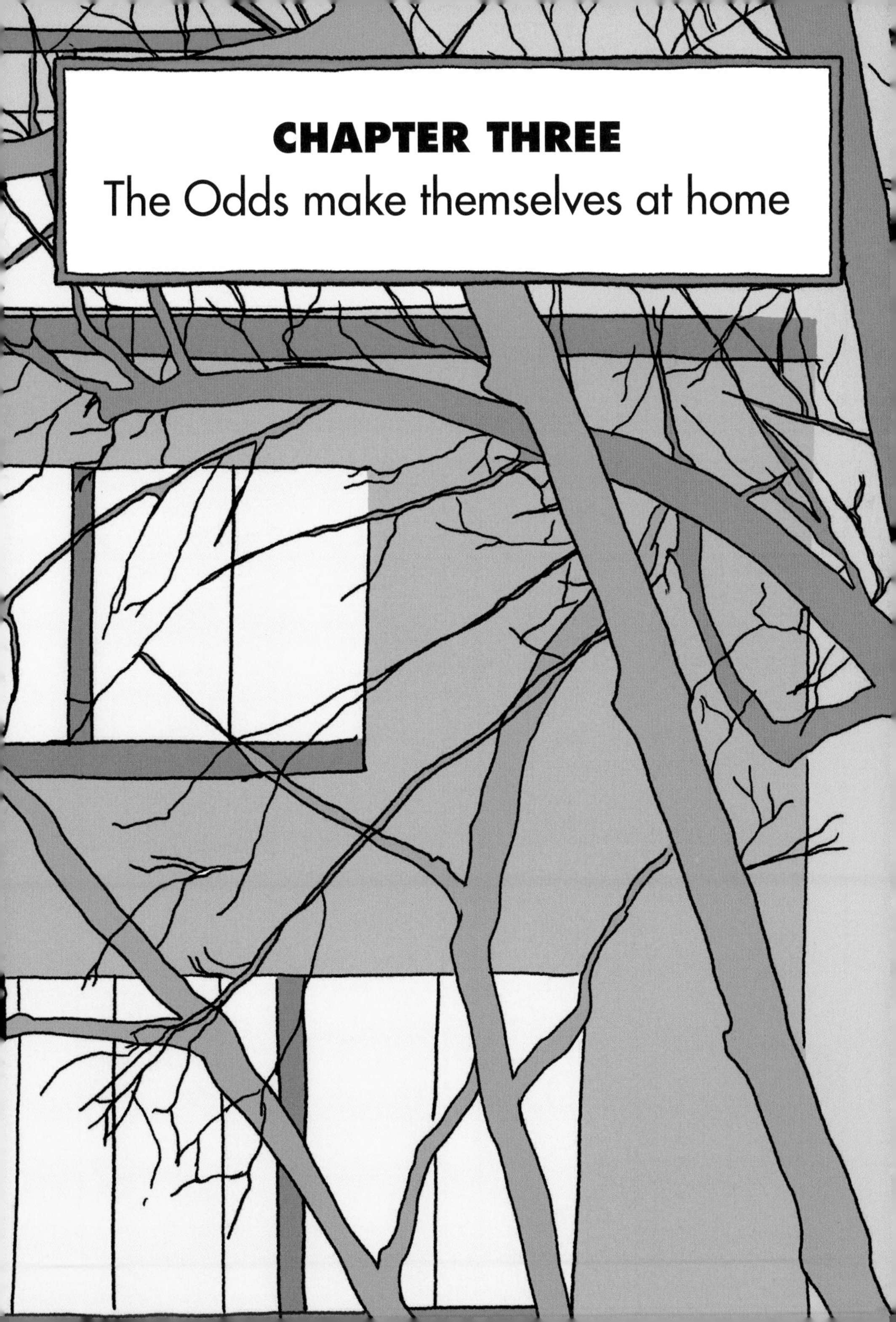

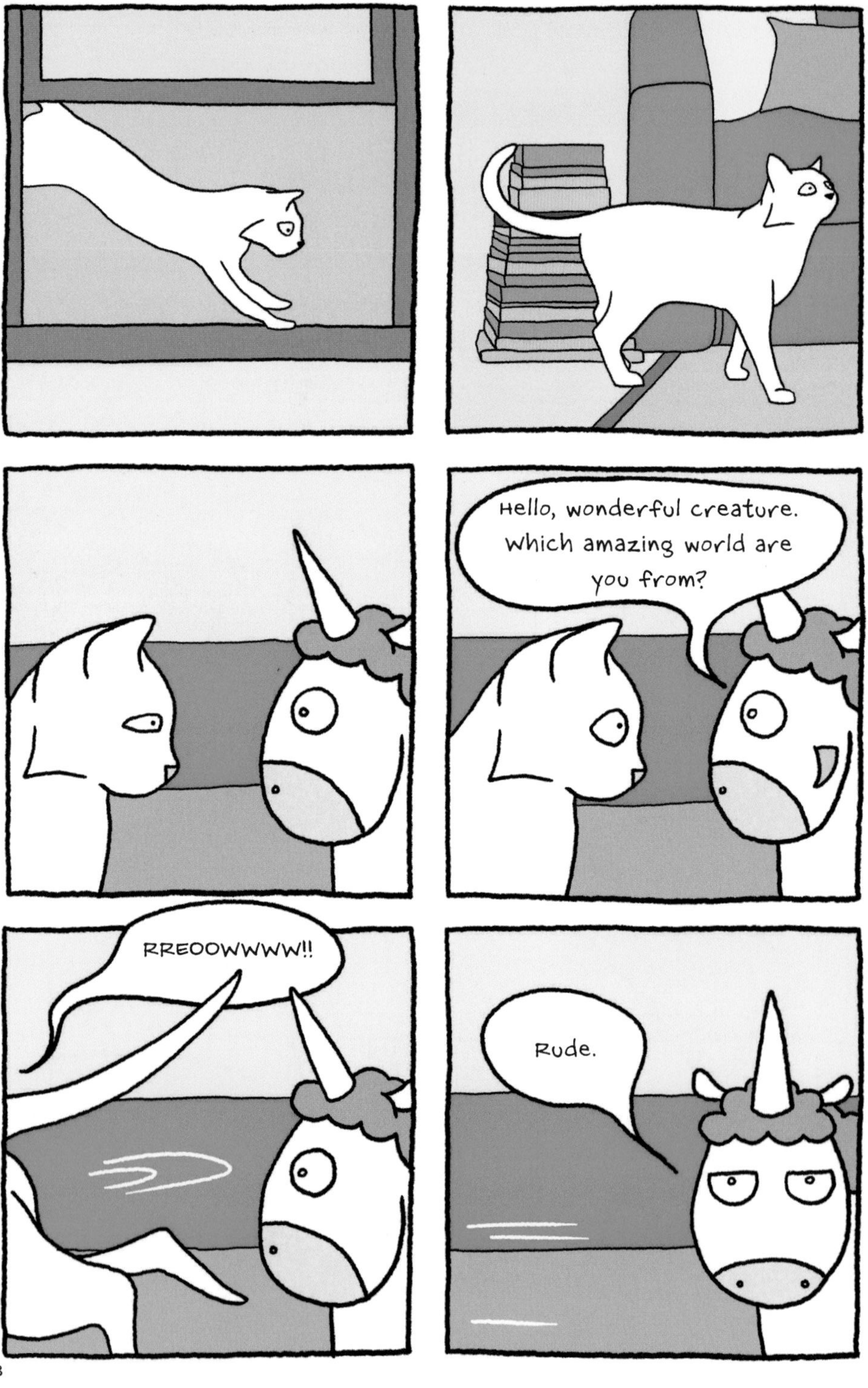
Hello, wonderful creature. Which amazing world are you from?
RREOOWWWW!!
Rude.

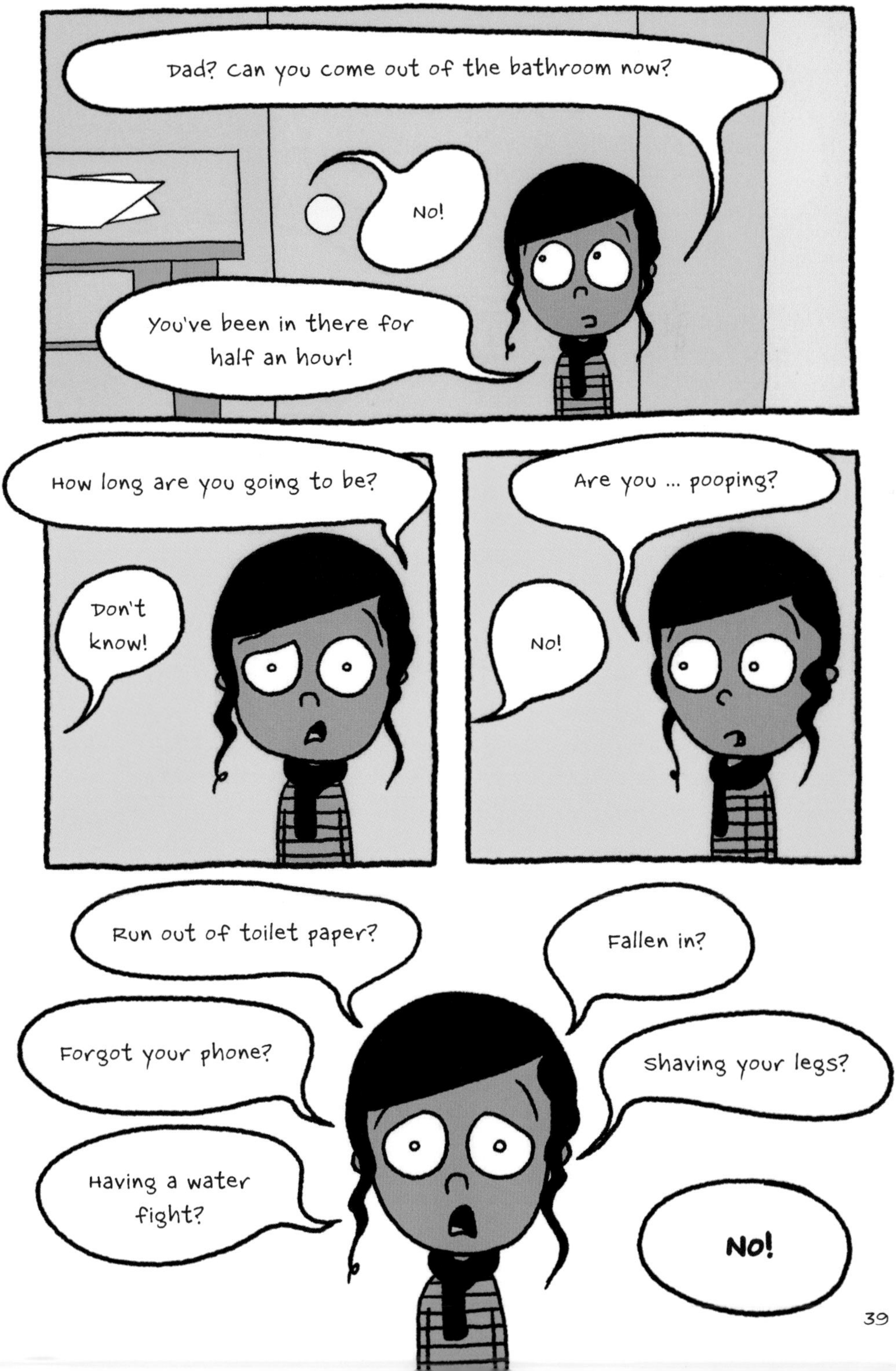
Dad? Can you come out of the bathroom now?
No!
You've been in there for half an hour!
How long are you going to be?
Don't know!
Are you ... pooping?
No!
Run out of toilet paper?
Fallen in?
Forgot your phone?
Shaving your legs?
Having a water fight?
NO!

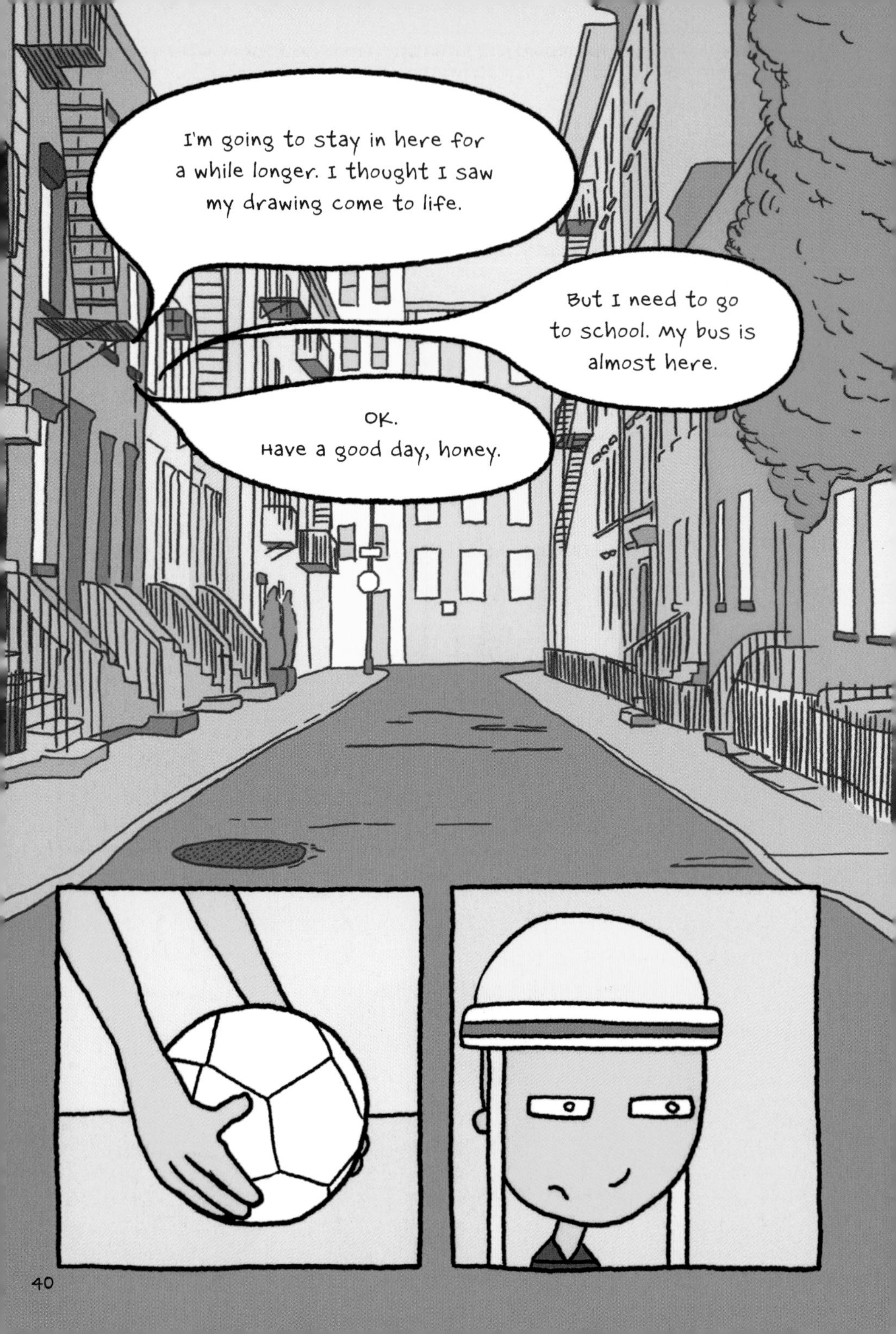
I'm going to stay in here for a while longer. I thought I saw my drawing come to life.
But I need to go to school. My bus is almost here.
OK.
Have a good day, honey.

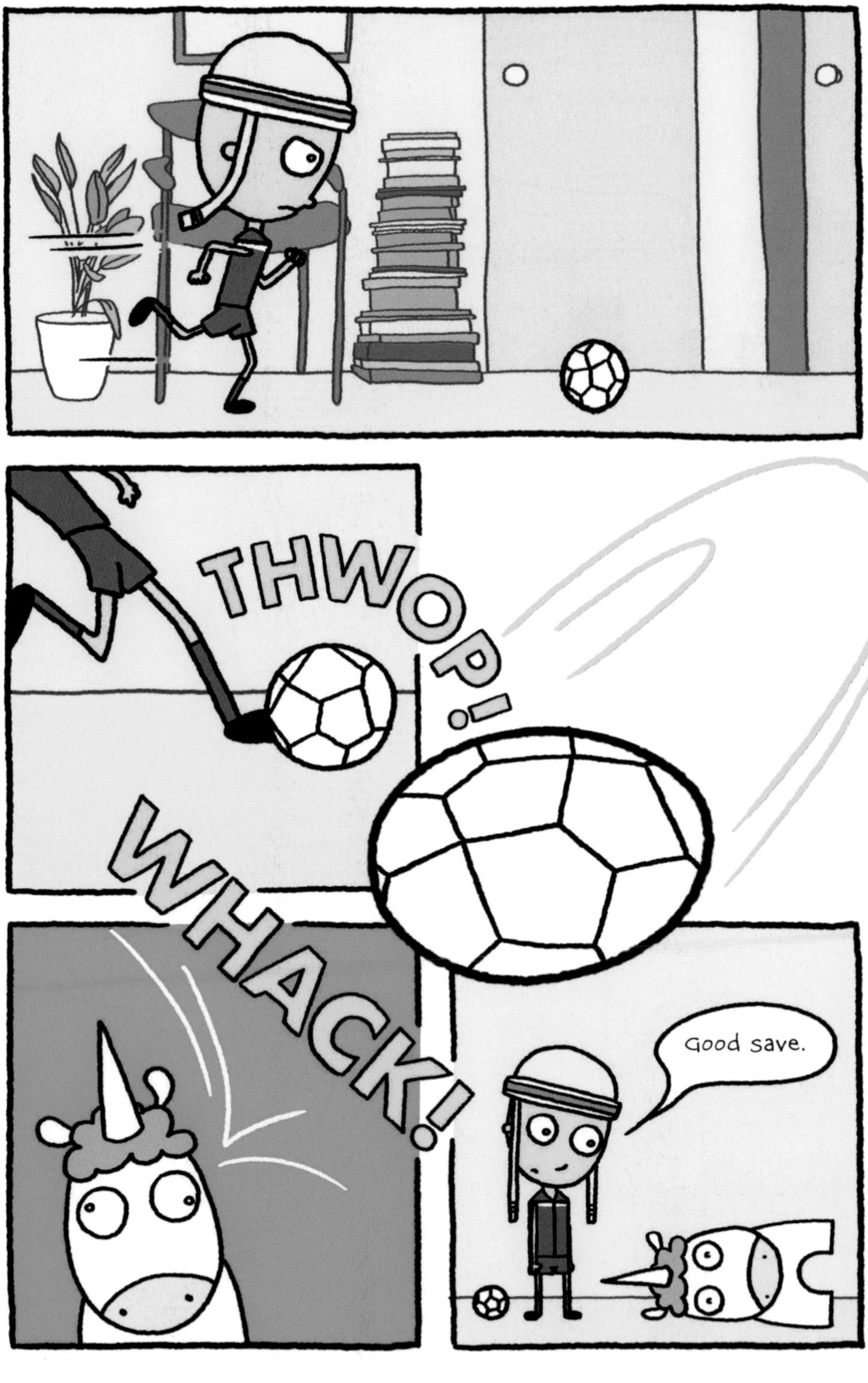
THWOP!
WHACK!
Good save.

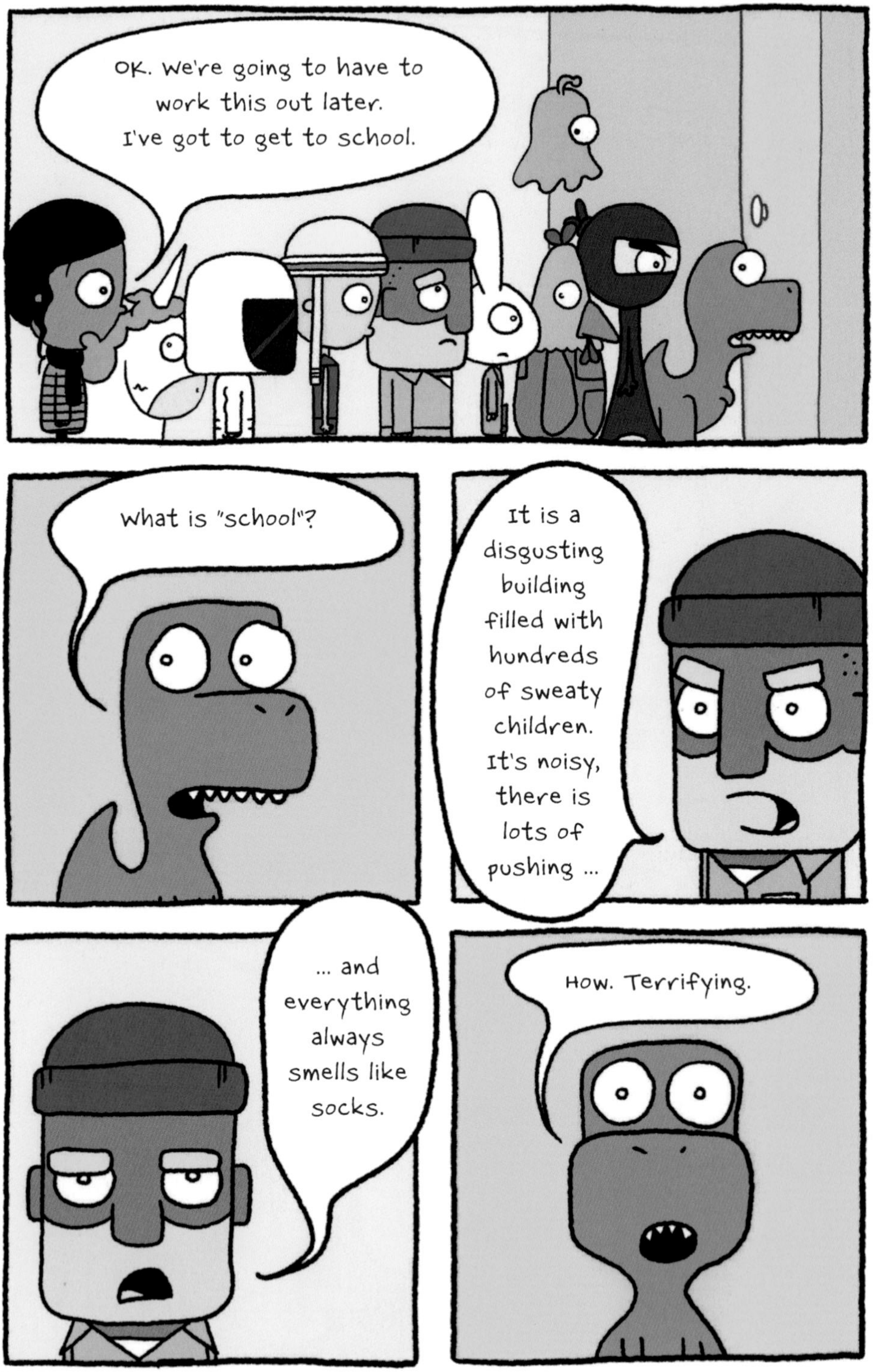
OK. We're going to have to work this out later. I've got to get to school.
What is "school"?
It is a disgusting building filled with hundreds of sweaty children. It's noisy, there is lots of pushing ...
... and everything always smells like socks.
How. Terrifying.

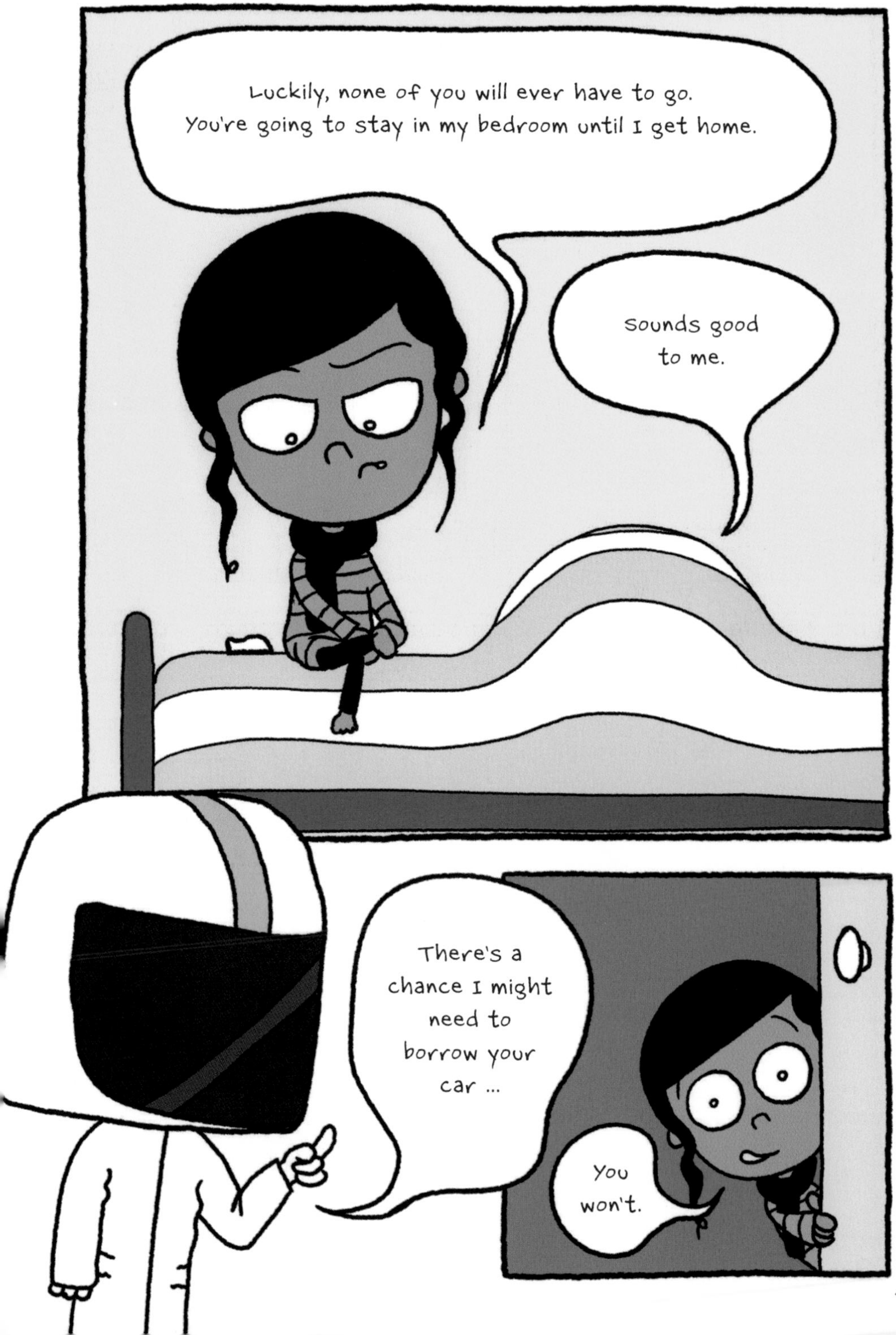
Luckily, none of you will ever have to go. You're going to stay in my bedroom until I get home.
Sounds good to me.
There's a chance I might need to borrow your car ...
You won't.

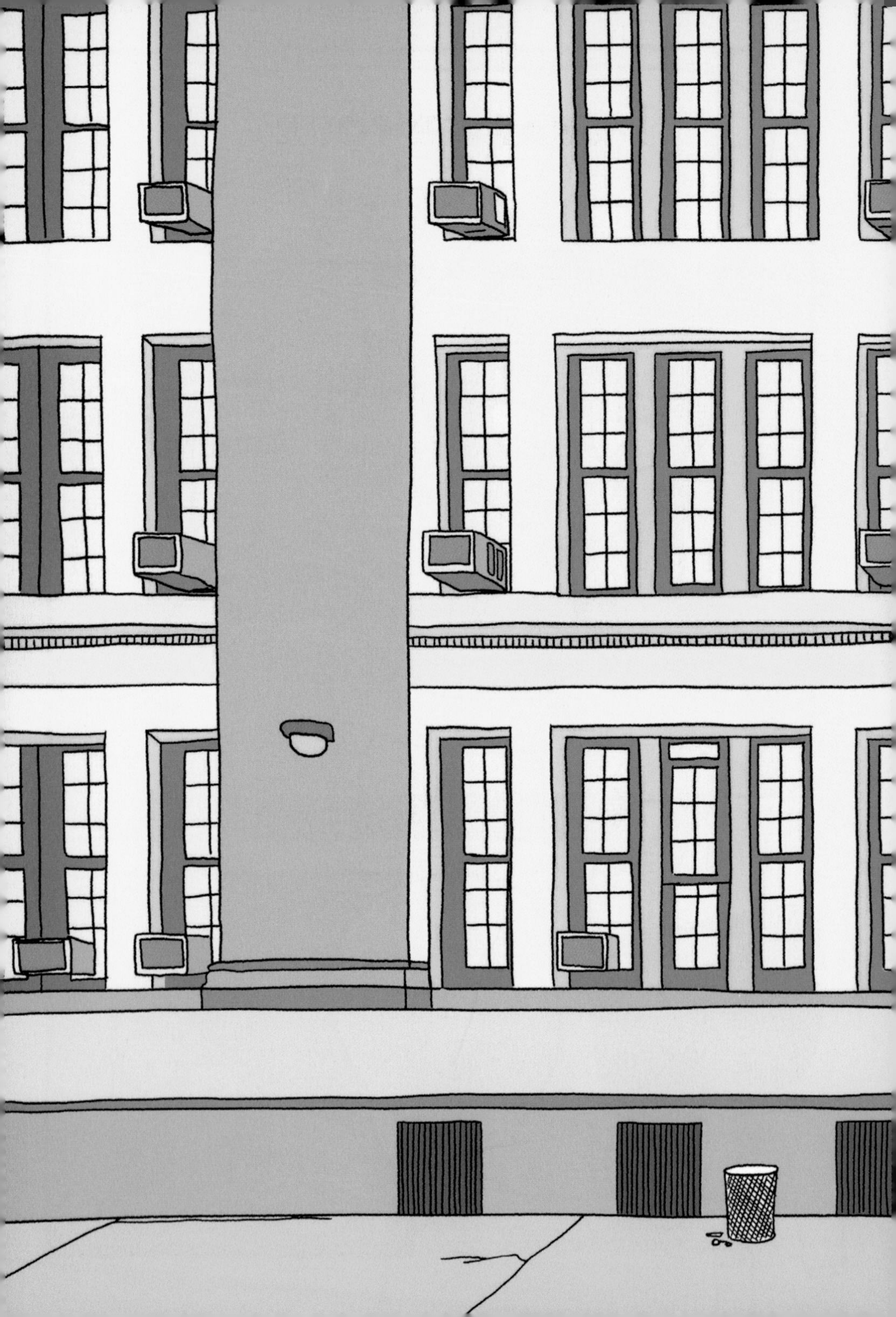

CHAPTER FOUR
The odd one out

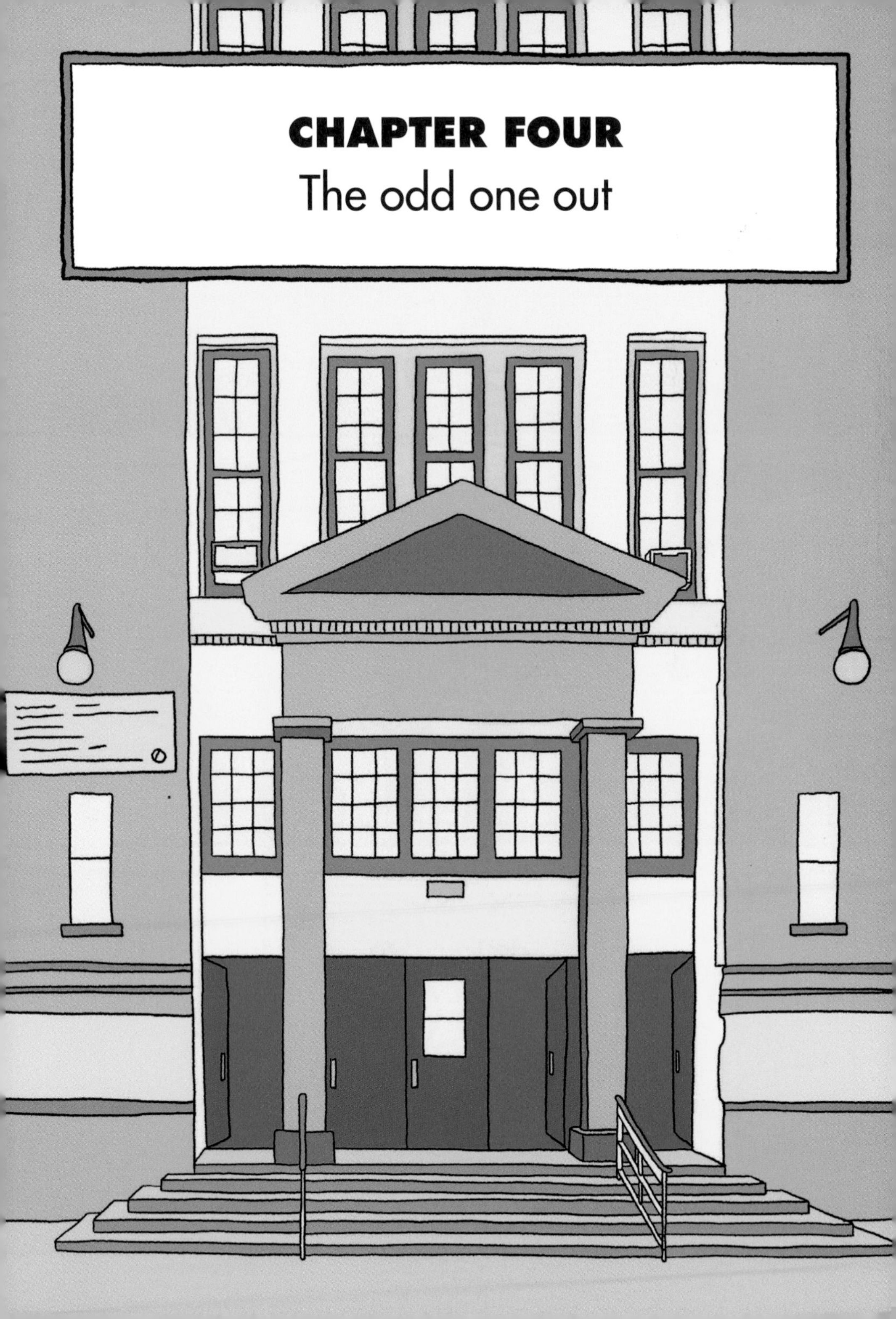

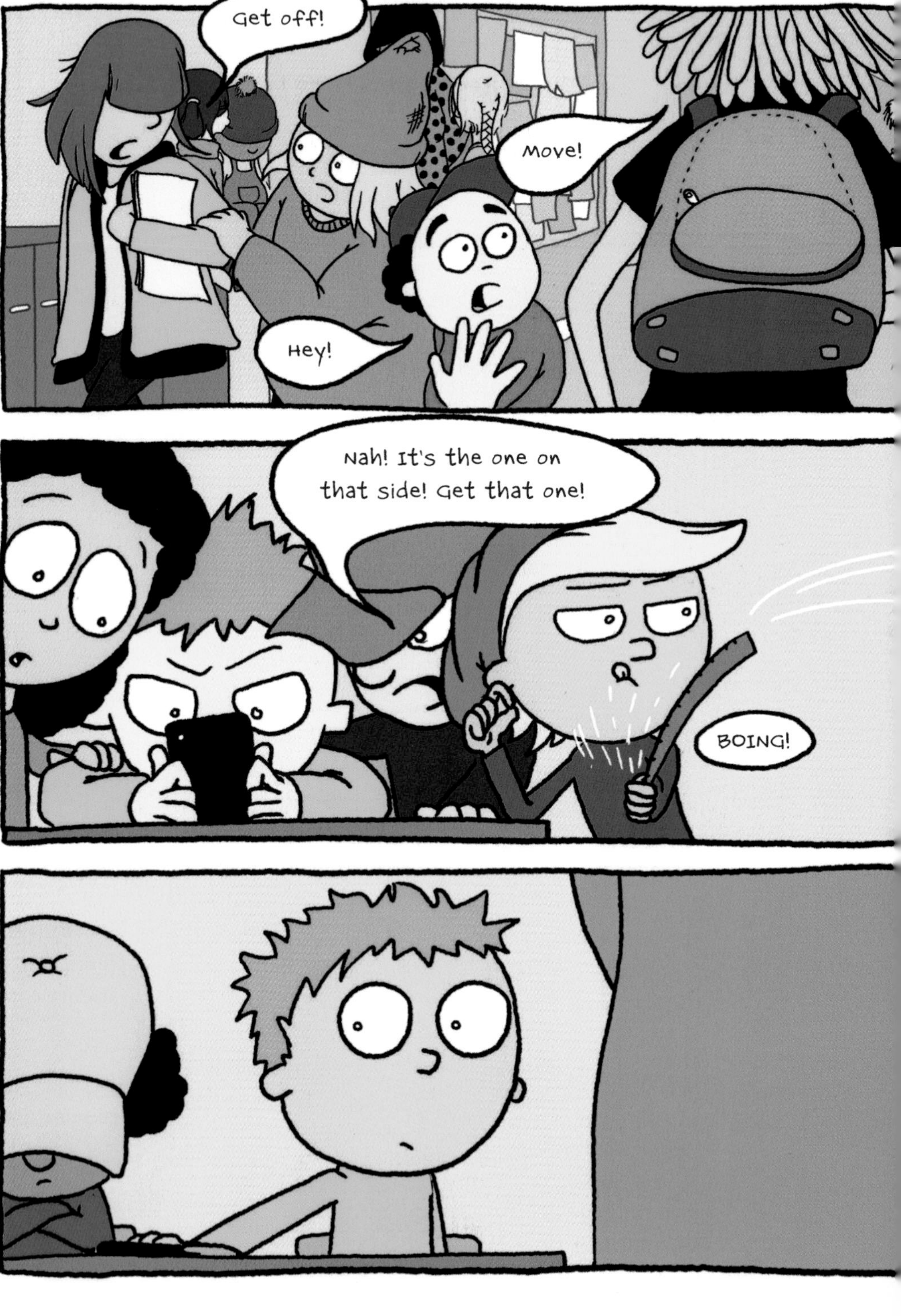
Get off!
Move!
Hey!
Nah! It's the one on that side! Get that one!
BOING!

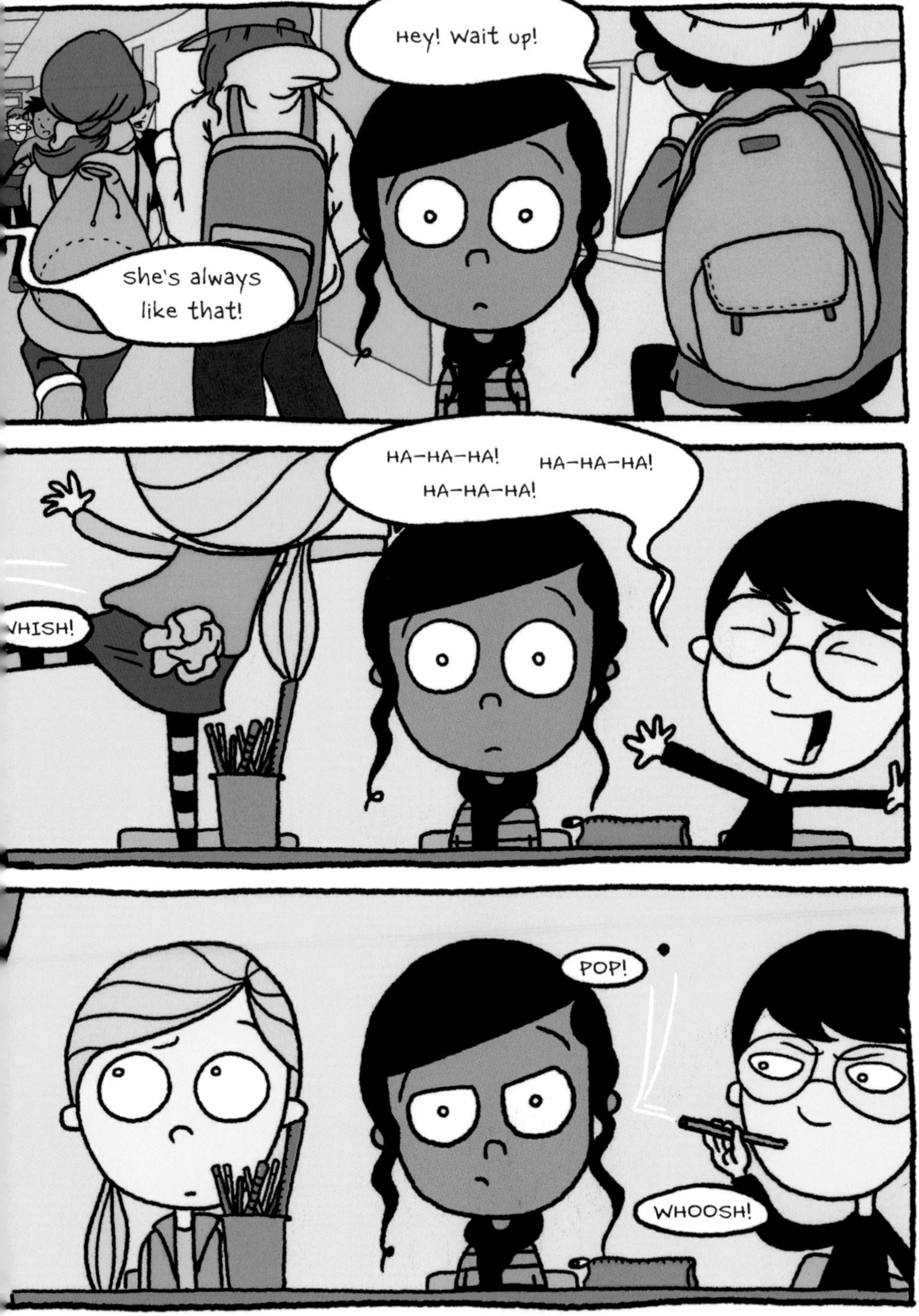
Hey! Wait up!
she's always like that!
HA-HA-HA! HA-HA-HA! HA-HA-HA!
WHISH!
POP!
WHOOSH!

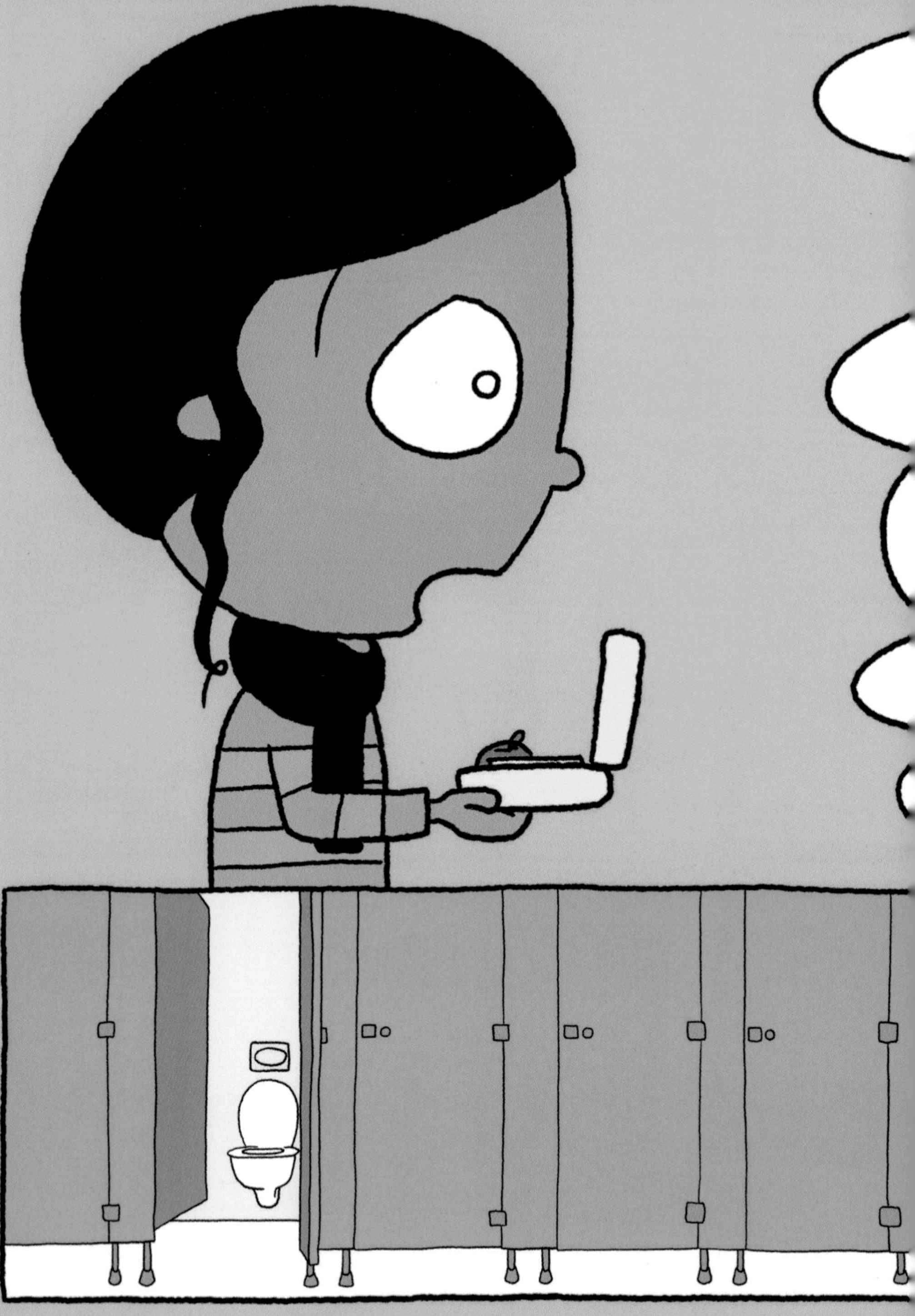

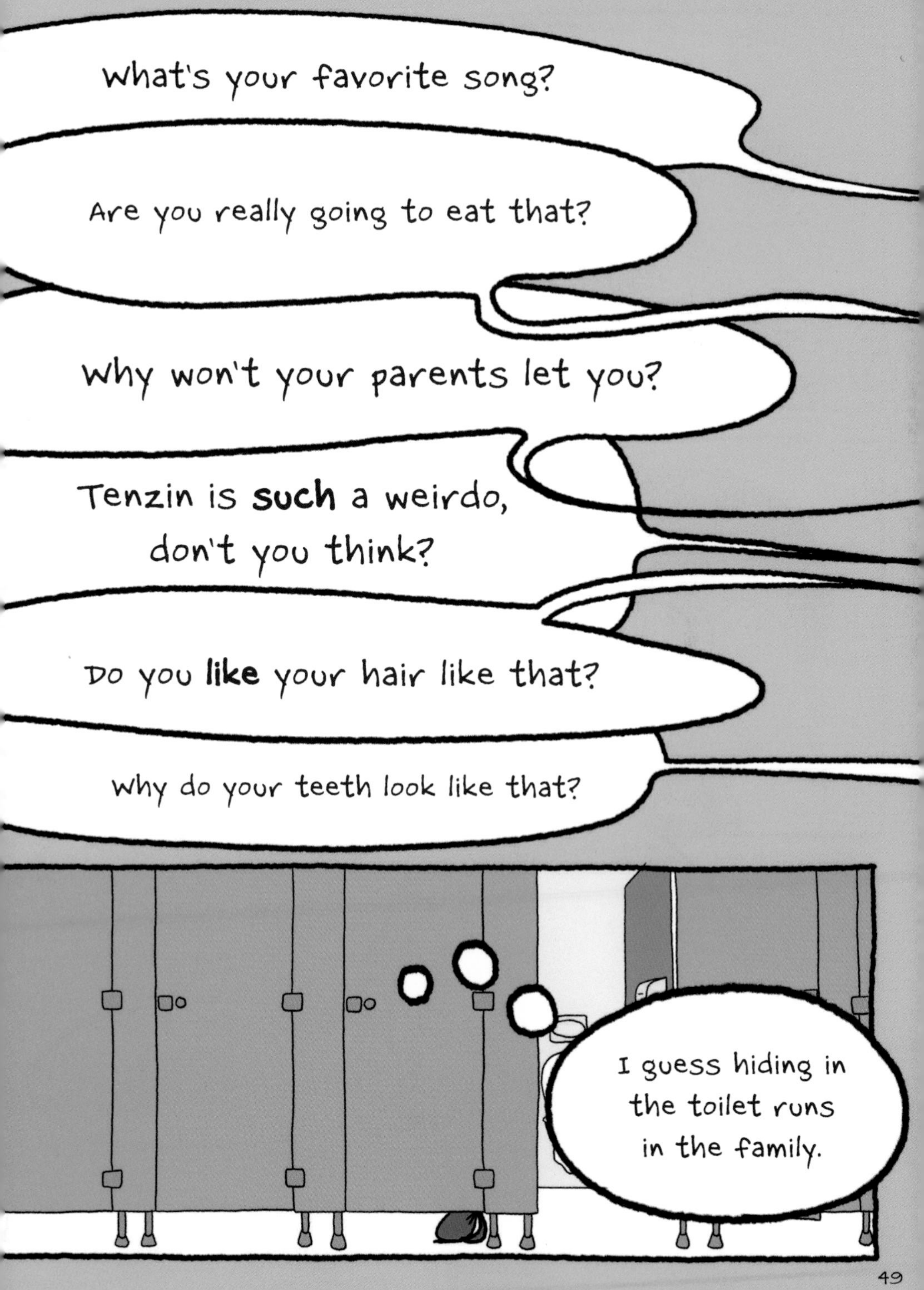
What's your favorite song?
Are you really going to eat that?
Why won't your parents let you?
Tenzin is **such** a weirdo, don't you think?
Do you **like** your hair like that?
Why do your teeth look like that?
I guess hiding in the toilet runs in the family.

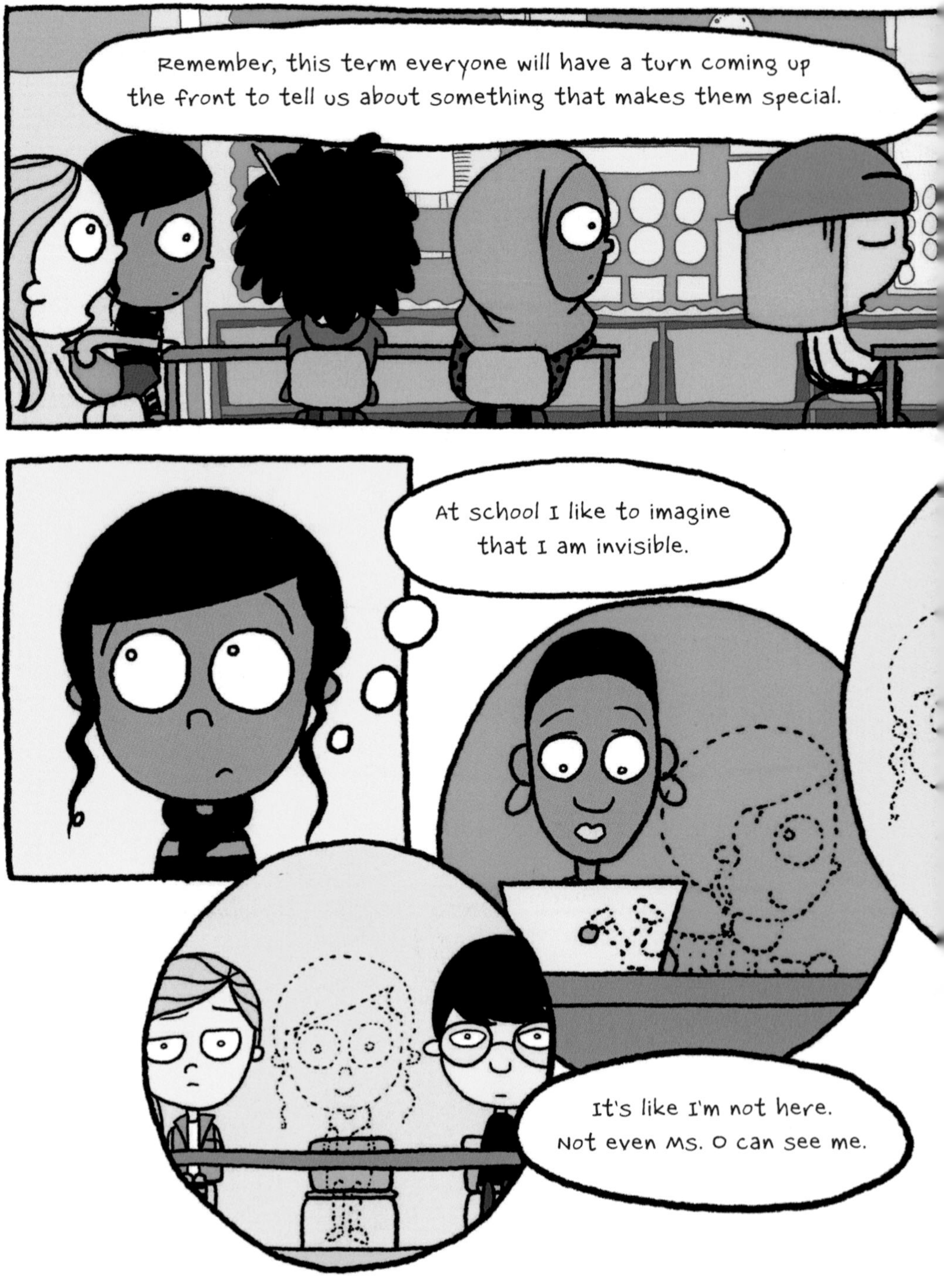
Remember, this term everyone will have a turn coming up the front to tell us about something that makes them special.
At school I like to imagine that I am invisible.
It's like I'm not here. Not even Ms. O can see me.

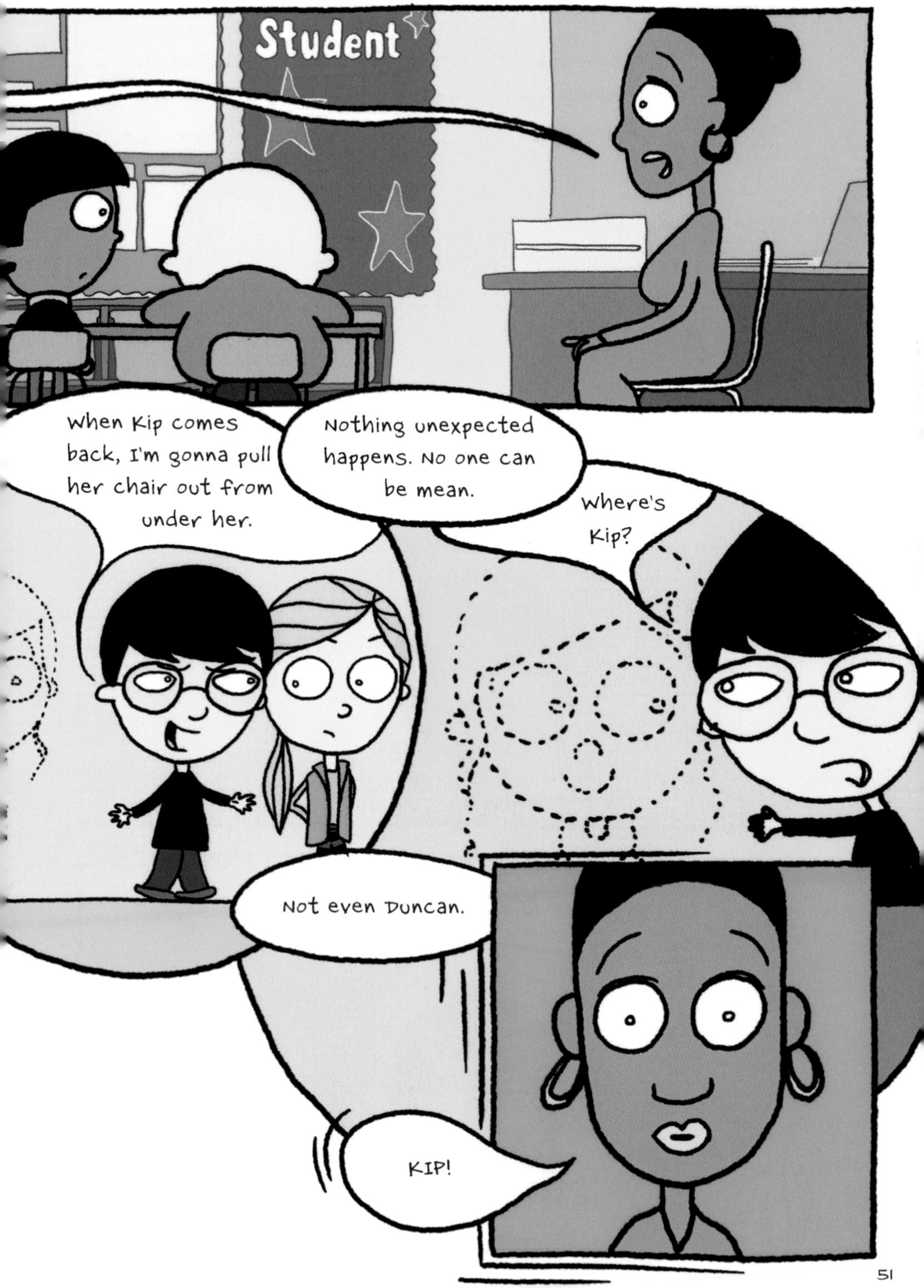
Student
When Kip comes back, I'm gonna pull her chair out from under her.
Nothing unexpected happens. No one can be mean.
Where's Kip?
Not even Duncan.
KIP!

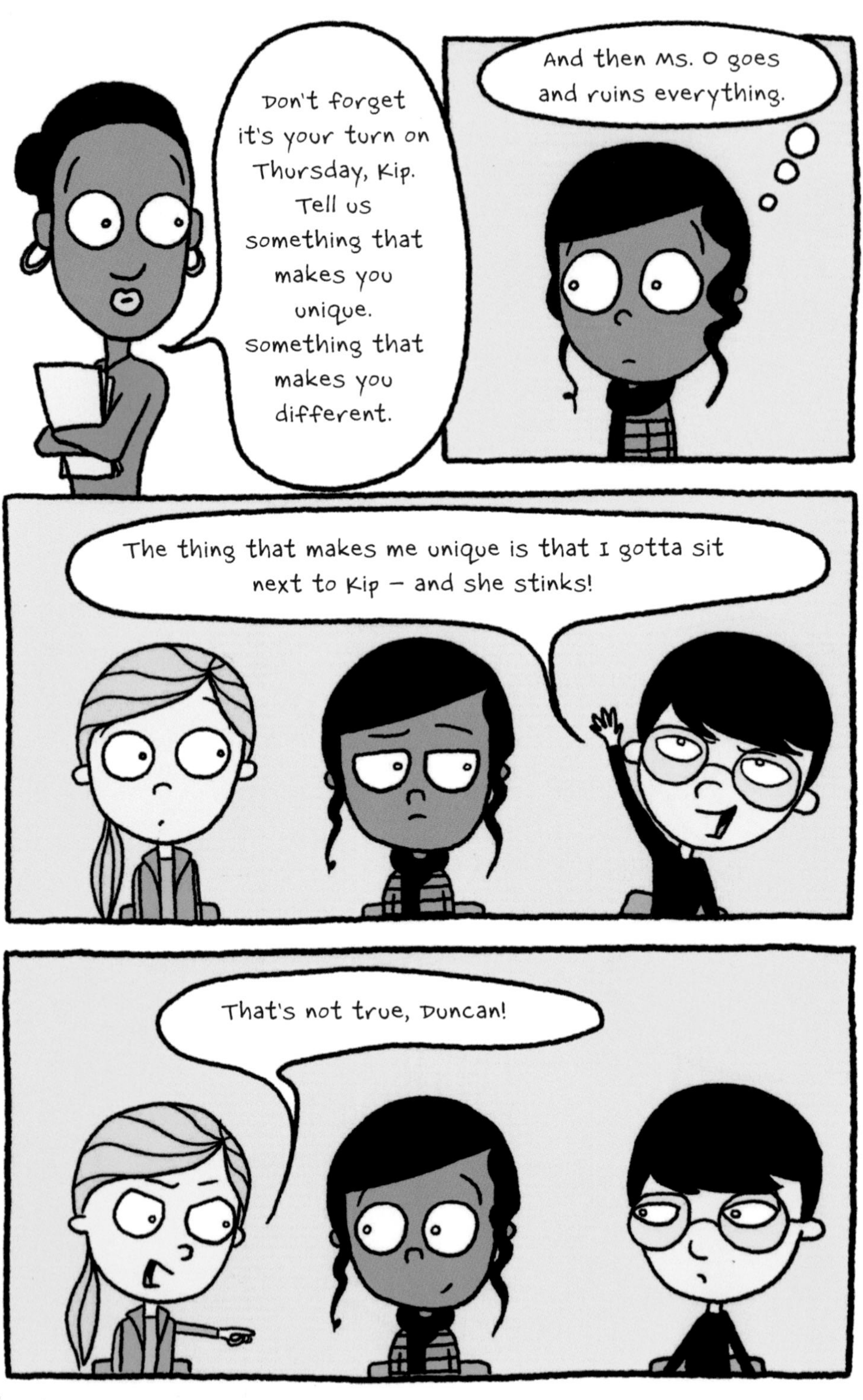
Don't forget it's your turn on Thursday, Kip. Tell us something that makes you unique. Something that makes you different.
And then Ms. O goes and ruins everything.
The thing that makes me unique is that I gotta sit next to Kip – and she stinks!
That's not true, Duncan!

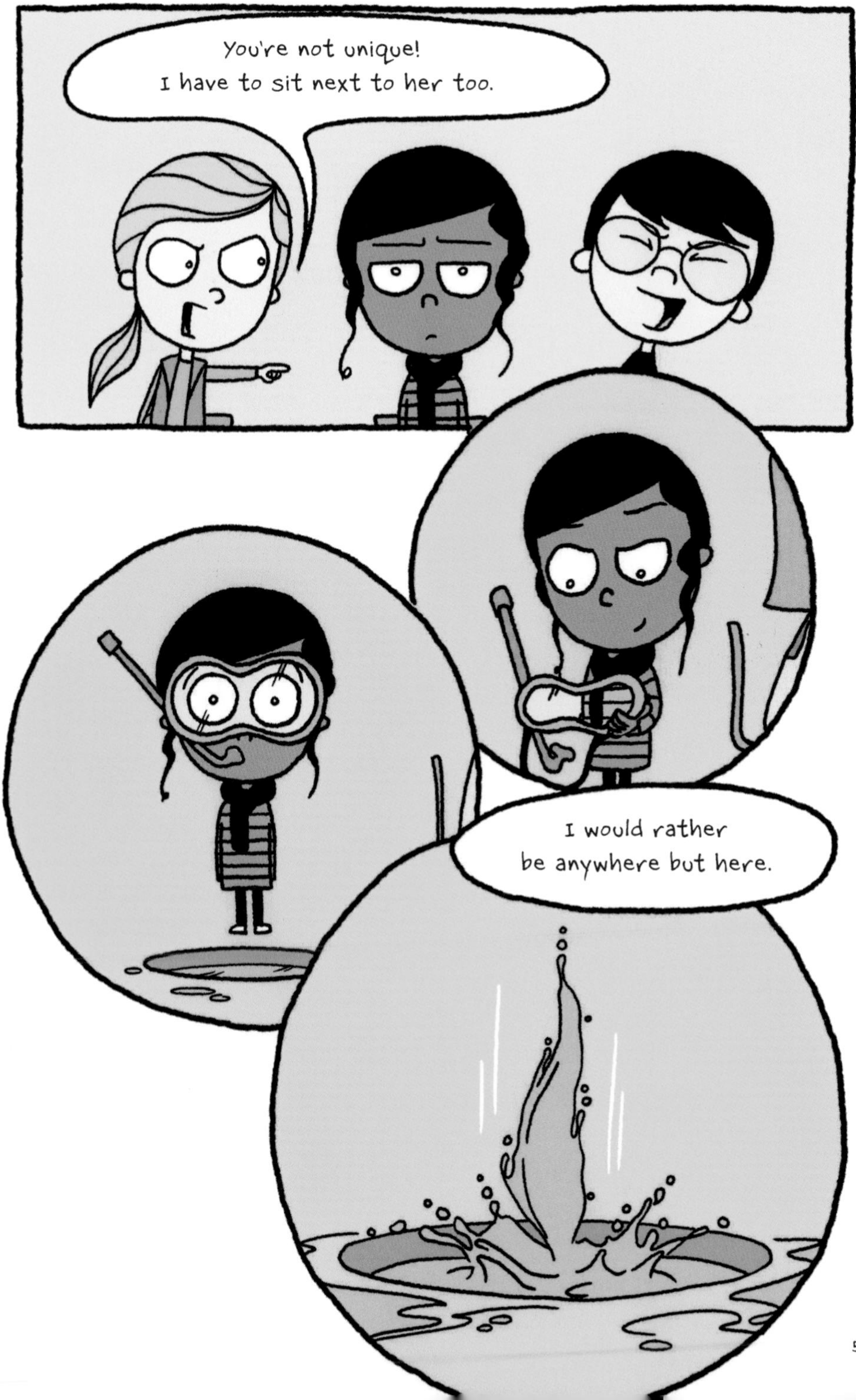
You're not unique!
I have to sit next to her too.
I would rather
be anywhere but here.

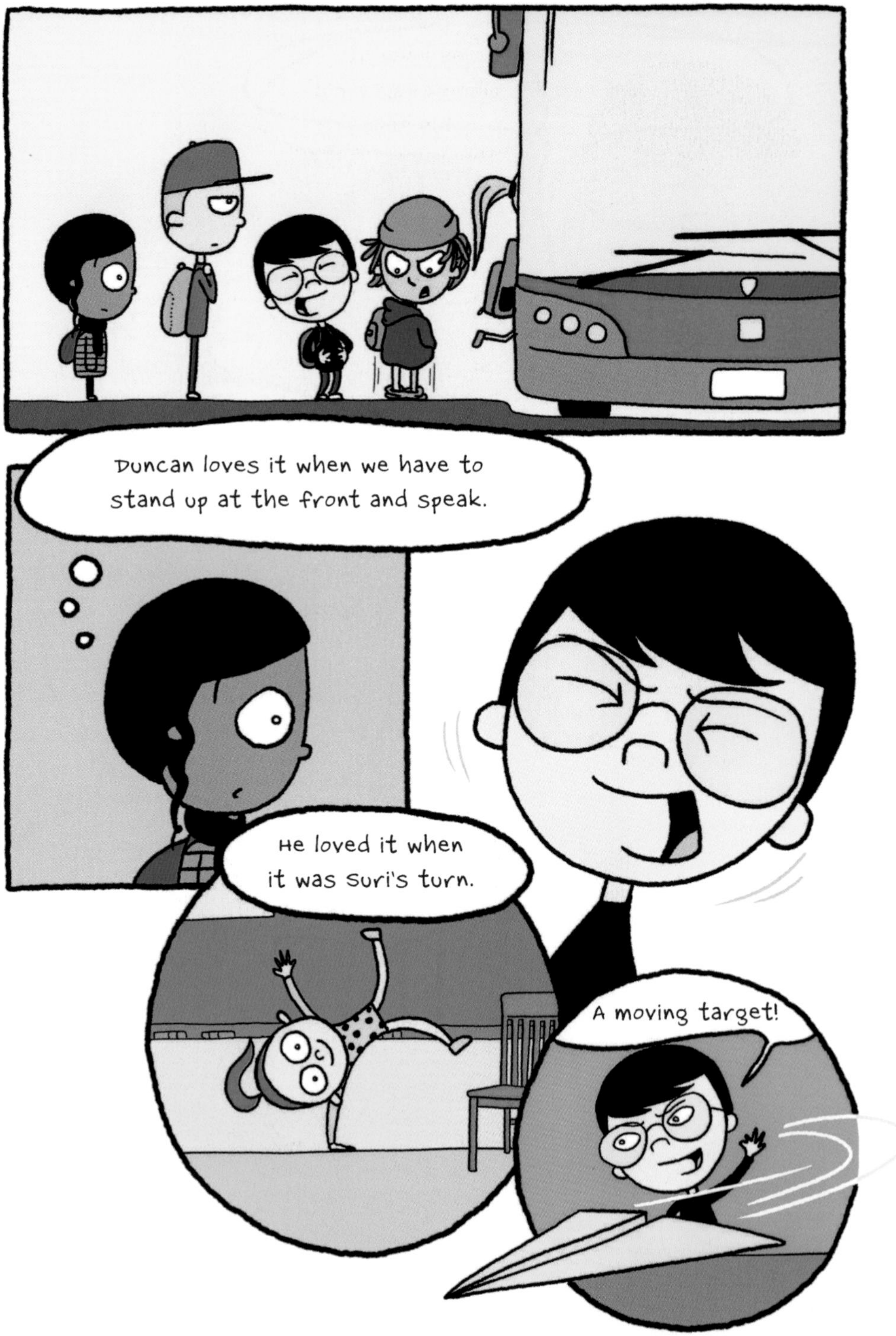
Duncan loves it when we have to stand up at the front and speak.
He loved it when it was Suri's turn.
A moving target!

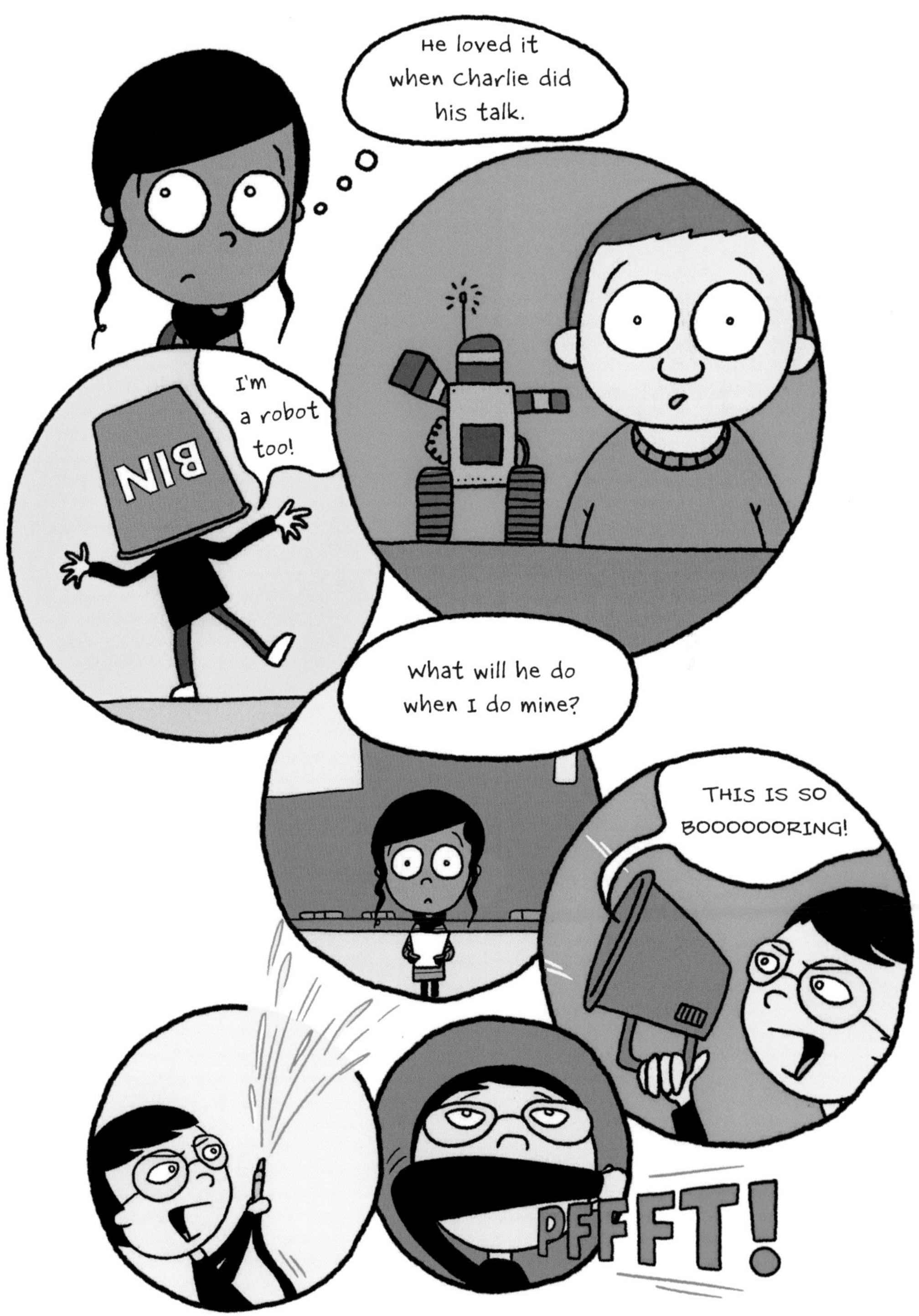

He loved it when Charlie did his talk.
I'm a robot too!
BIN
What will he do when I do mine?
THIS IS SO BOOOOOORING!
PFFFT!

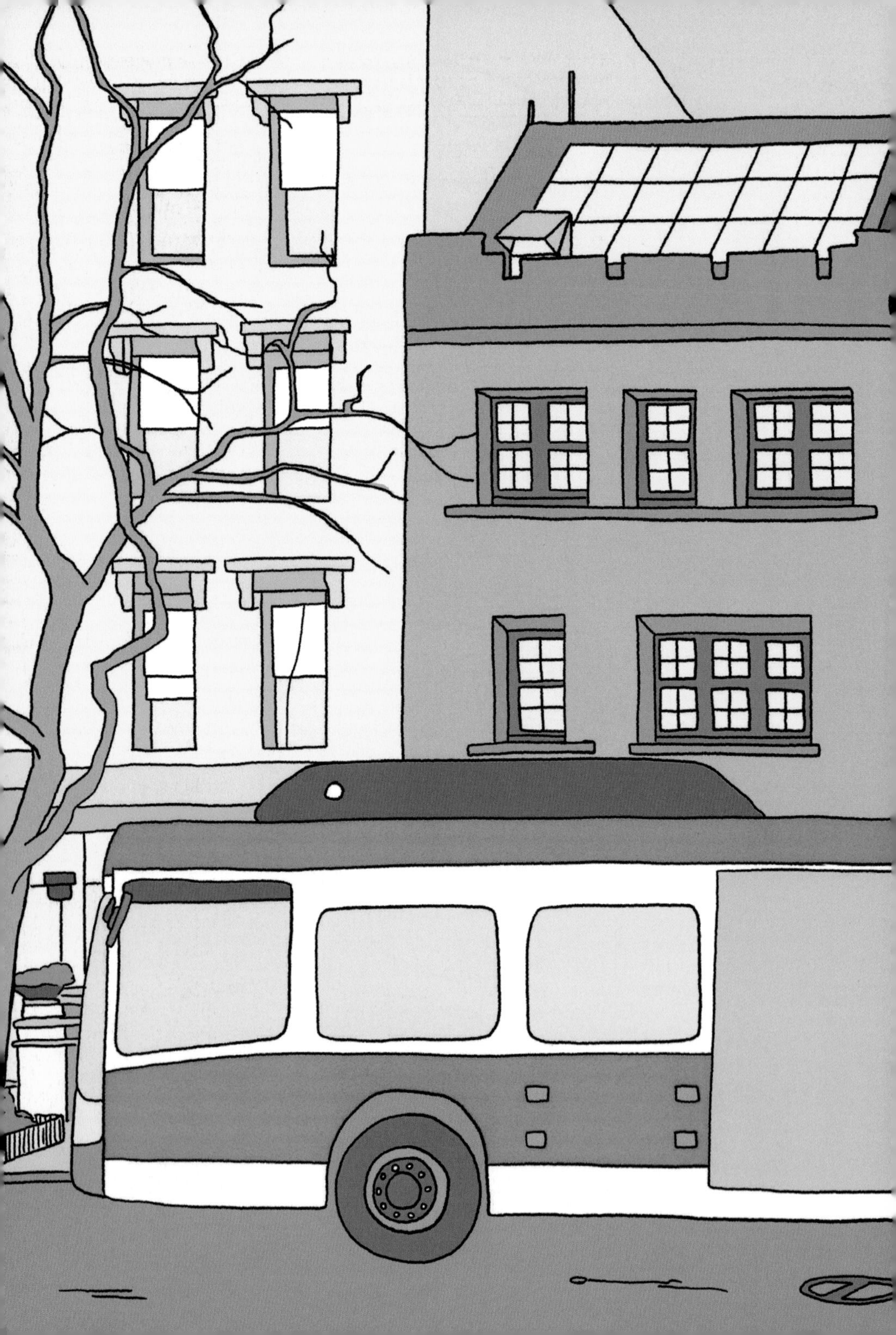

CHAPTER FIVE
The Odds take charge

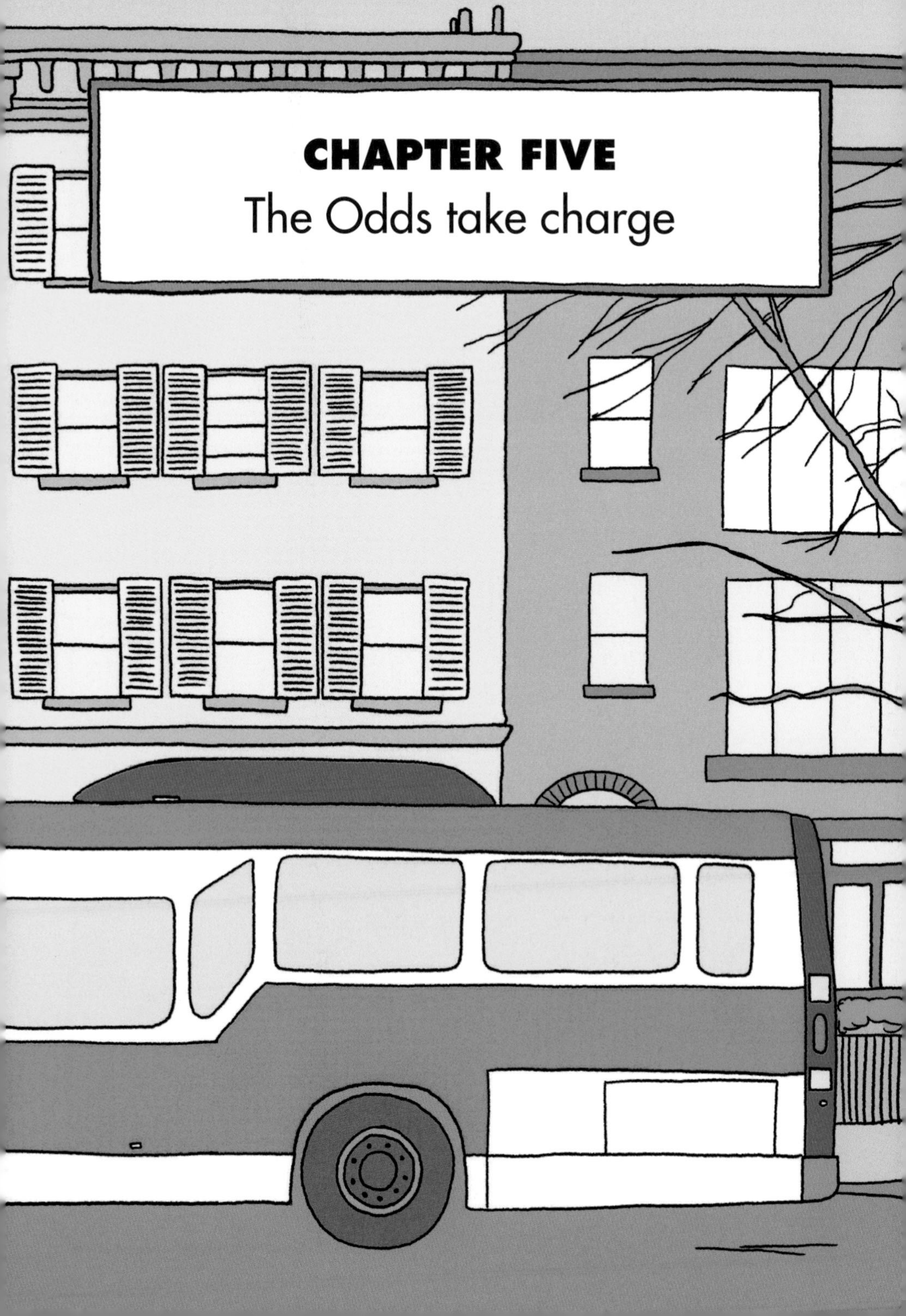

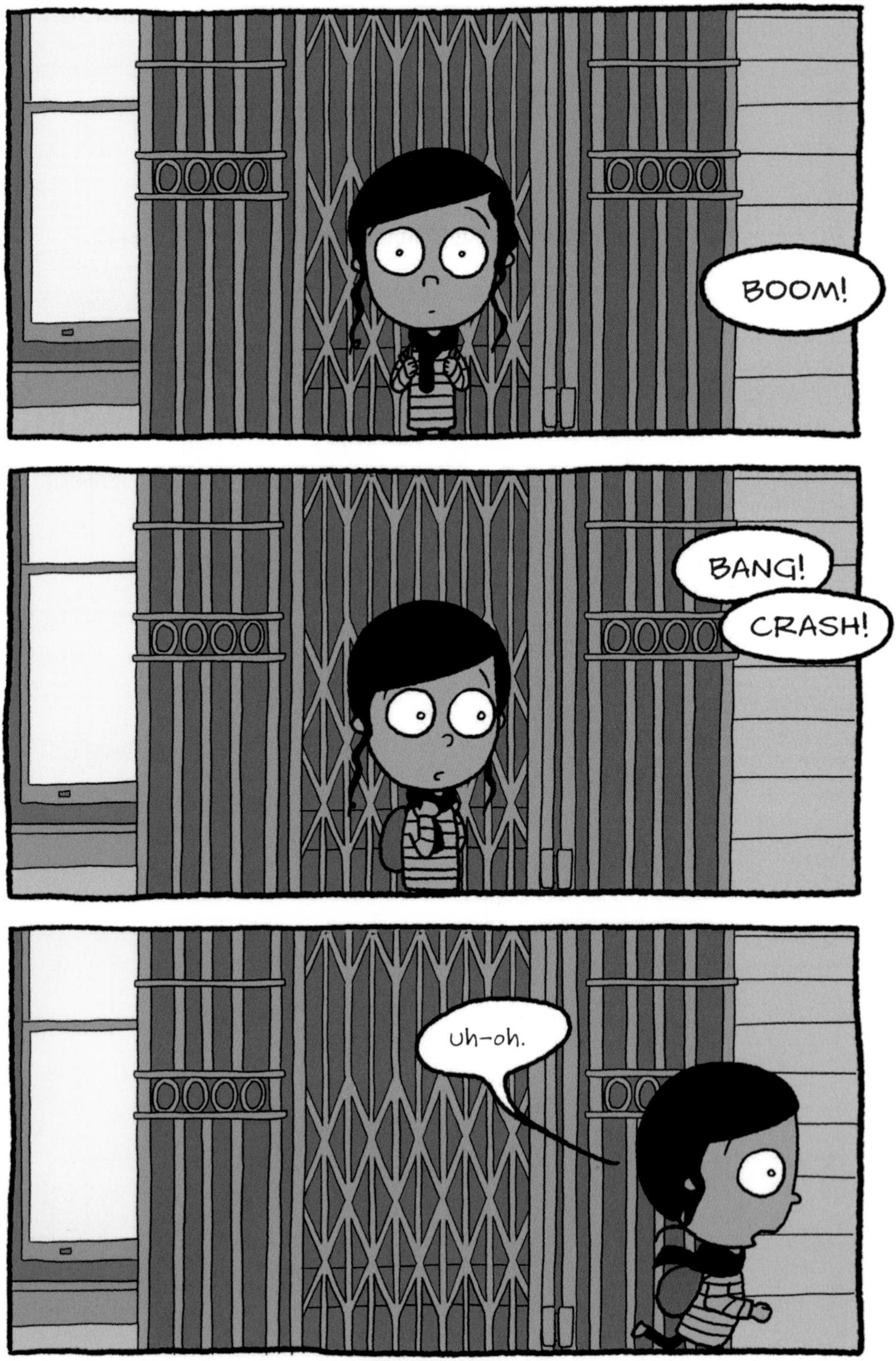
BOOM!
BANG!
CRASH!
Uh-oh.

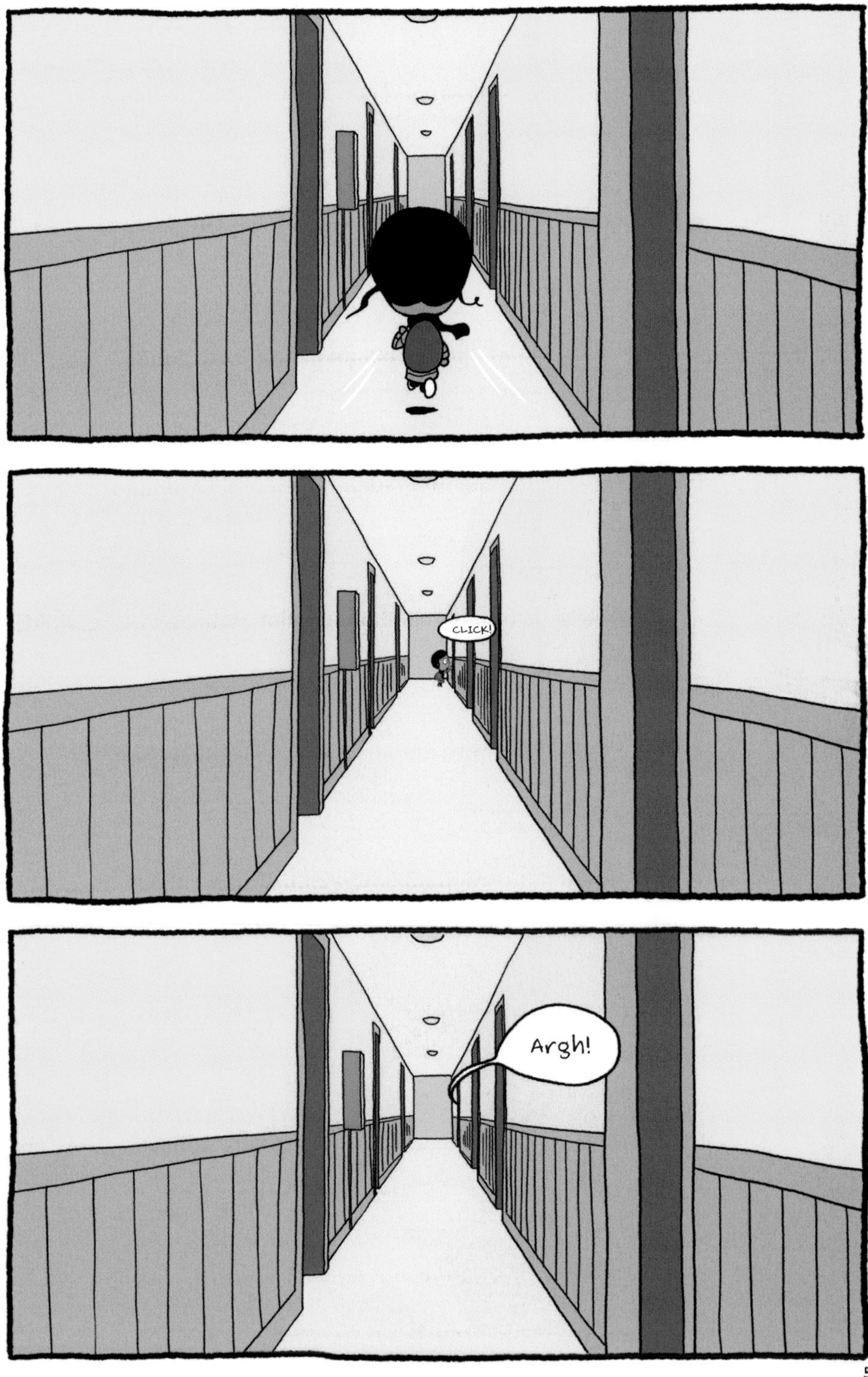
CLICK!
Argh!

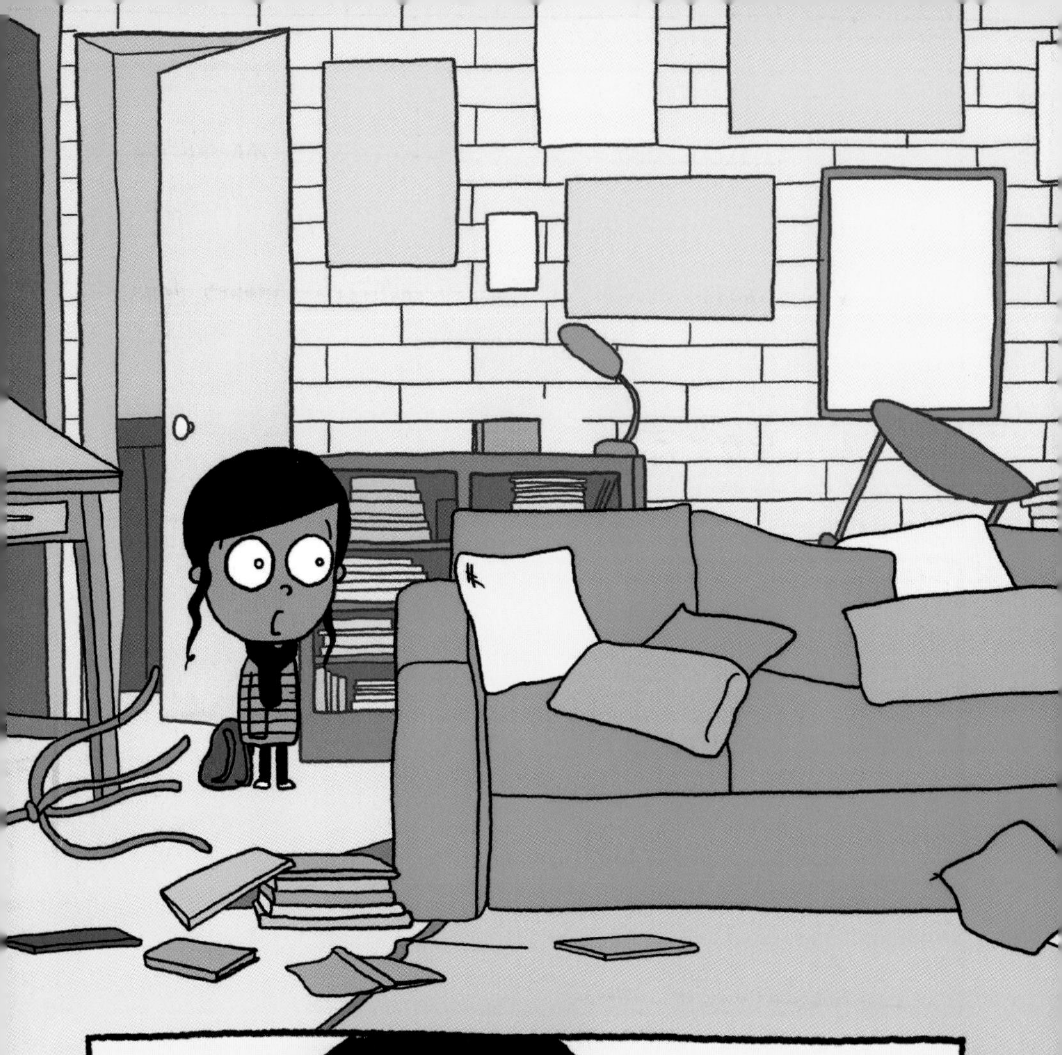

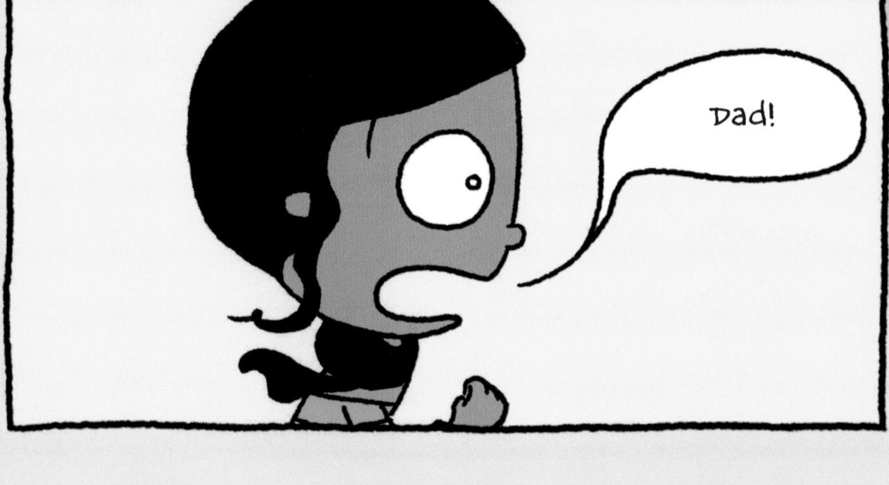
Dad!

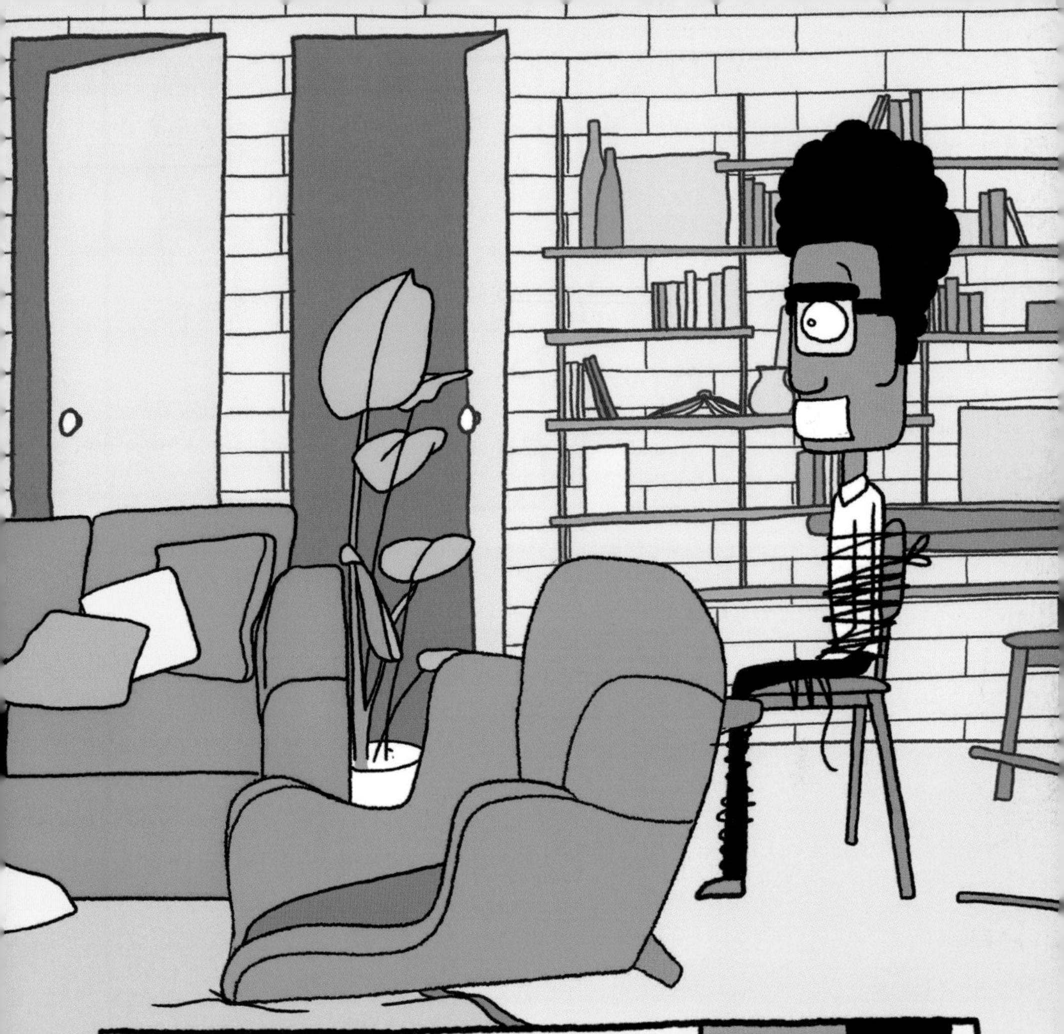

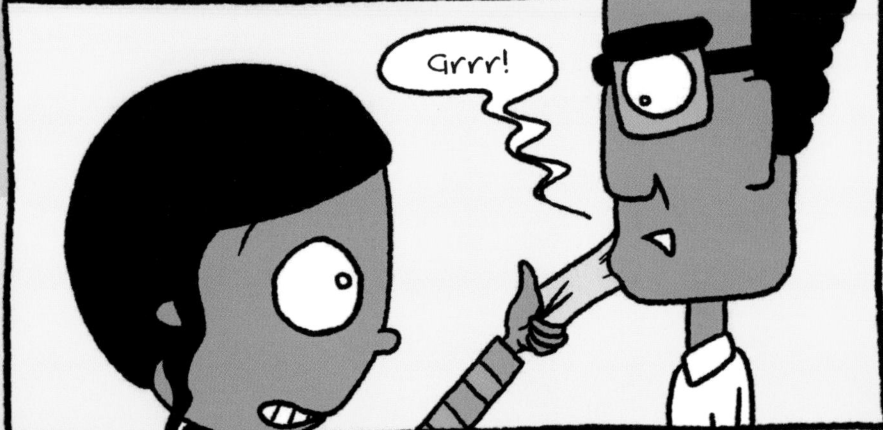
Grrr!

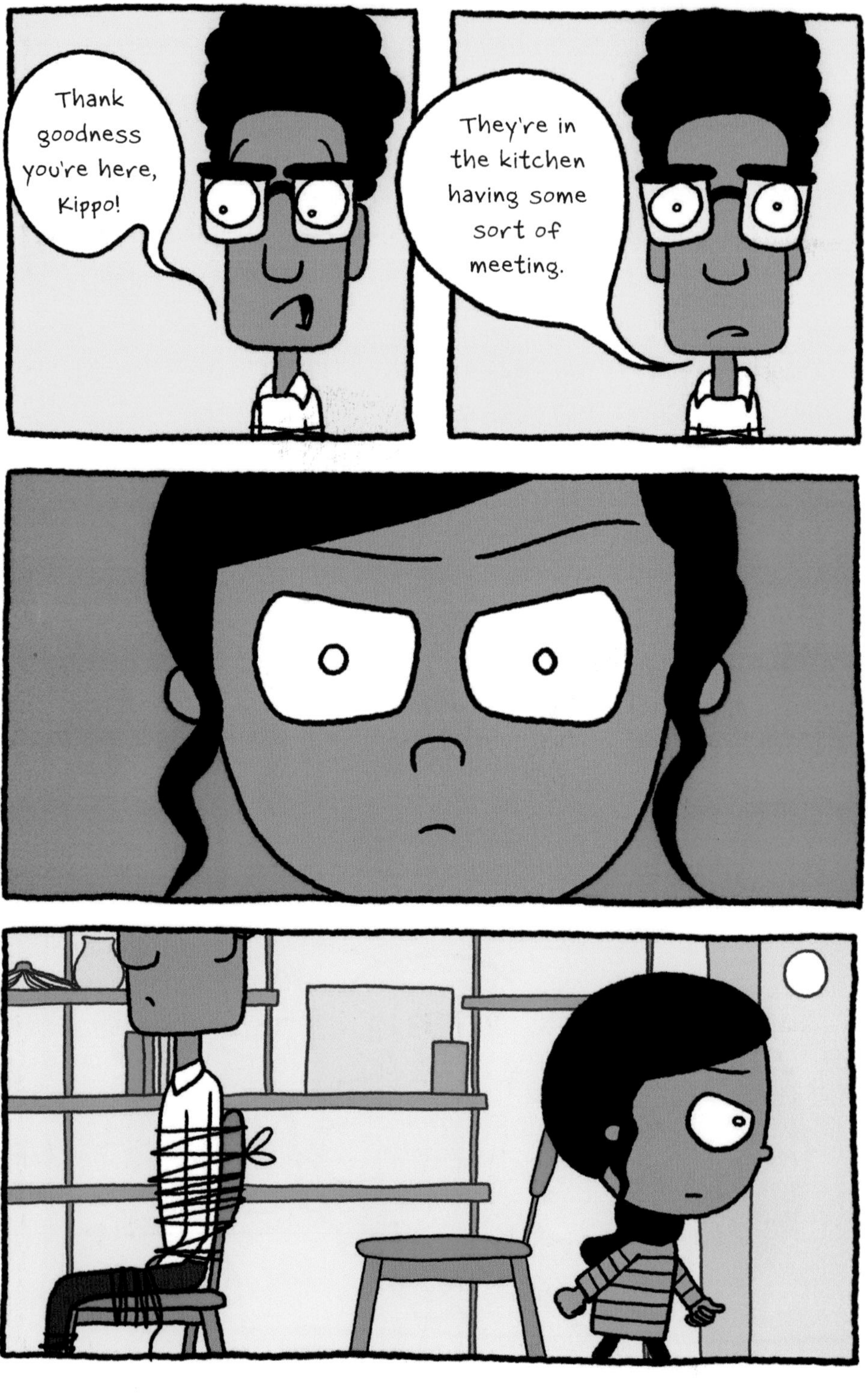
Thank goodness you're here, Kippo!
They're in the kitchen having some sort of meeting.

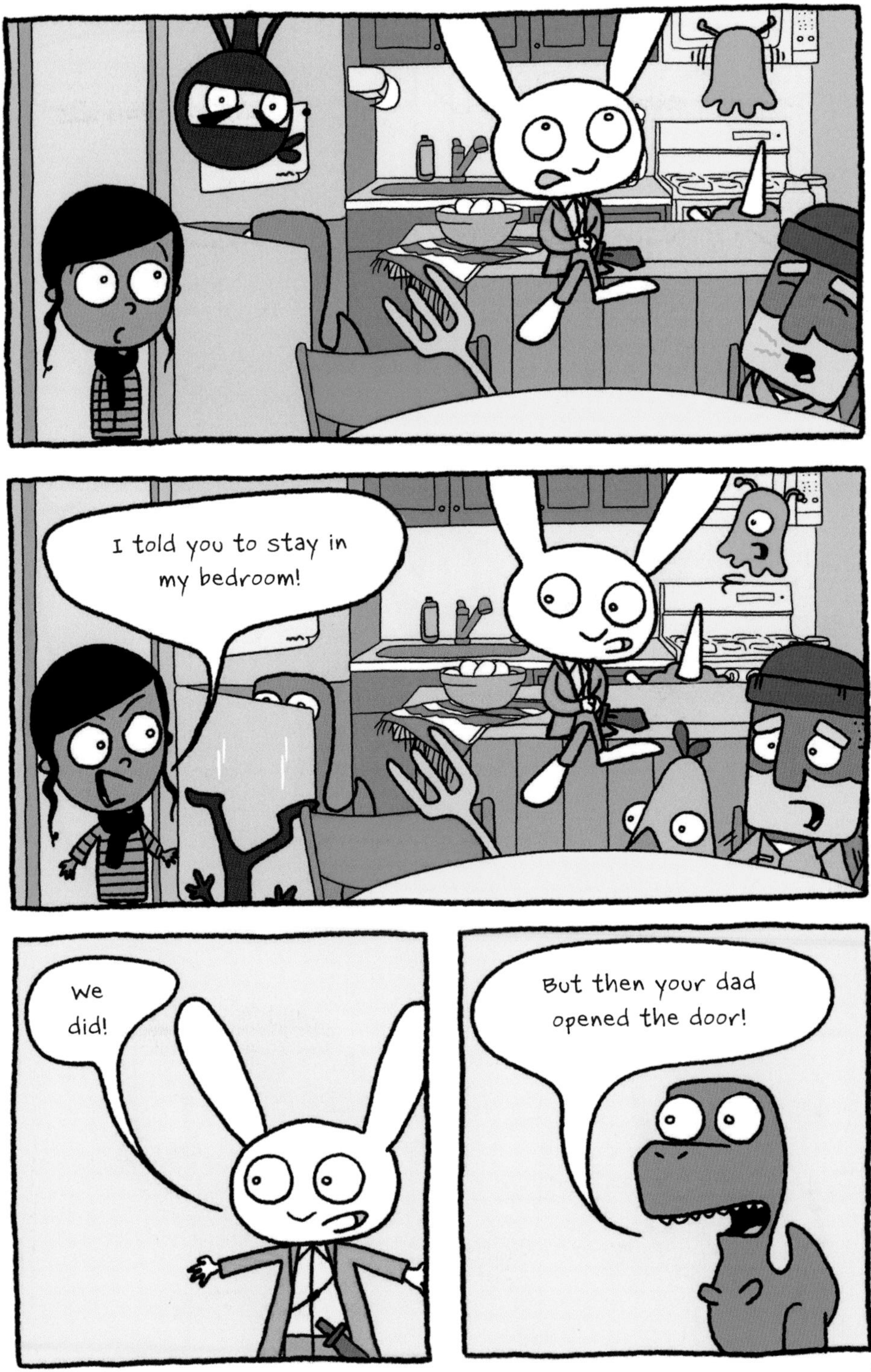

I told you to stay in my bedroom!
We did!
But then your dad opened the door!

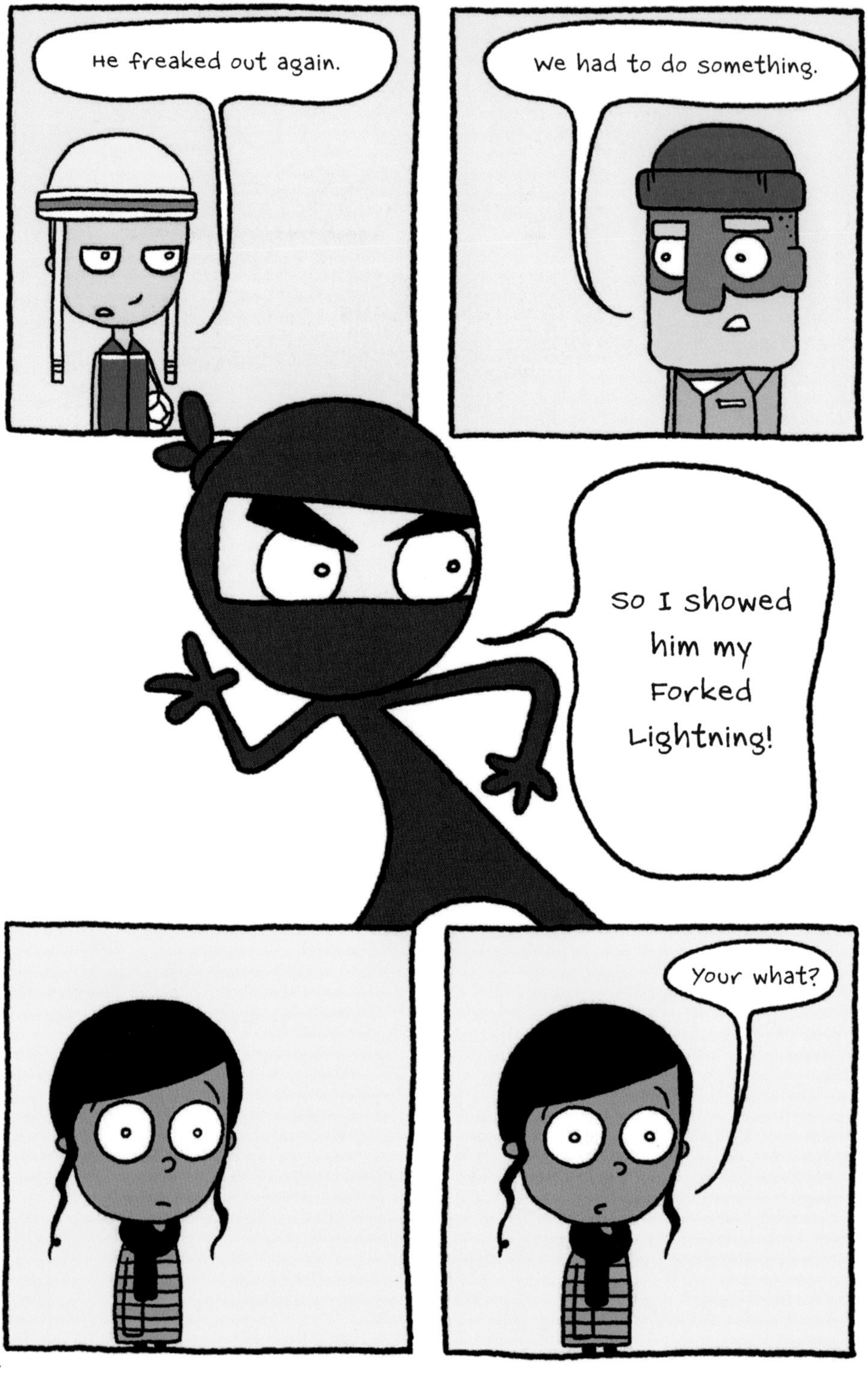
He freaked out again.
We had to do something.
So I showed him my Forked Lightning!
Your what?

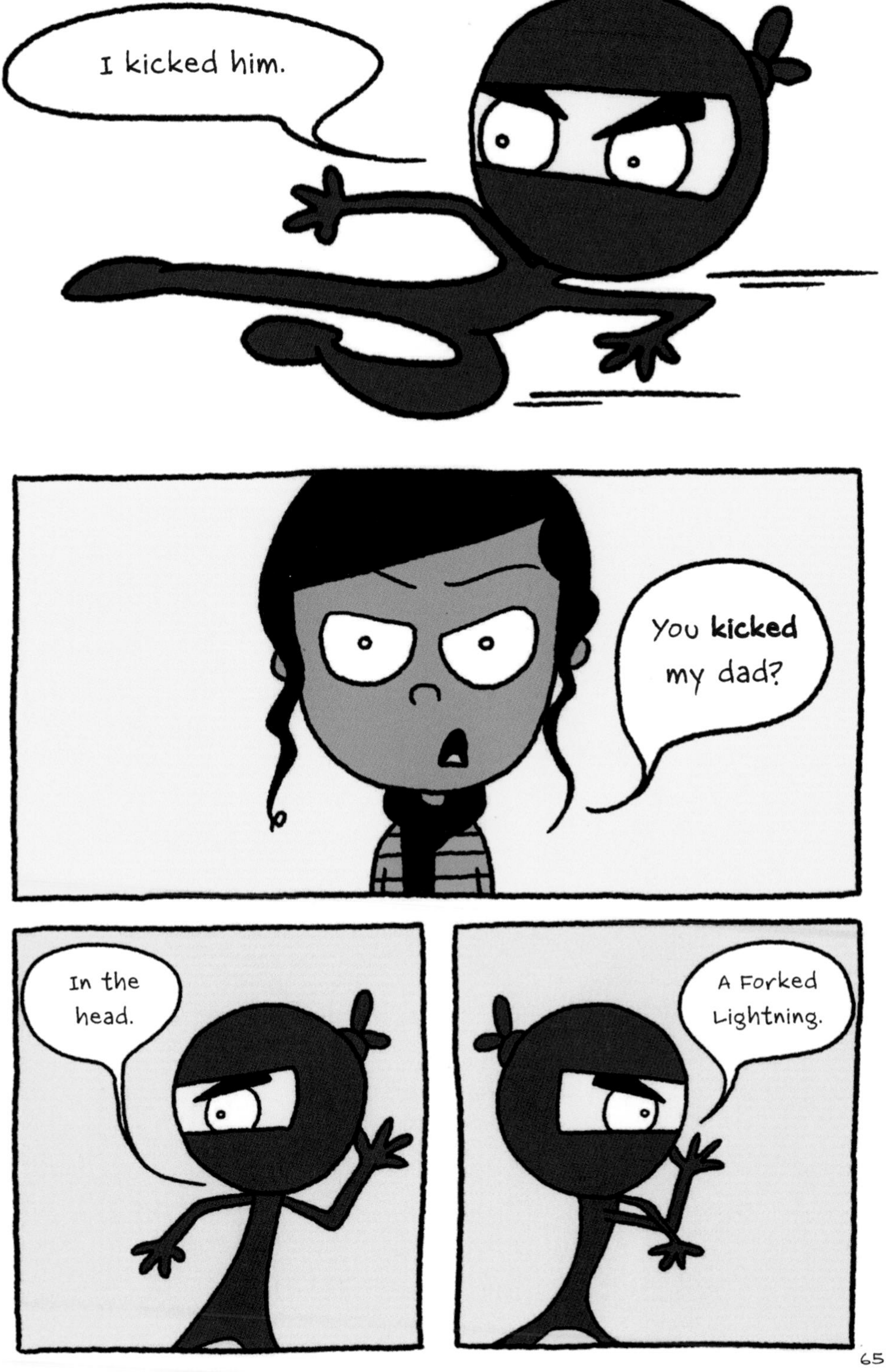
I kicked him.
You **kicked** my dad?
In the head.
A Forked Lightning.

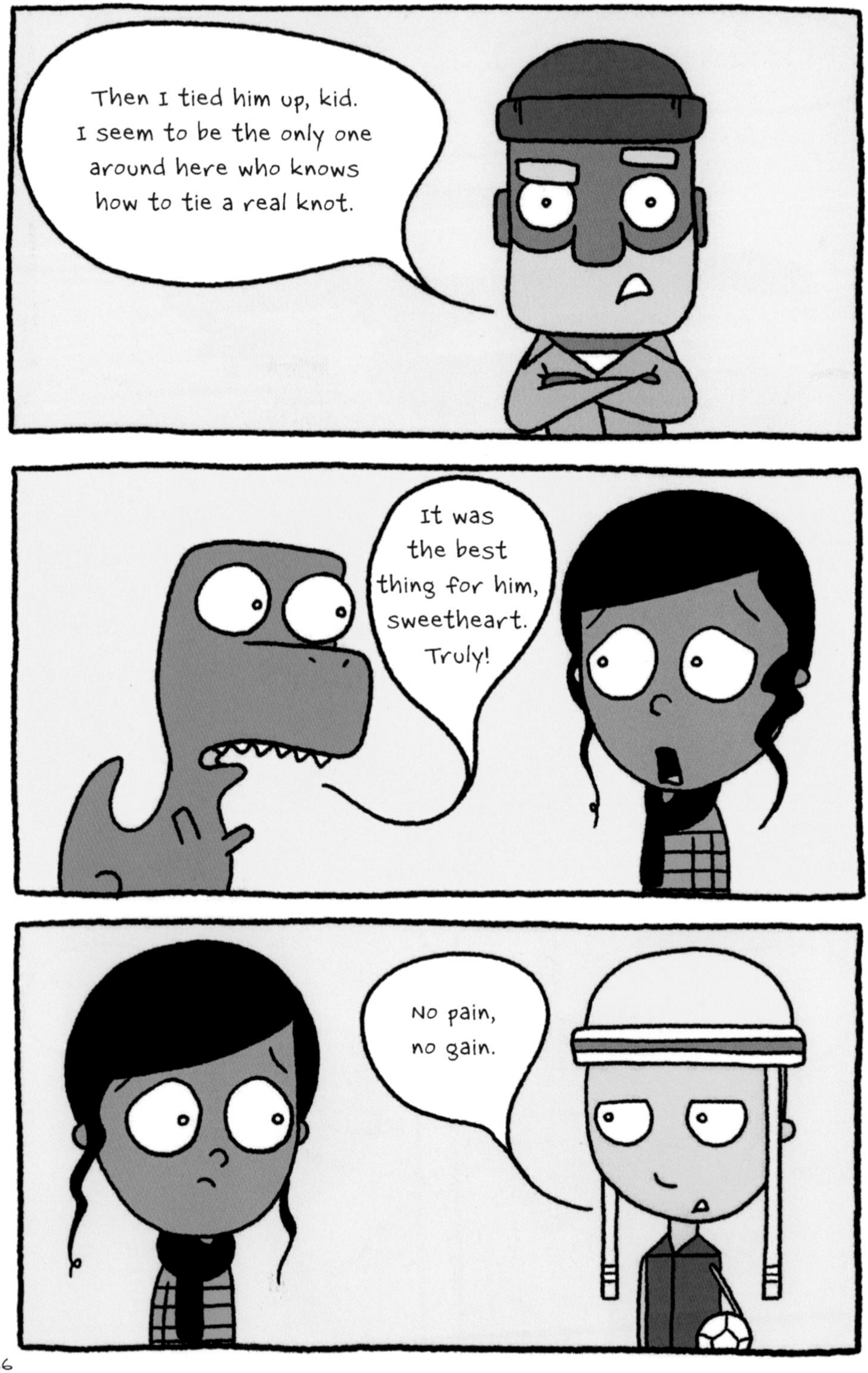
Then I tied him up, kid. I seem to be the only one around here who knows how to tie a real knot.
It was the best thing for him, sweetheart. Truly!
No pain, no gain.

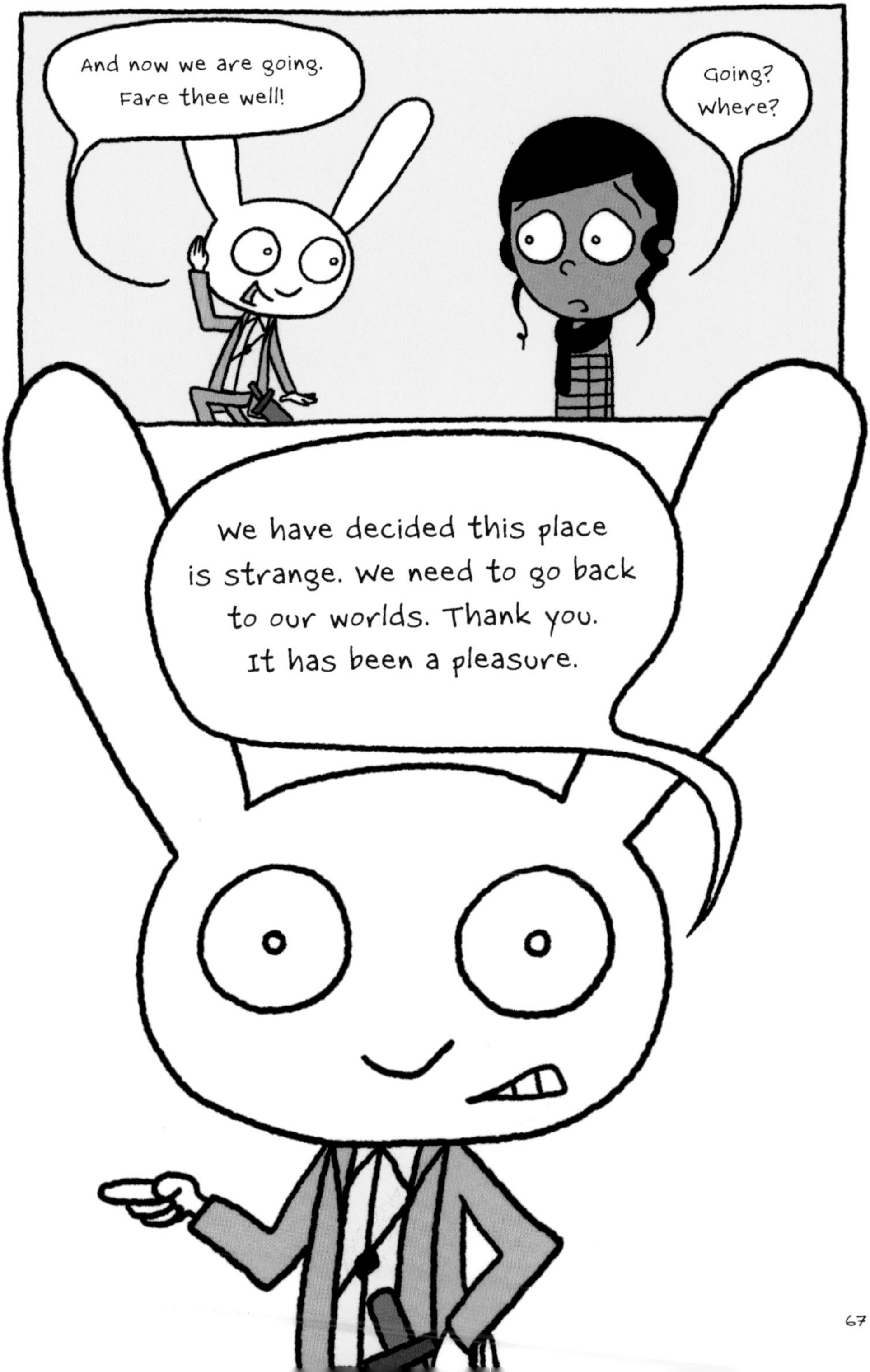
And now we are going. Fare thee well!
Going? Where?
We have decided this place is strange. We need to go back to our worlds. Thank you. It has been a pleasure.

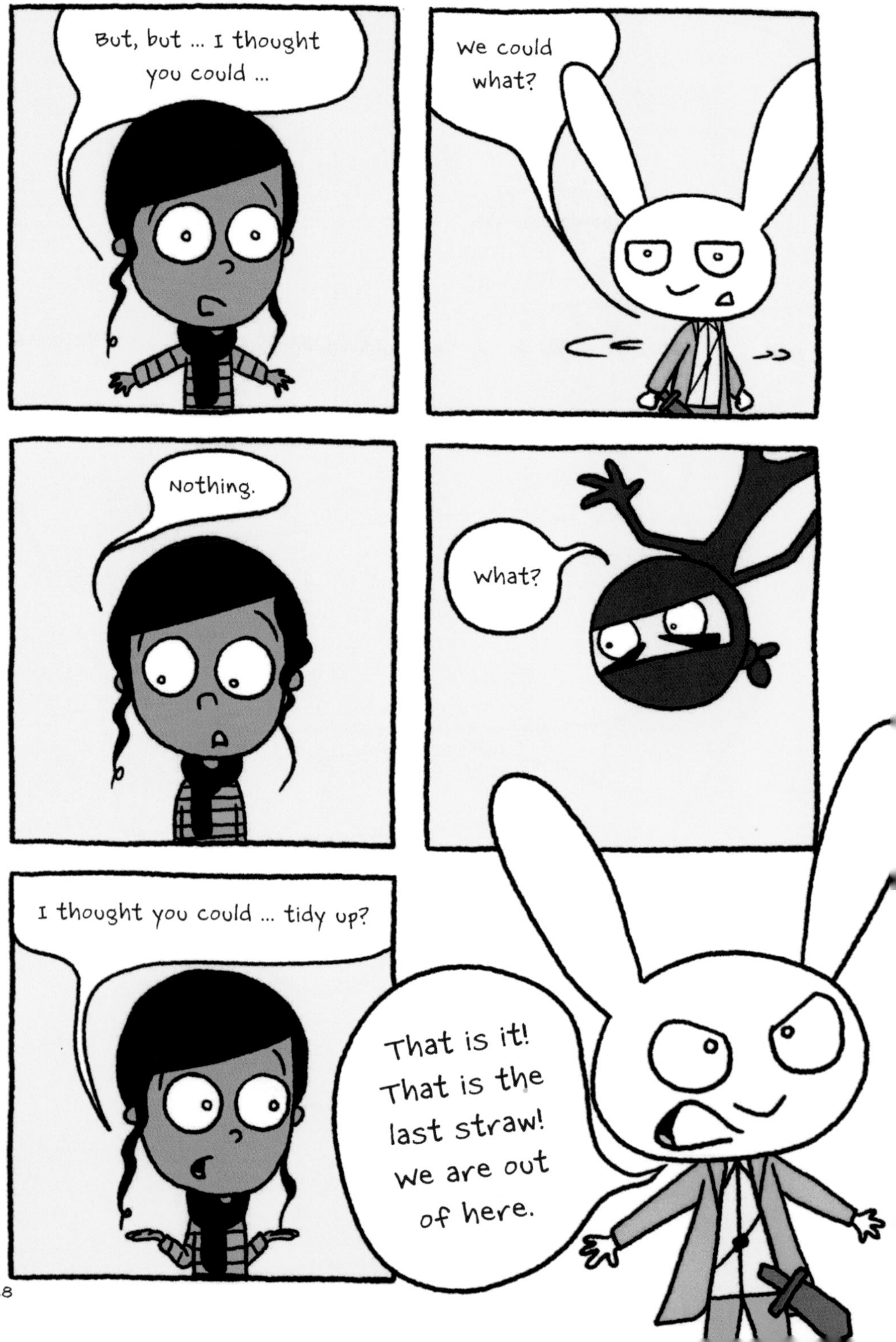
But, but ... I thought you could ...
We could what?
Nothing.
What?
I thought you could ... tidy up?
That is it! That is the last straw! We are out of here.

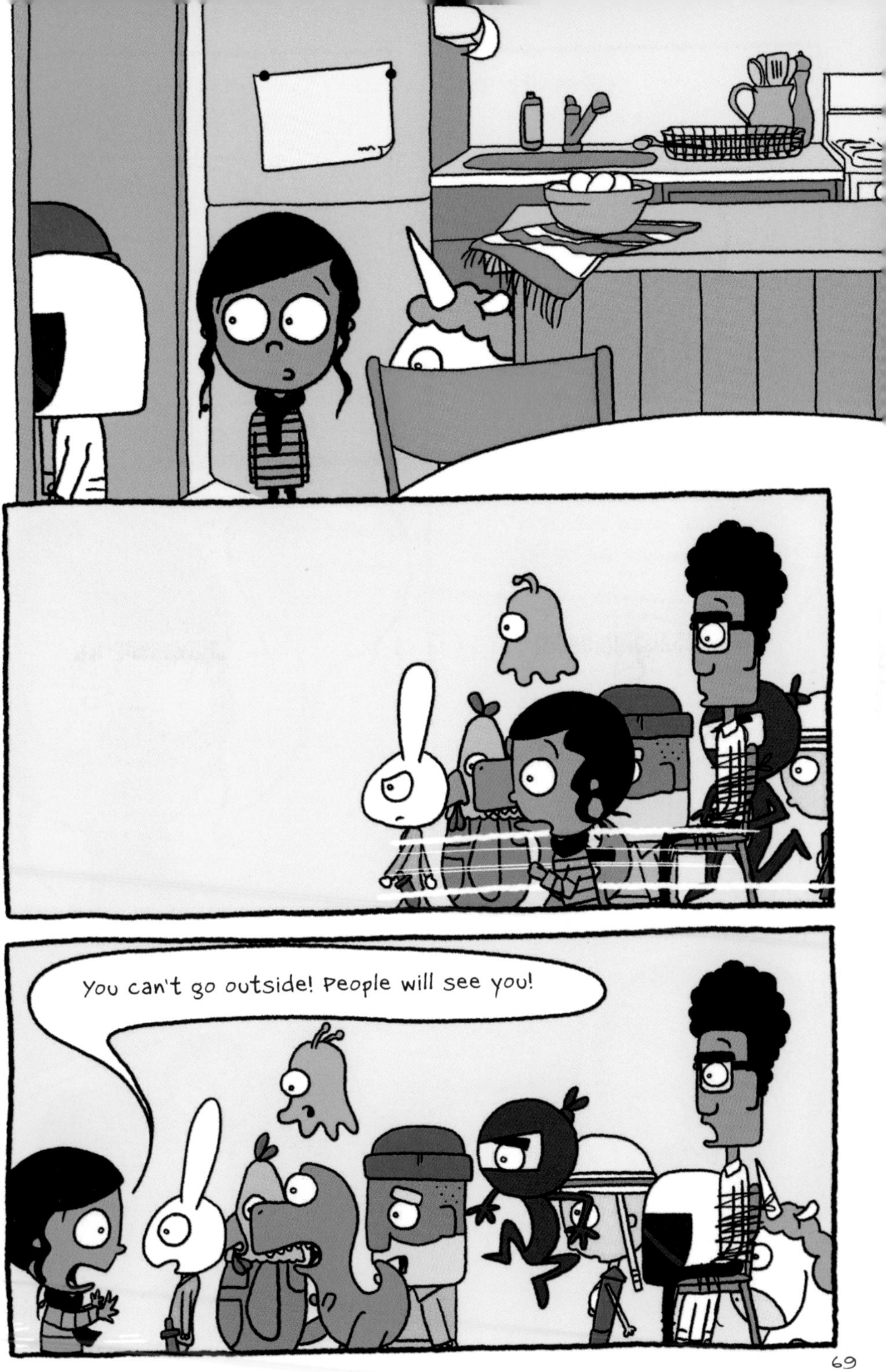
You can't go outside! People will see you!

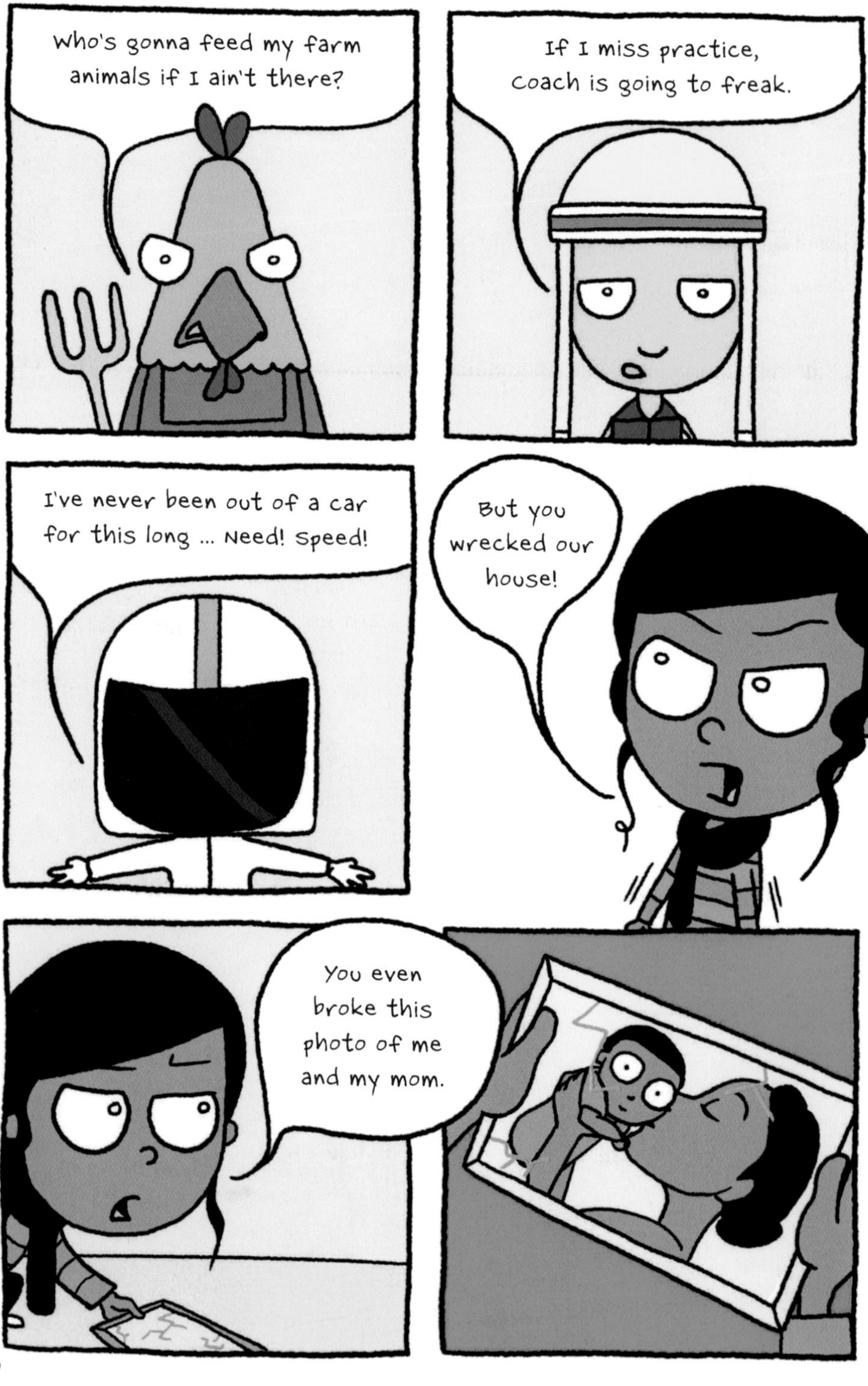
Who's gonna feed my farm animals if I ain't there?
If I miss practice, coach is going to freak.
I've never been out of a car for this long ... Need! Speed!
But you wrecked our house!
You even broke this photo of me and my mom.

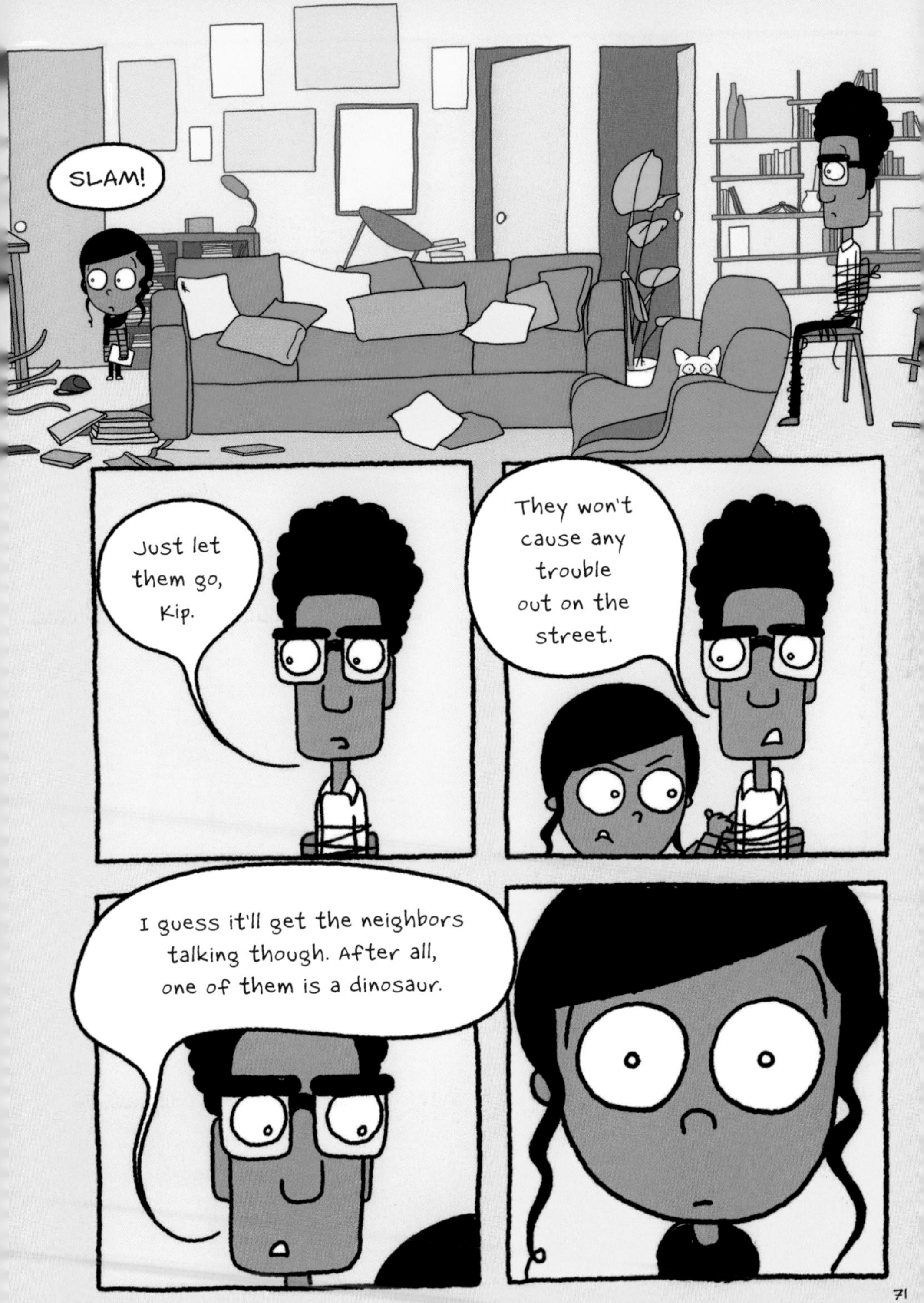
SLAM!
Just let them go, Kip.
They won't cause any trouble out on the street.
I guess it'll get the neighbors talking though. After all, one of them is a dinosaur.

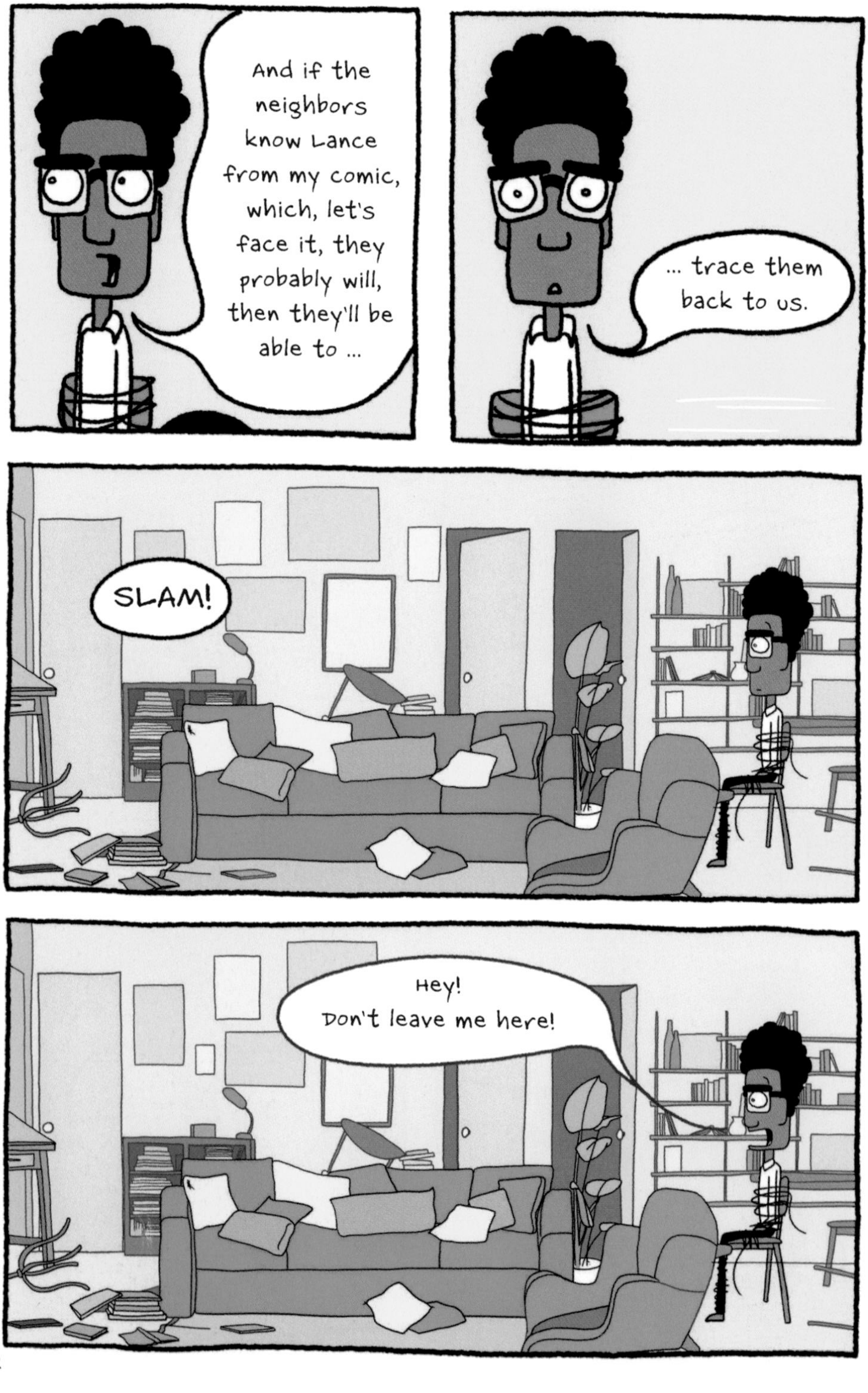
And if the neighbors know Lance from my comic, which, let's face it, they probably will, then they'll be able to ...
... trace them back to us.
SLAM!
Hey!
Don't leave me here!

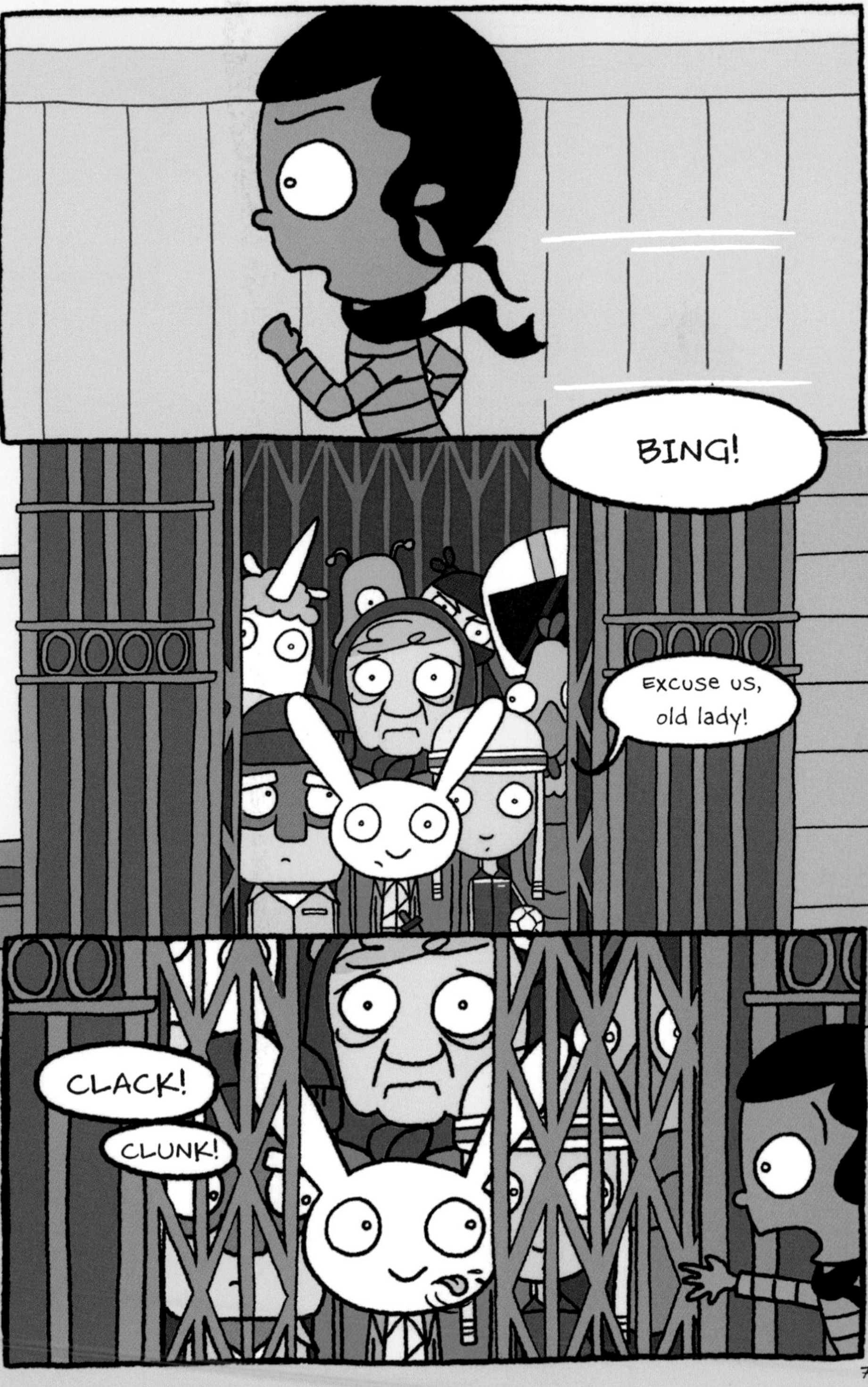
BING!
Excuse us, old lady!
CLACK!
CLUNK!

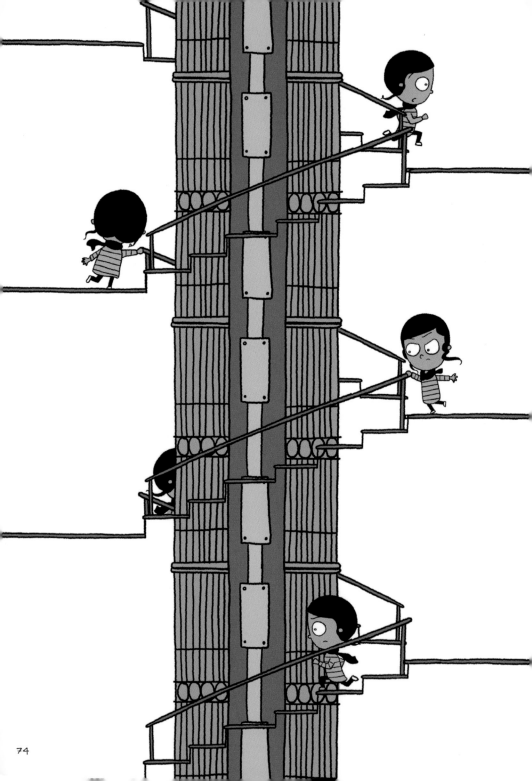

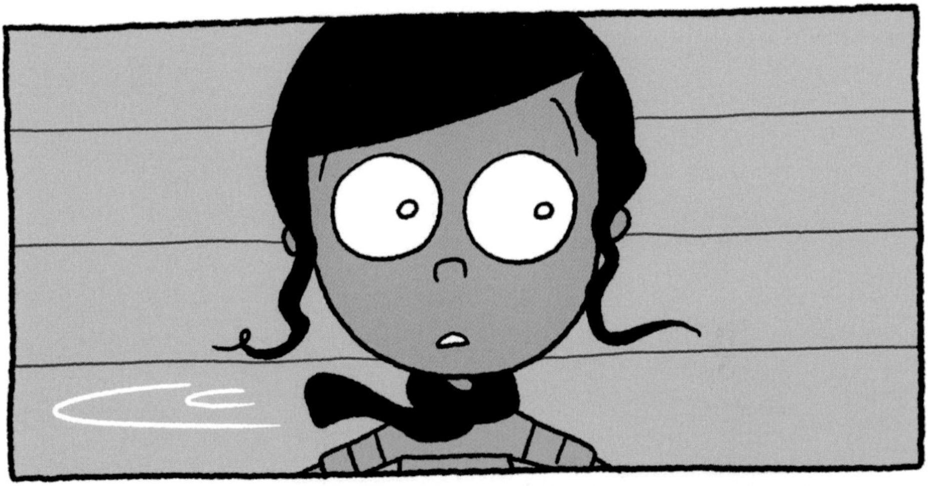

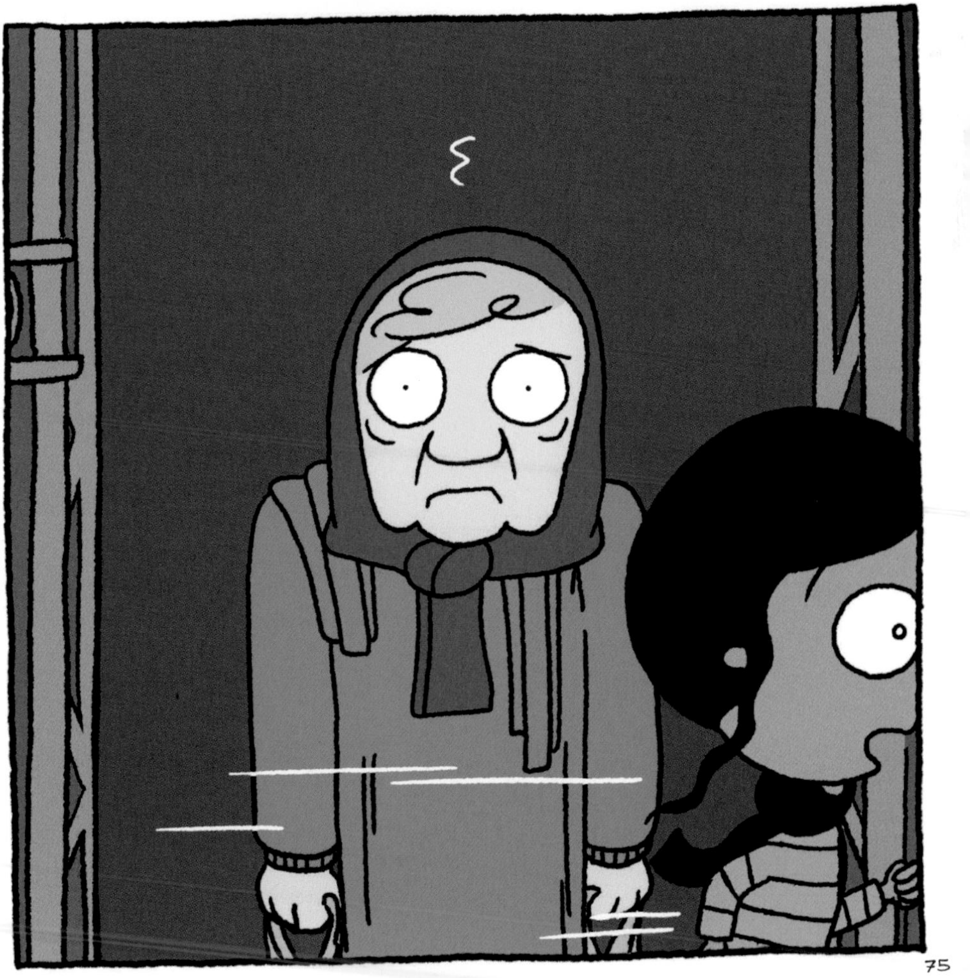

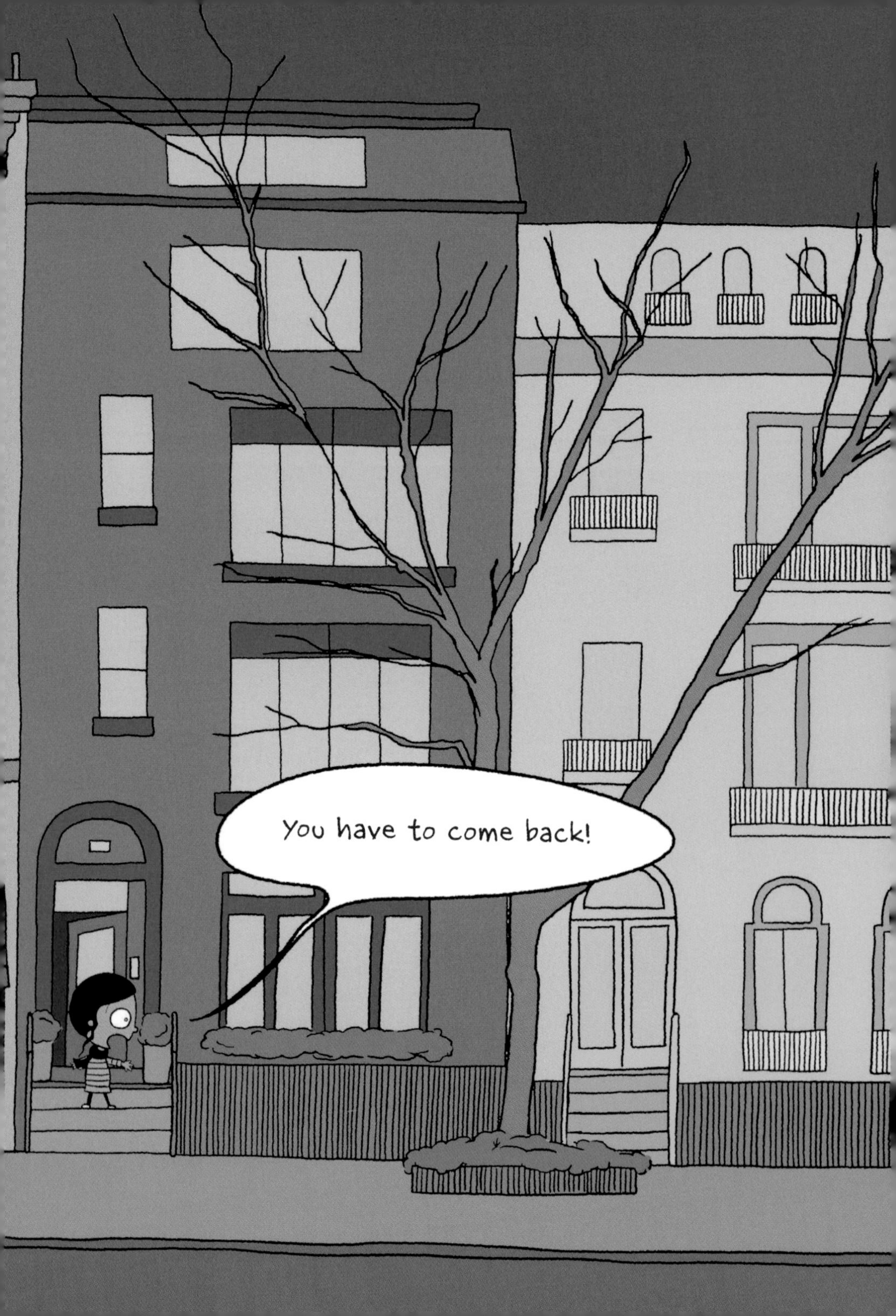
You have to come back!

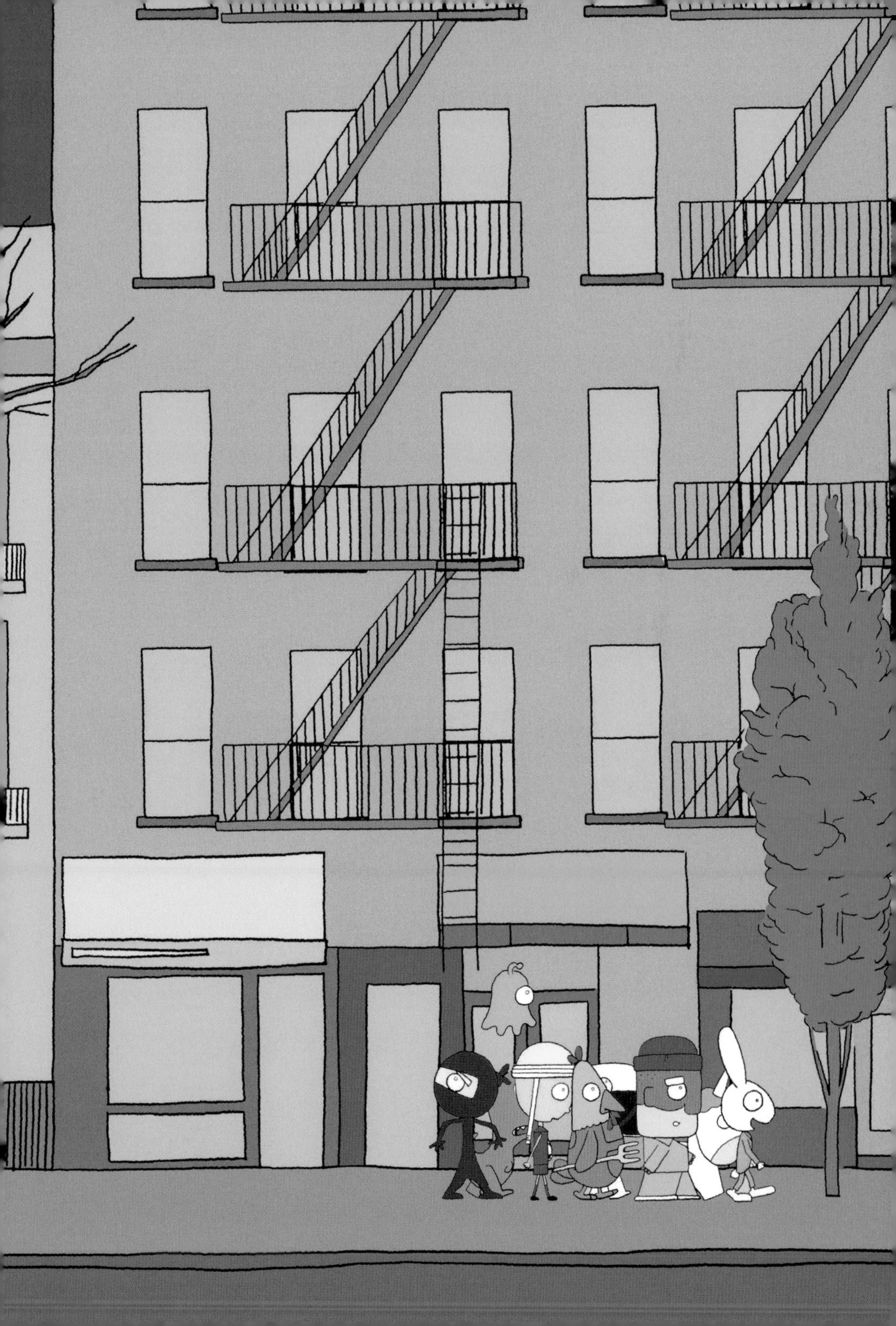

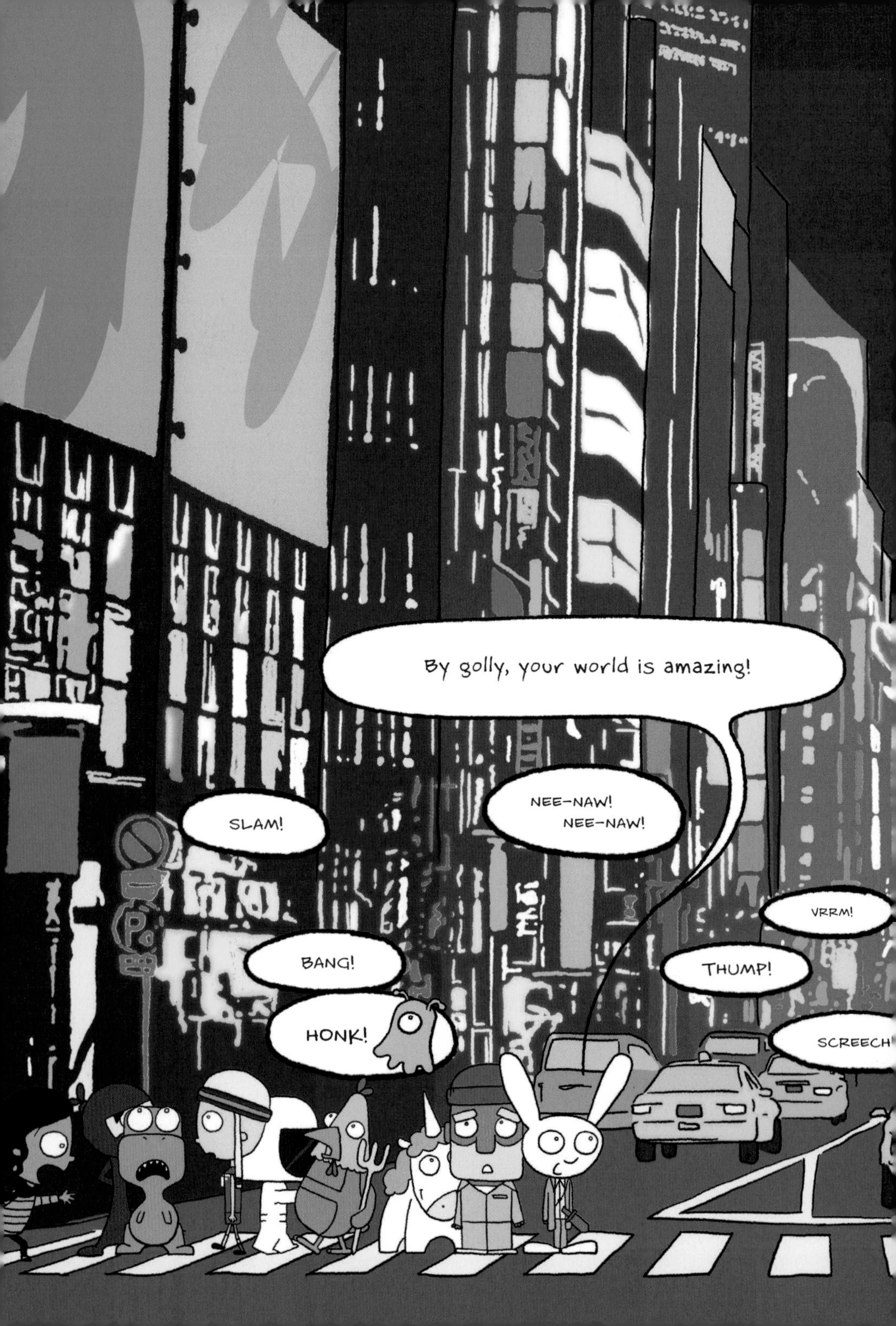
By golly, your world is amazing!
SLAM!
NEE-NAW! NEE-NAW!
VRRM!
BANG!
THUMP!
HONK!
SCREECH

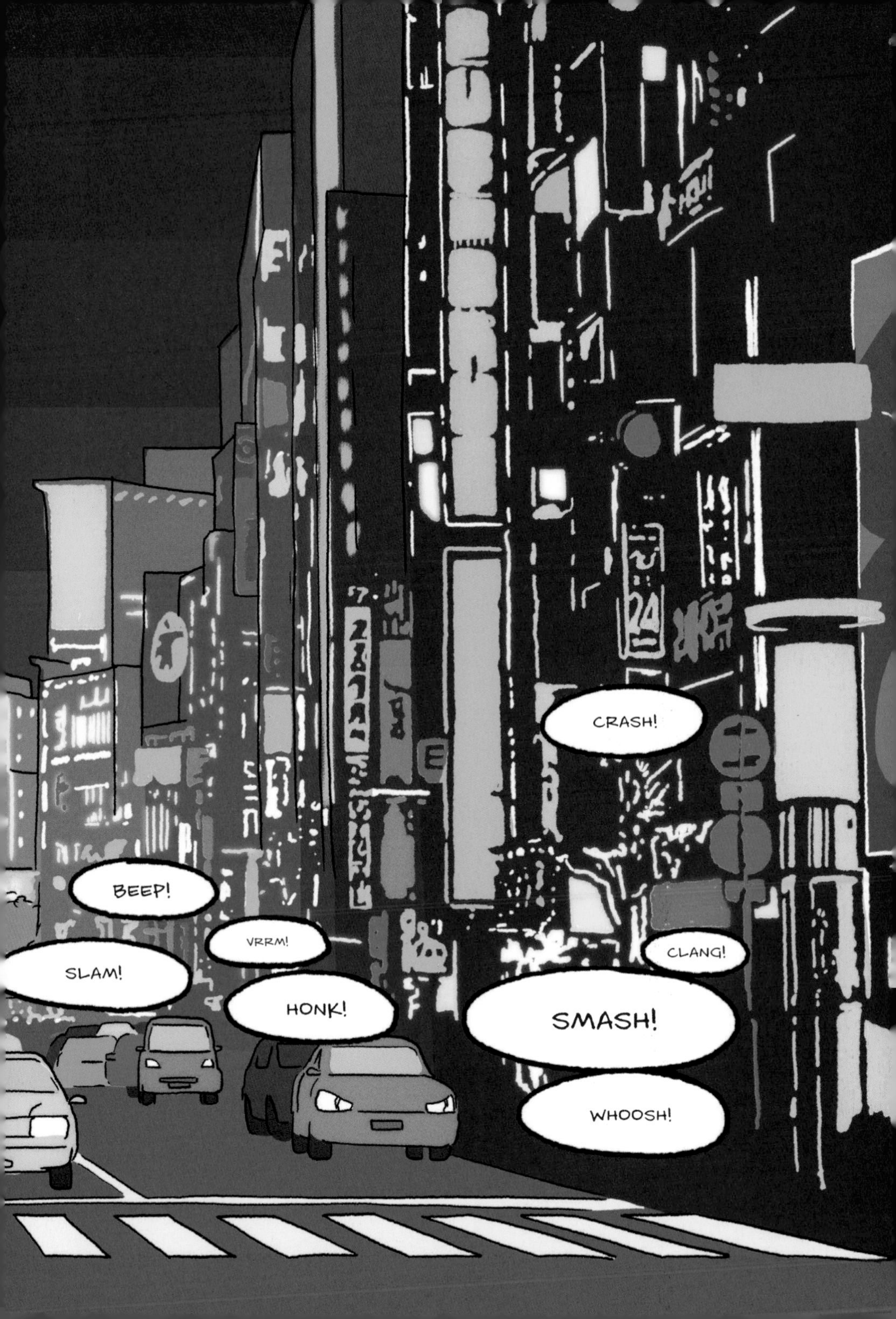
CRASH!
BEEP!
VRRM!
SLAM!
CLANG!
HONK!
SMASH!
WHOOSH!

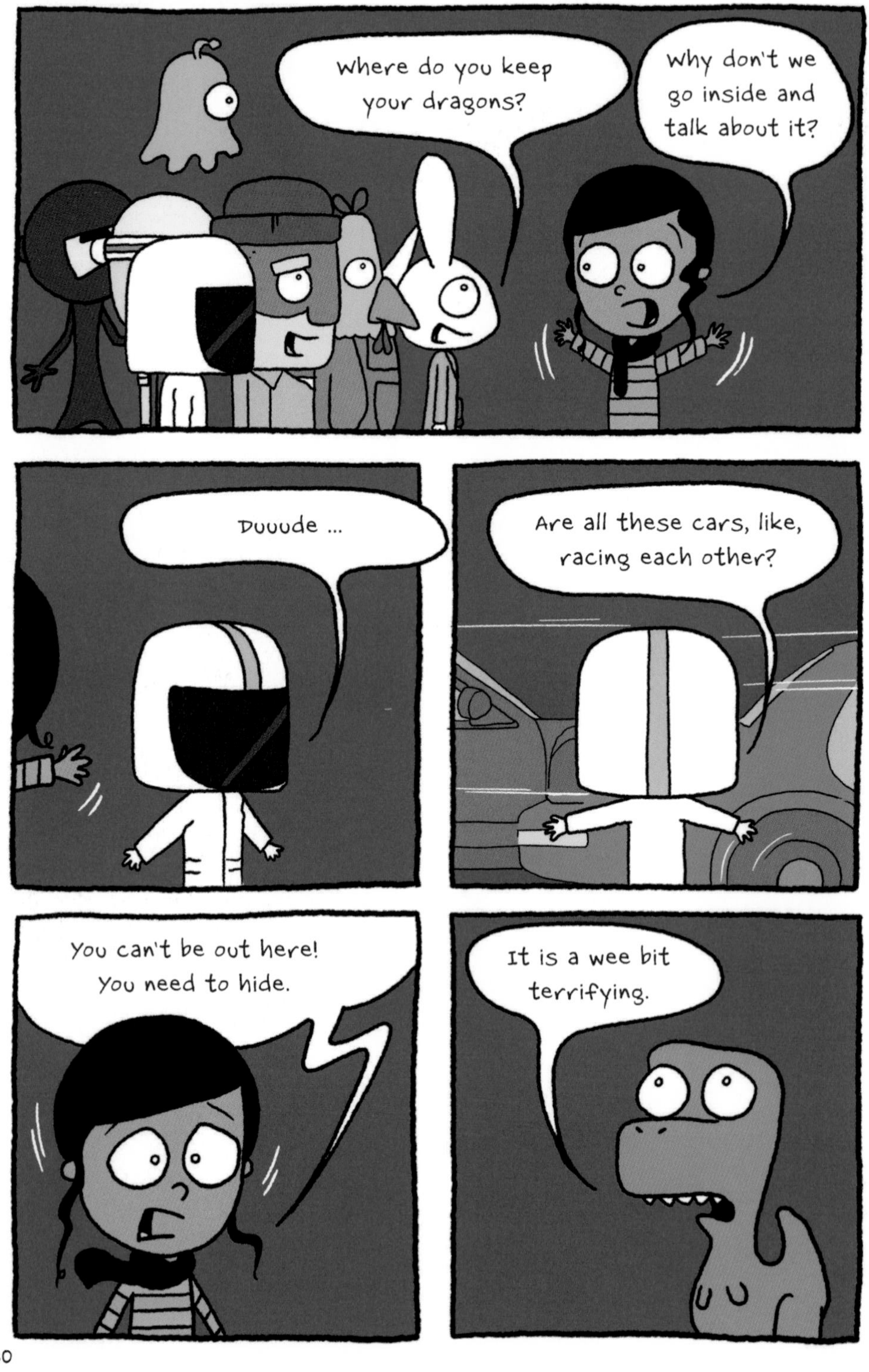
Where do you keep your dragons?
Why don't we go inside and talk about it?
Duuude ...
Are all these cars, like, racing each other?
You can't be out here! You need to hide.
It is a wee bit terrifying.

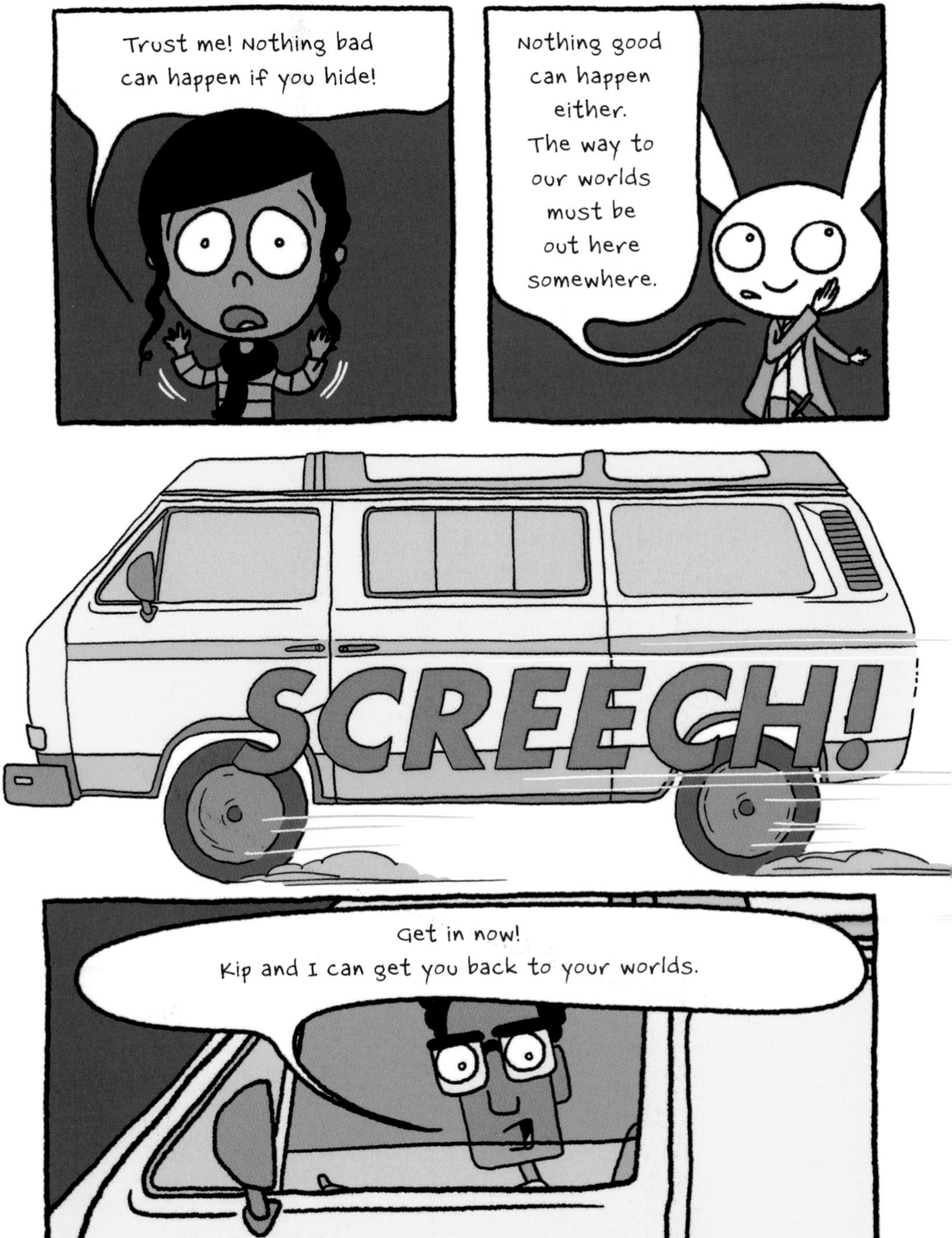
Trust me! Nothing bad can happen if you hide!
Nothing good can happen either. The way to our worlds must be out here somewhere.
SCREECH!
Get in now! Kip and I can get you back to your worlds.

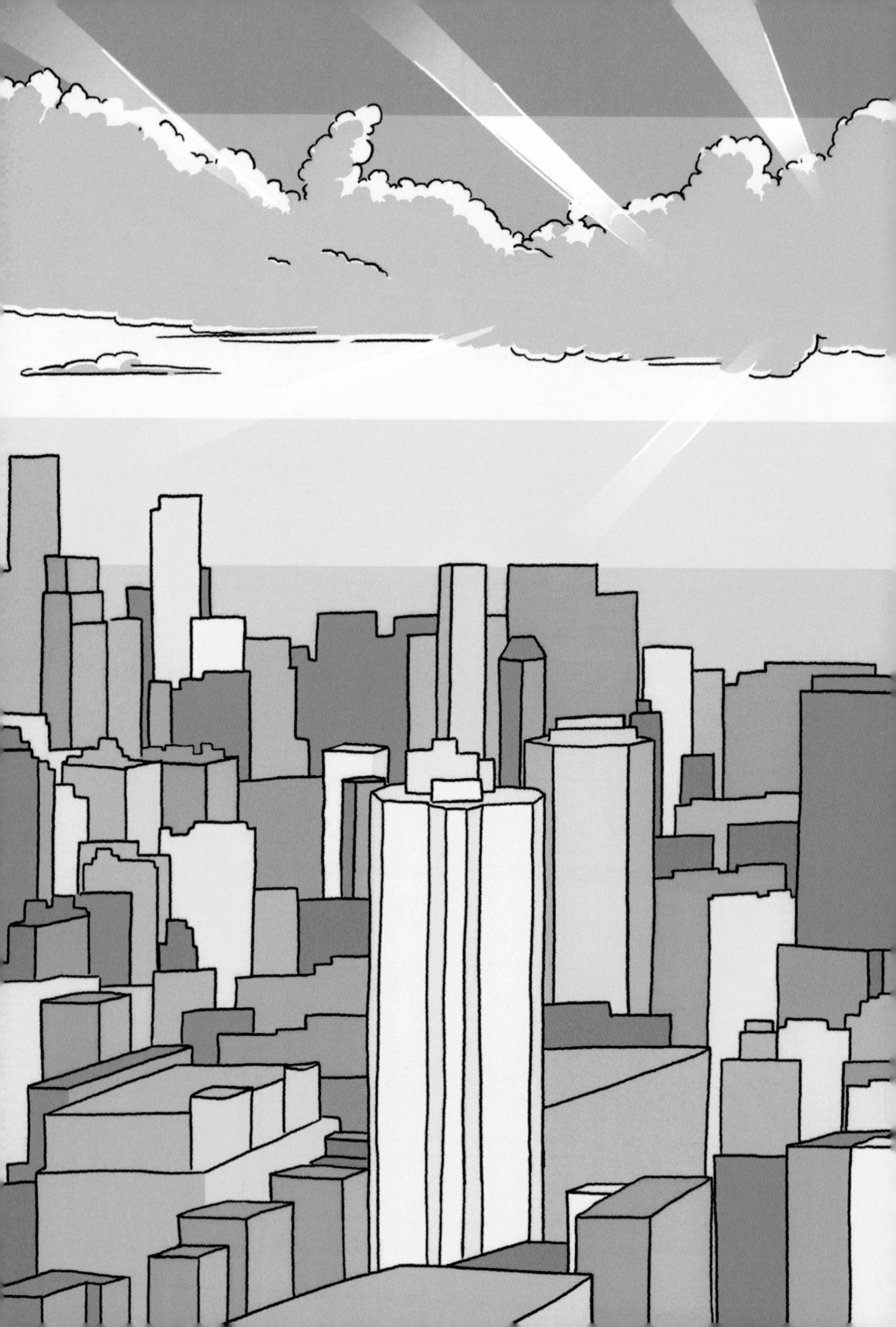

CHAPTER SIX
The Odds need to go

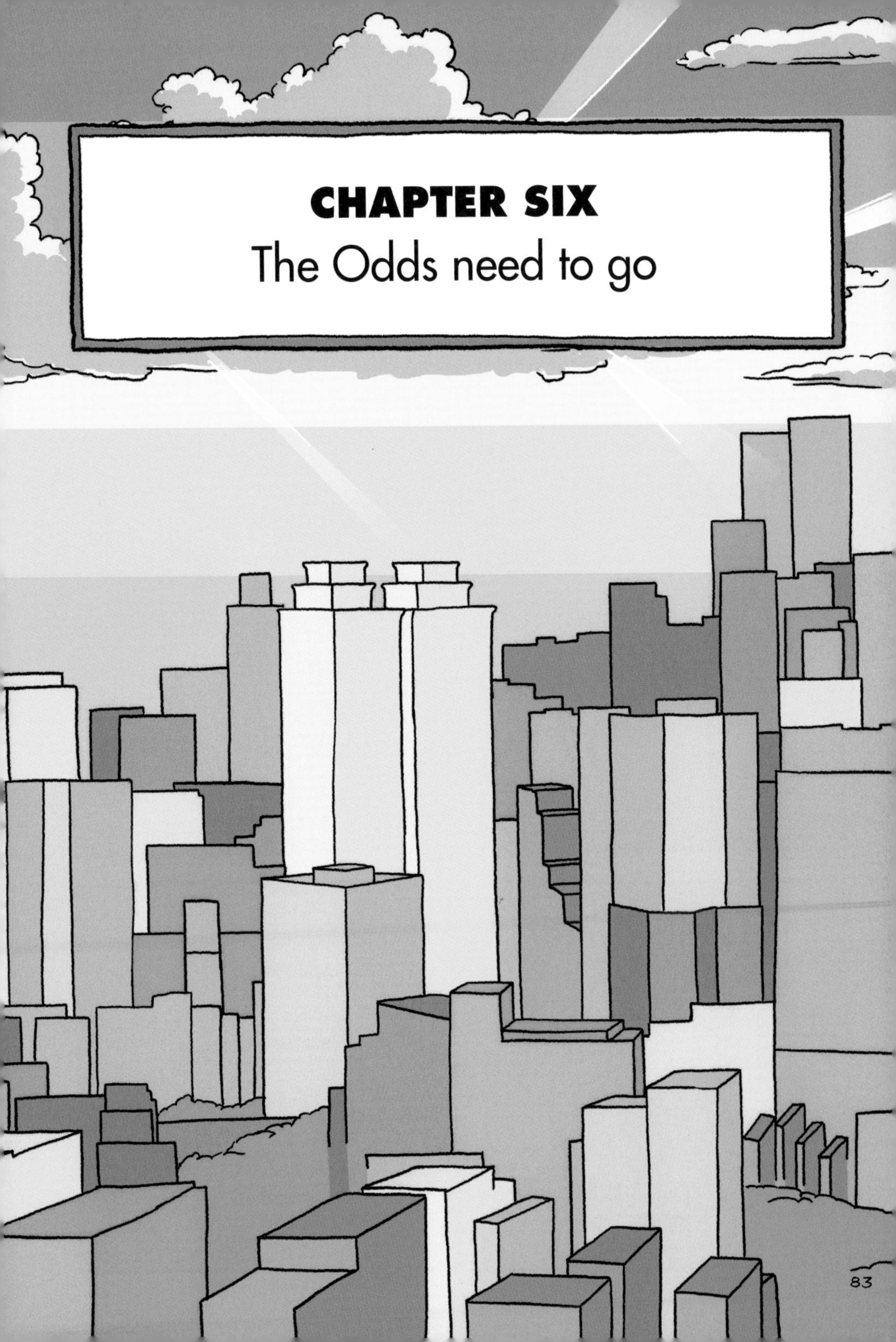

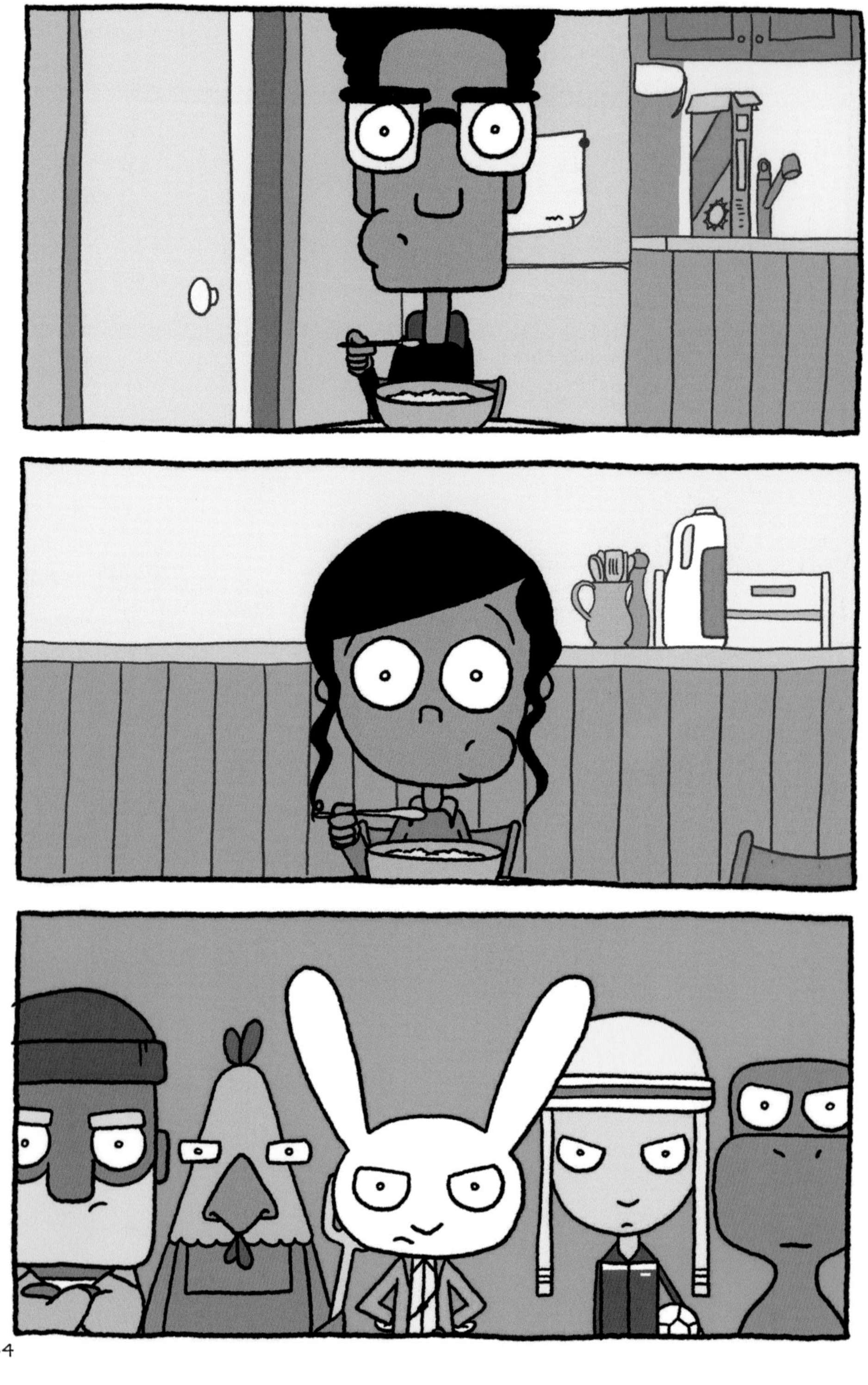

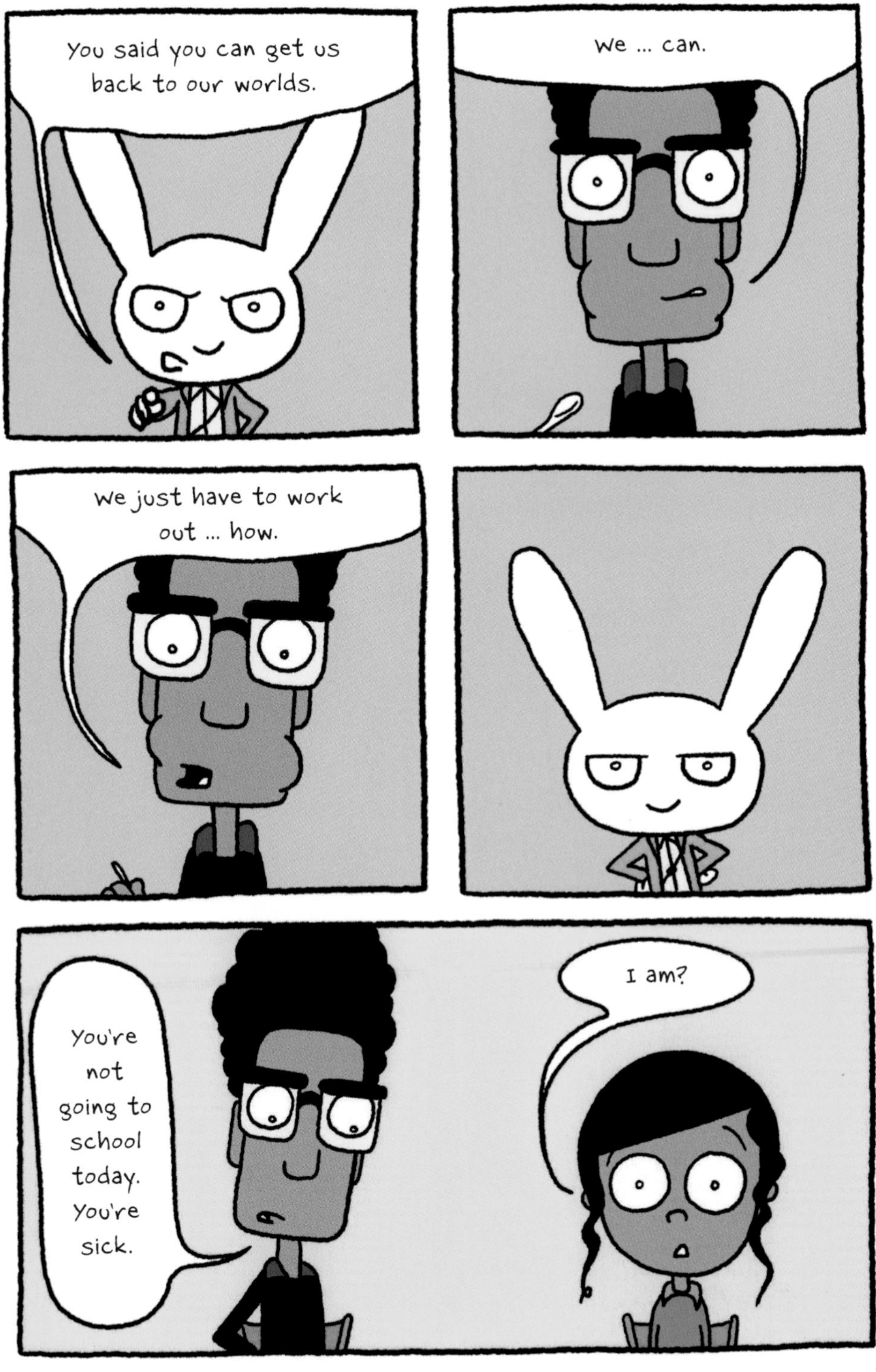
You said you can get us back to our worlds.
We ... can.
We just have to work out ... how.
You're not going to school today. You're sick.
I am?

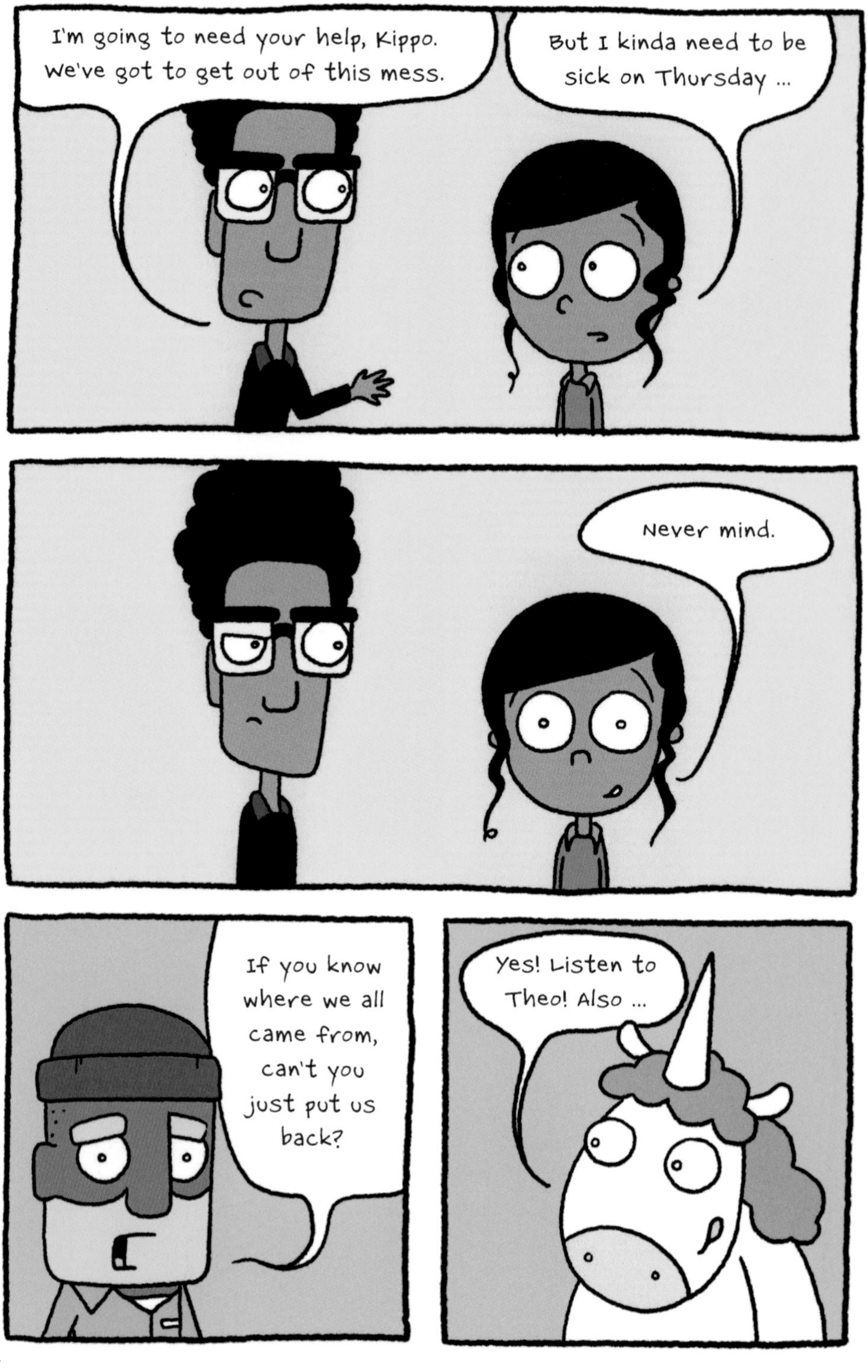
I'm going to need your help, Kippo. We've got to get out of this mess.
But I kinda need to be sick on Thursday ...
Never mind.
If you know where we all came from, can't you just put us back?
Yes! Listen to Theo! Also ...

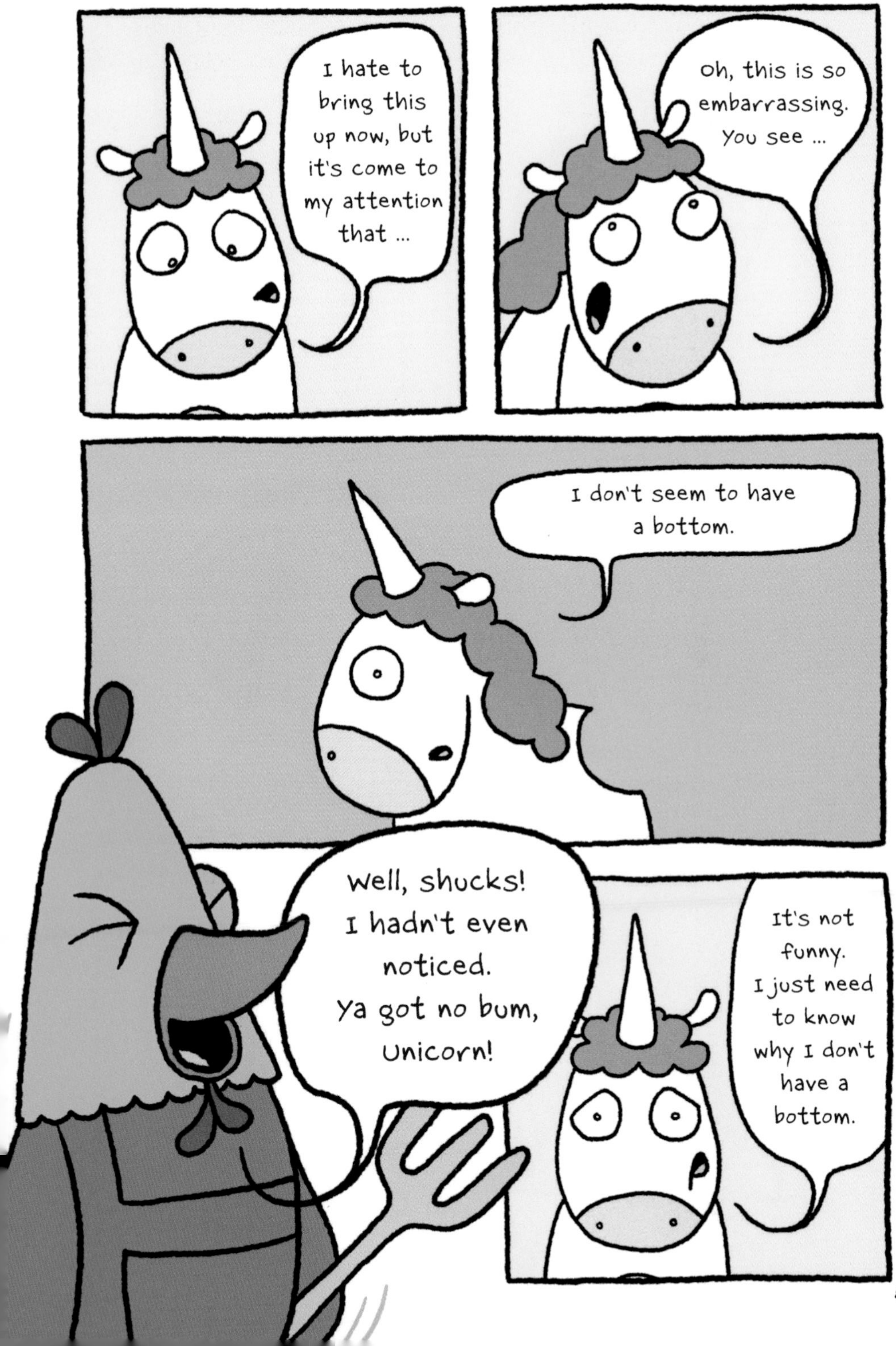
I hate to bring this up now, but it's come to my attention that ...
Oh, this is so embarrassing. You see ...
I don't seem to have a bottom.
Well, shucks! I hadn't even noticed. Ya got no bum, Unicorn!
It's not funny. I just need to know why I don't have a bottom.

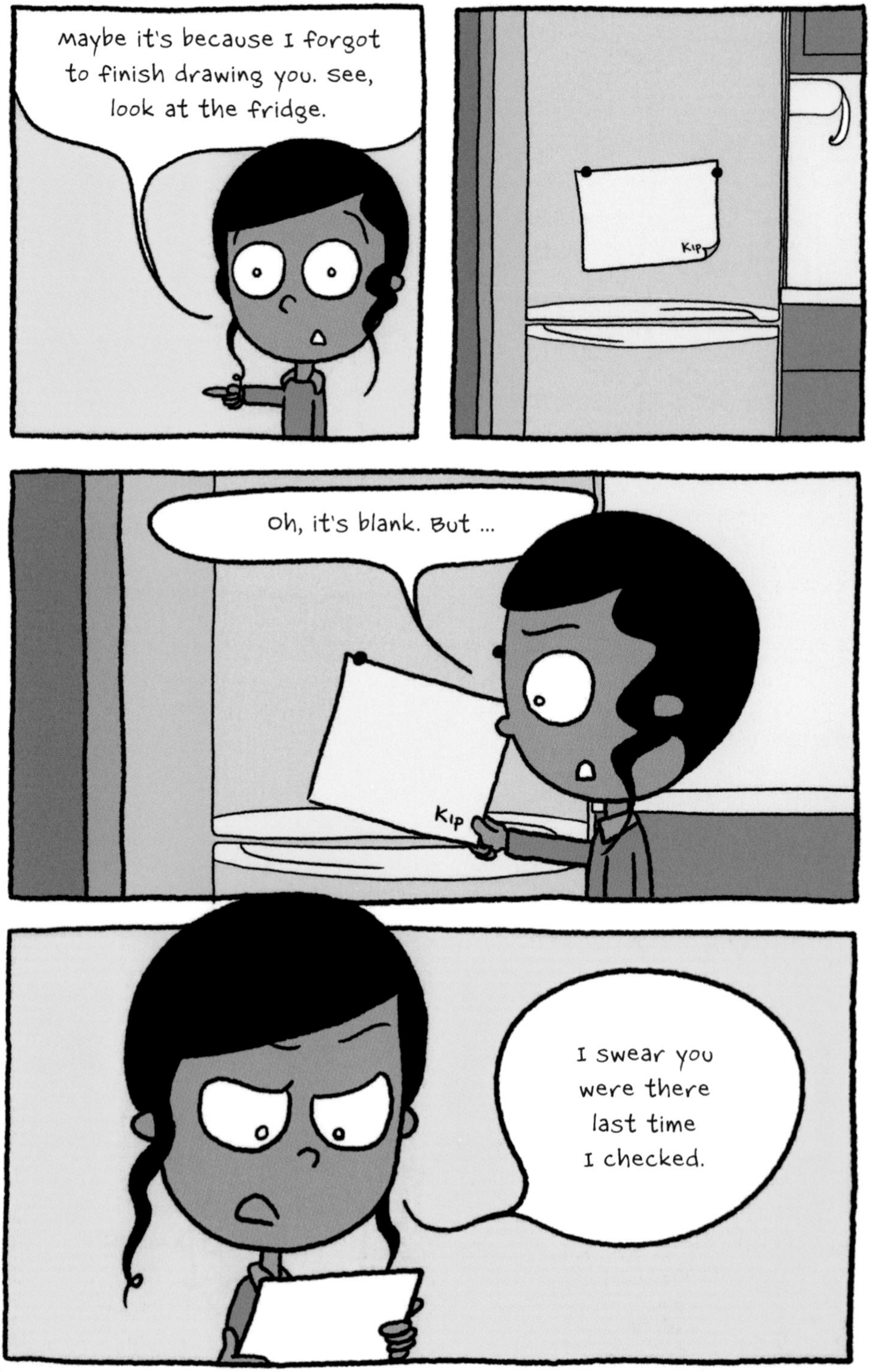
Maybe it's because I forgot to finish drawing you. See, look at the fridge.
Kip
Oh, it's blank. But ...
Kip
I swear you were there last time I checked.

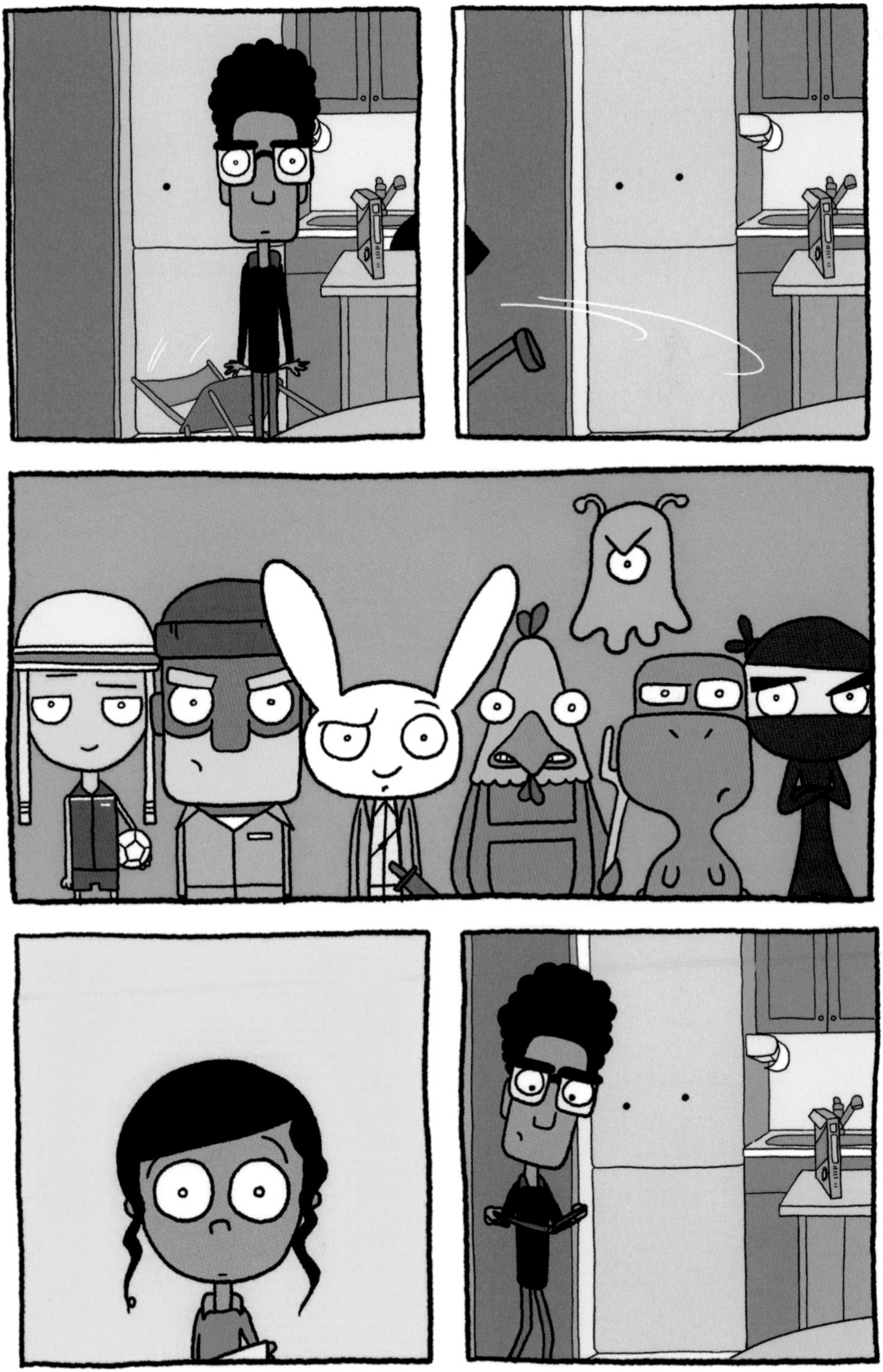

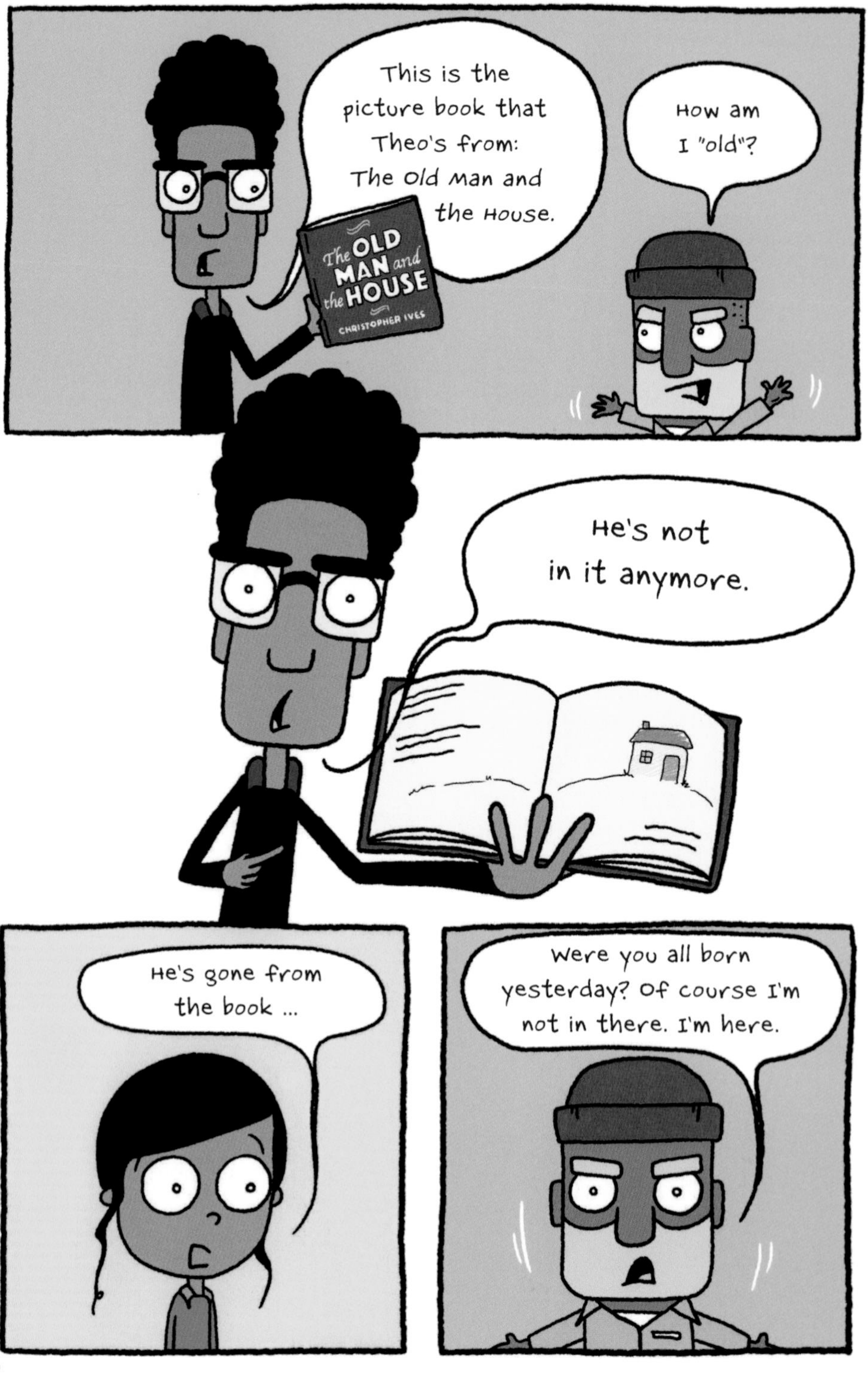
This is the picture book that Theo's from: The Old Man and the House.
The OLD MAN and the HOUSE
CHRISTOPHER IVES
How am I "old"?
He's not in it anymore.
He's gone from the book ...
Were you all born yesterday? Of course I'm not in there. I'm here.

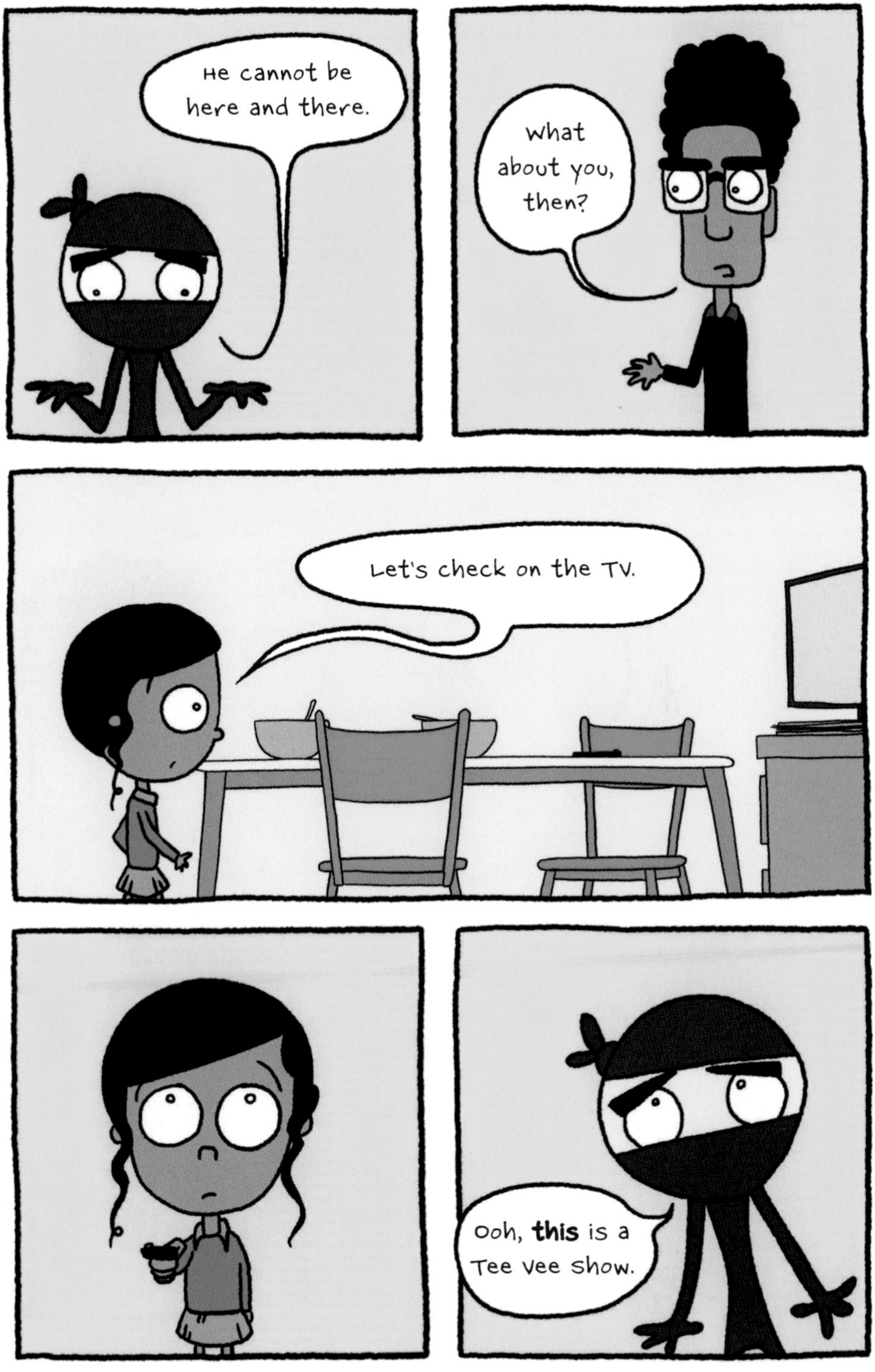
He cannot be here and there.
What about you, then?
Let's check on the TV.
Ooh, **this** is a Tee Vee show.

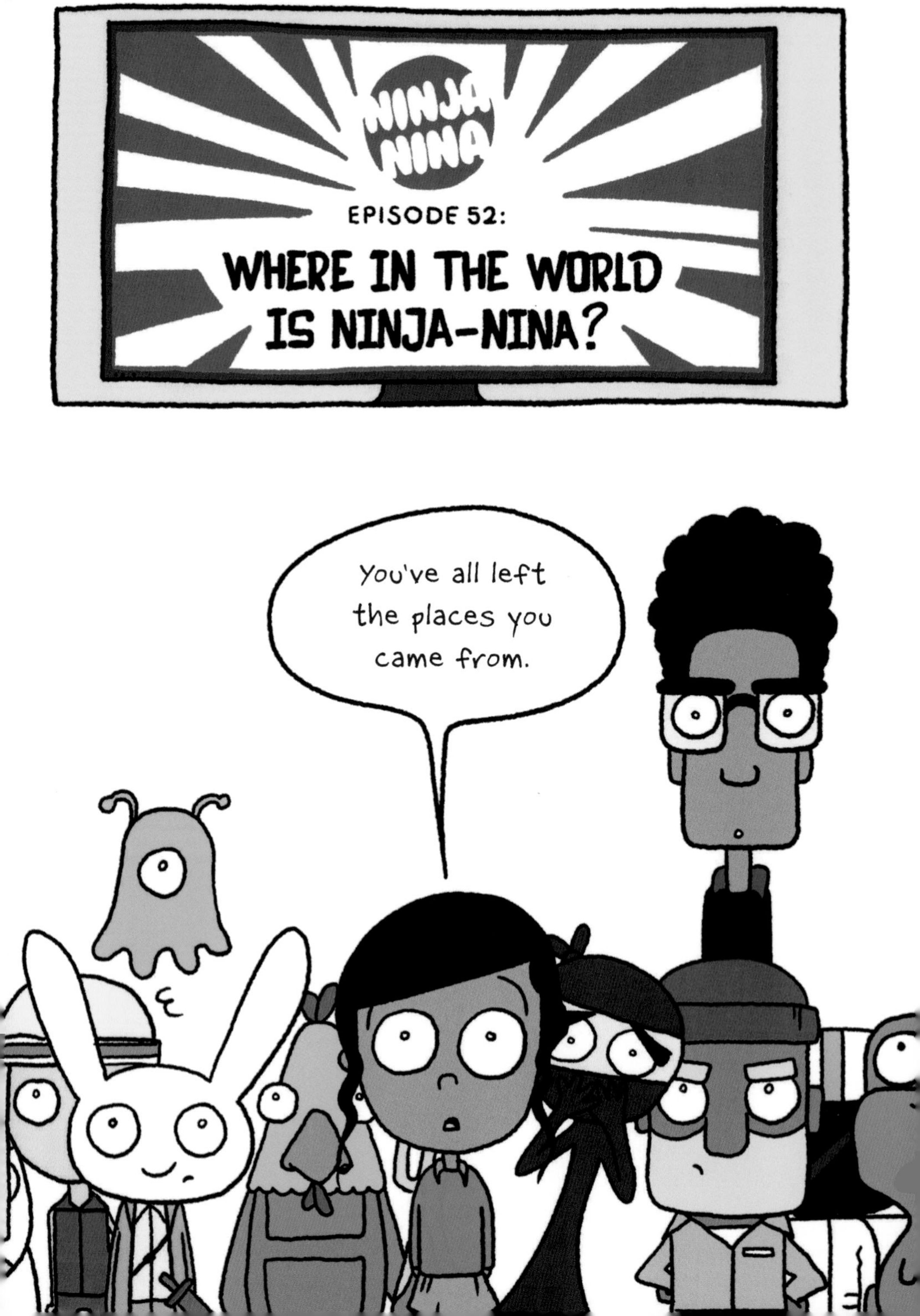
NINJA NINA
EPISODE 52:
WHERE IN THE WORLD IS NINJA-NINA?
You've all left the places you came from.

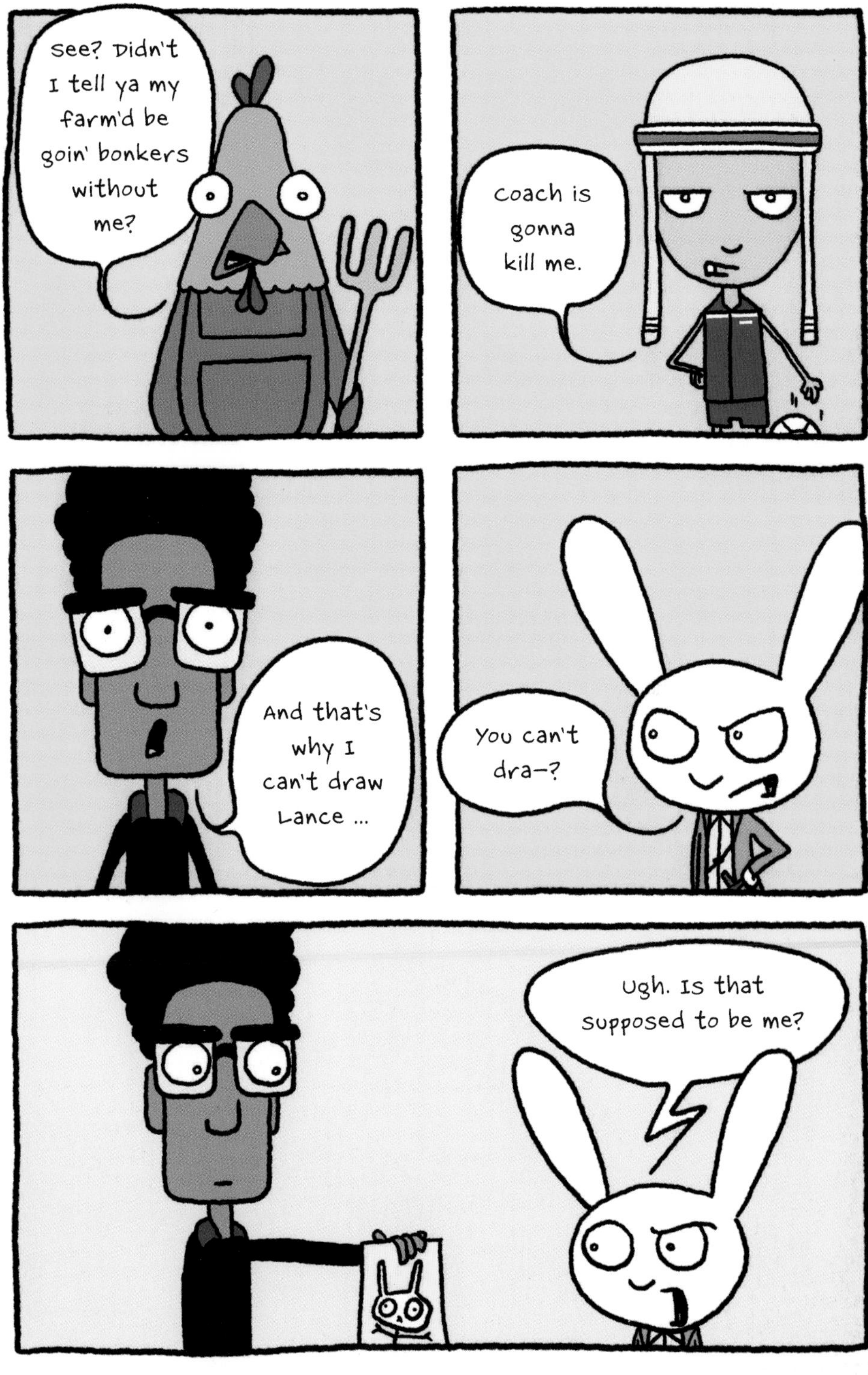
See? Didn't I tell ya my farm'd be goin' bonkers without me?
Coach is gonna kill me.
And that's why I can't draw Lance ...
You can't dra–?
Ugh. Is that supposed to be me?

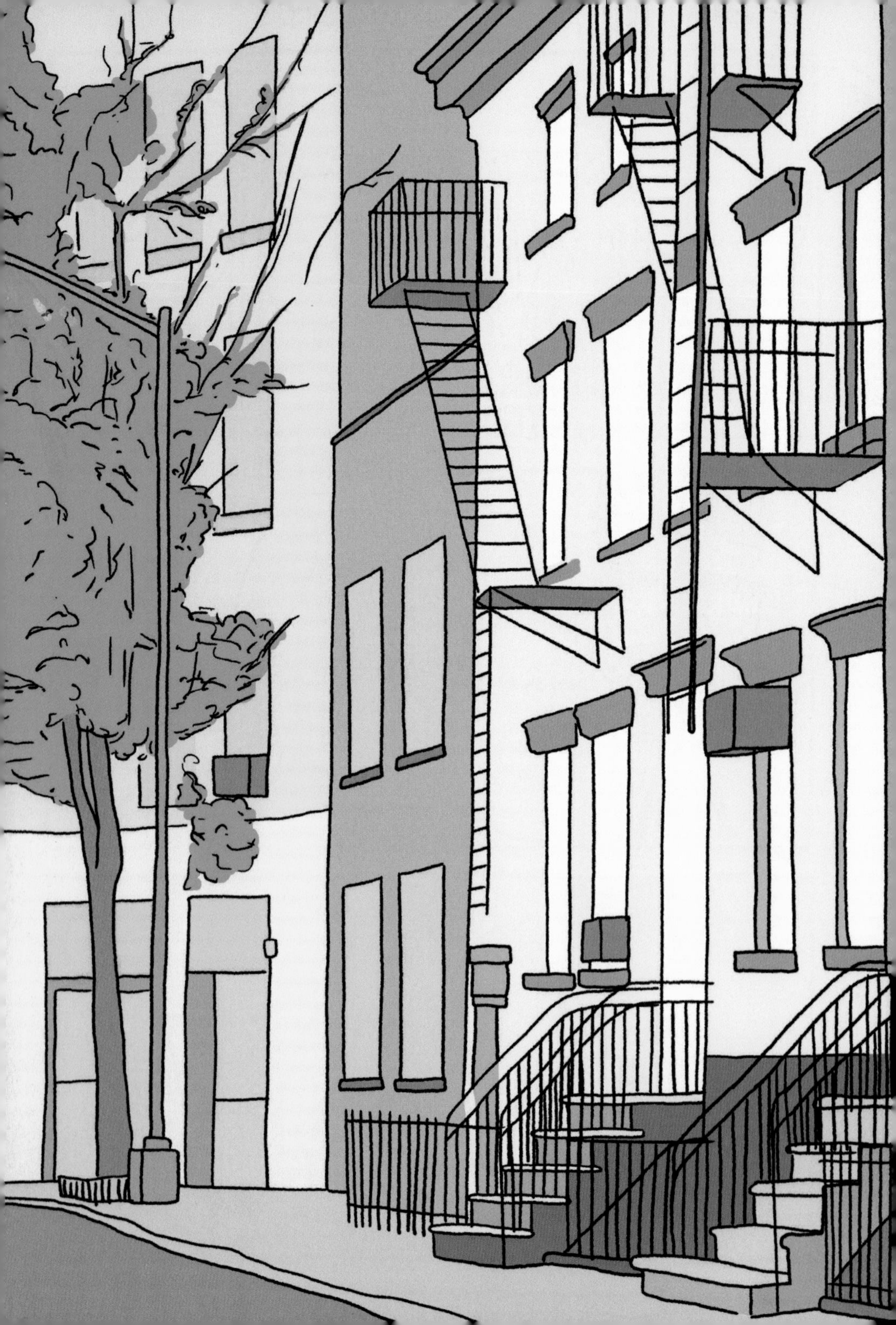

CHAPTER SEVEN
The Odds try everything

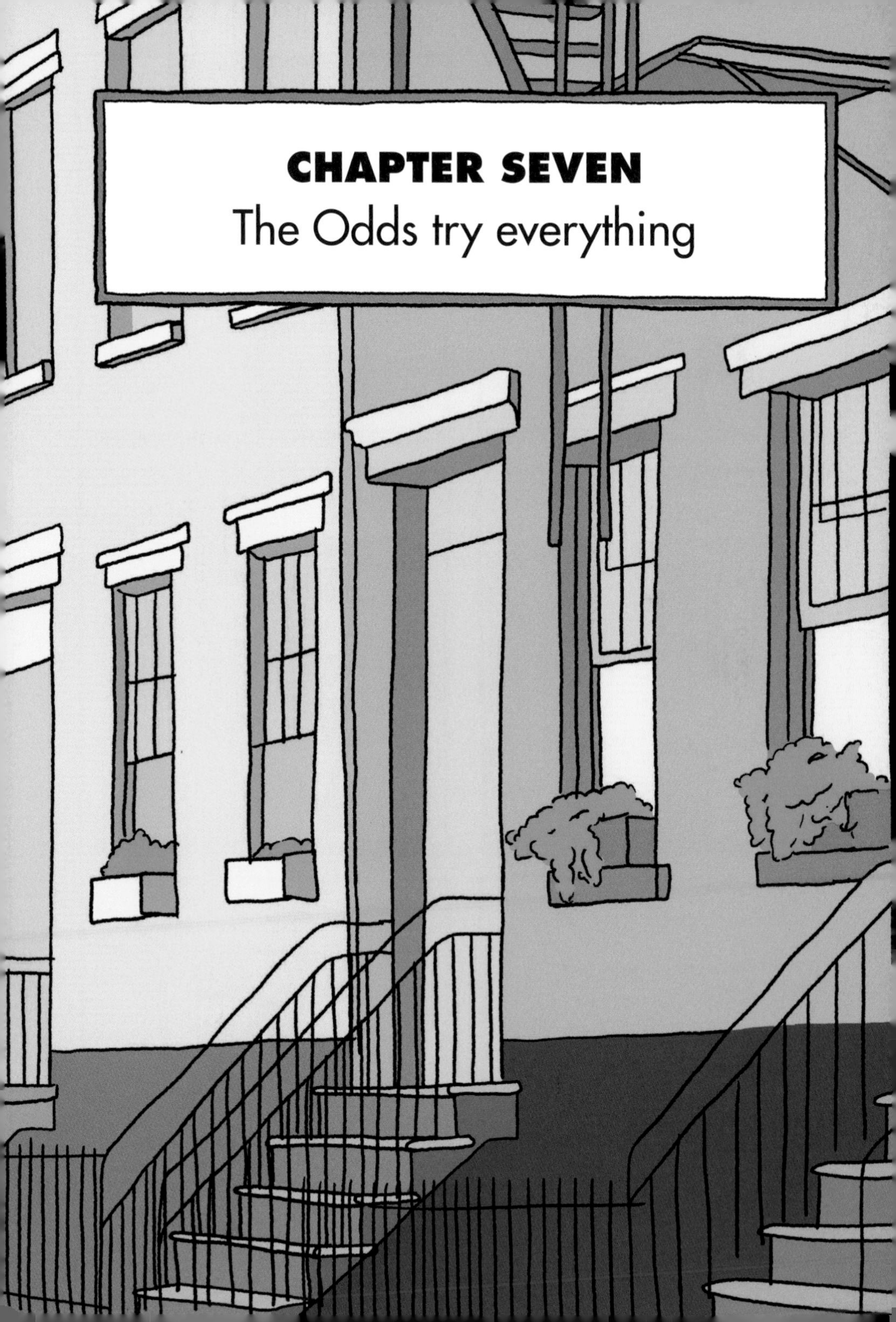

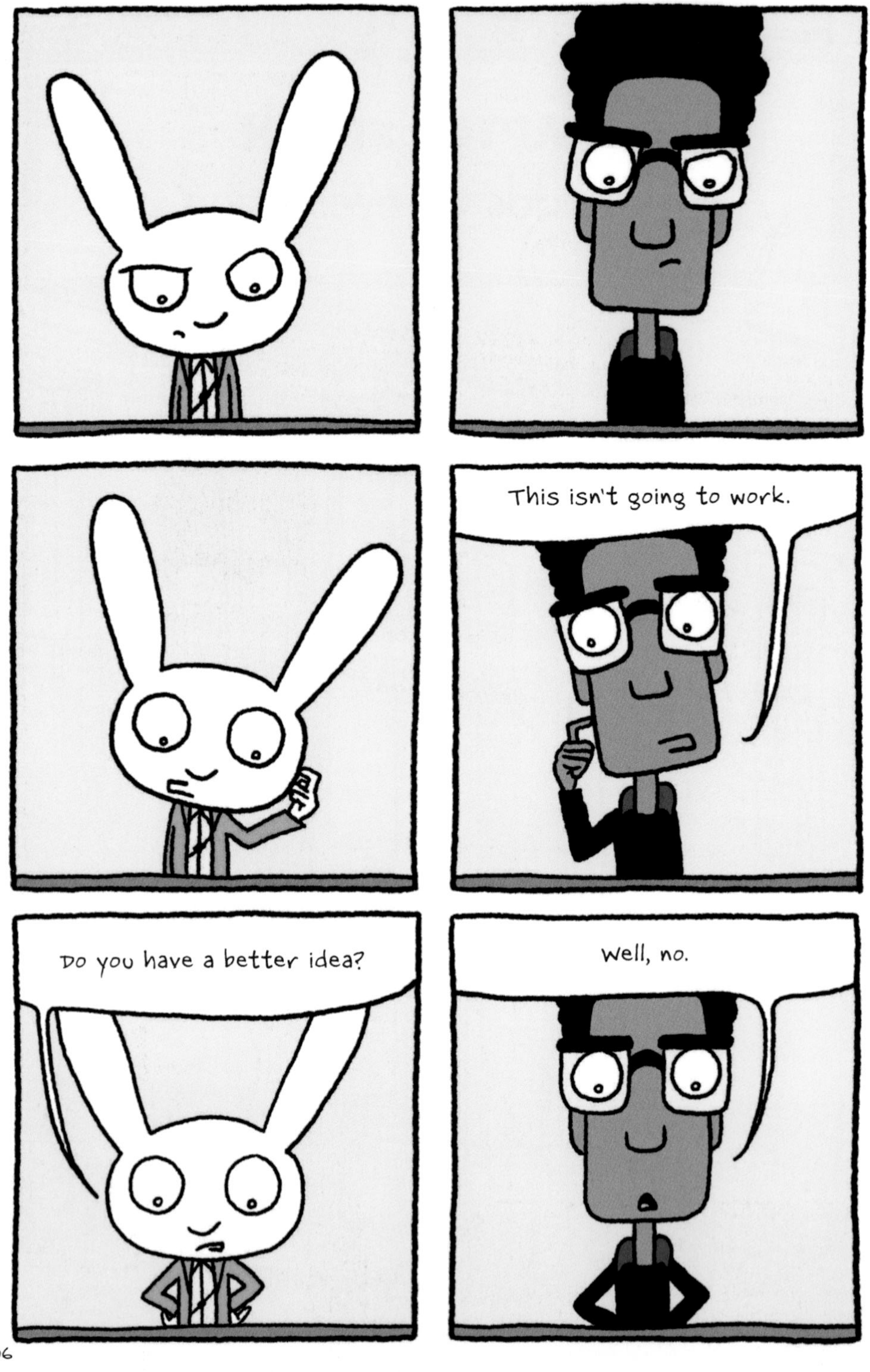
This isn't going to work.
Do you have a better idea?
Well, no.

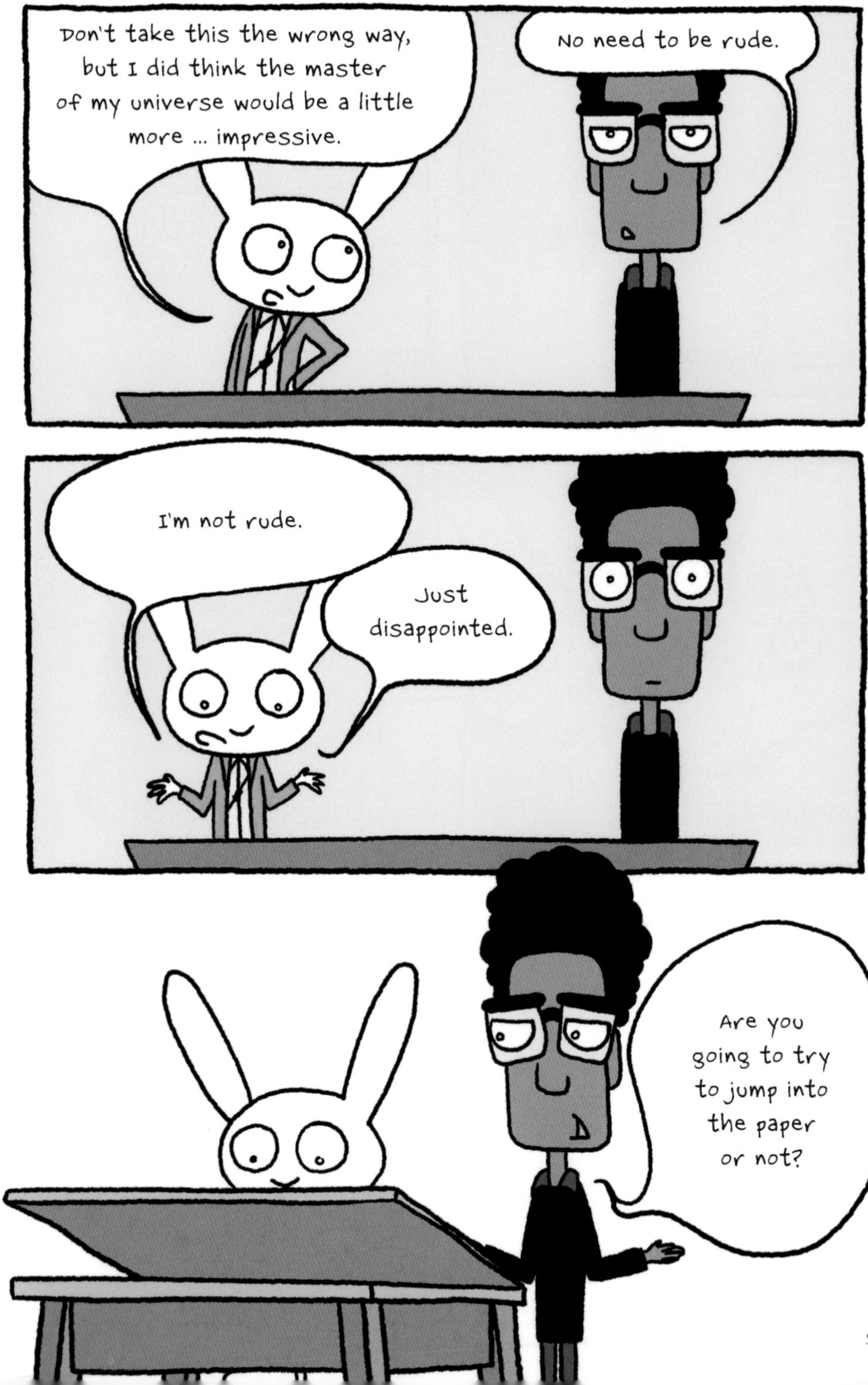
Don't take this the wrong way, but I did think the master of my universe would be a little more ... impressive.
No need to be rude.
I'm not rude.
Just disappointed.
Are you going to try to jump into the paper or not?

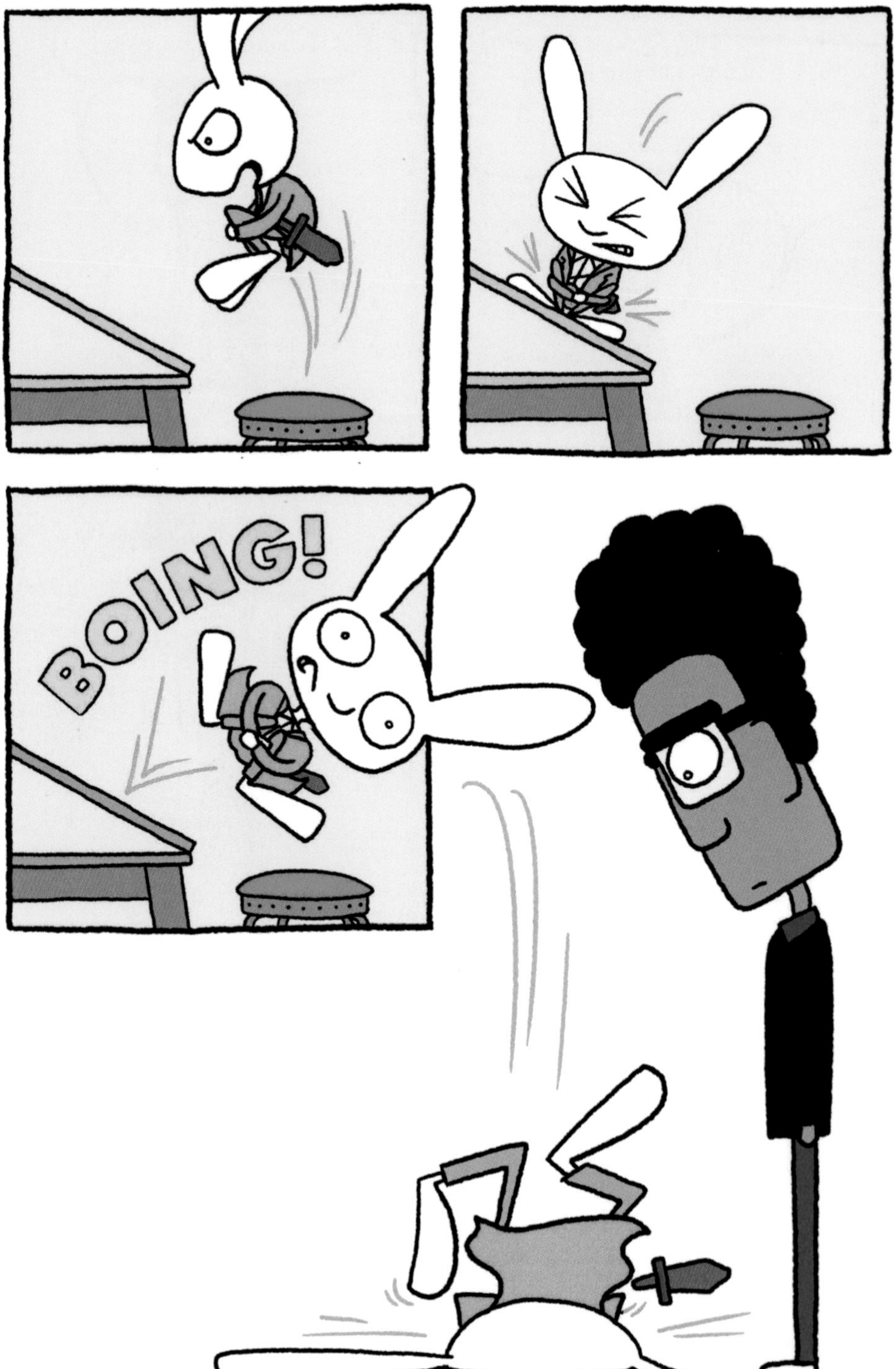
BOING!

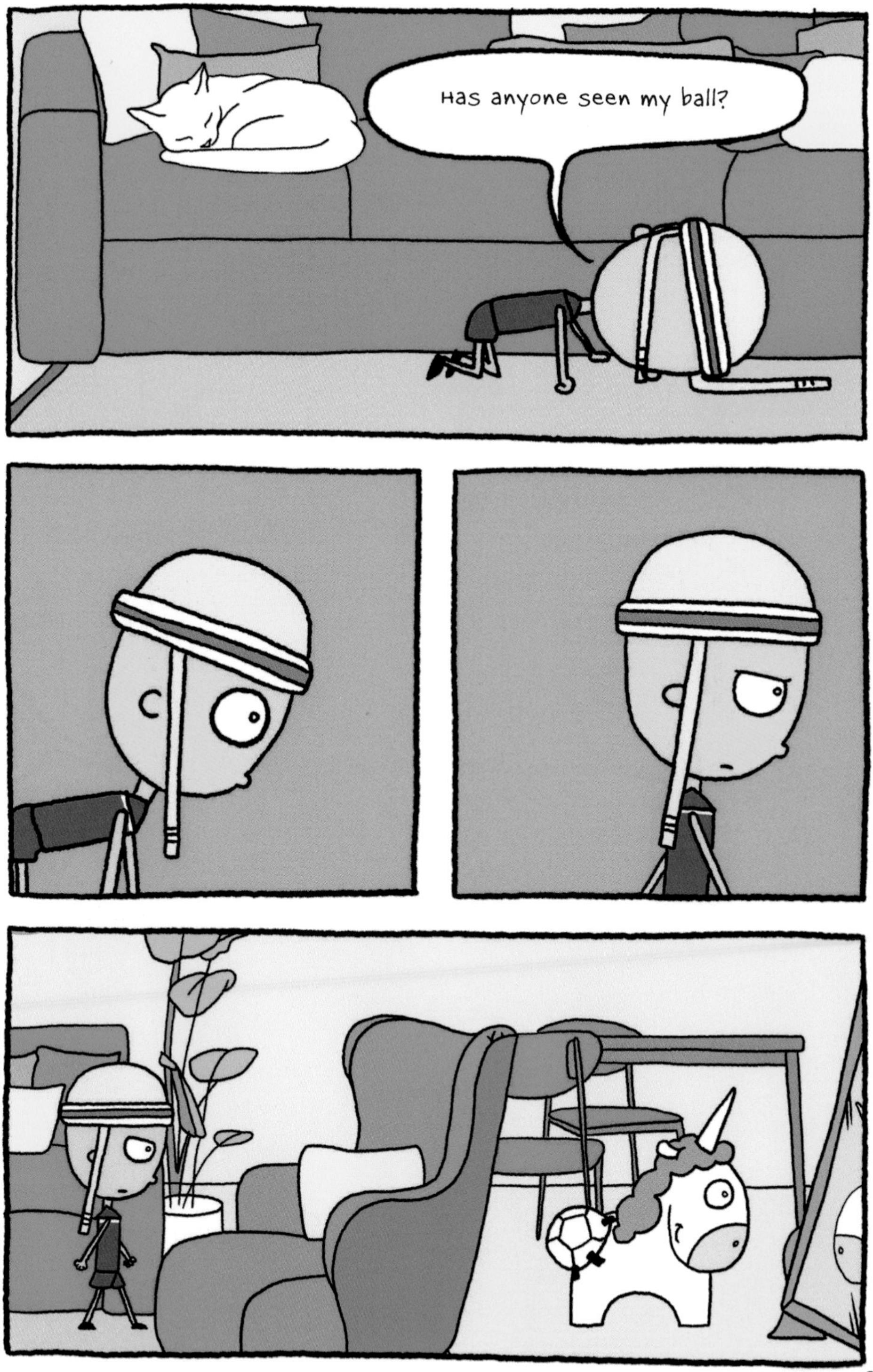
Has anyone seen my ball?

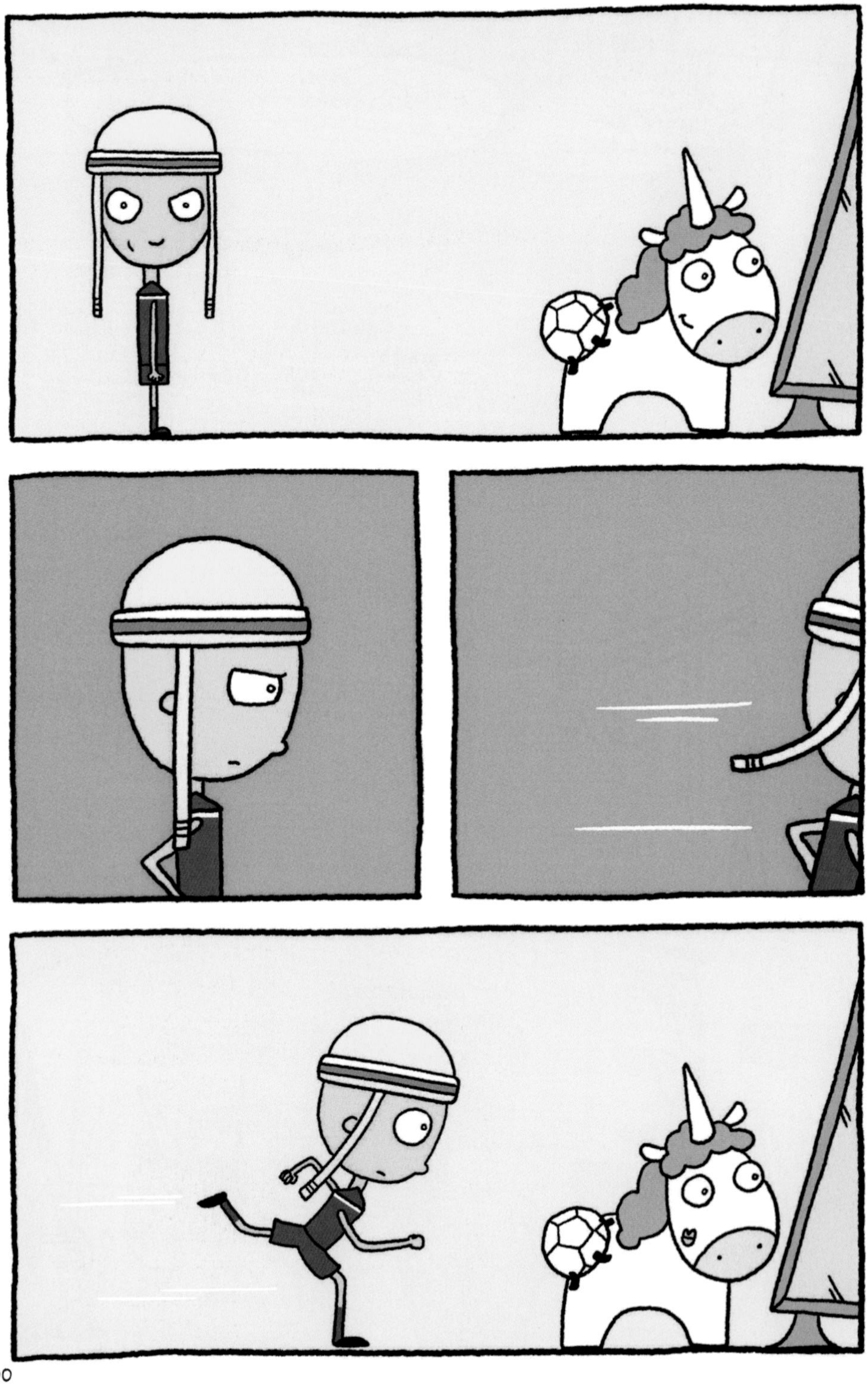

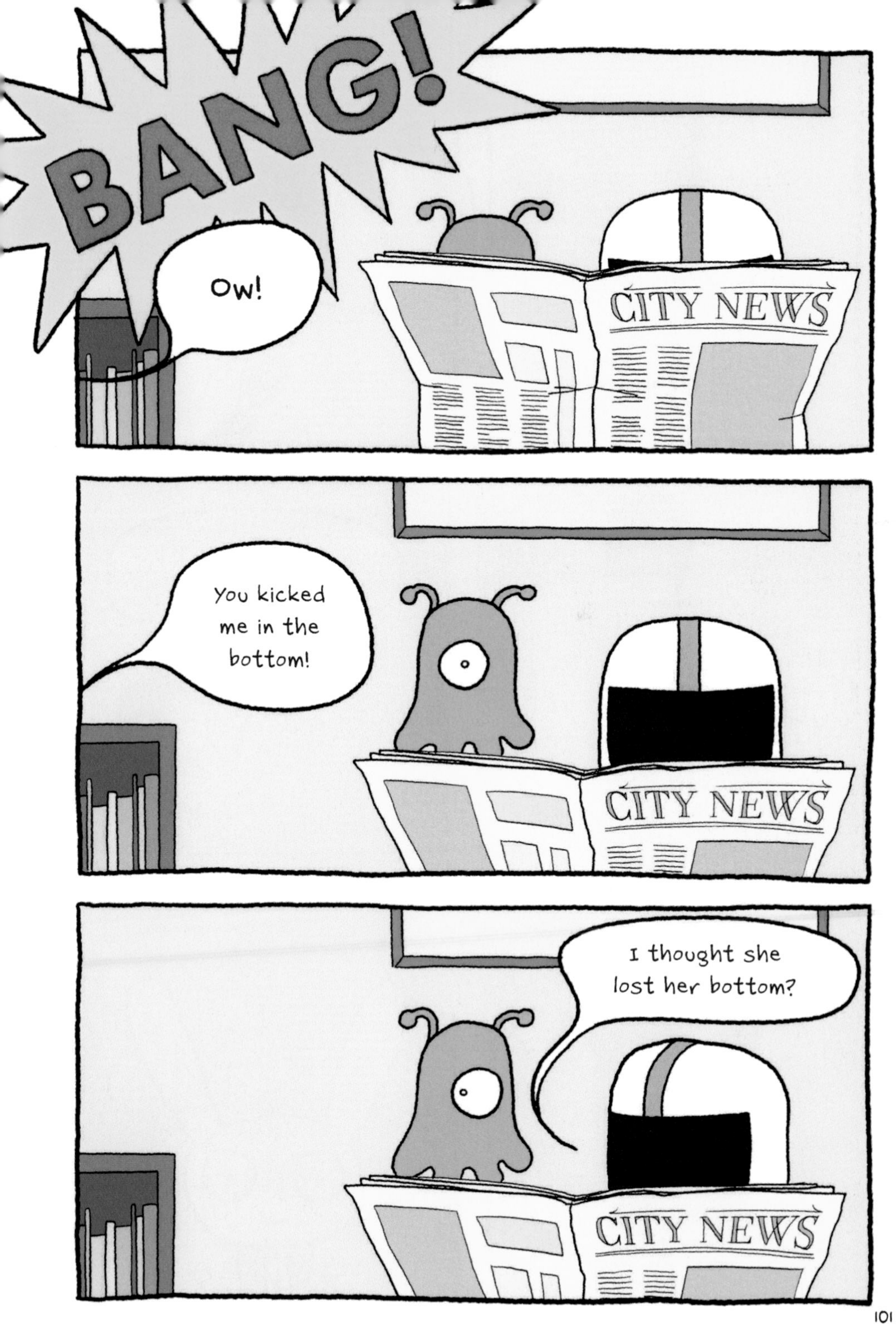
BANG!
Ow!
CITY NEWS
You kicked me in the bottom!
CITY NEWS
I thought she lost her bottom?
CITY NEWS

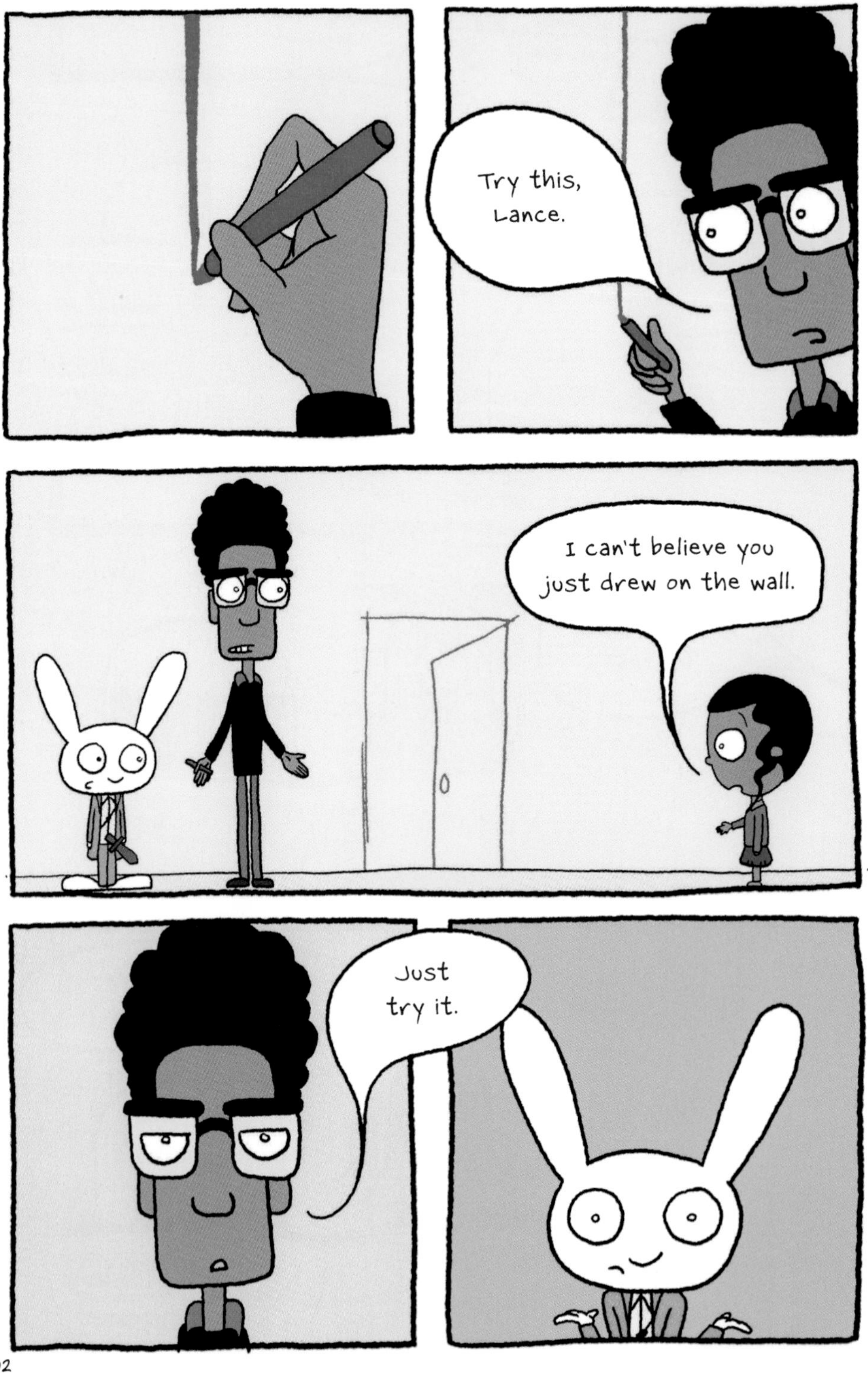
Try this, Lance.
I can't believe you just drew on the wall.
Just try it.

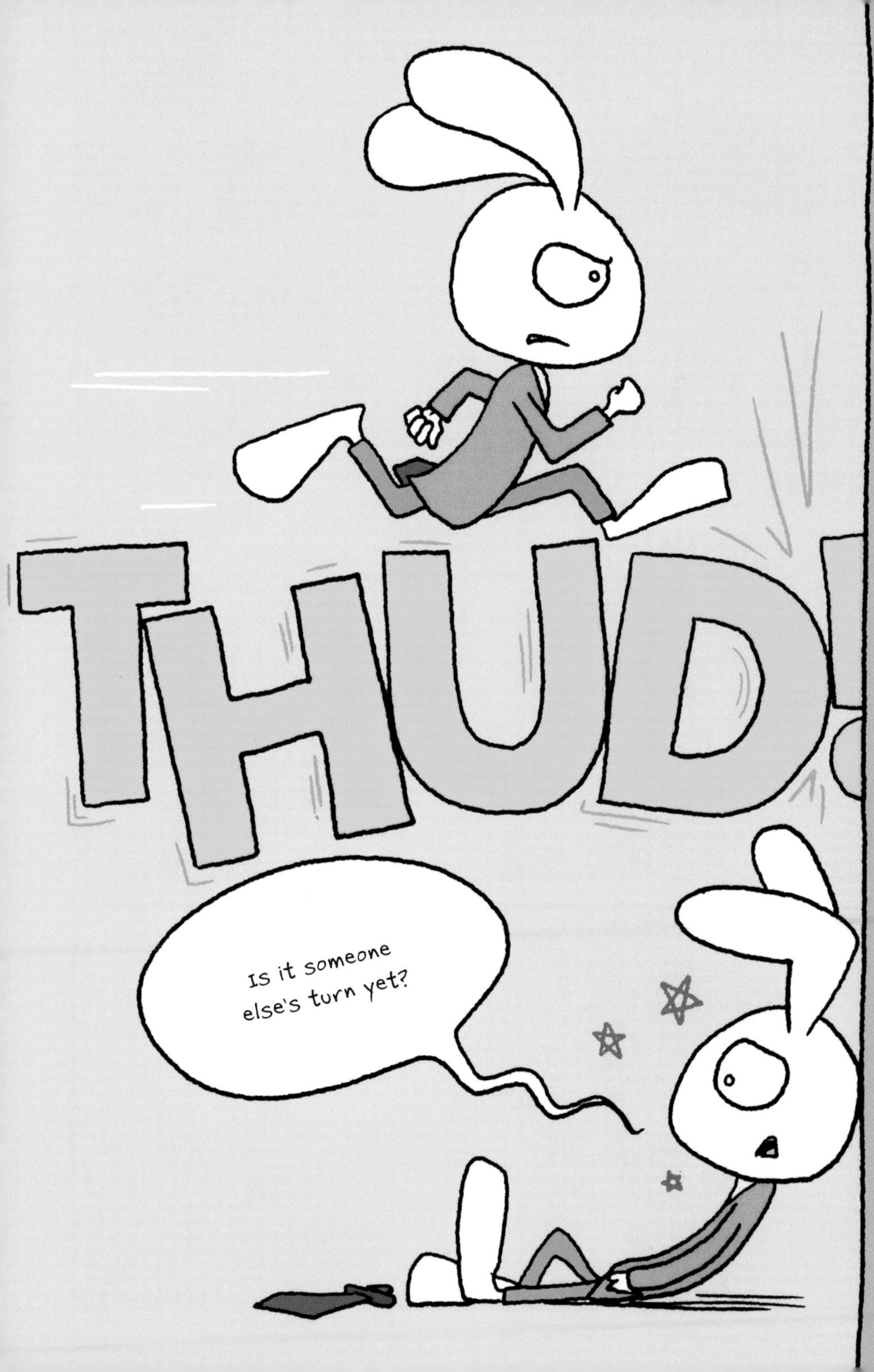
THUD!
Is it someone else's turn yet?

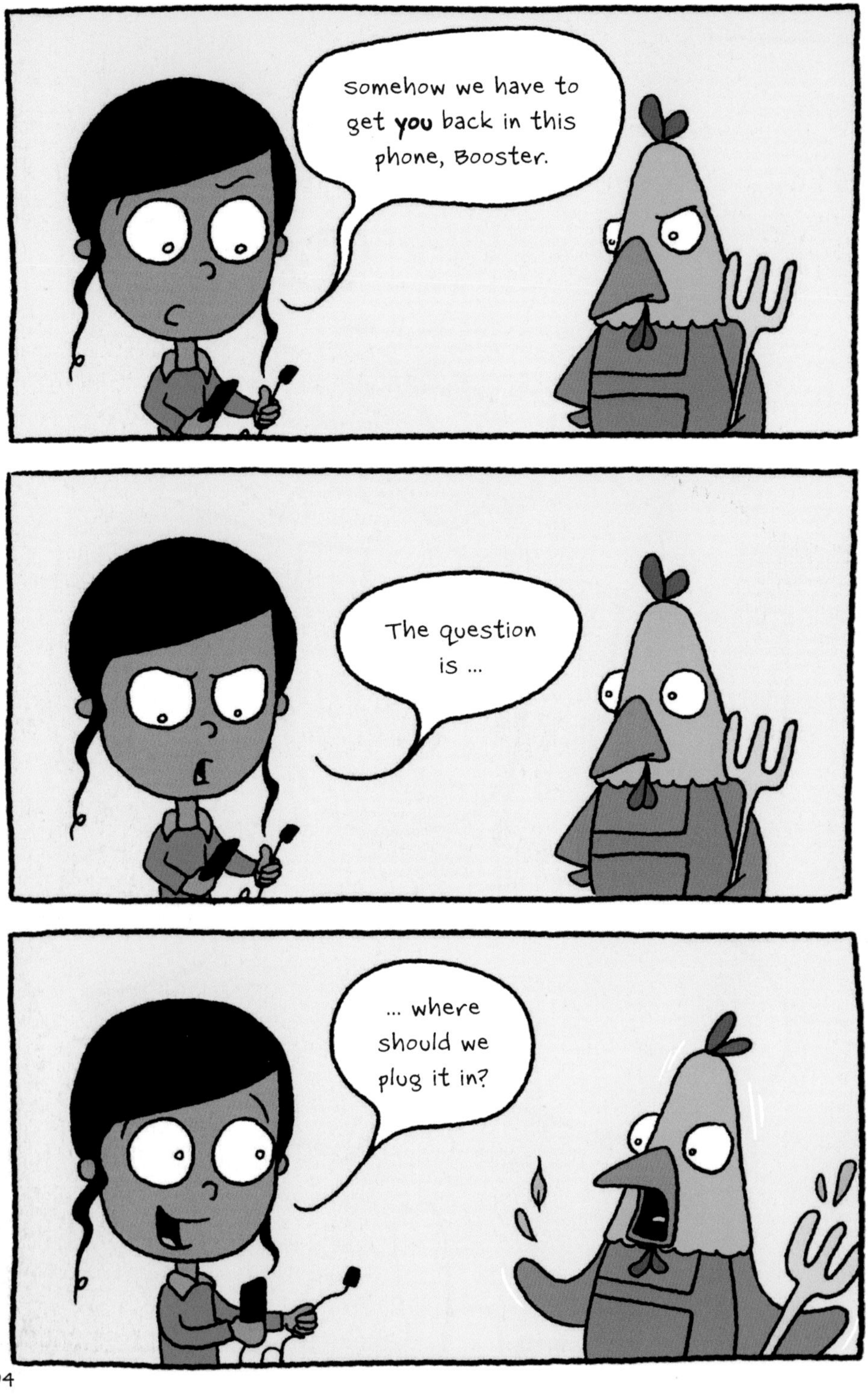
Somehow we have to get **you** back in this phone, Booster.
The question is ...
... where should we plug it in?

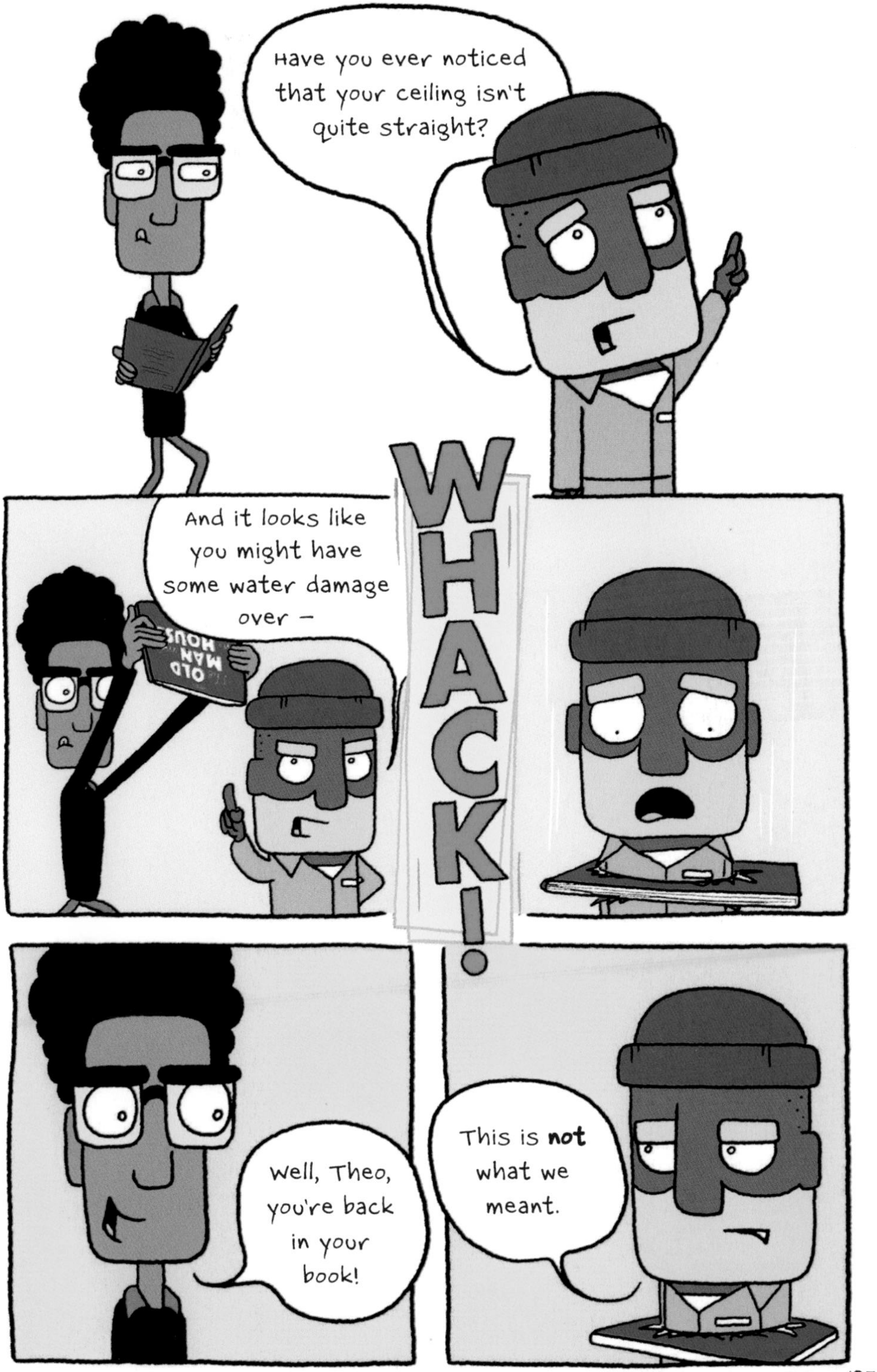
Have you ever noticed that your ceiling isn't quite straight?
And it looks like you might have some water damage over –
OLD MAN HOUS
WHACK!
Well, Theo, you're back in your book!
This is **not** what we meant.

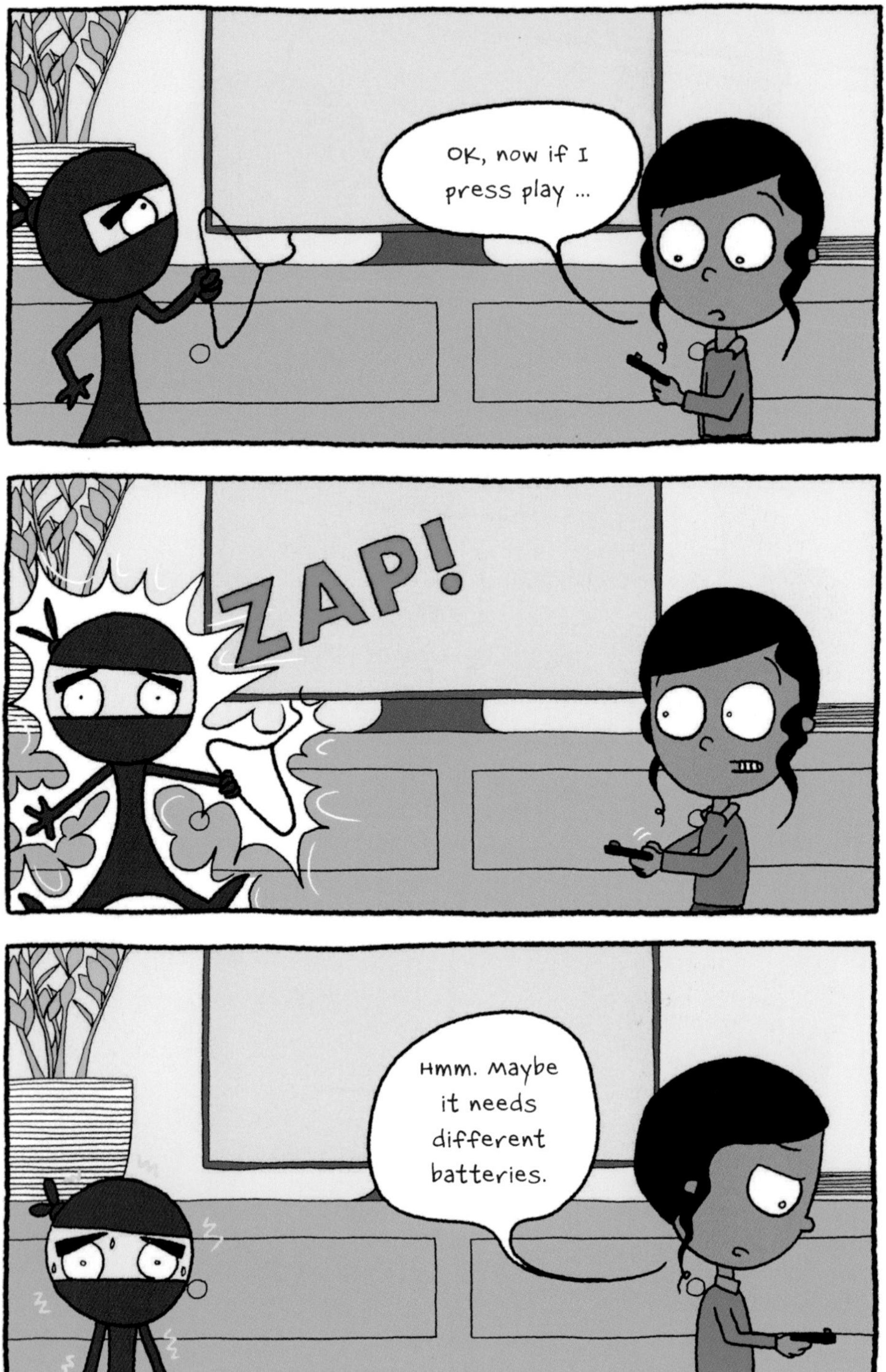
OK, now if I press play ...
ZAP!
Hmm. Maybe it needs different batteries.

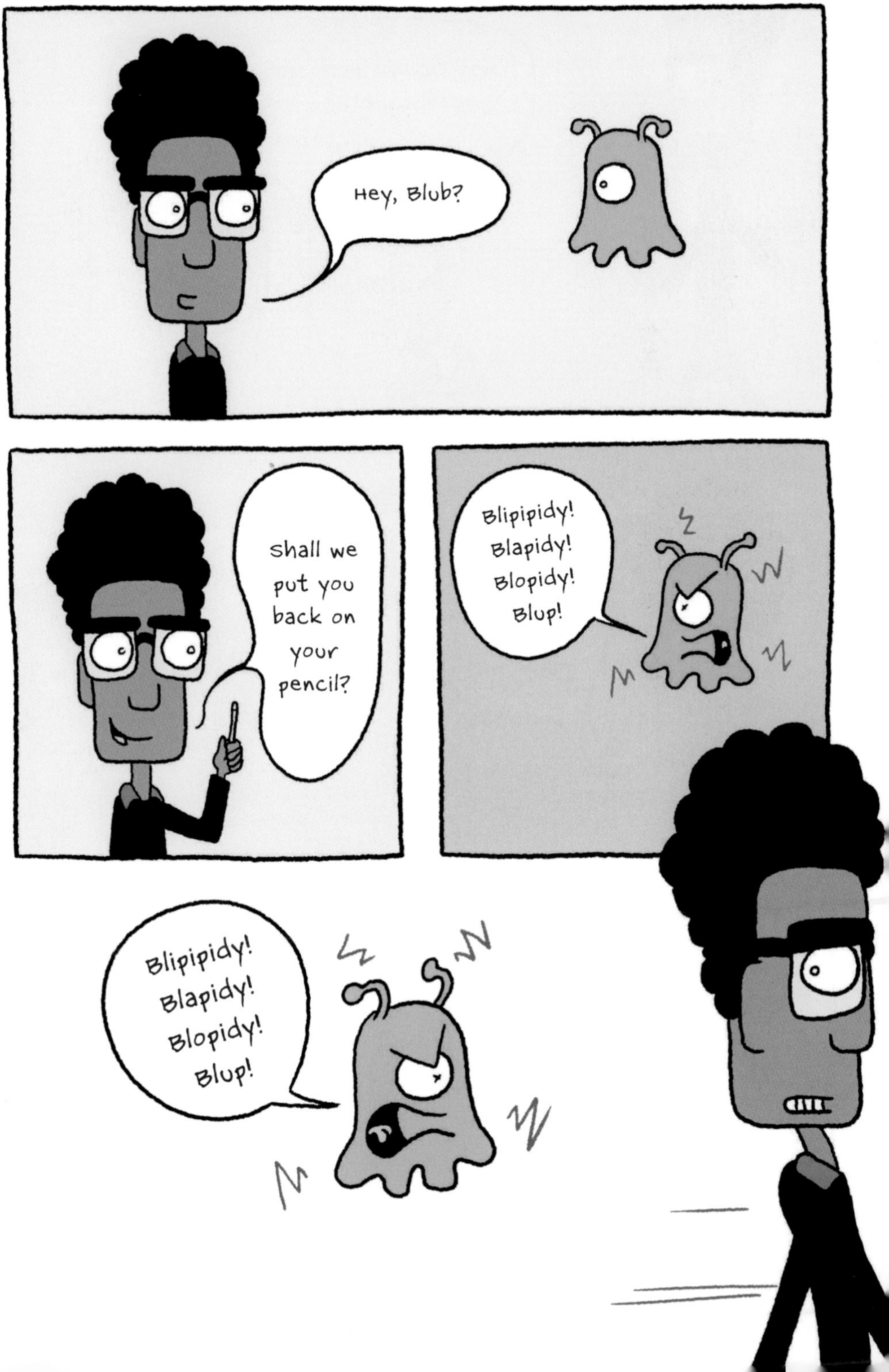
Hey, Blub?
Shall we put you back on your pencil?
Blipipidy! Blapidy! Blopidy! Blup!
Blipipidy! Blapidy! Blopidy! Blup!

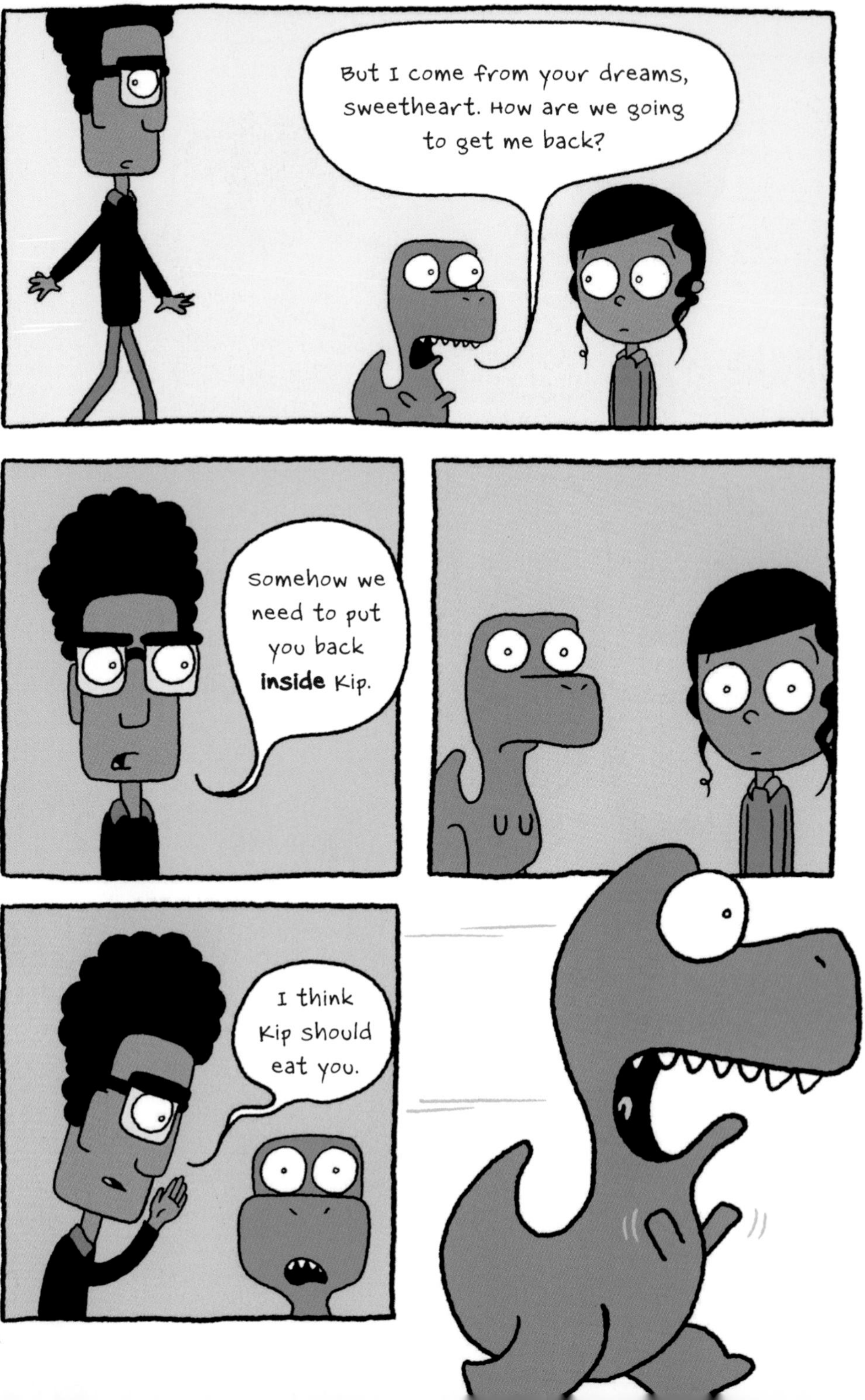
But I come from your dreams, sweetheart. How are we going to get me back?
Somehow we need to put you back **inside** Kip.
I think Kip should eat you.

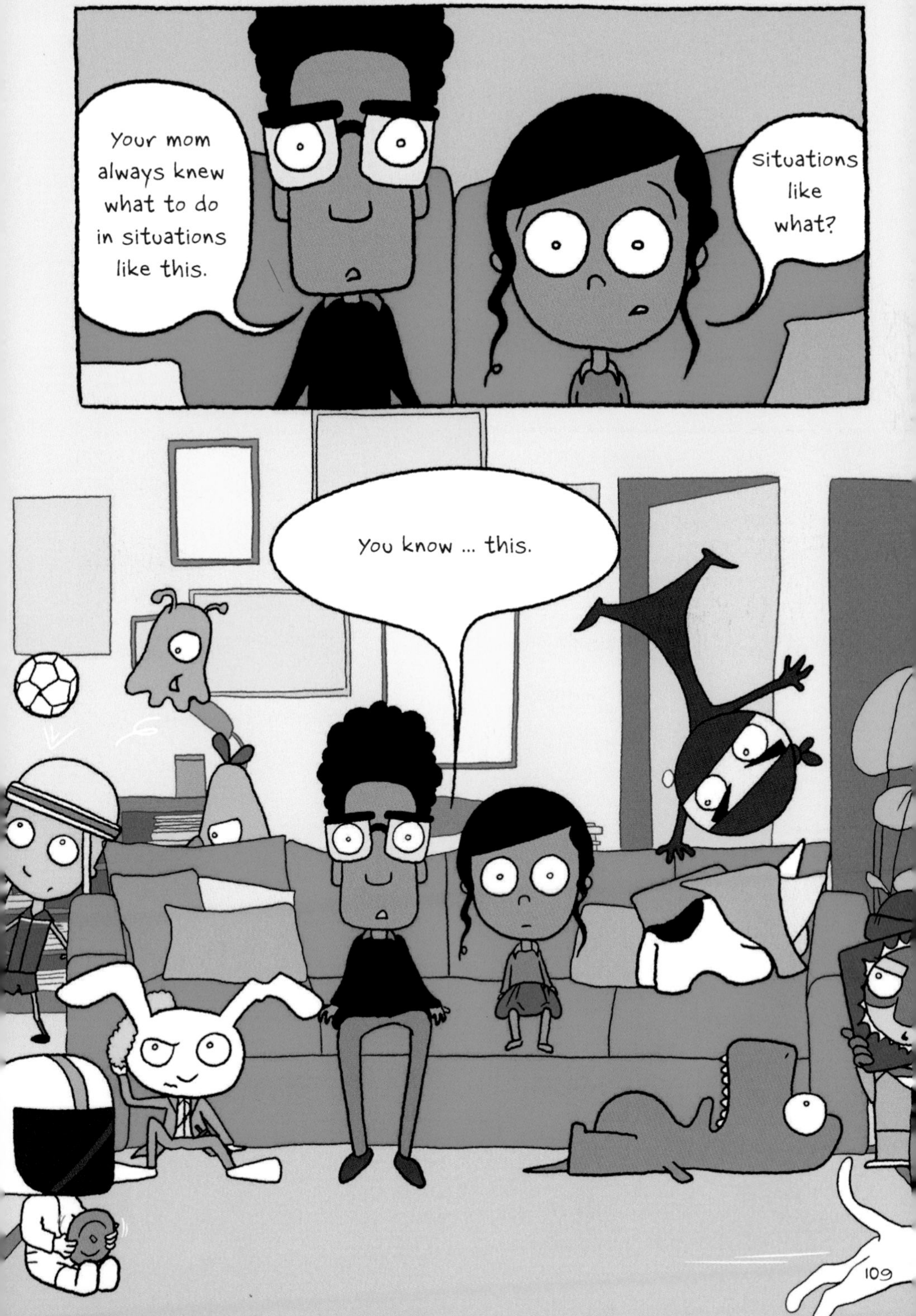
Your mom always knew what to do in situations like this.
Situations like what?
You know ... this.

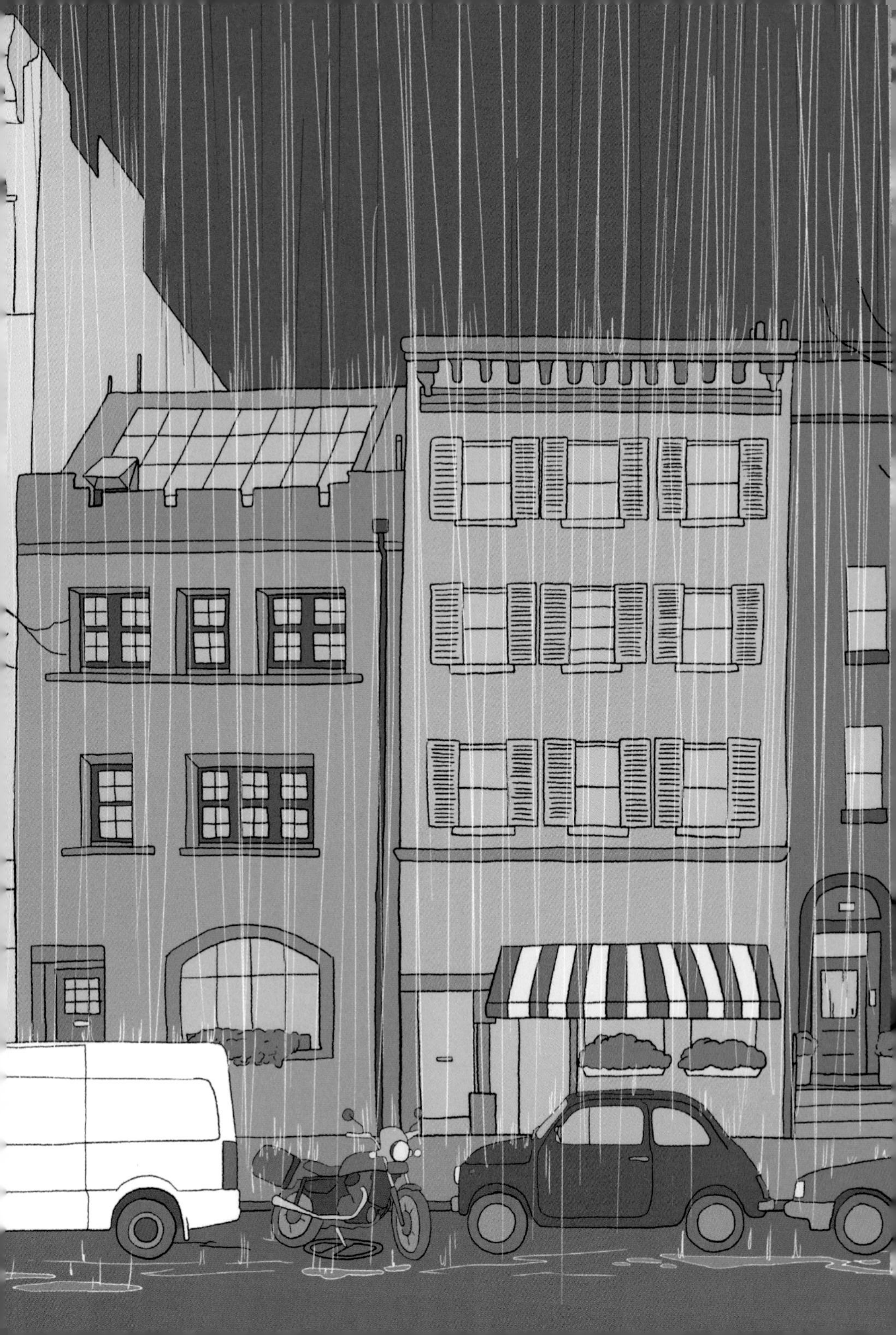

CHAPTER EIGHT
Nine out of ten Odds

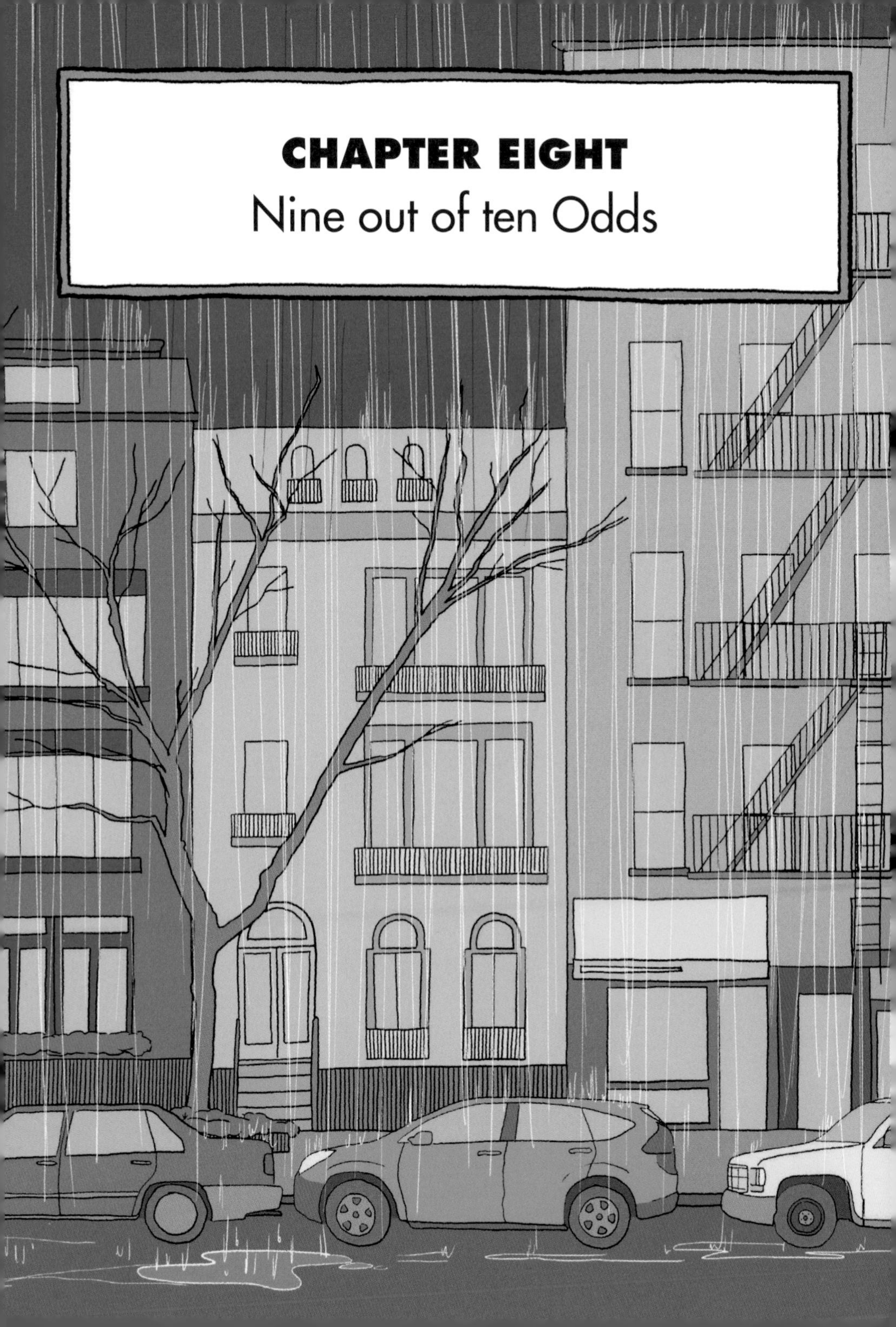

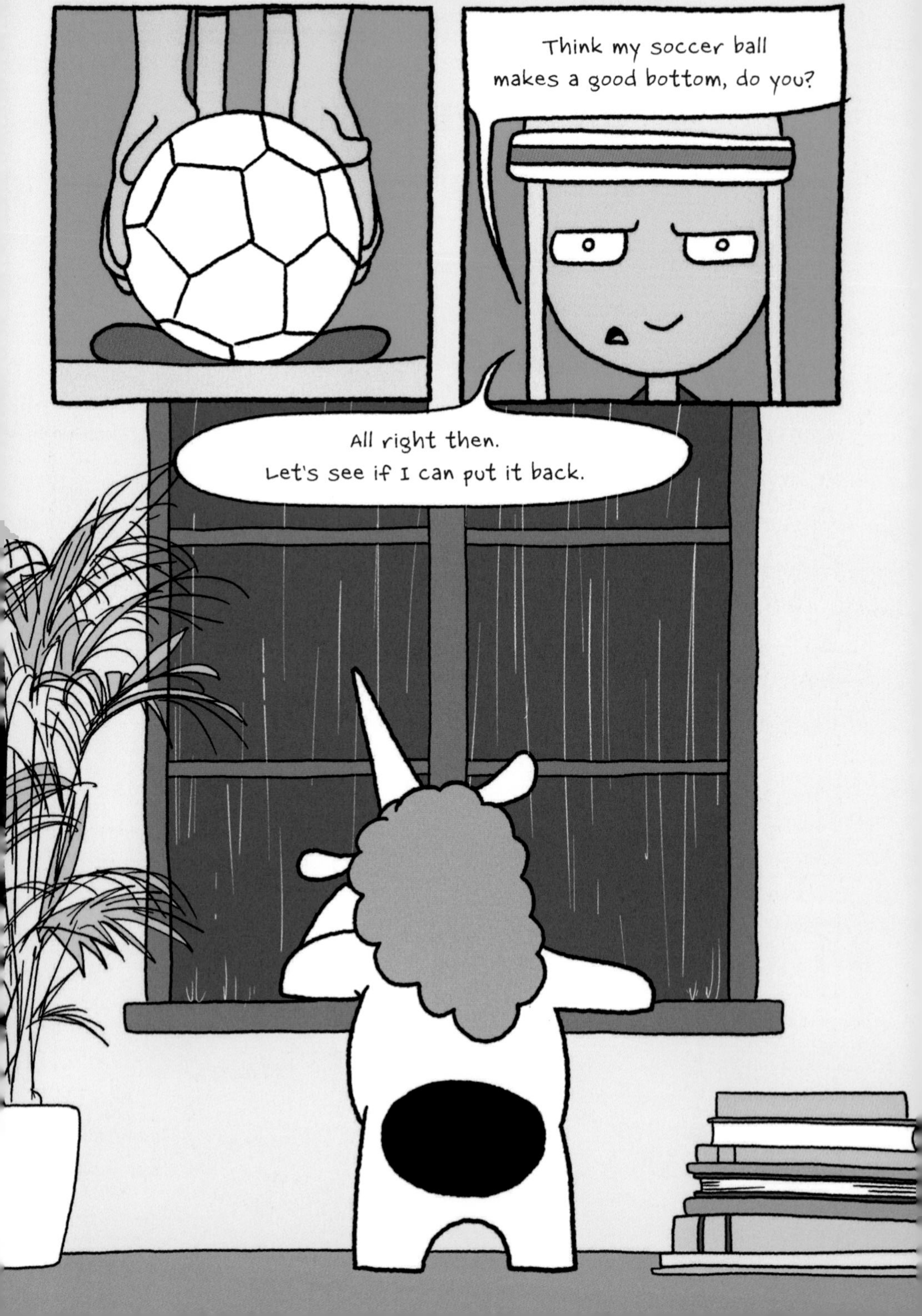
Think my soccer ball makes a good bottom, do you?
All right then. Let's see if I can put it back.

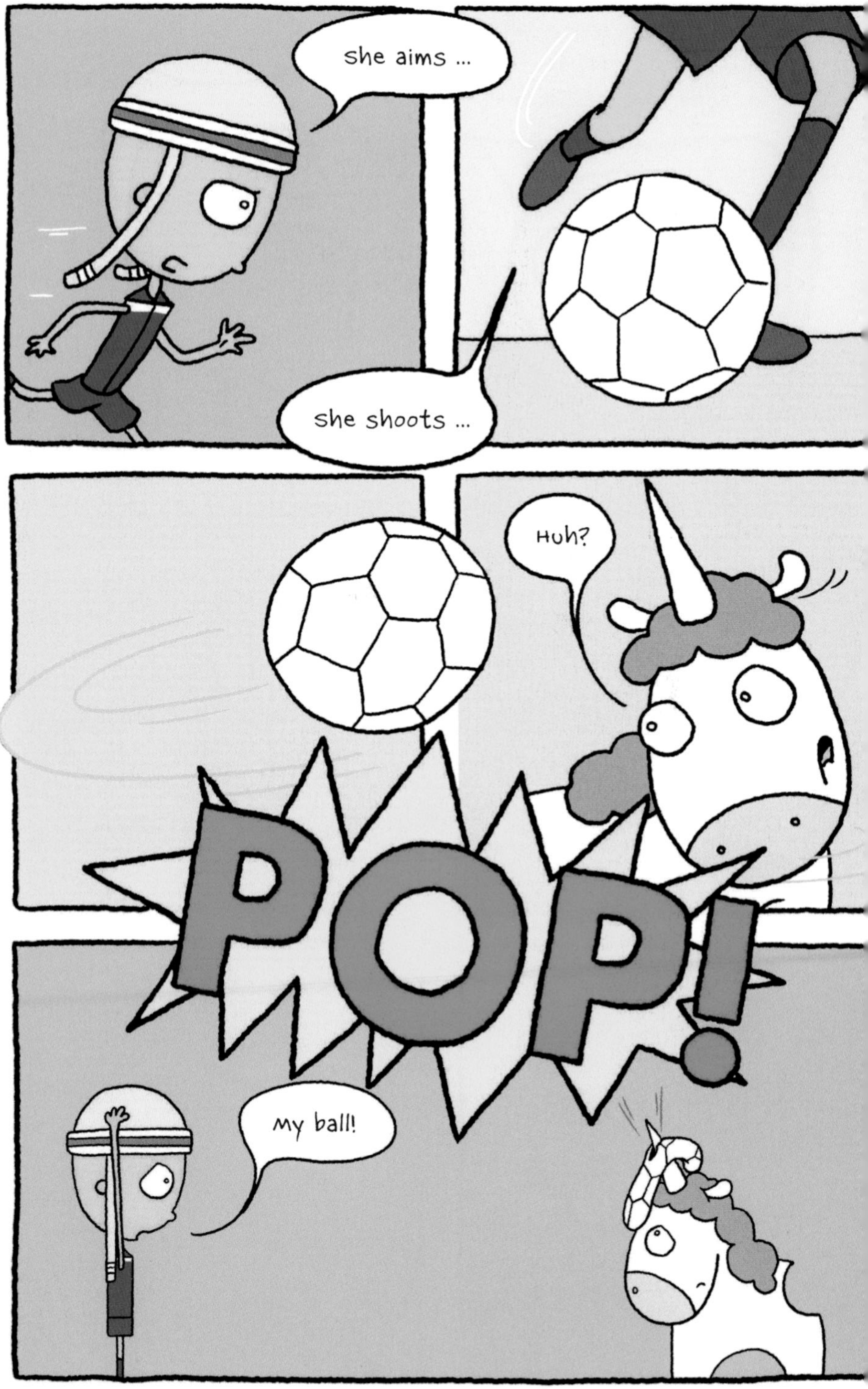
she aims ...
she shoots ...
Huh?
POP!
My ball!

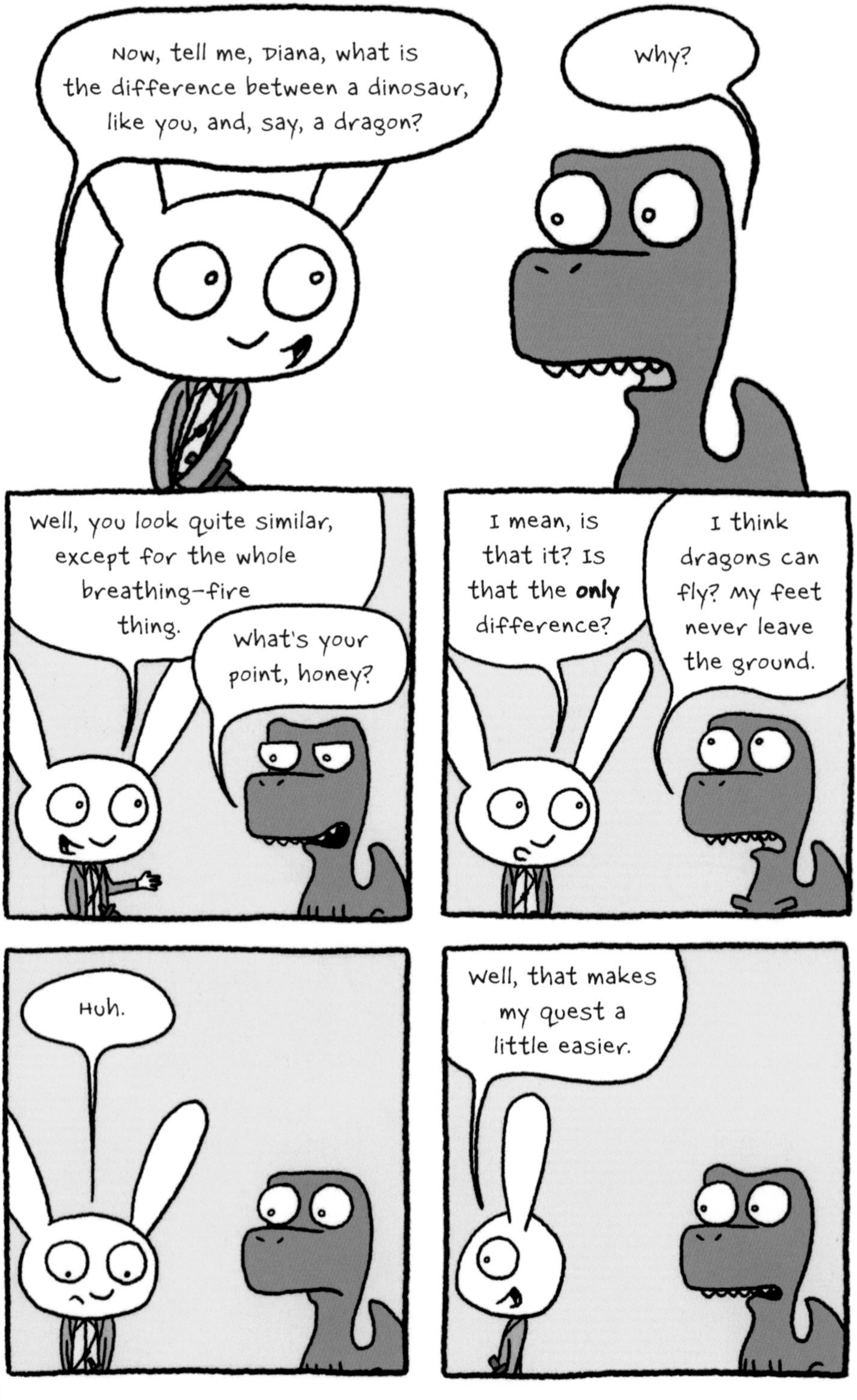
Now, tell me, Diana, what is the difference between a dinosaur, like you, and, say, a dragon?
Why?
Well, you look quite similar, except for the whole breathing-fire thing.
What's your point, honey?
I mean, is that it? Is that the **only** difference?
I think dragons can fly? My feet never leave the ground.
Huh.
Well, that makes my quest a little easier.

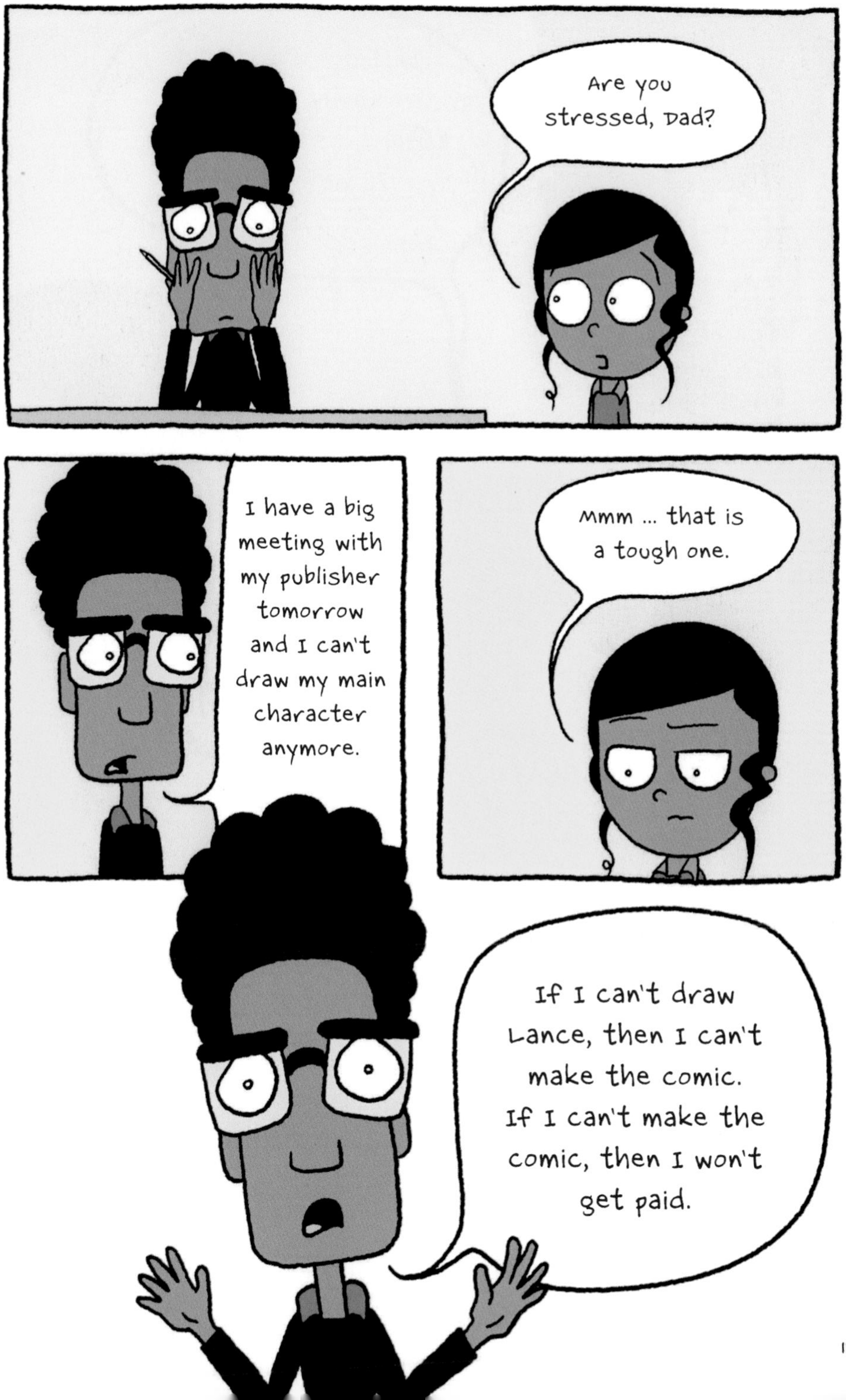
Are you stressed, Dad?
I have a big meeting with my publisher tomorrow and I can't draw my main character anymore.
Mmm ... that is a tough one.
If I can't draw Lance, then I can't make the comic. If I can't make the comic, then I won't get paid.

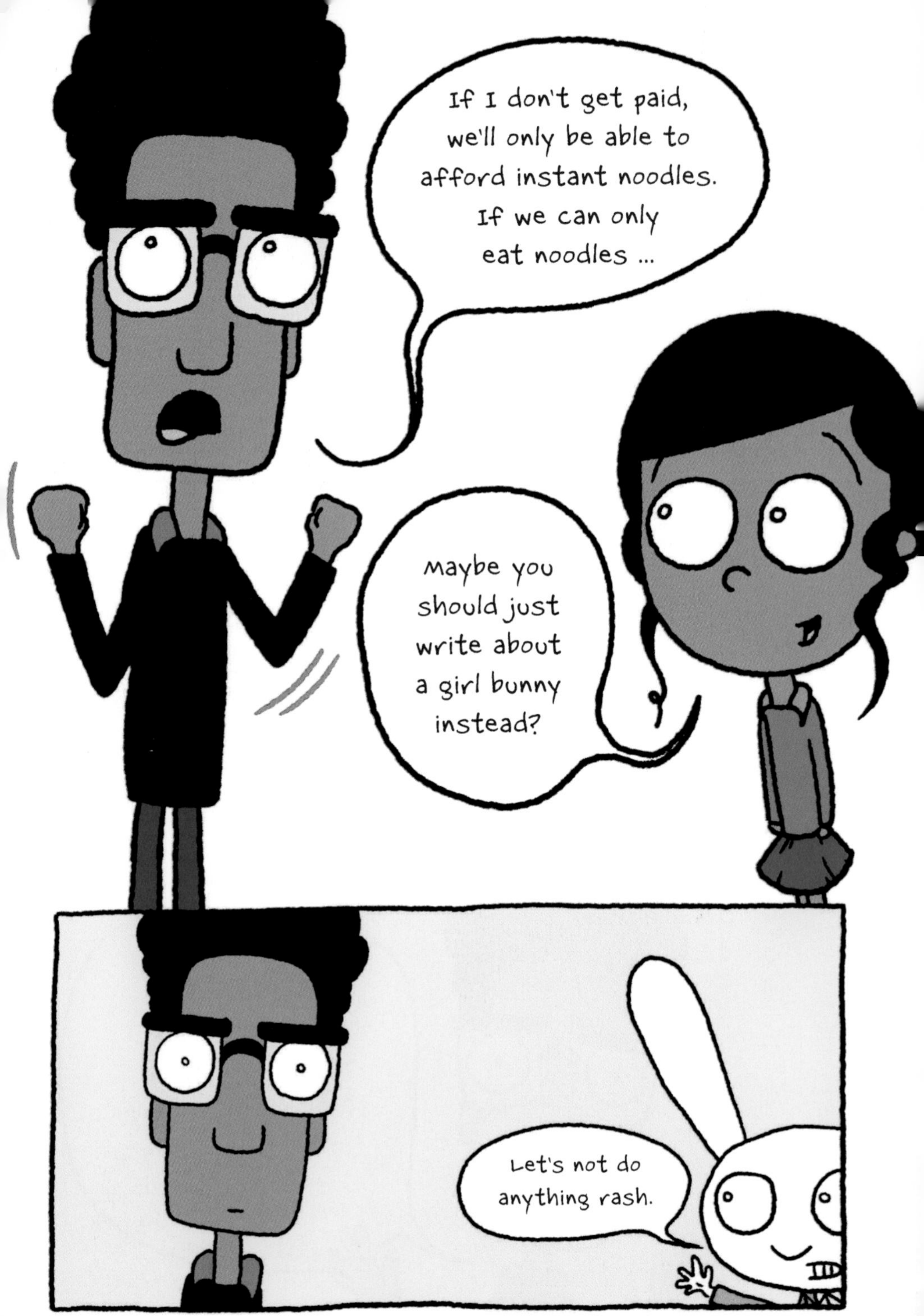
If I don't get paid, we'll only be able to afford instant noodles. If we can only eat noodles ...
Maybe you should just write about a girl bunny instead?
Let's not do anything rash.

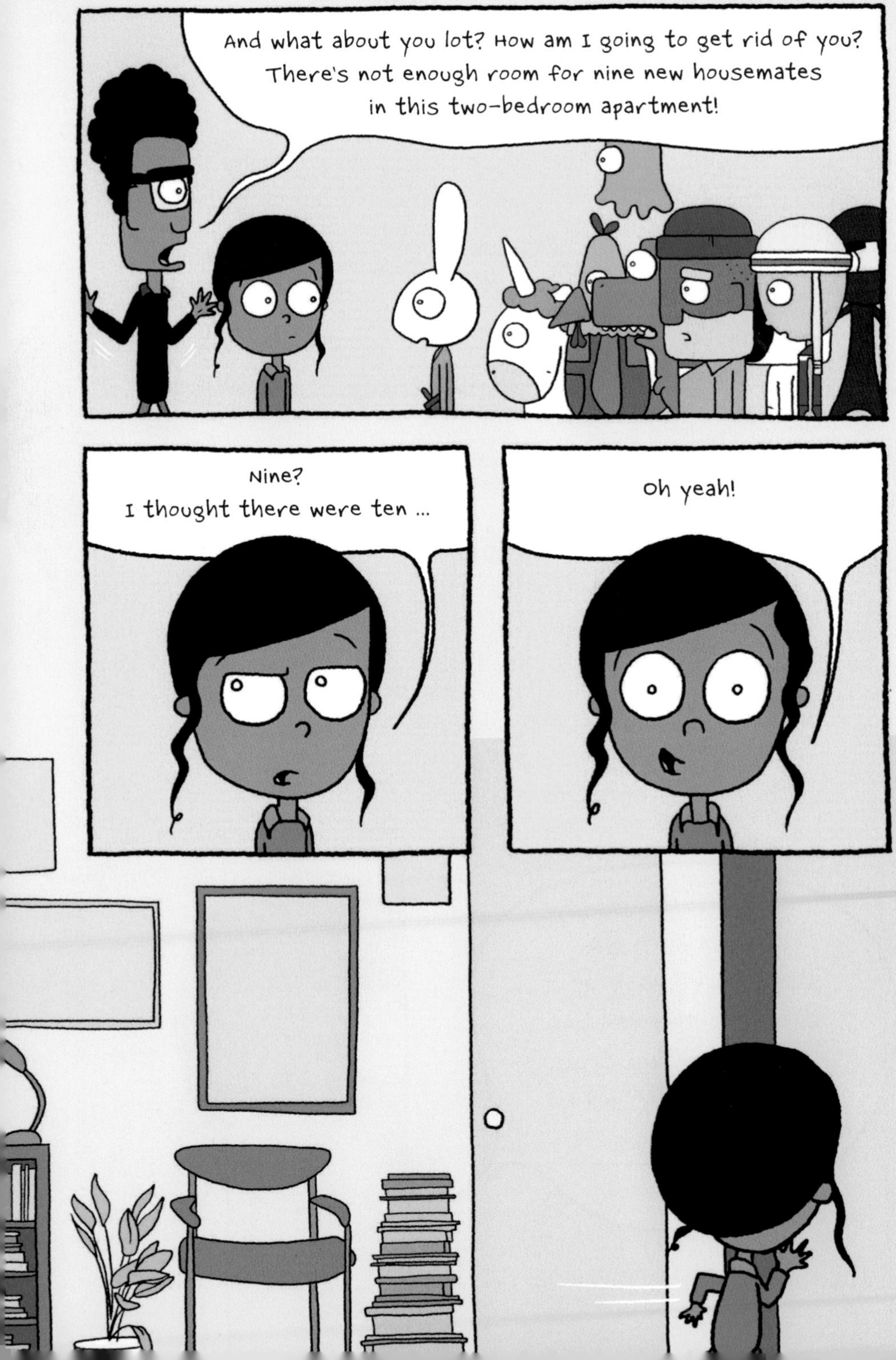
And what about you lot? How am I going to get rid of you? There's not enough room for nine new housemates in this two-bedroom apartment!
Nine? I thought there were ten ...
Oh yeah!

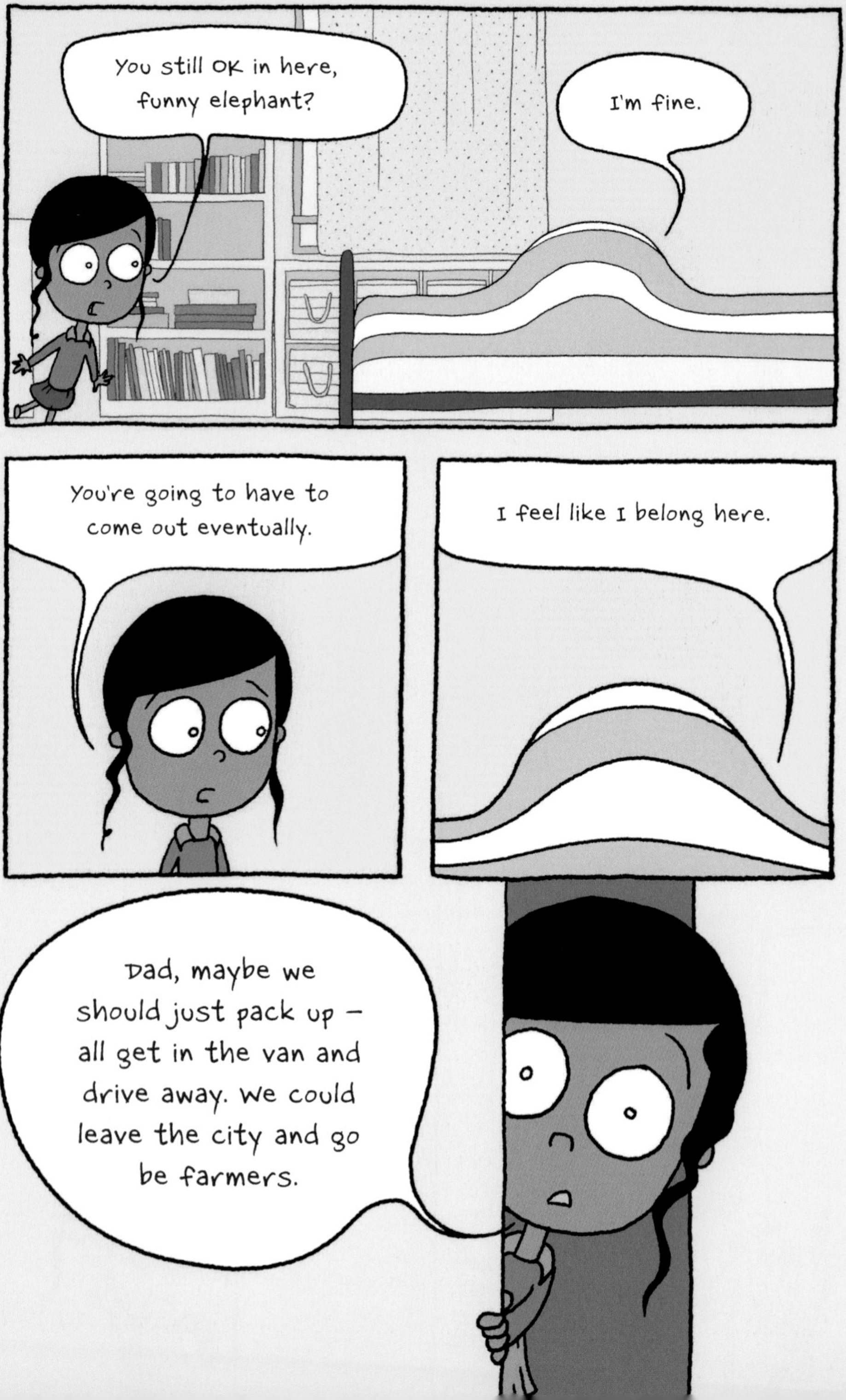
You still OK in here, funny elephant?
I'm fine.
You're going to have to come out eventually.
I feel like I belong here.
Dad, maybe we should just pack up – all get in the van and drive away. We could leave the city and go be farmers.

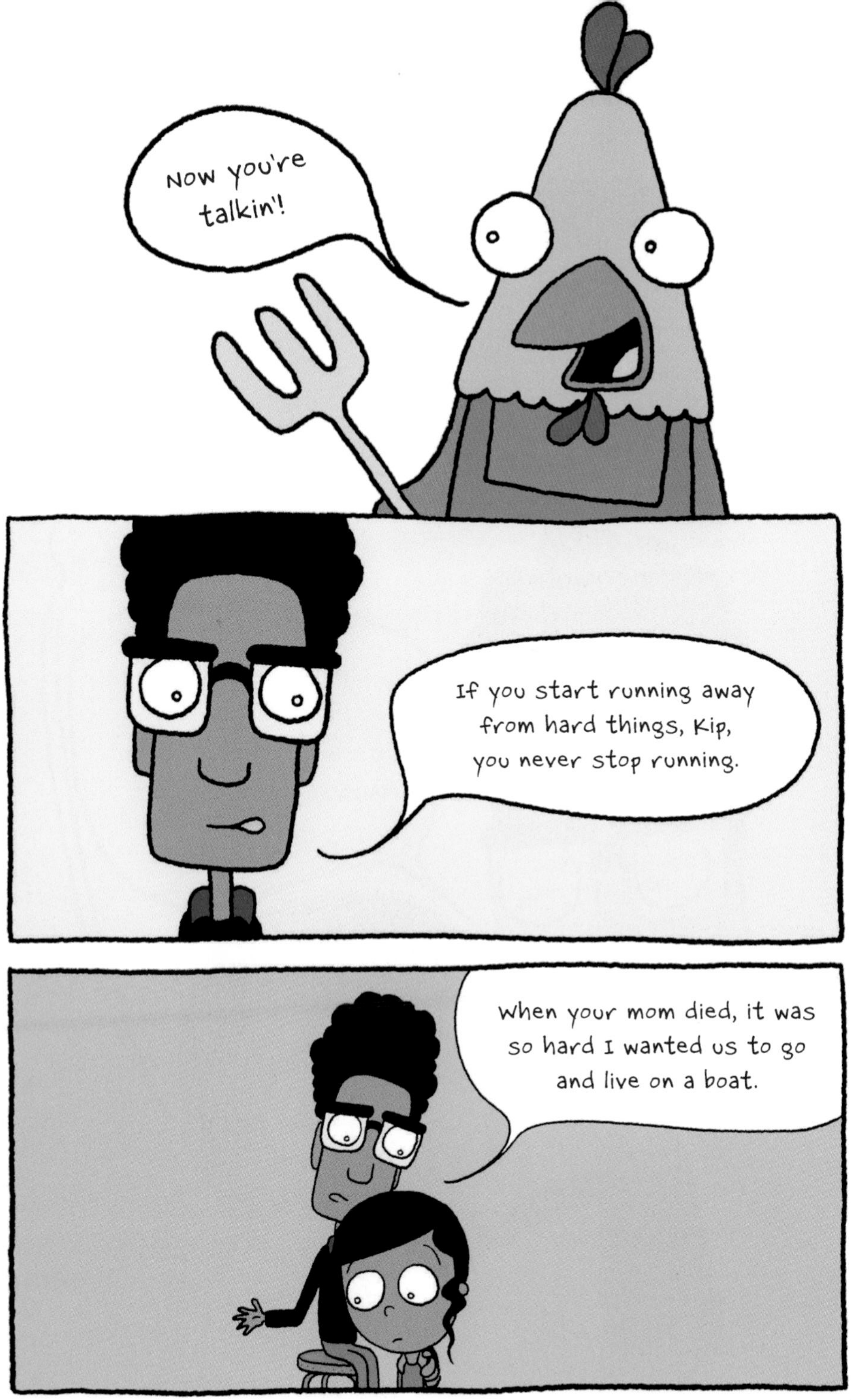
Now you're talkin'!
If you start running away from hard things, Kip, you never stop running.
When your mom died, it was so hard I wanted us to go and live on a boat.

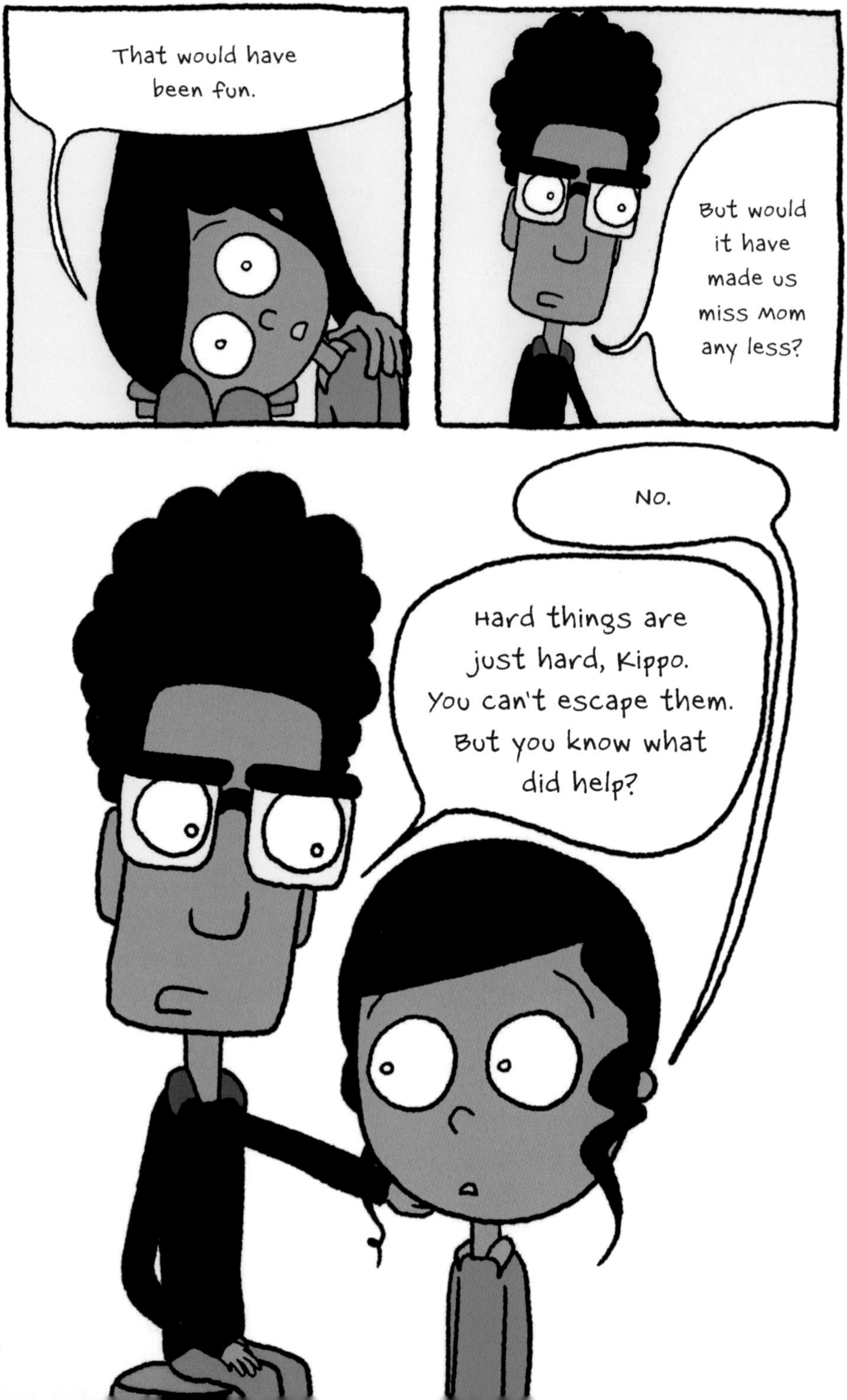
That would have been fun.
But would it have made us miss Mom any less?
No.
Hard things are just hard, Kippo. You can't escape them. But you know what did help?

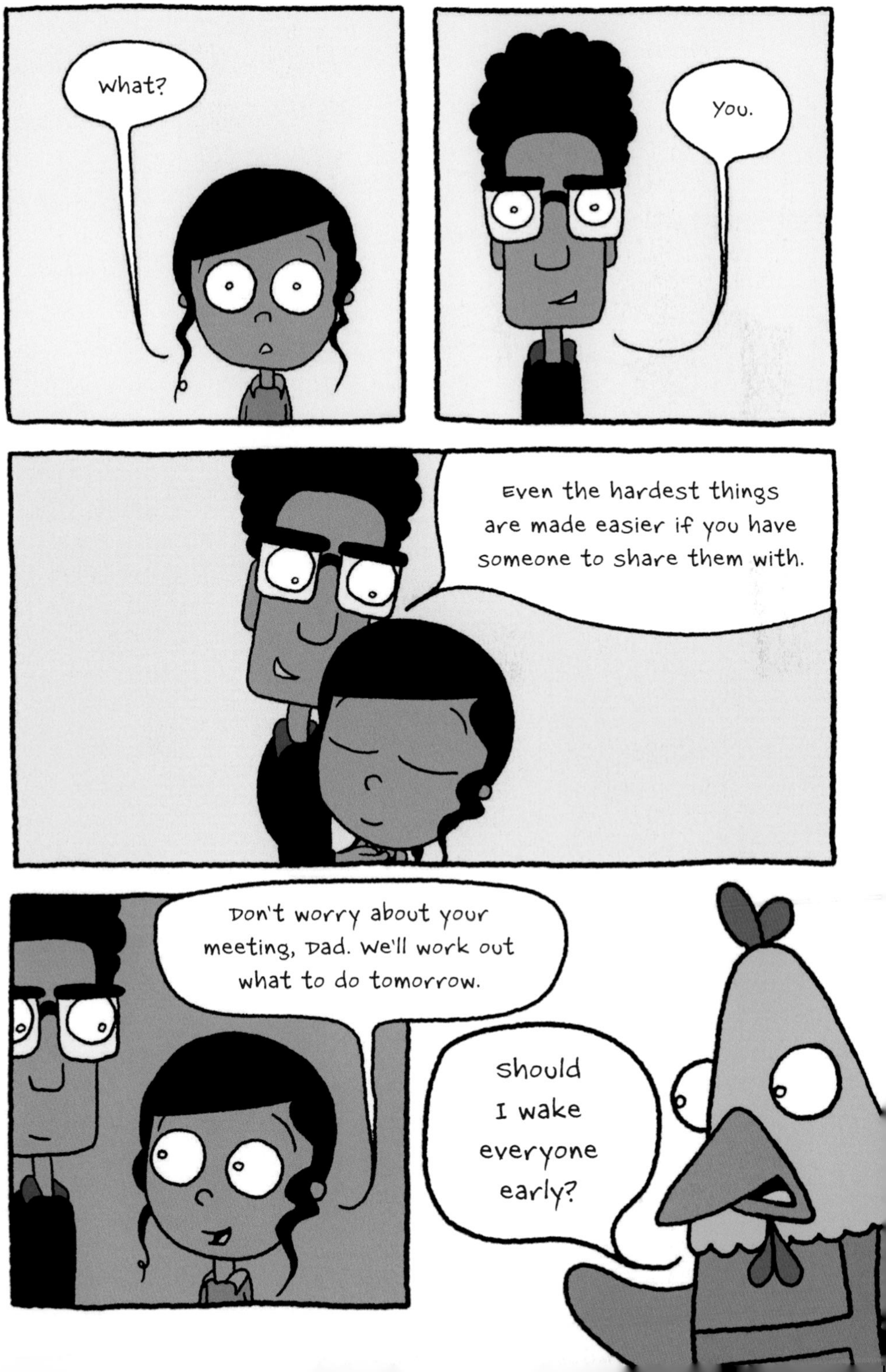
What?
You.
Even the hardest things are made easier if you have someone to share them with.
Don't worry about your meeting, Dad. We'll work out what to do tomorrow.
Should I wake everyone early?

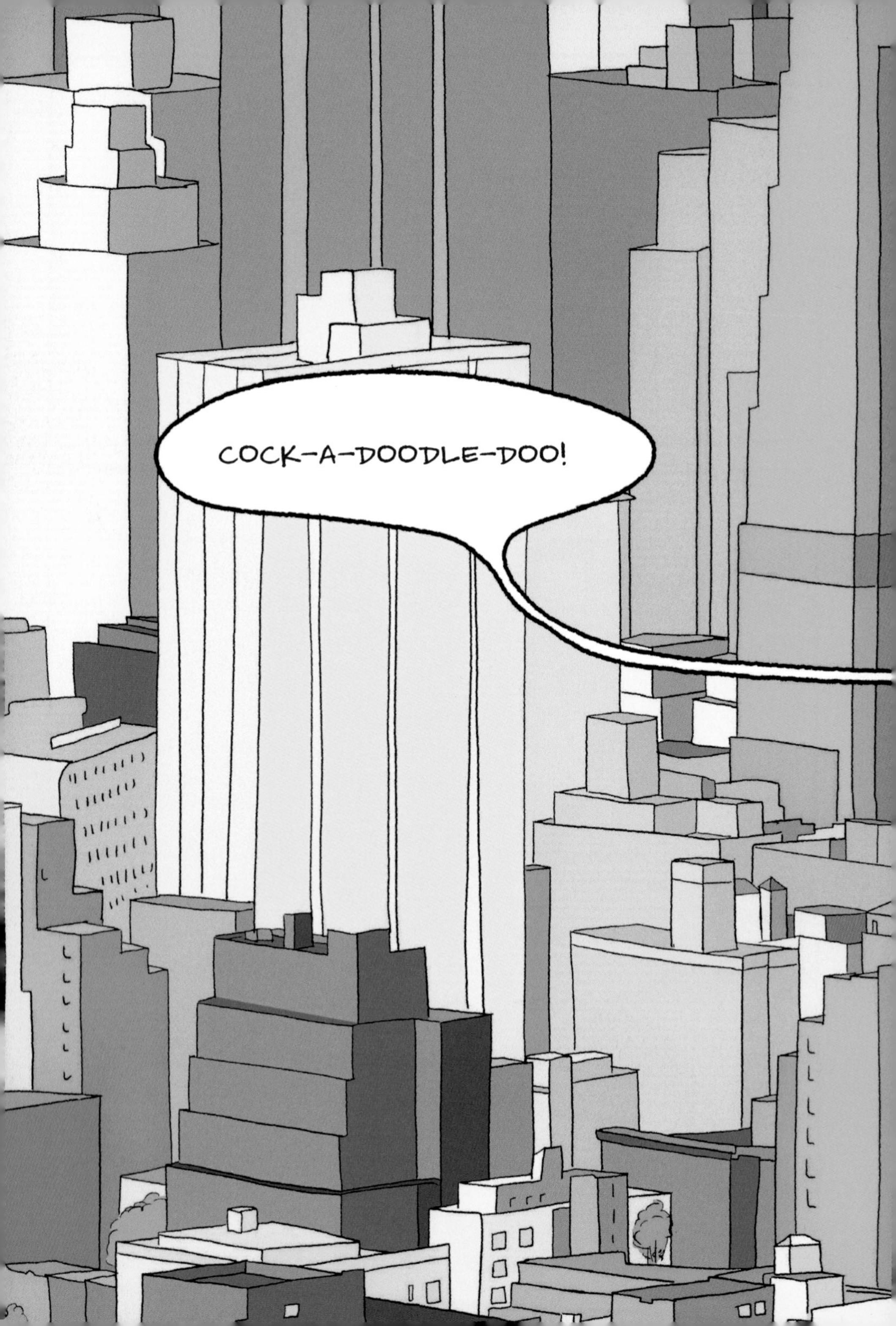
COCK-A-DOODLE-DOO!

CHAPTER NINE
The Odds get a secret base

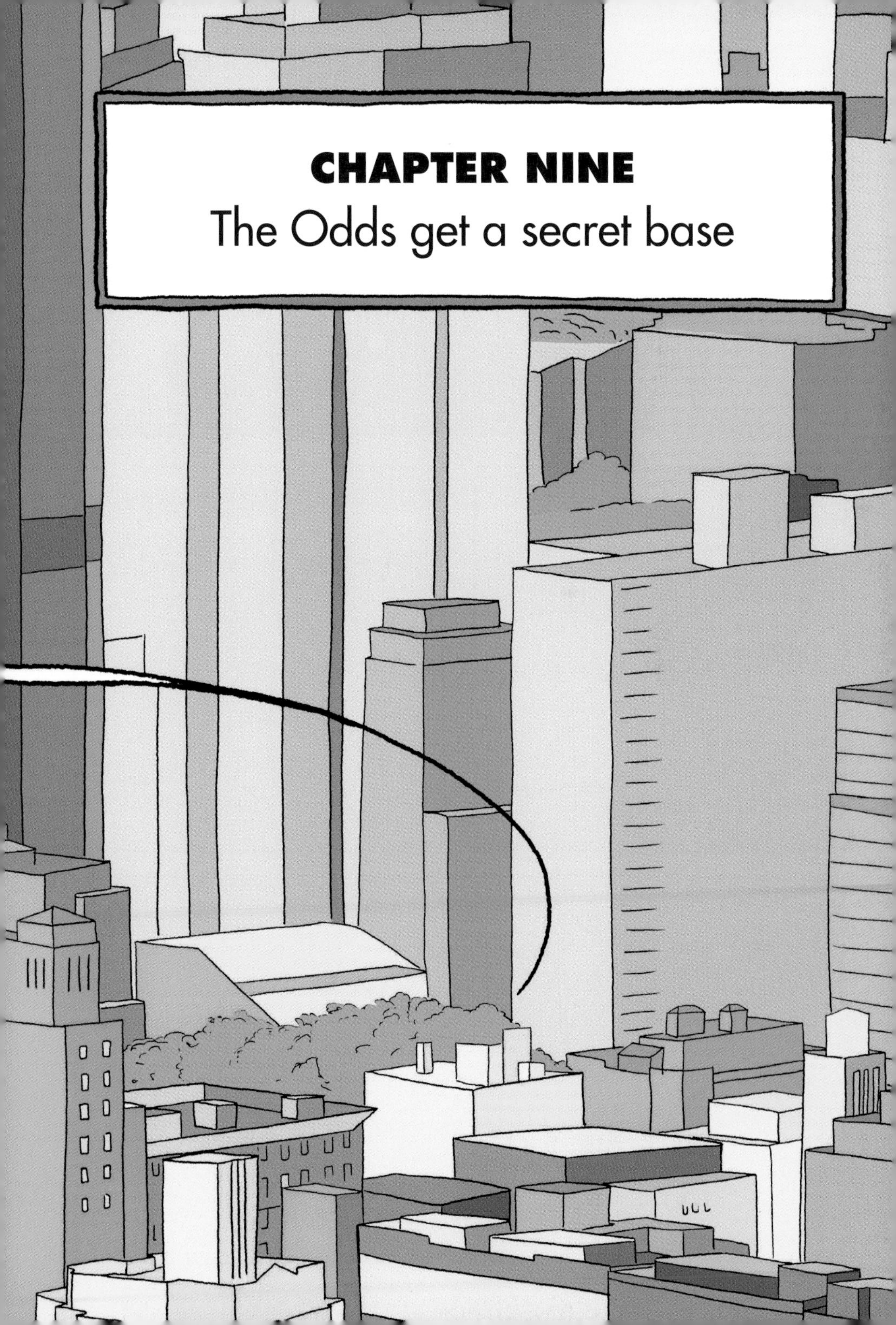

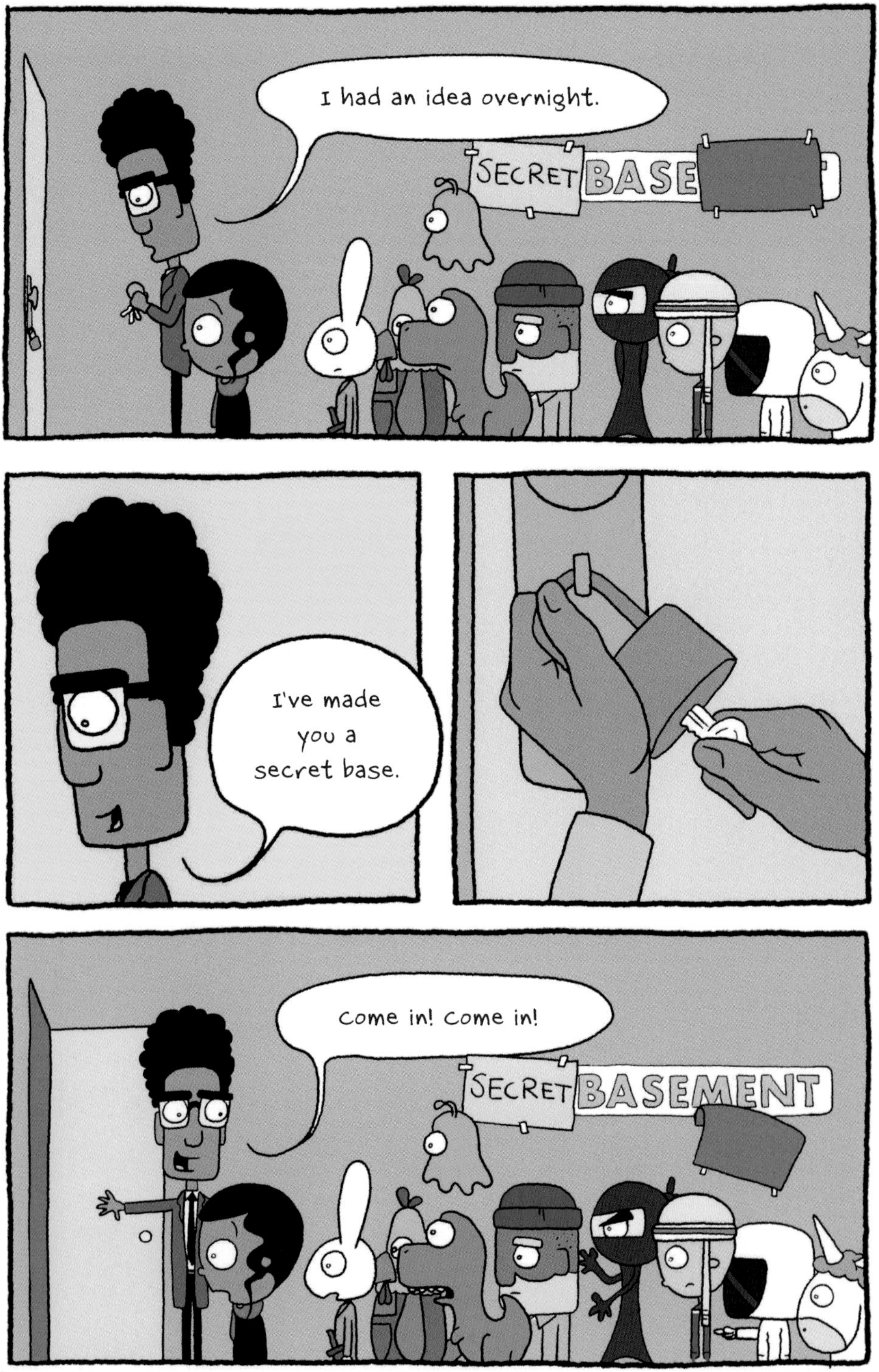
I had an idea overnight.
SECRET BASE
I've made you a secret base.
Come in! Come in!
SECRET BASEMENT

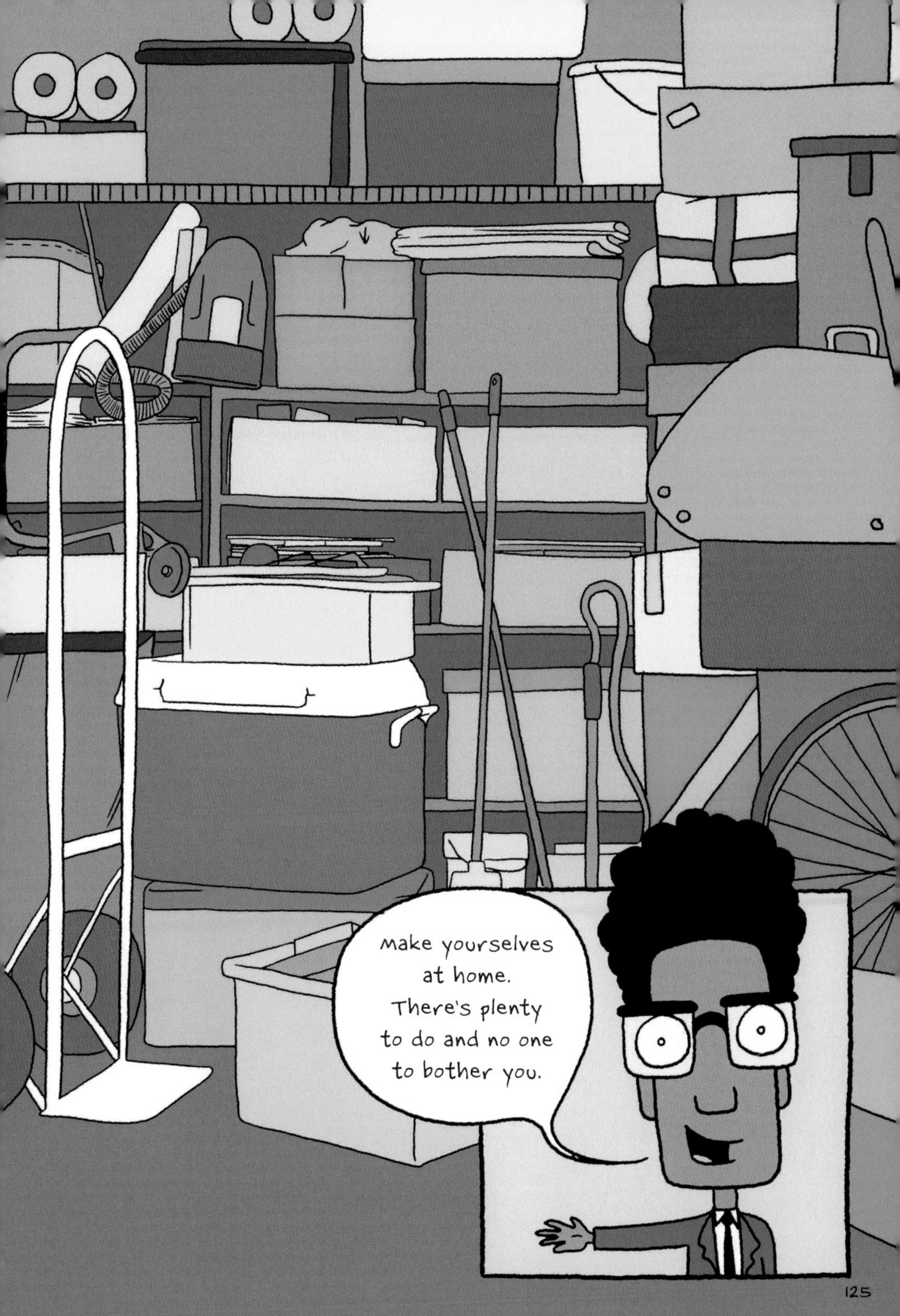
Make yourselves at home. There's plenty to do and no one to bother you.

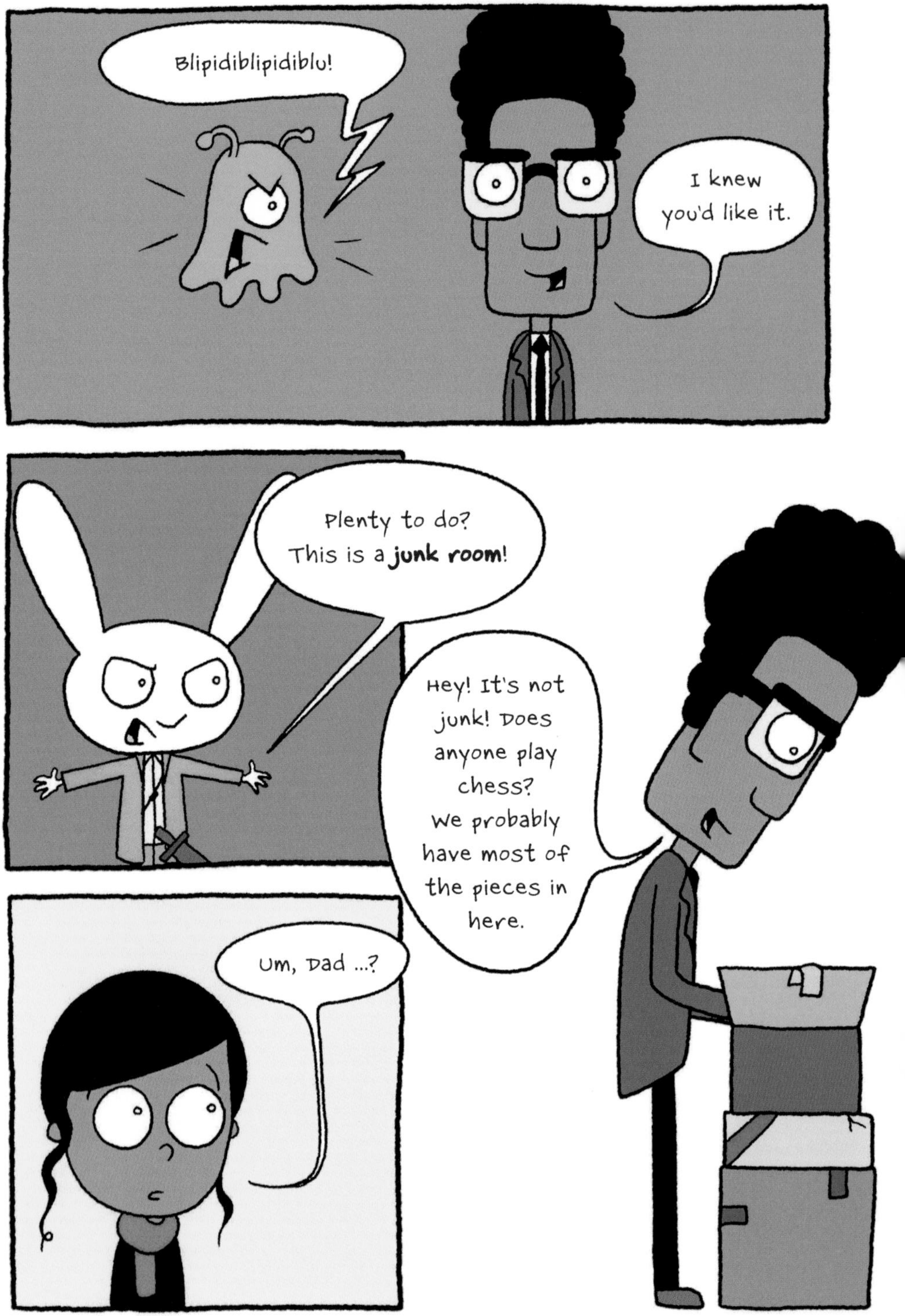

Blipidiblipidiblu!
I knew you'd like it.
Plenty to do? This is a **junk room**!
Hey! It's not junk! Does anyone play chess? We probably have most of the pieces in here.
Um, Dad ...?

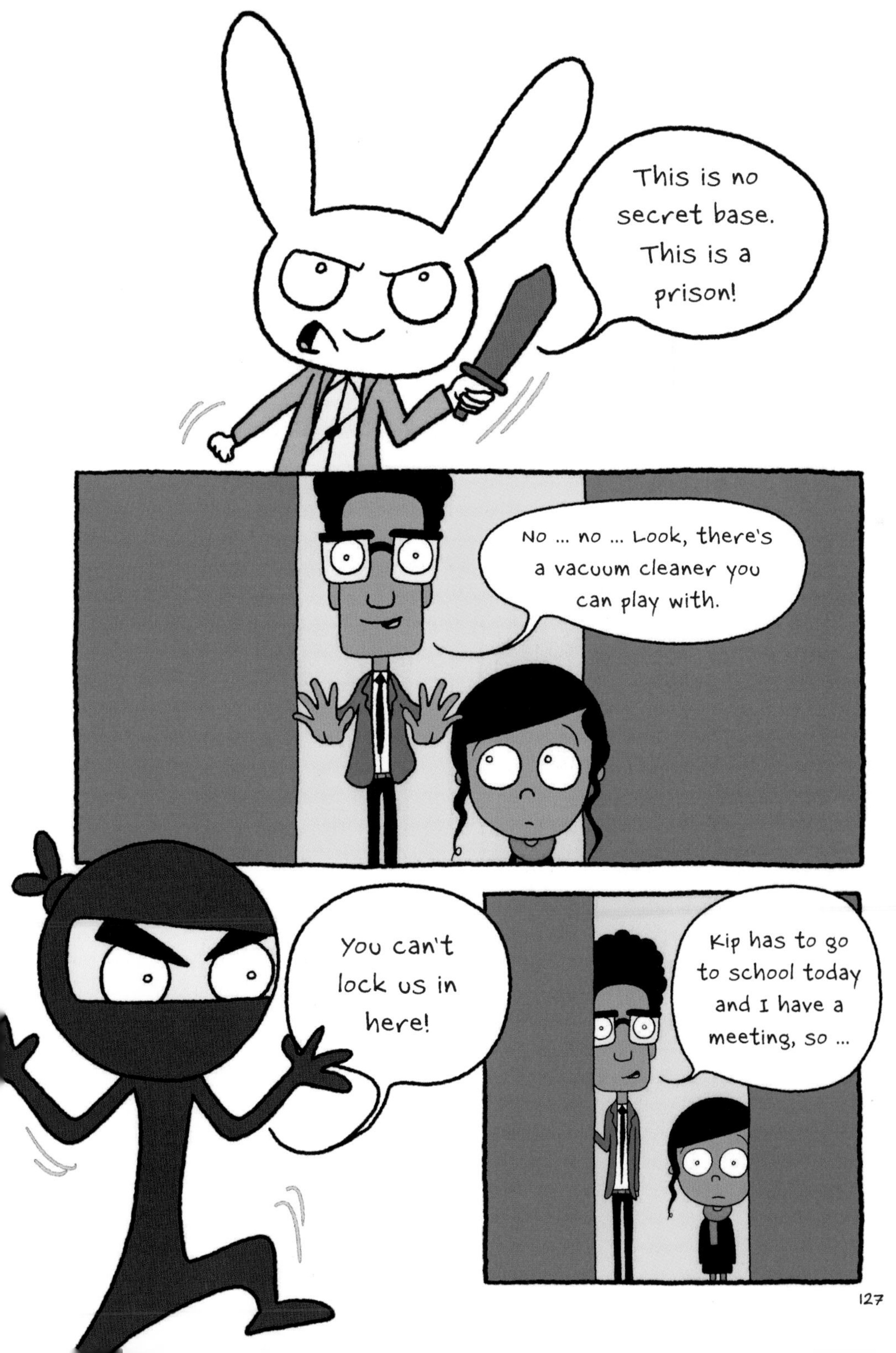
This is no secret base. This is a prison!
No ... no ... Look, there's a vacuum cleaner you can play with.
You can't lock us in here!
Kip has to go to school today and I have a meeting, so ...

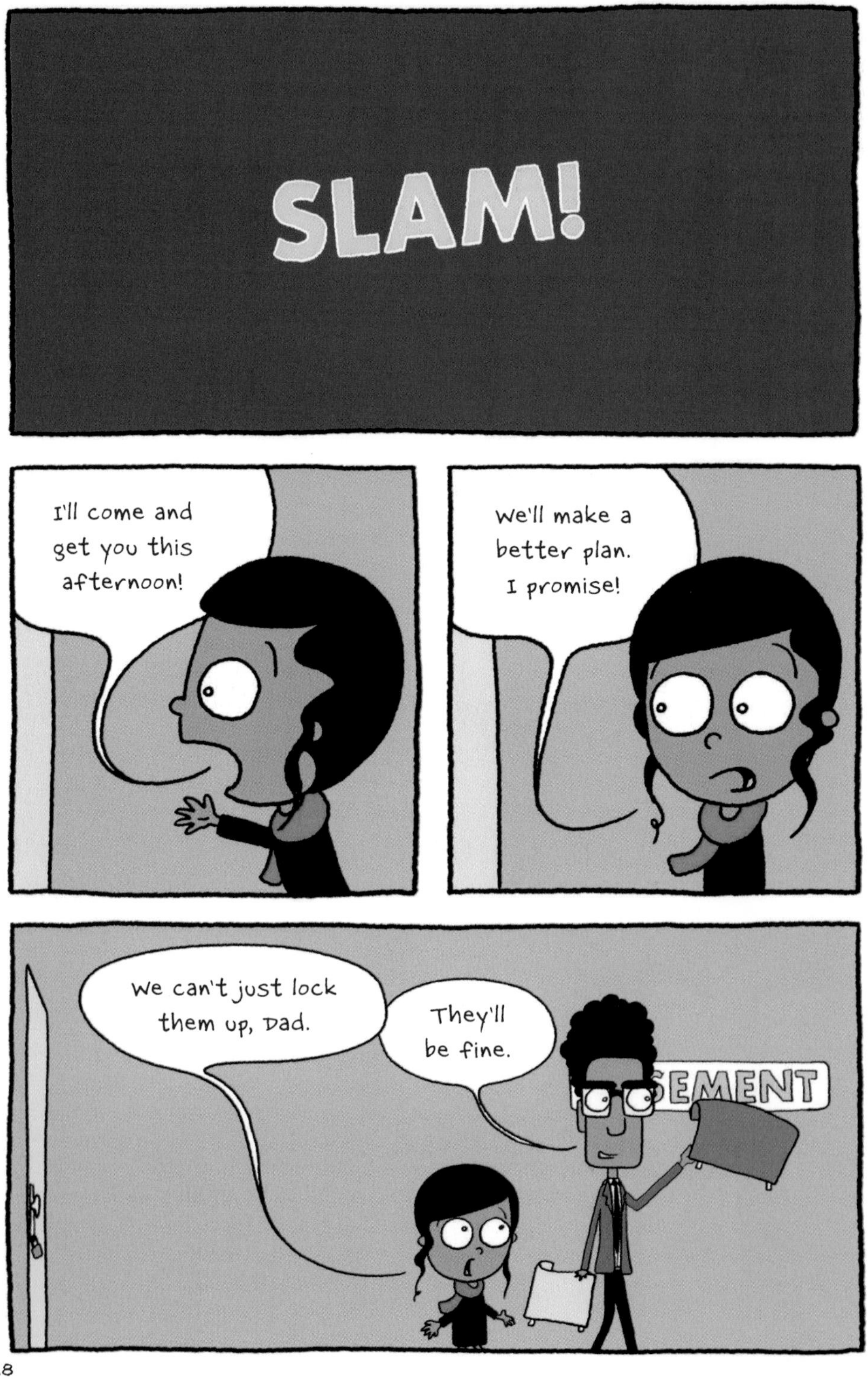
SLAM!
I'll come and get you this afternoon!
We'll make a better plan. I promise!
We can't just lock them up, Dad.
They'll be fine.
SEMENT

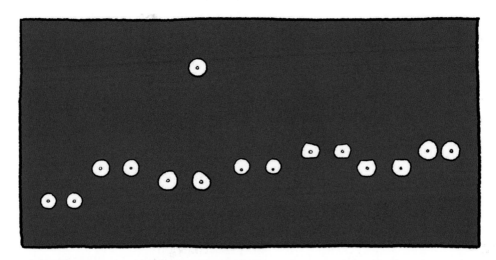

Booster! You're sucking my tail with the vacuum cleaner, you crazy rooster!

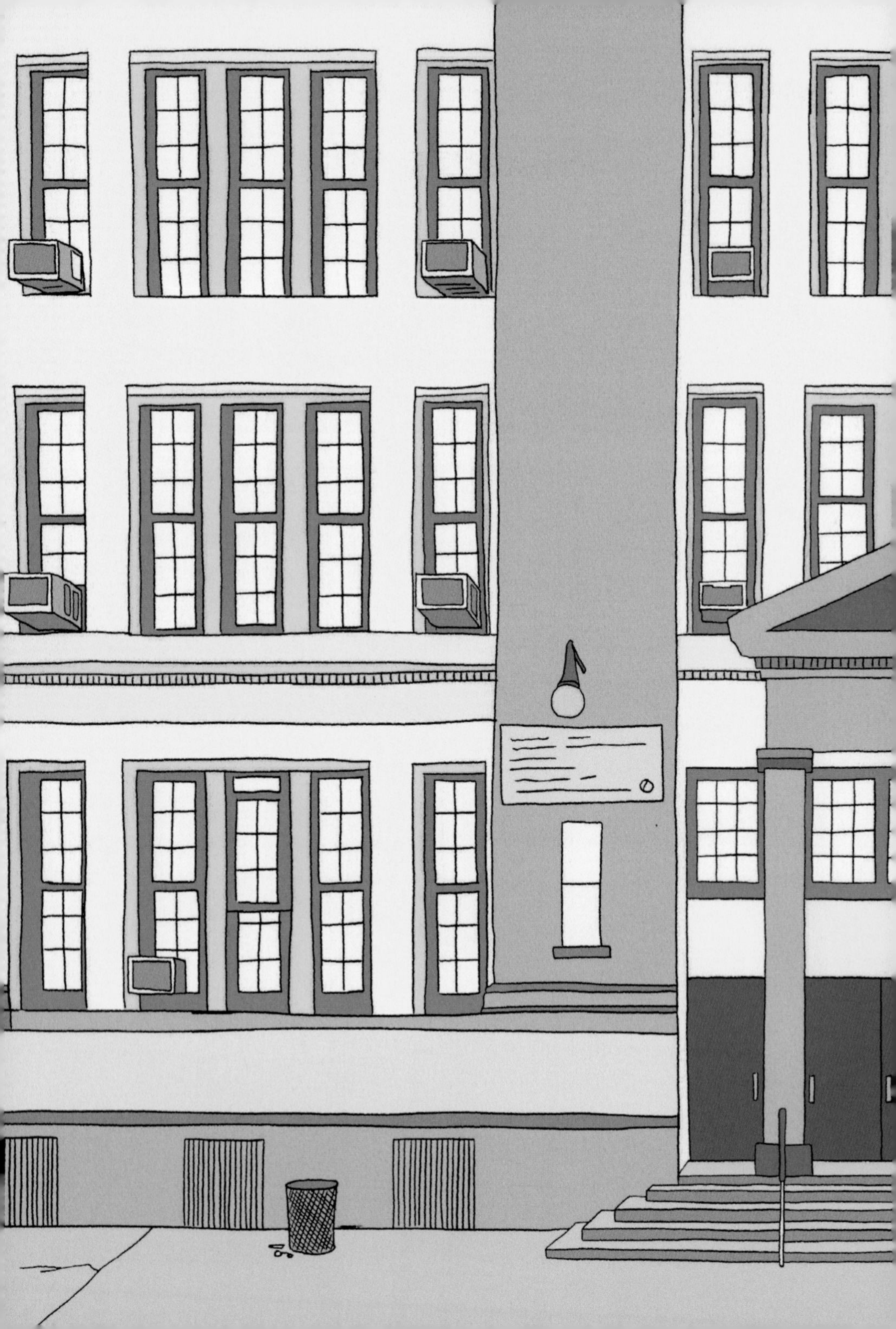

CHAPTER TEN
An odd imagination

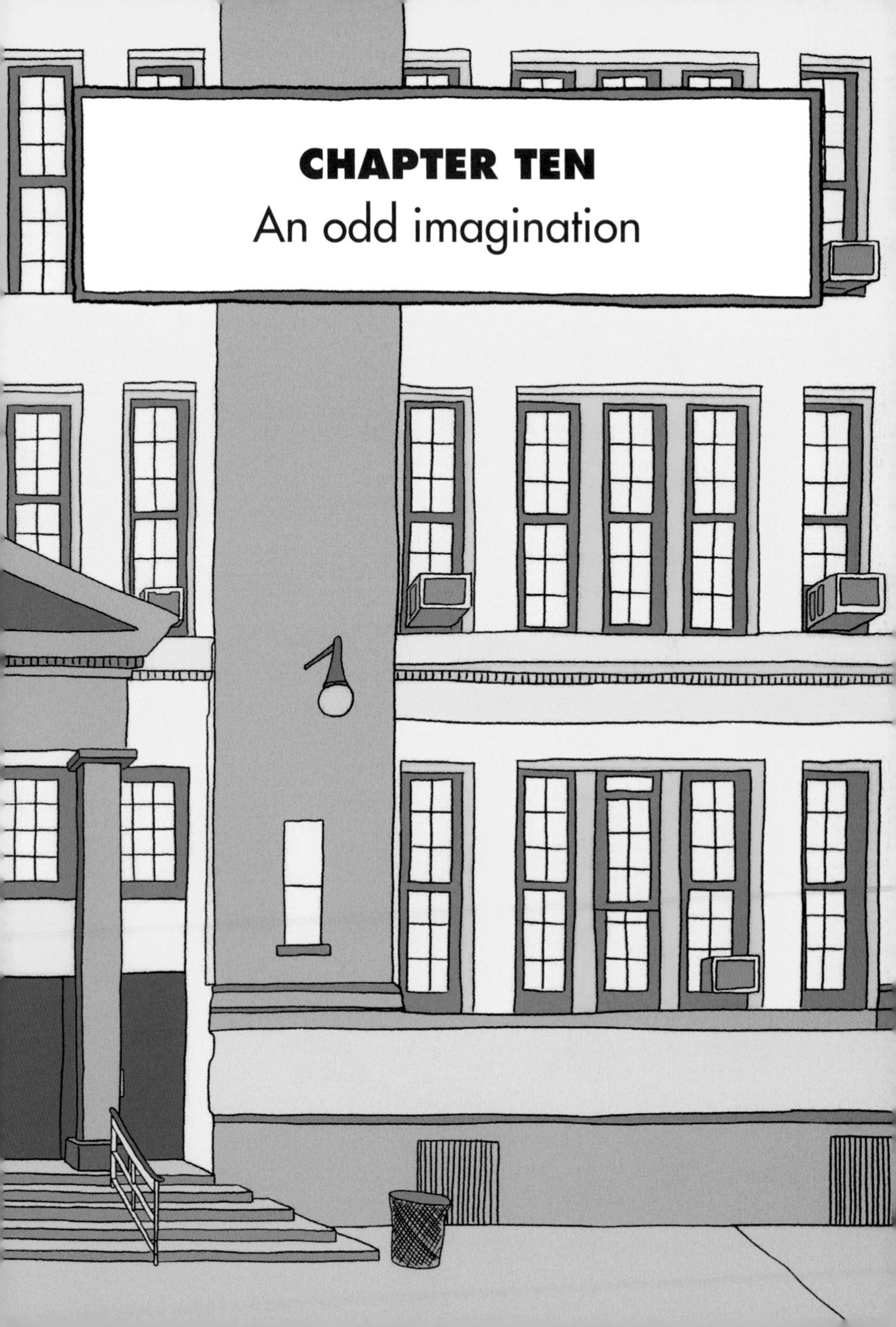

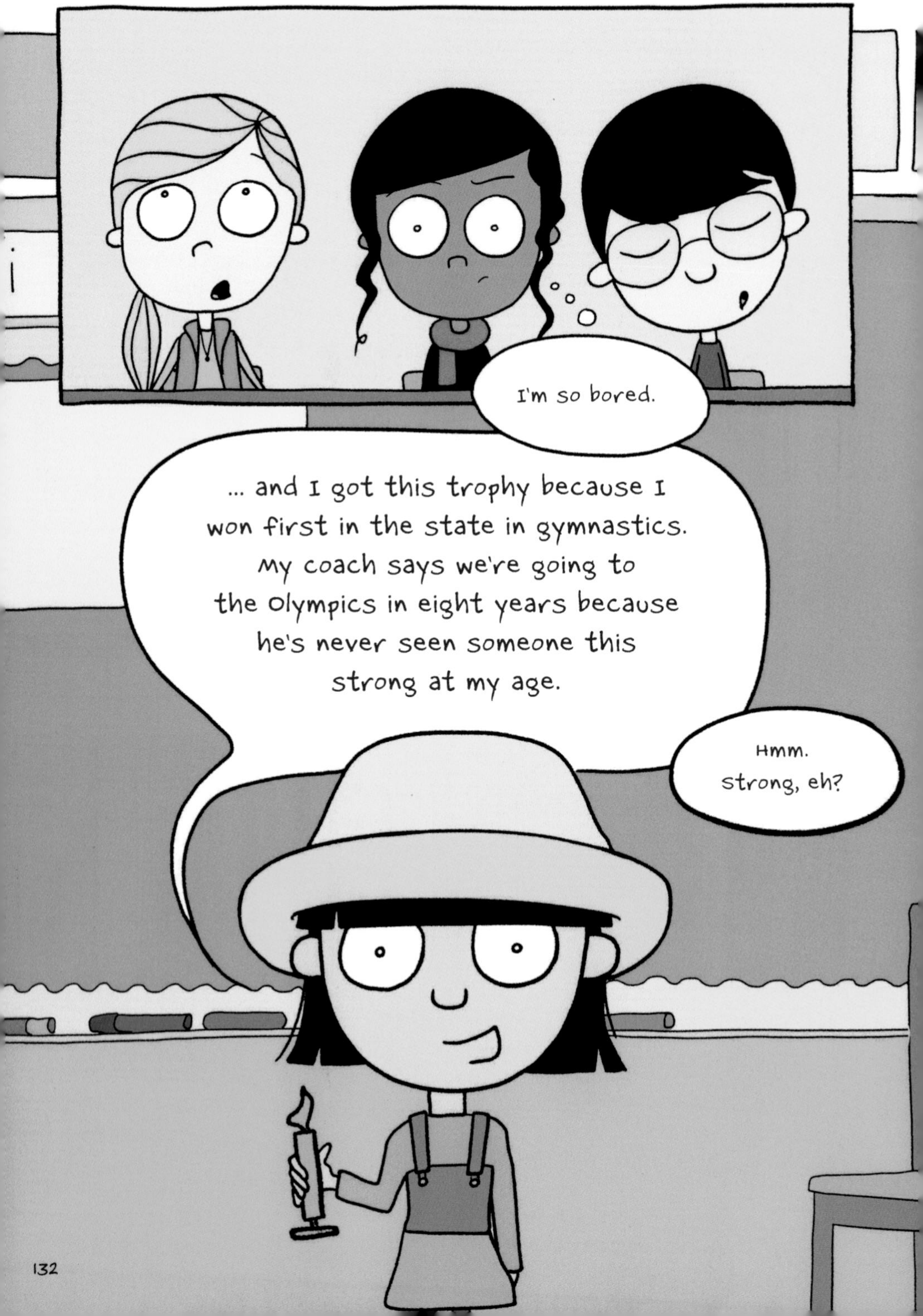
I'm so bored.
... and I got this trophy because I won first in the state in gymnastics. My coach says we're going to the Olympics in eight years because he's never seen someone this strong at my age.
Hmm. Strong, eh?

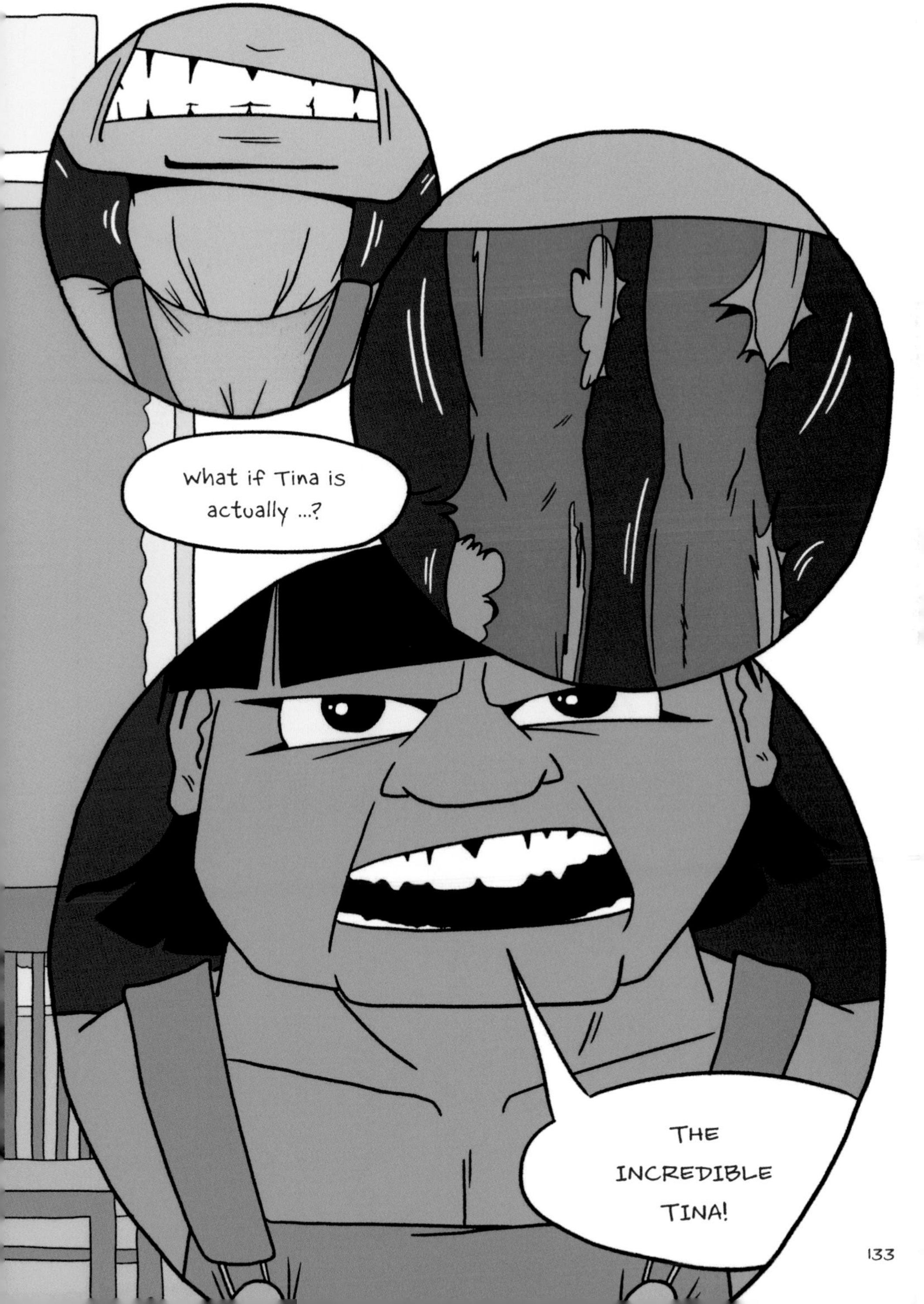
What if Tina is actually ...?
THE INCREDIBLE TINA!

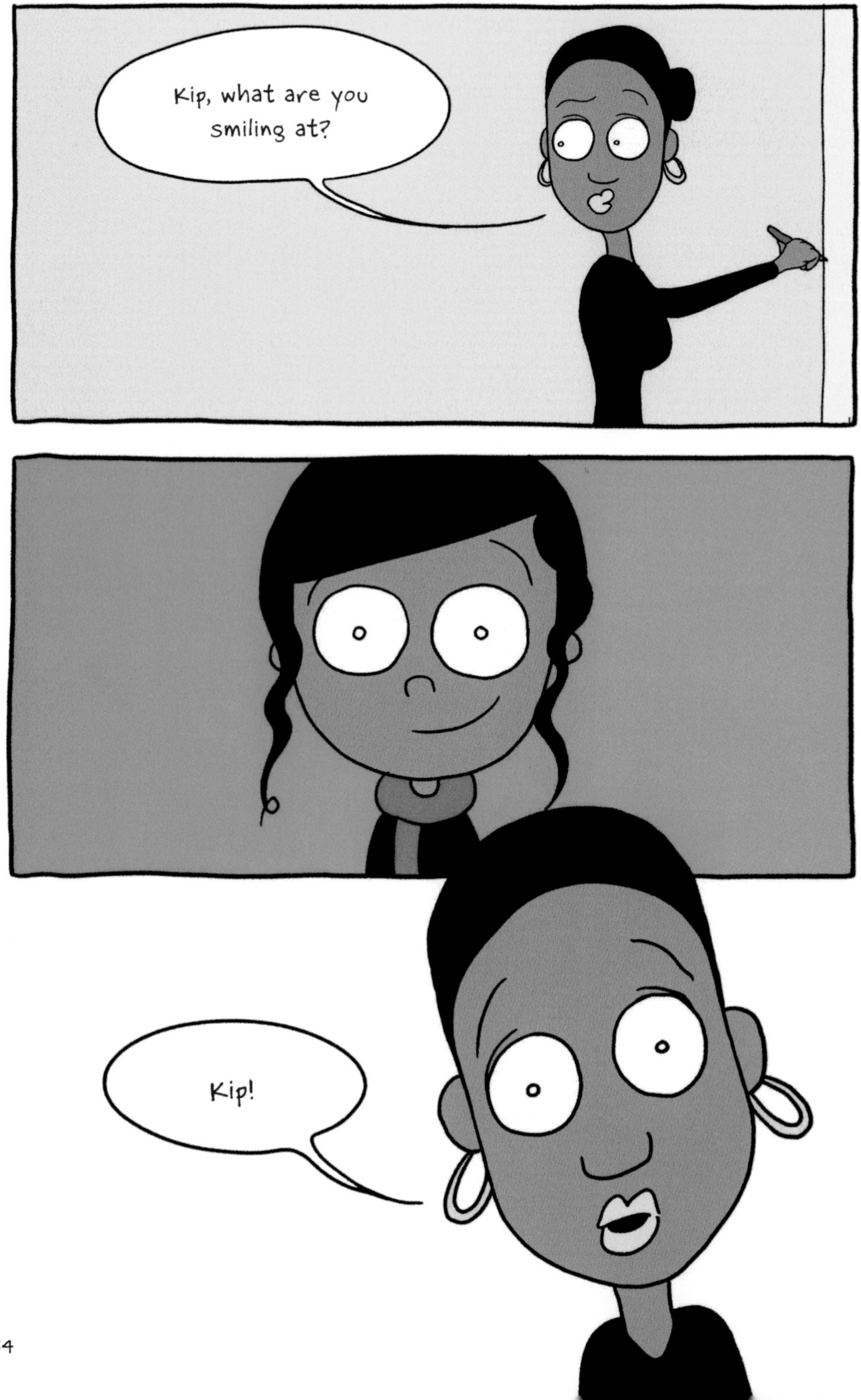
Kip, what are you smiling at?
Kip!

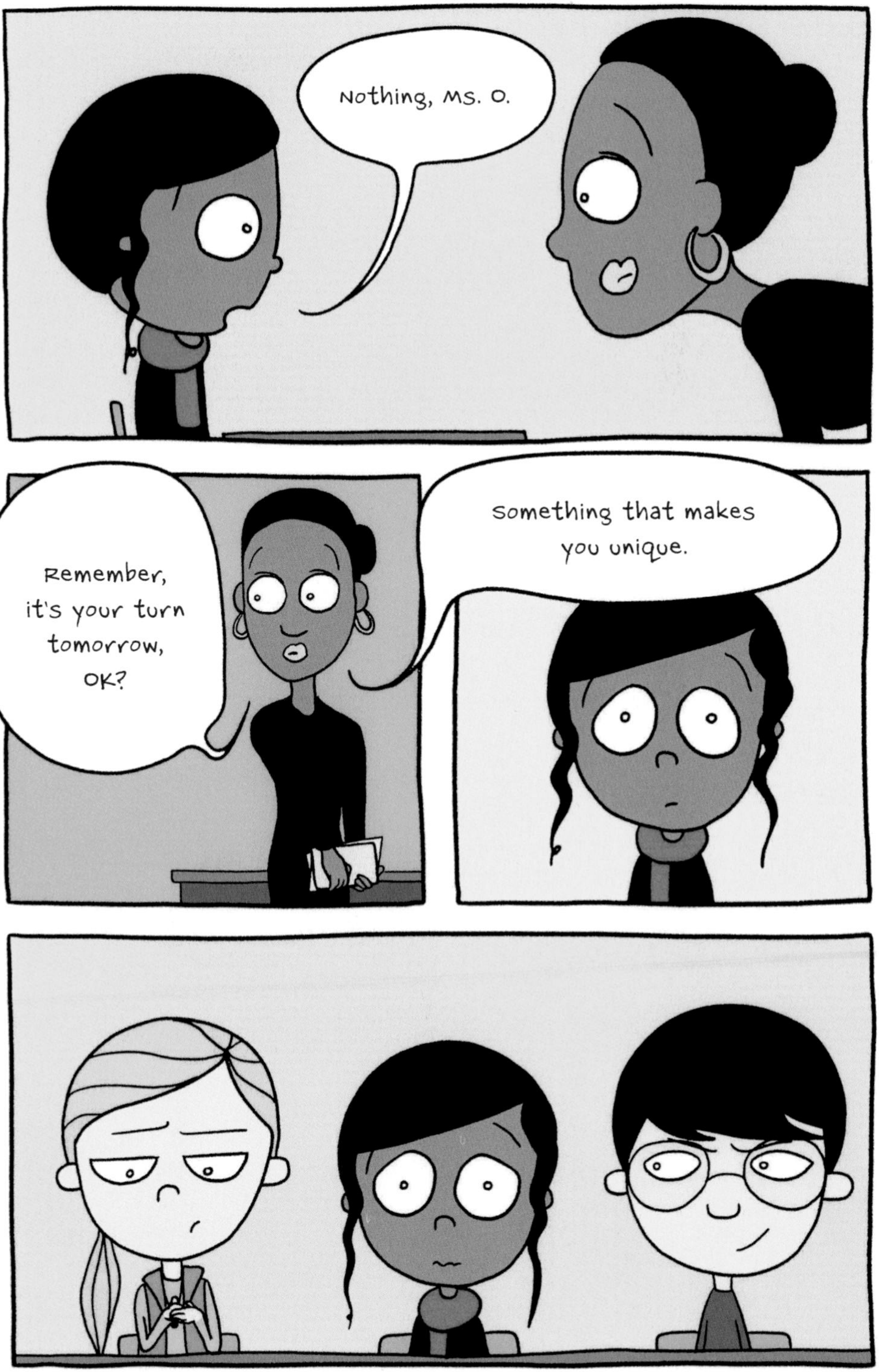
Nothing, Ms. O.
Remember, it's your turn tomorrow, OK?
Something that makes you unique.

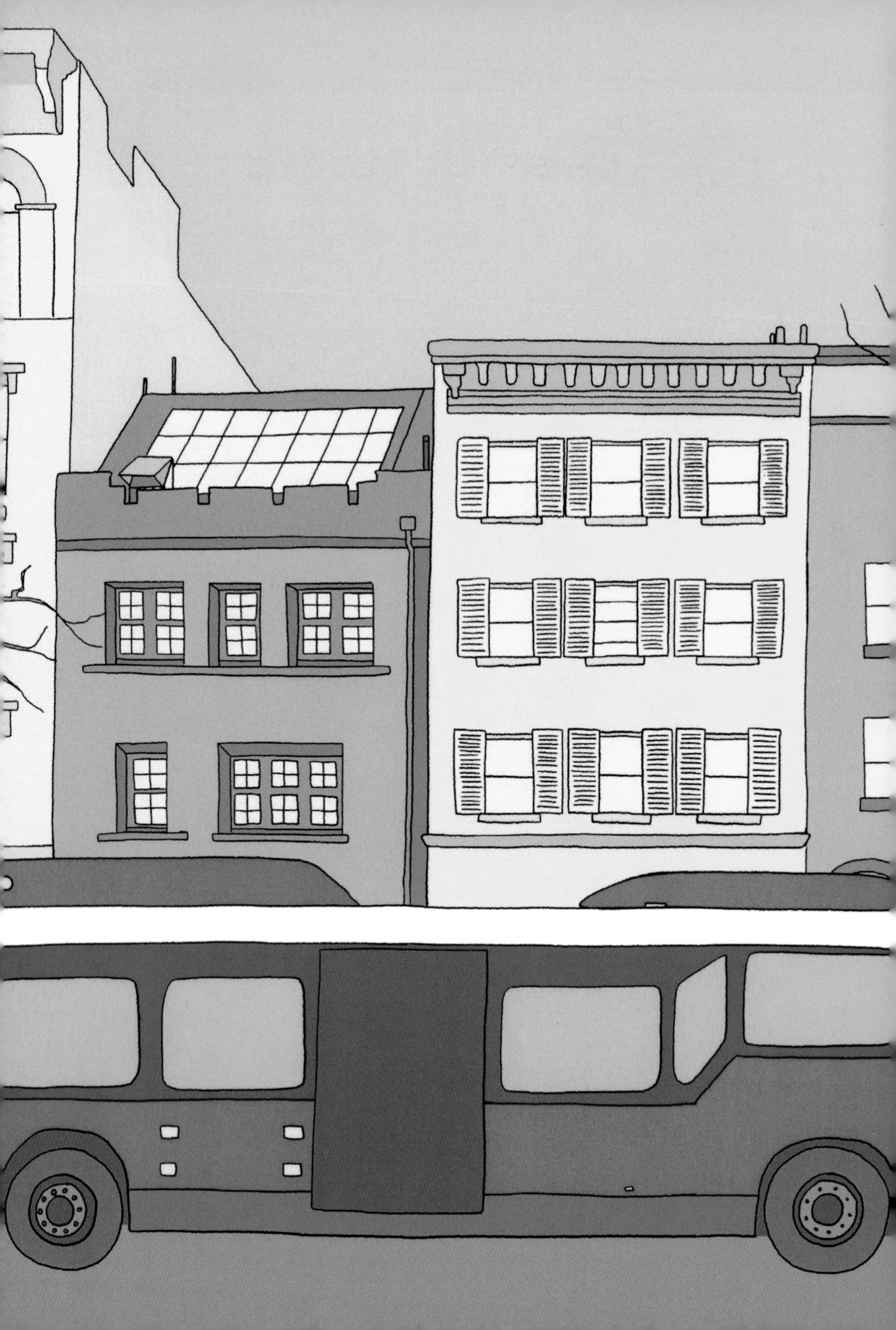

CHAPTER ELEVEN

The Odds escape

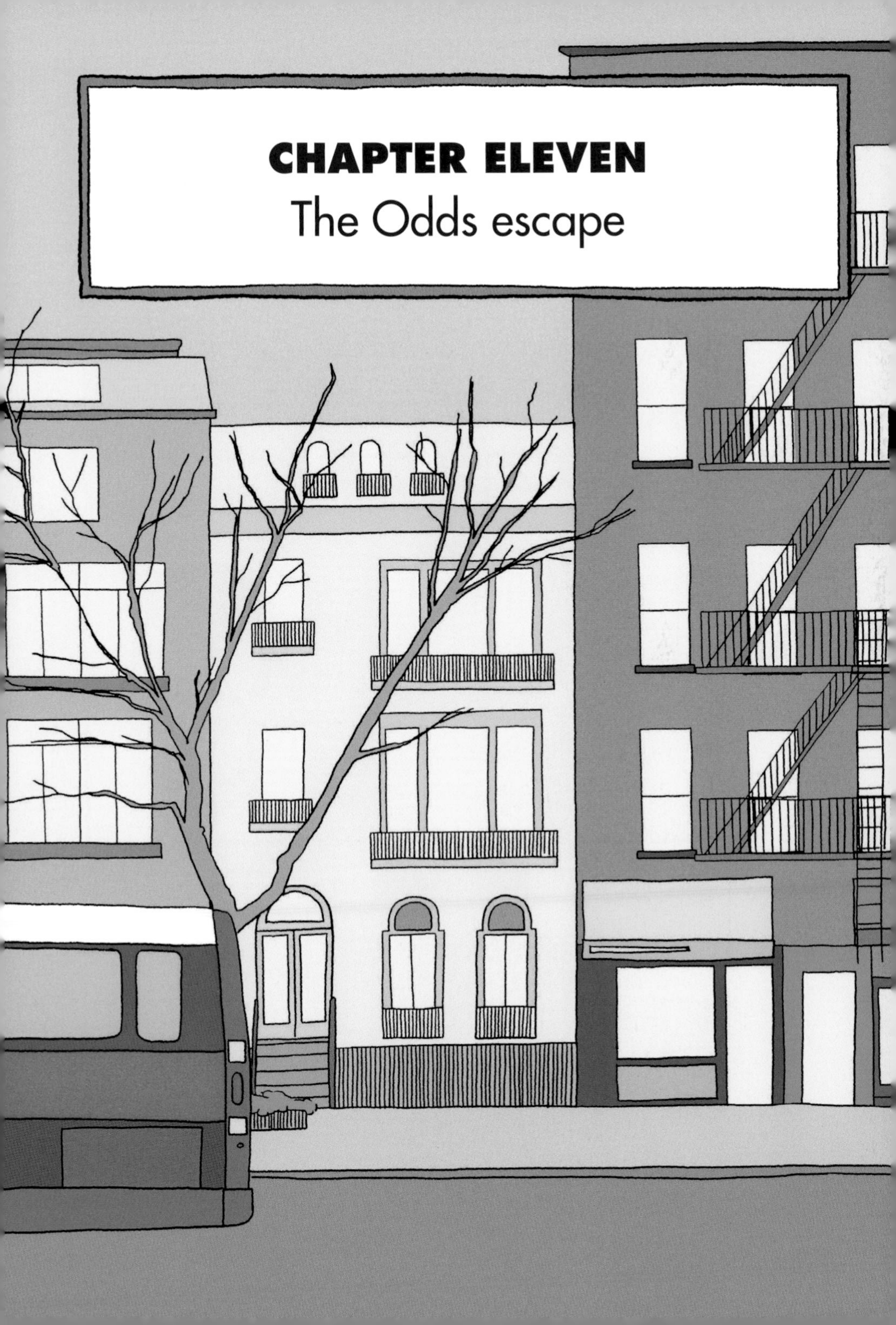

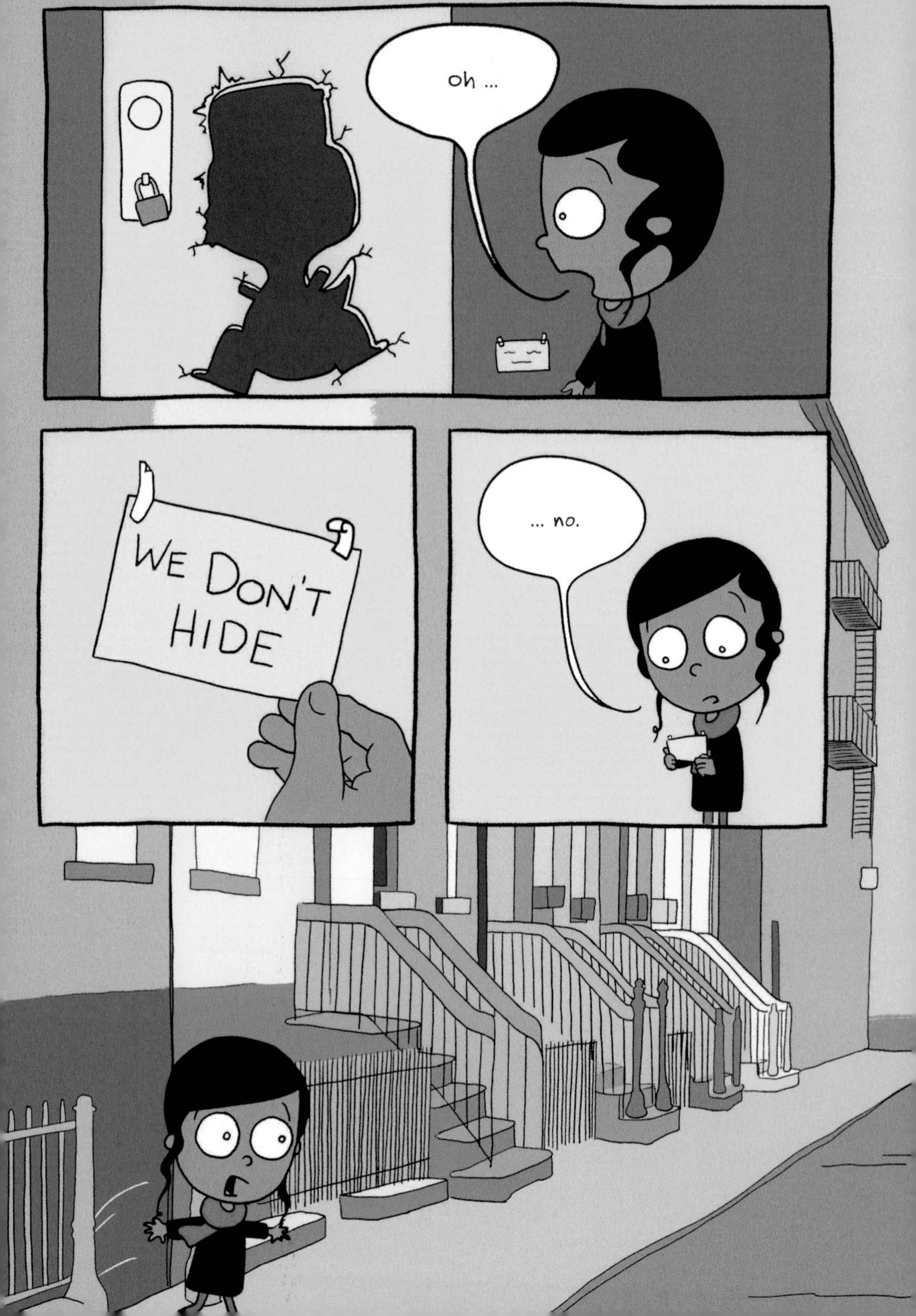
oh ...
WE DON'T HIDE
... no.

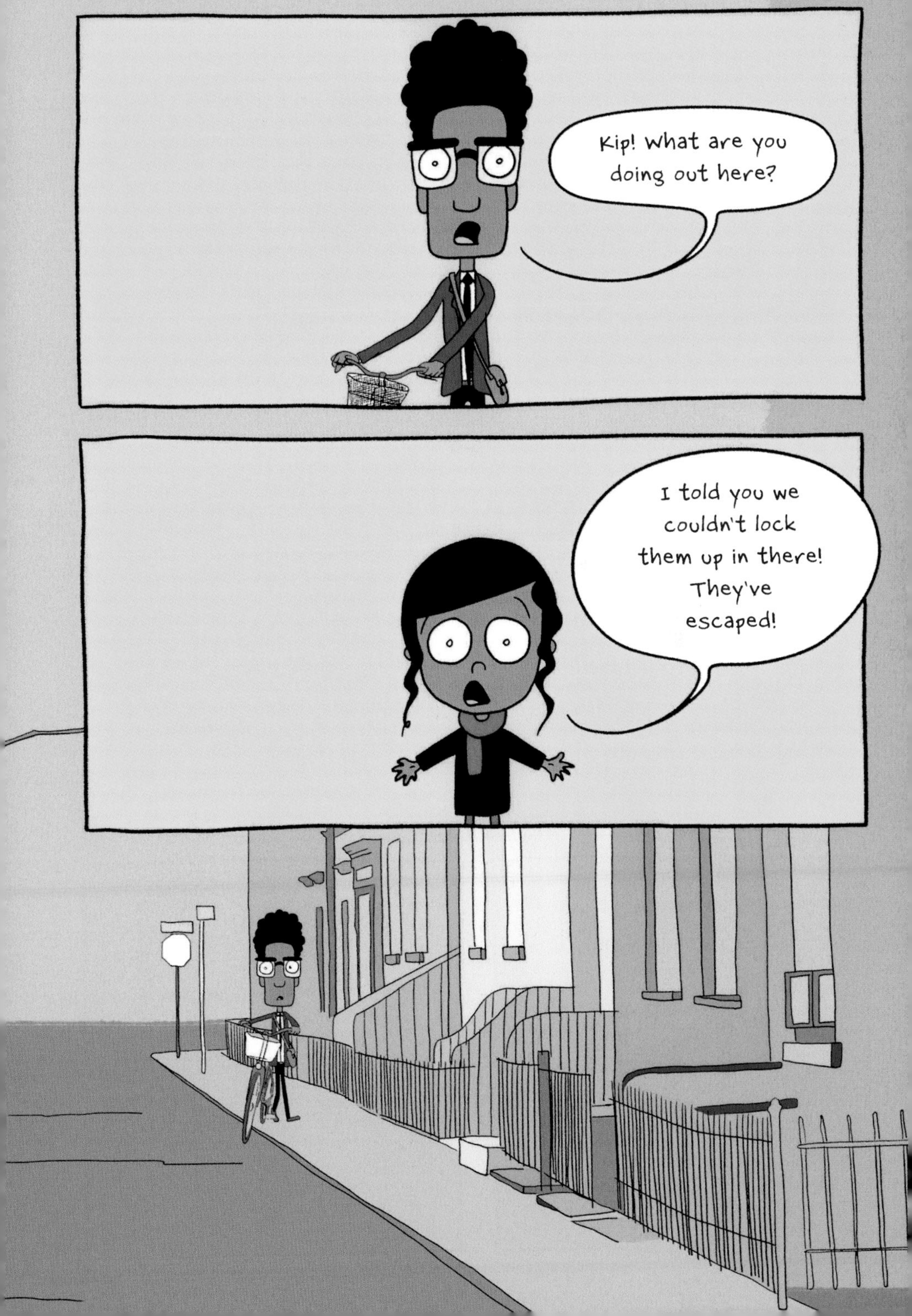
Kip! What are you doing out here?
I told you we couldn't lock them up in there! They've escaped!

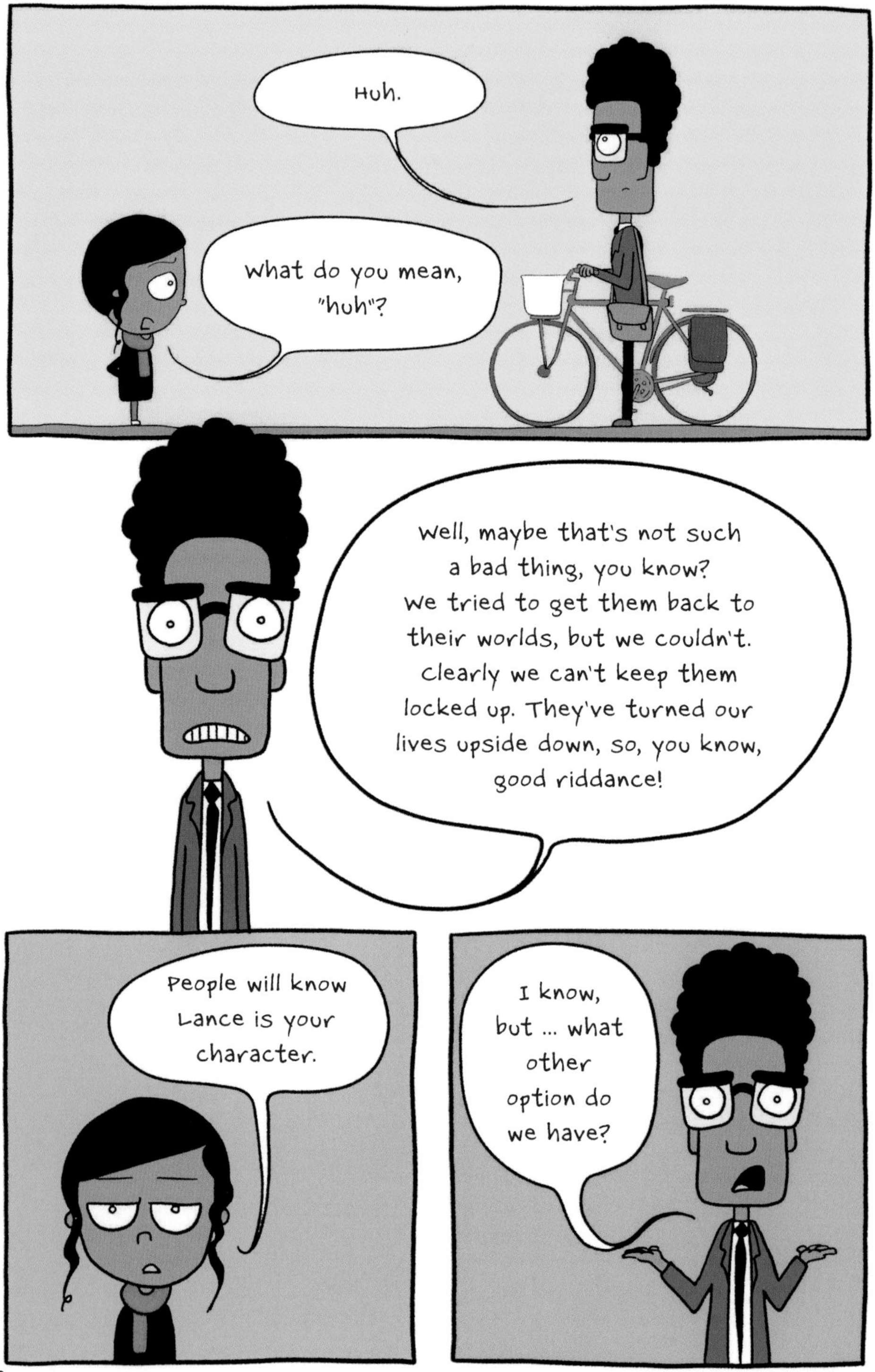
Huh.
What do you mean, "huh"?
Well, maybe that's not such a bad thing, you know? We tried to get them back to their worlds, but we couldn't. Clearly we can't keep them locked up. They've turned our lives upside down, so, you know, good riddance!
People will know Lance is your character.
I know, but ... what other option do we have?

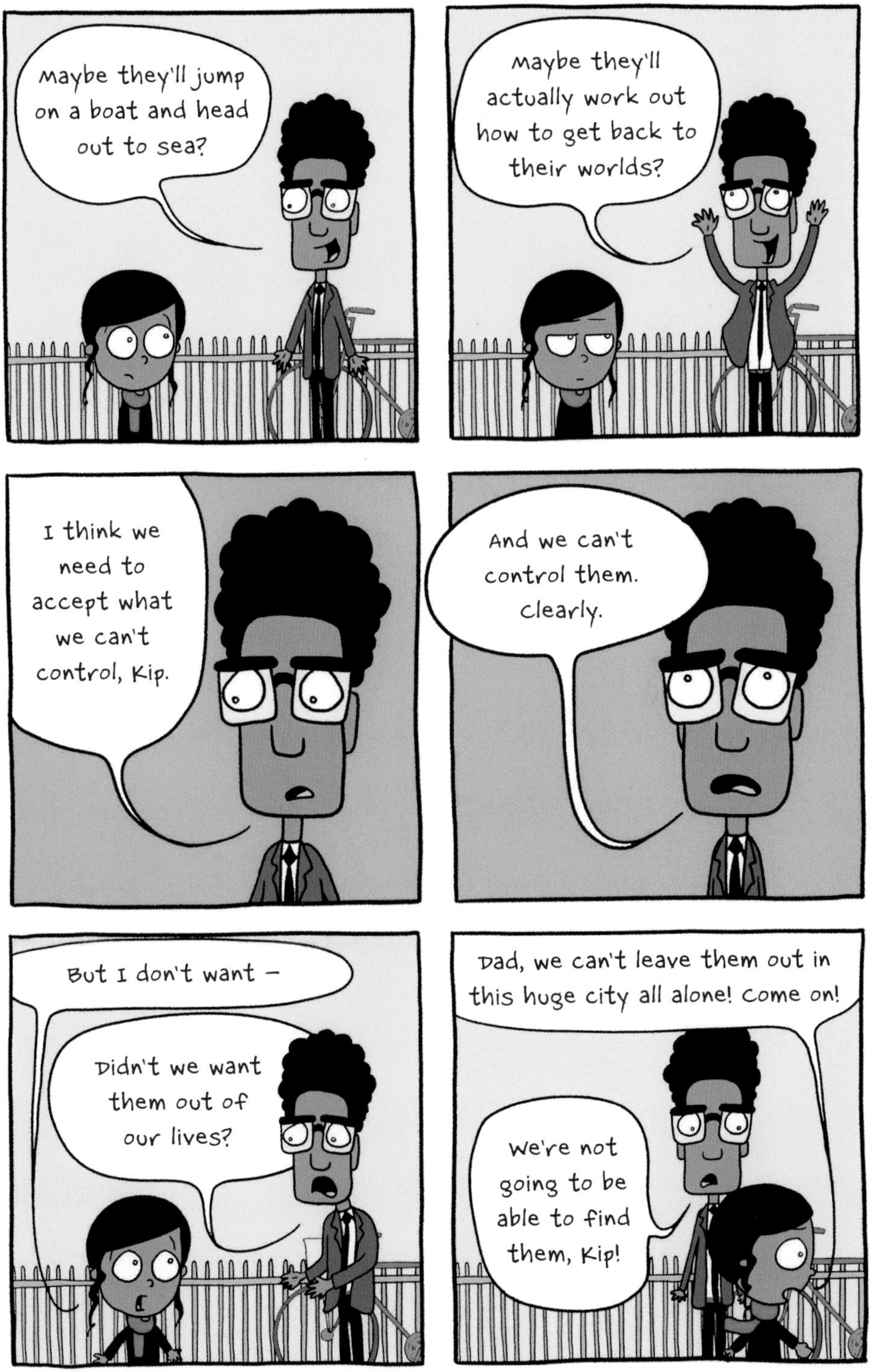
Maybe they'll jump on a boat and head out to sea?
Maybe they'll actually work out how to get back to their worlds?
I think we need to accept what we can't control, Kip.
And we can't control them. Clearly.
But I don't want –
Didn't we want them out of our lives?
Dad, we can't leave them out in this huge city all alone! Come on!
We're not going to be able to find them, Kip!

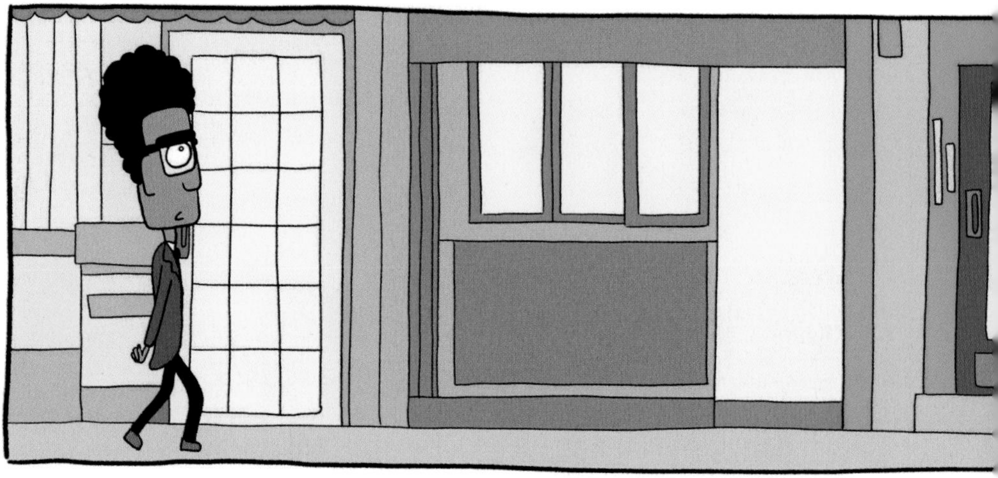

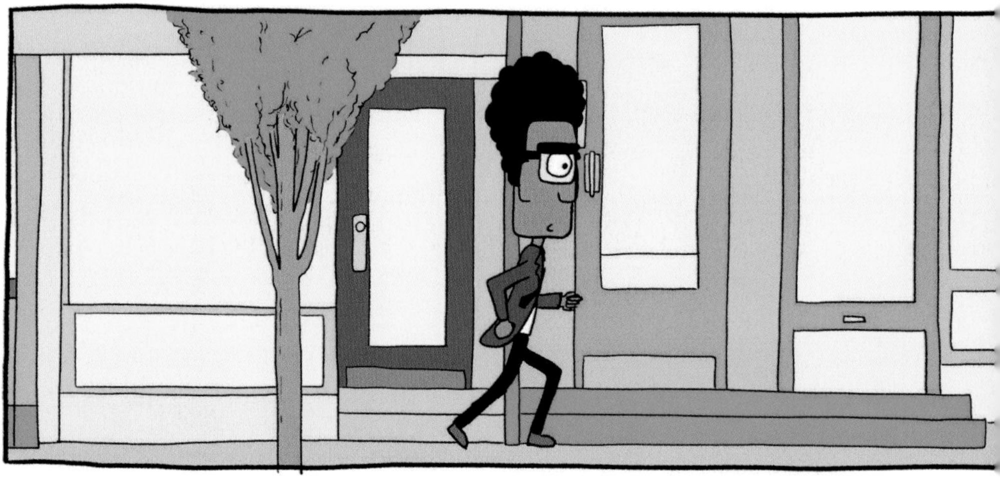

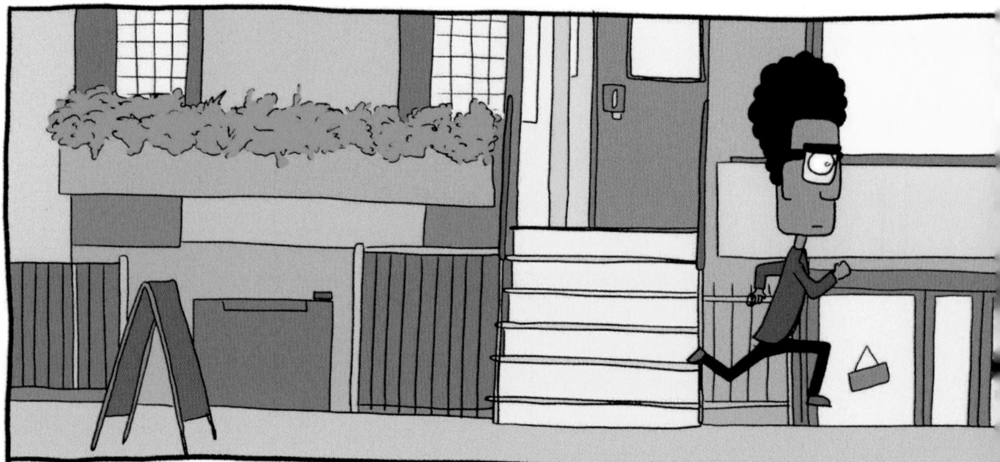

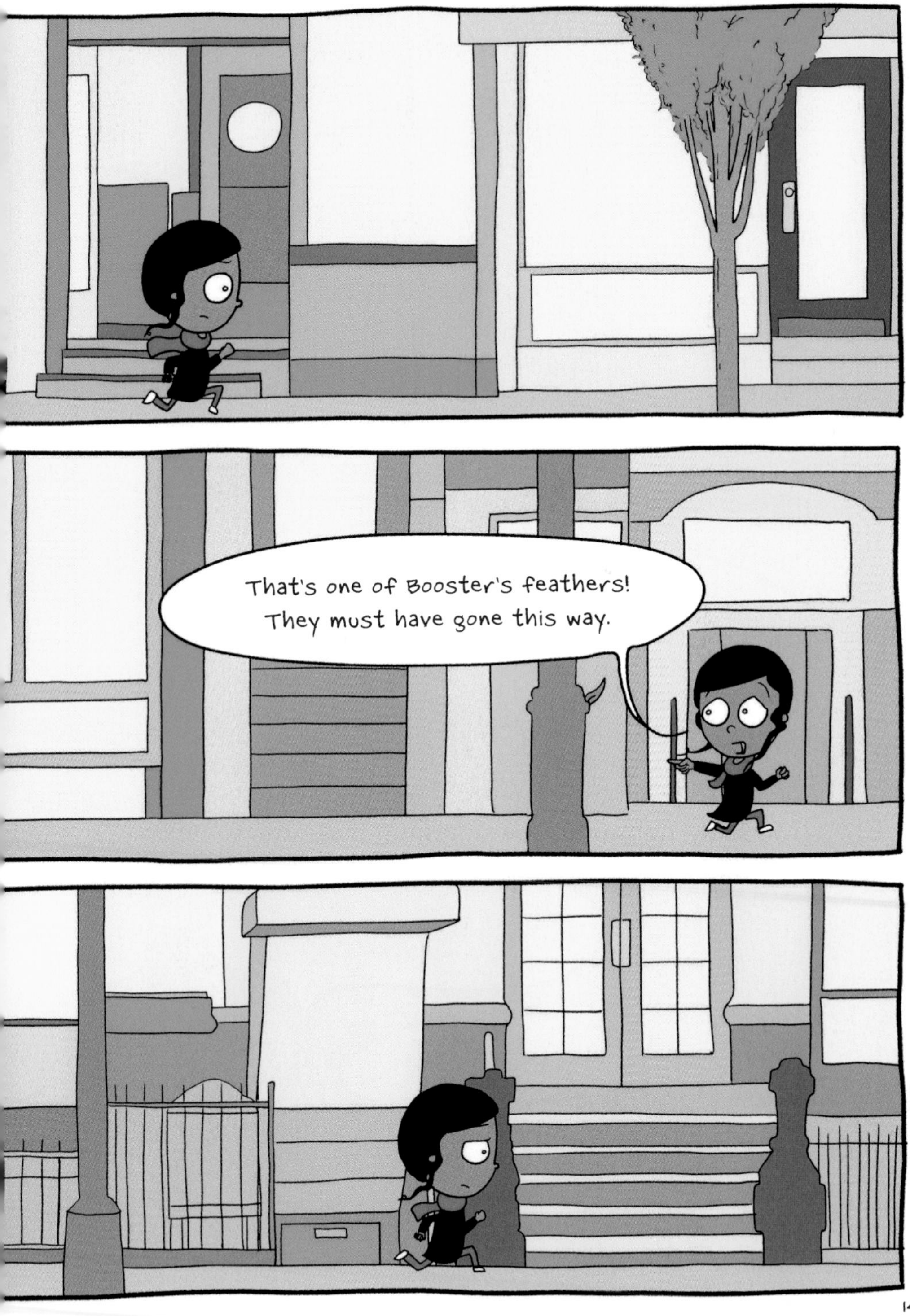
That's one of Booster's feathers! They must have gone this way.

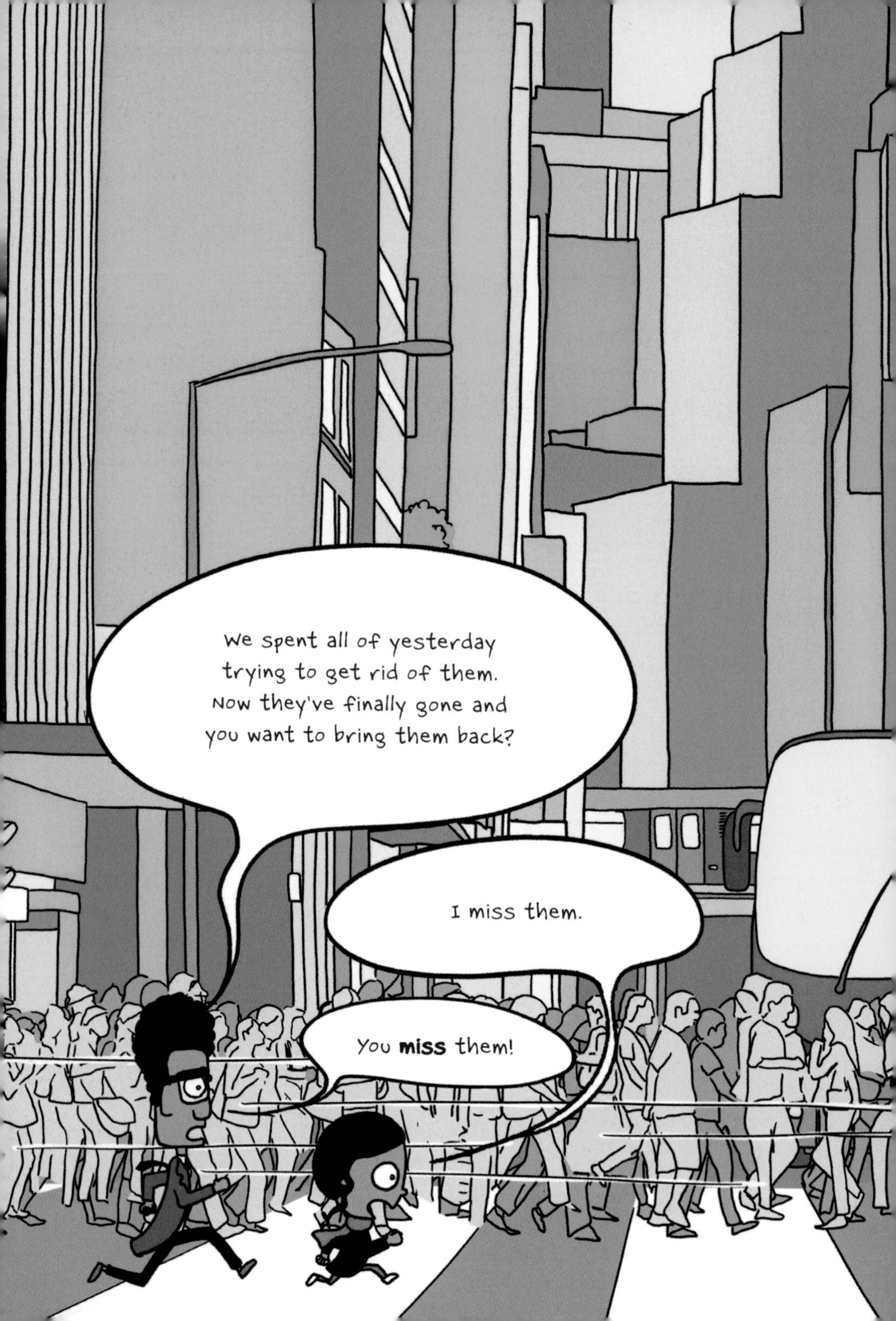
We spent all of yesterday trying to get rid of them. Now they've finally gone and you want to bring them back?
I miss them.
You **miss** them!

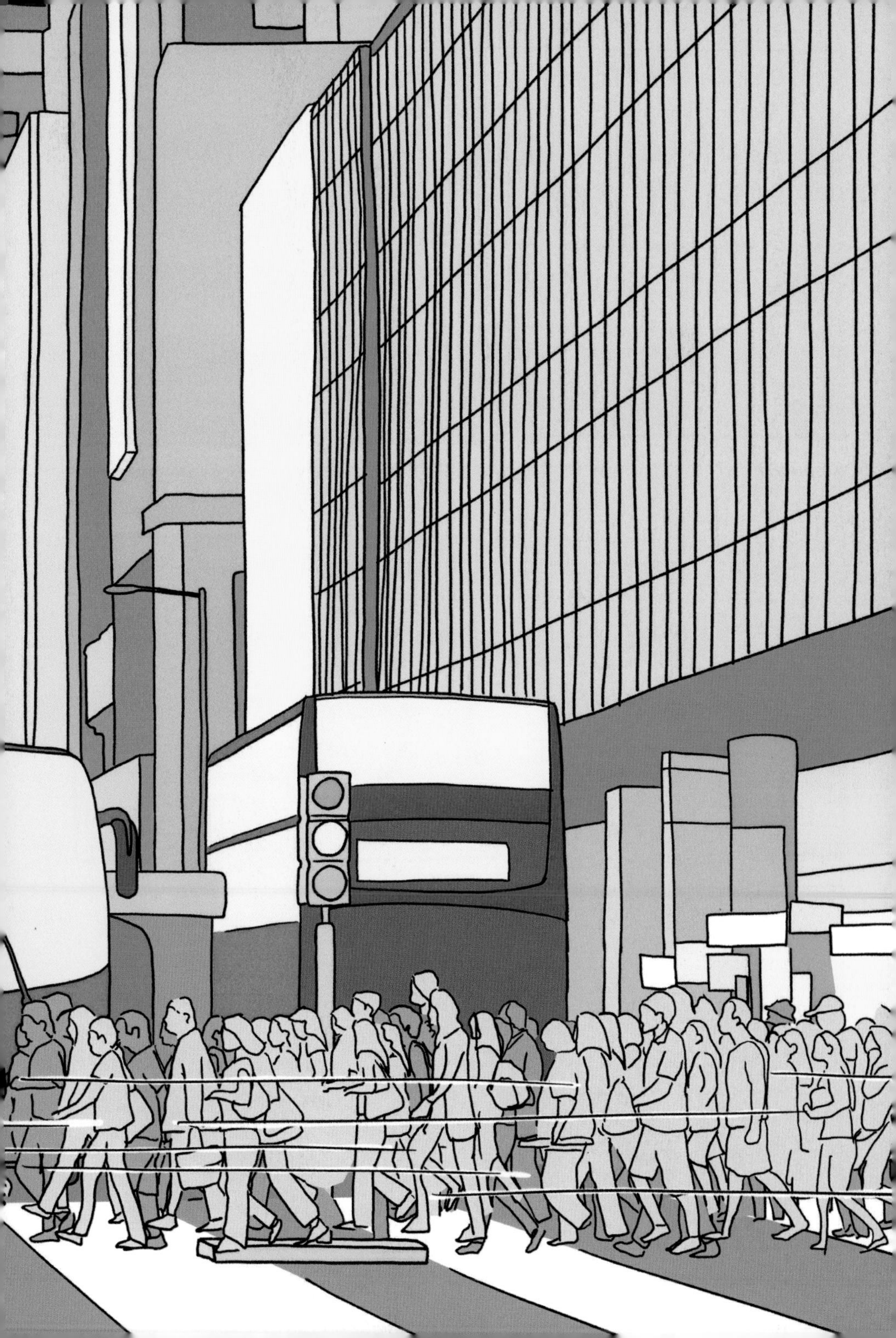

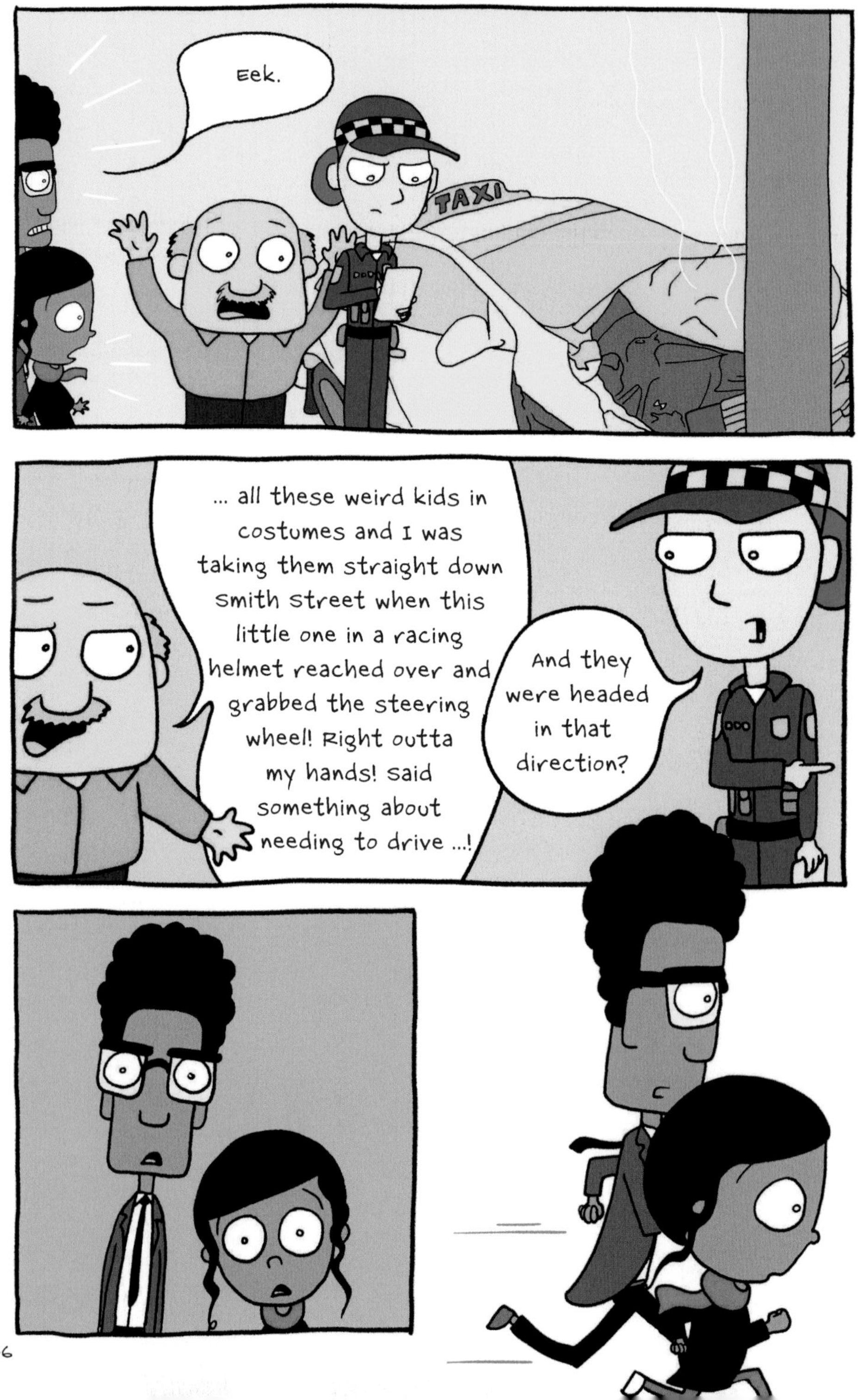
Eek.
... all these weird kids in costumes and I was taking them straight down Smith Street when this little one in a racing helmet reached over and grabbed the steering wheel! Right outta my hands! Said something about needing to drive ...!
And they were headed in that direction?
TAXI

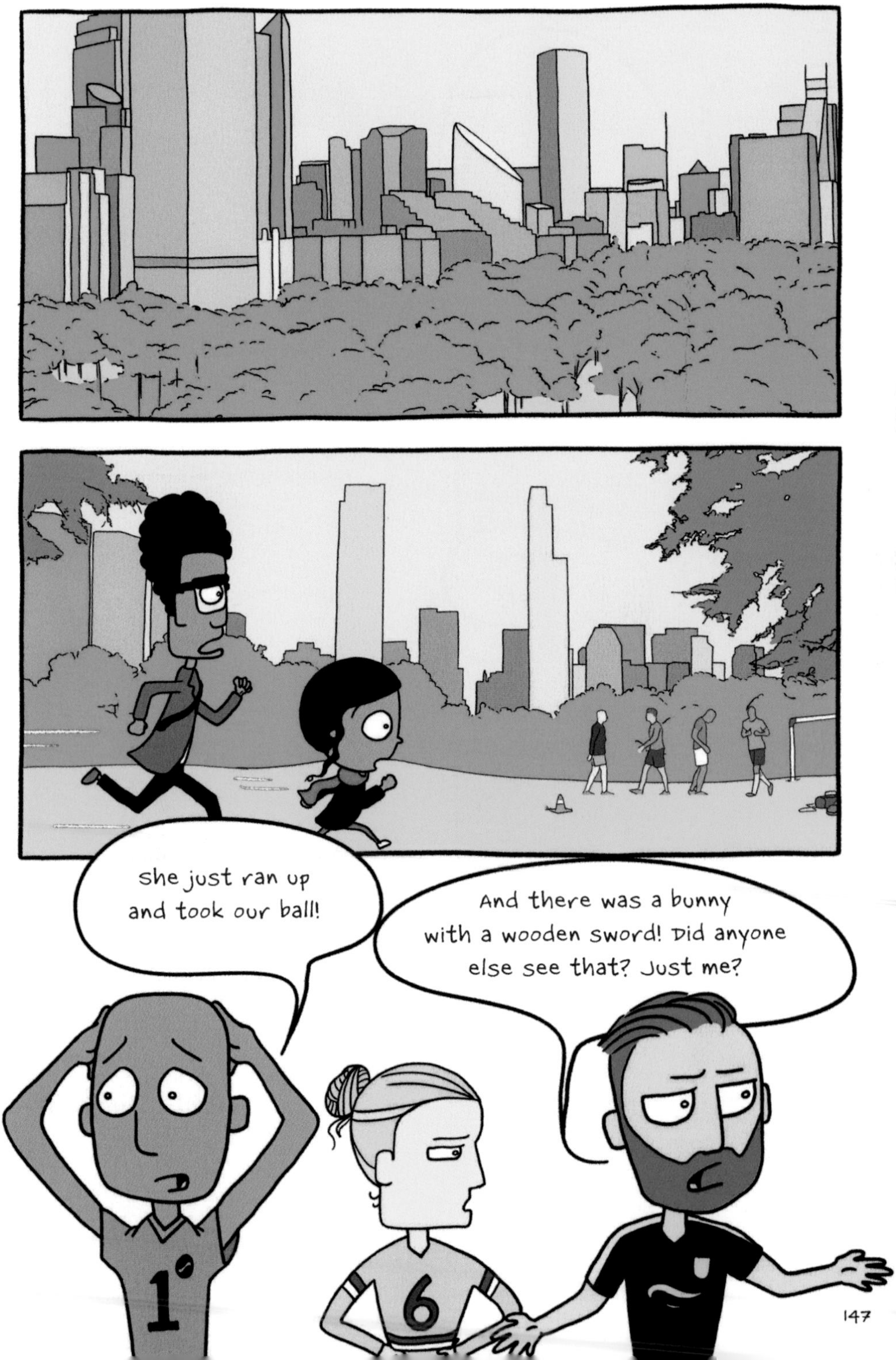
she just ran up and took our ball!
And there was a bunny with a wooden sword! Did anyone else see that? Just me?

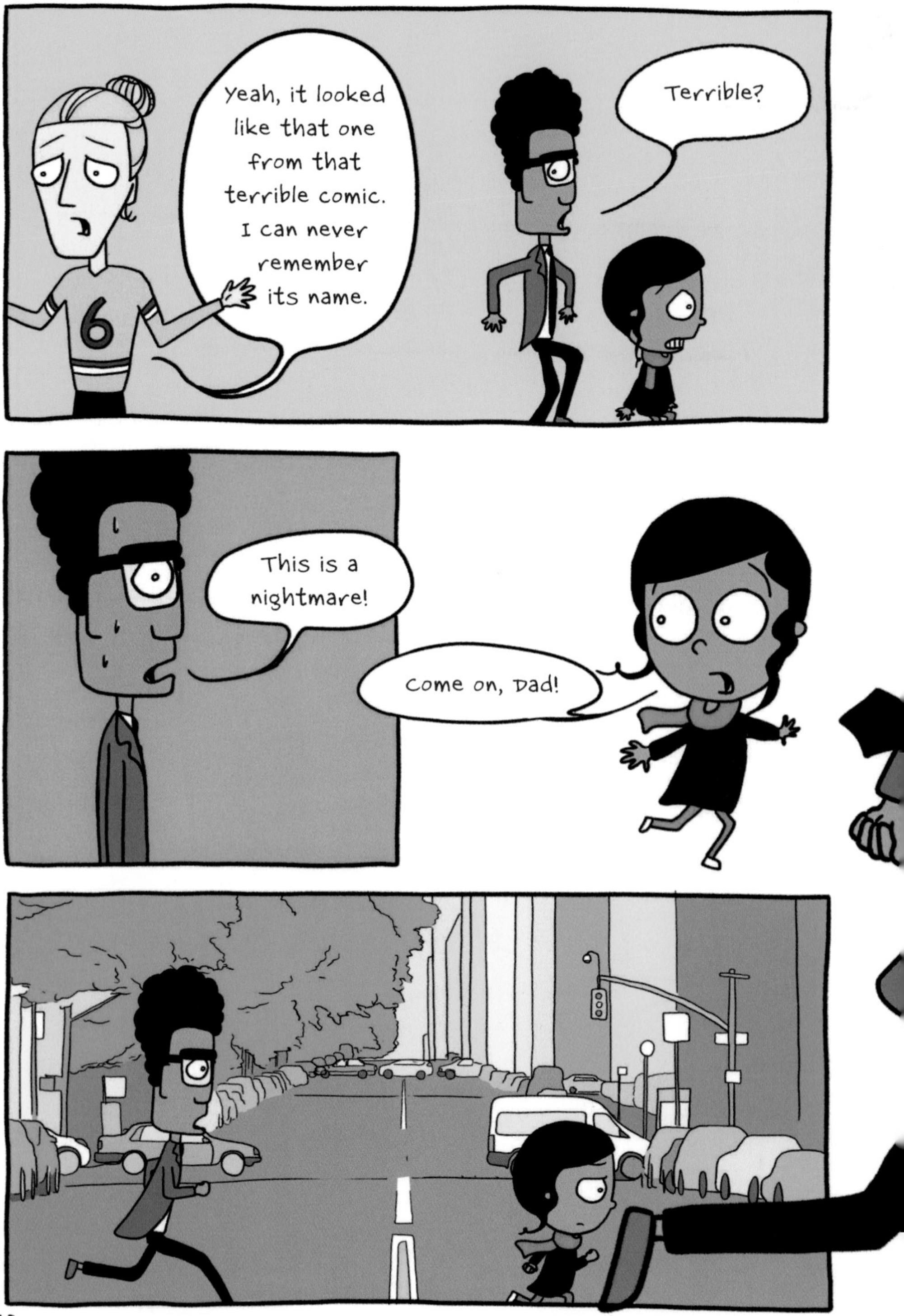

Yeah, it looked like that one from that terrible comic. I can never remember its name.
Terrible?
This is a nightmare!
Come on, Dad!

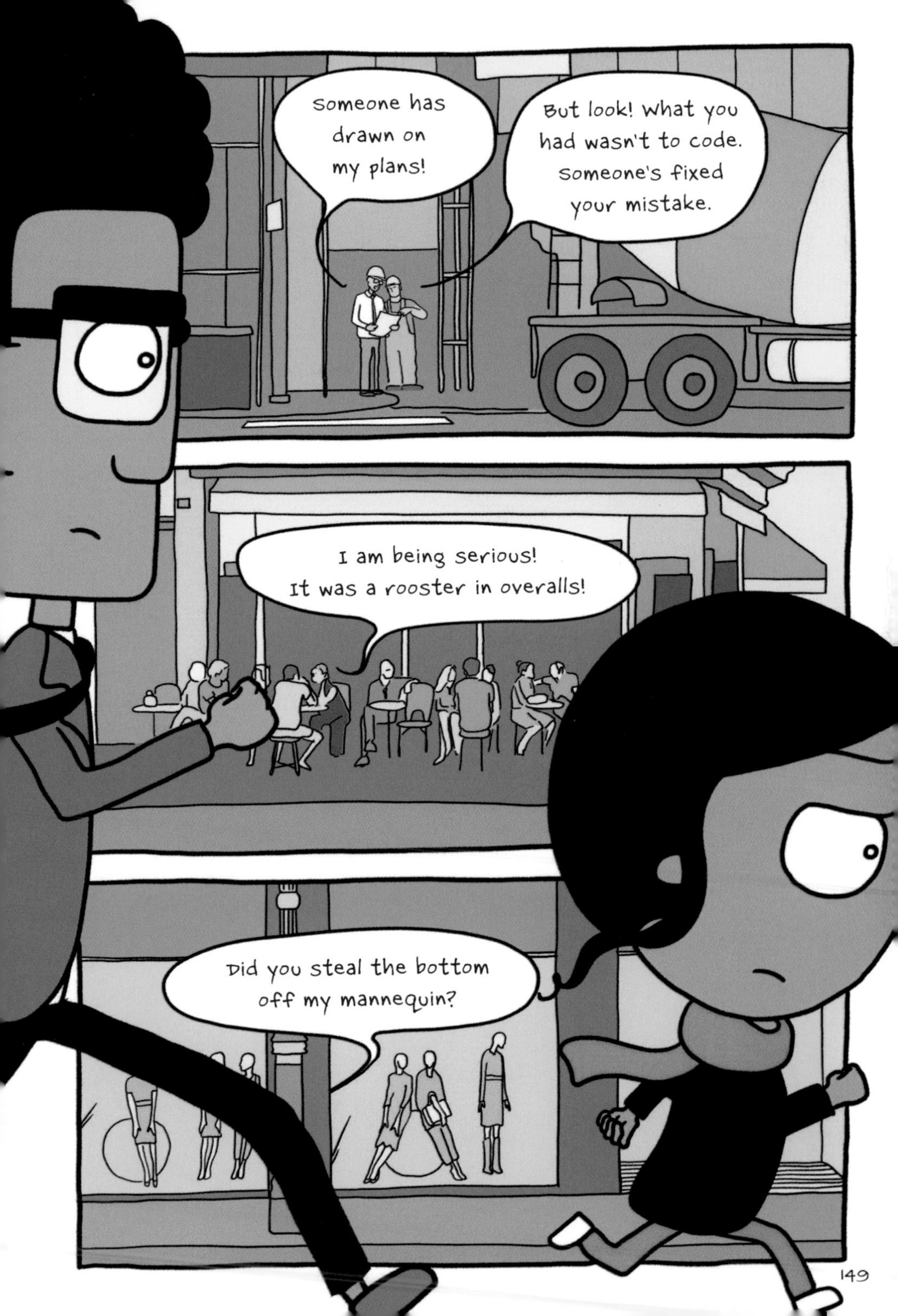
Someone has drawn on my plans!
But look! What you had wasn't to code. Someone's fixed your mistake.
I am being serious! It was a rooster in overalls!
Did you steal the bottom off my mannequin?

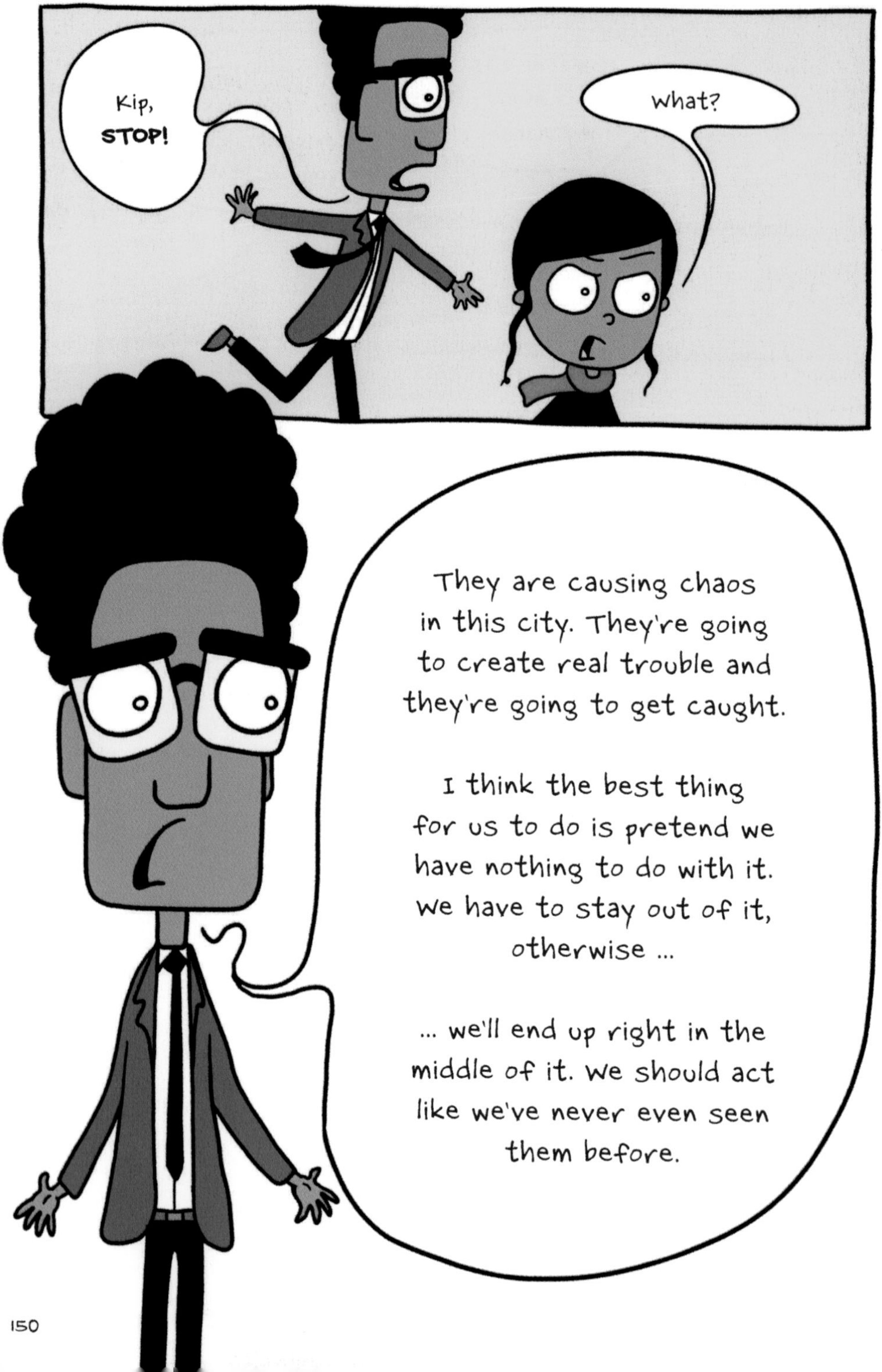
Kip, STOP!
what?
They are causing chaos in this city. They're going to create real trouble and they're going to get caught.
I think the best thing for us to do is pretend we have nothing to do with it. we have to stay out of it, otherwise ...
... we'll end up right in the middle of it. we should act like we've never even seen them before.

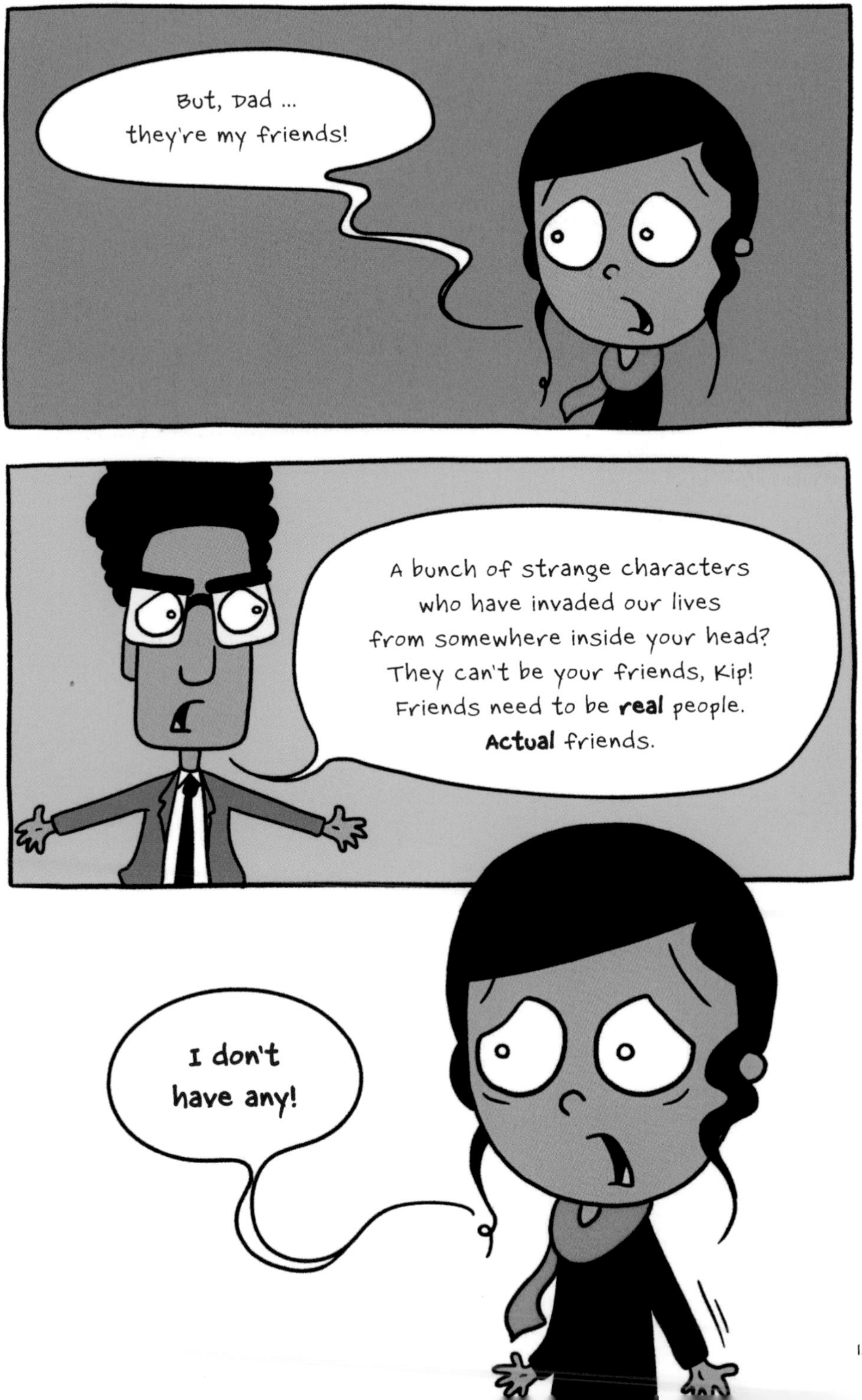

But, Dad ... they're my friends!
A bunch of strange characters who have invaded our lives from somewhere inside your head? They can't be your friends, Kip! Friends need to be **real** people. **Actual** friends.
I don't have any!

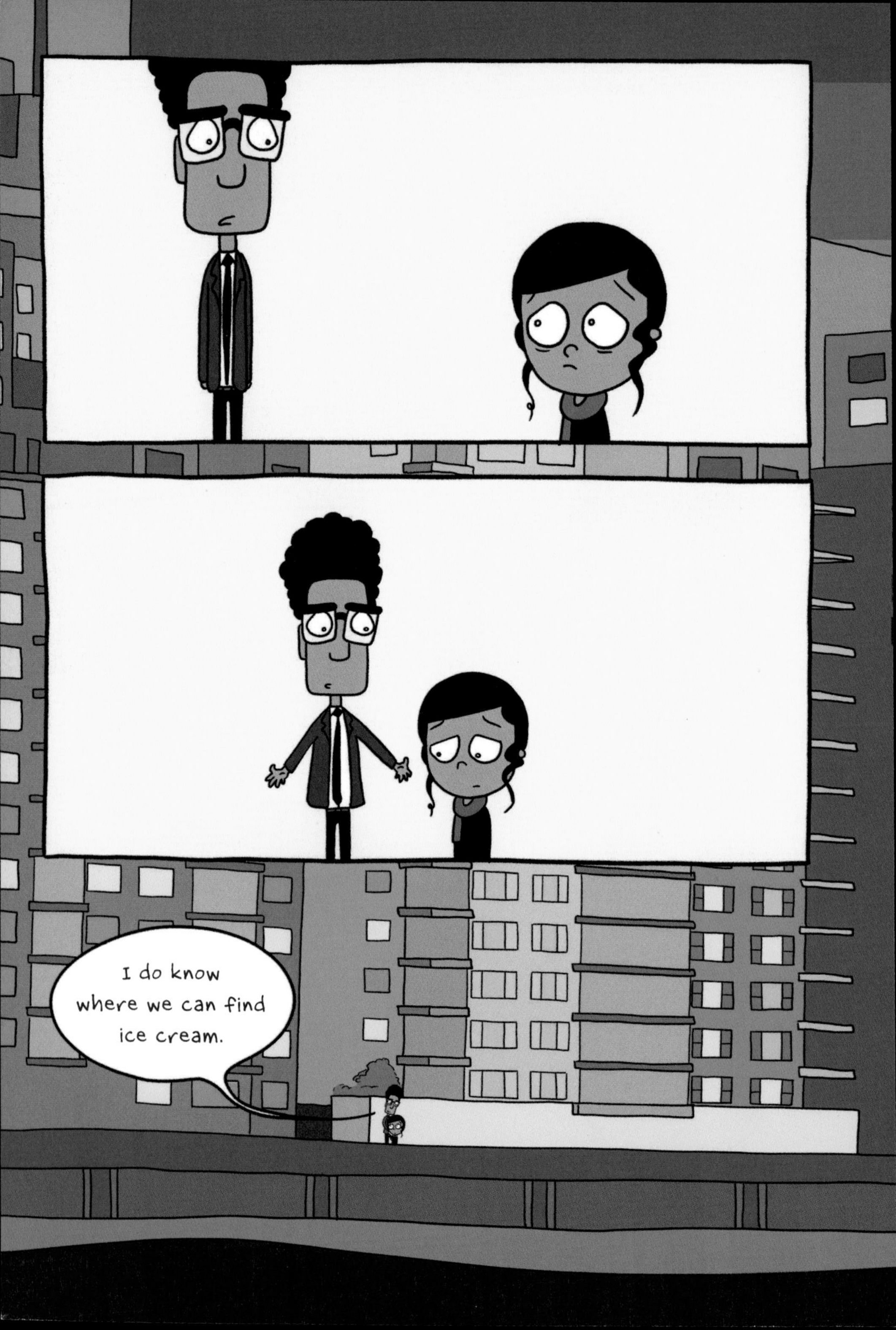
I do know where we can find ice cream.

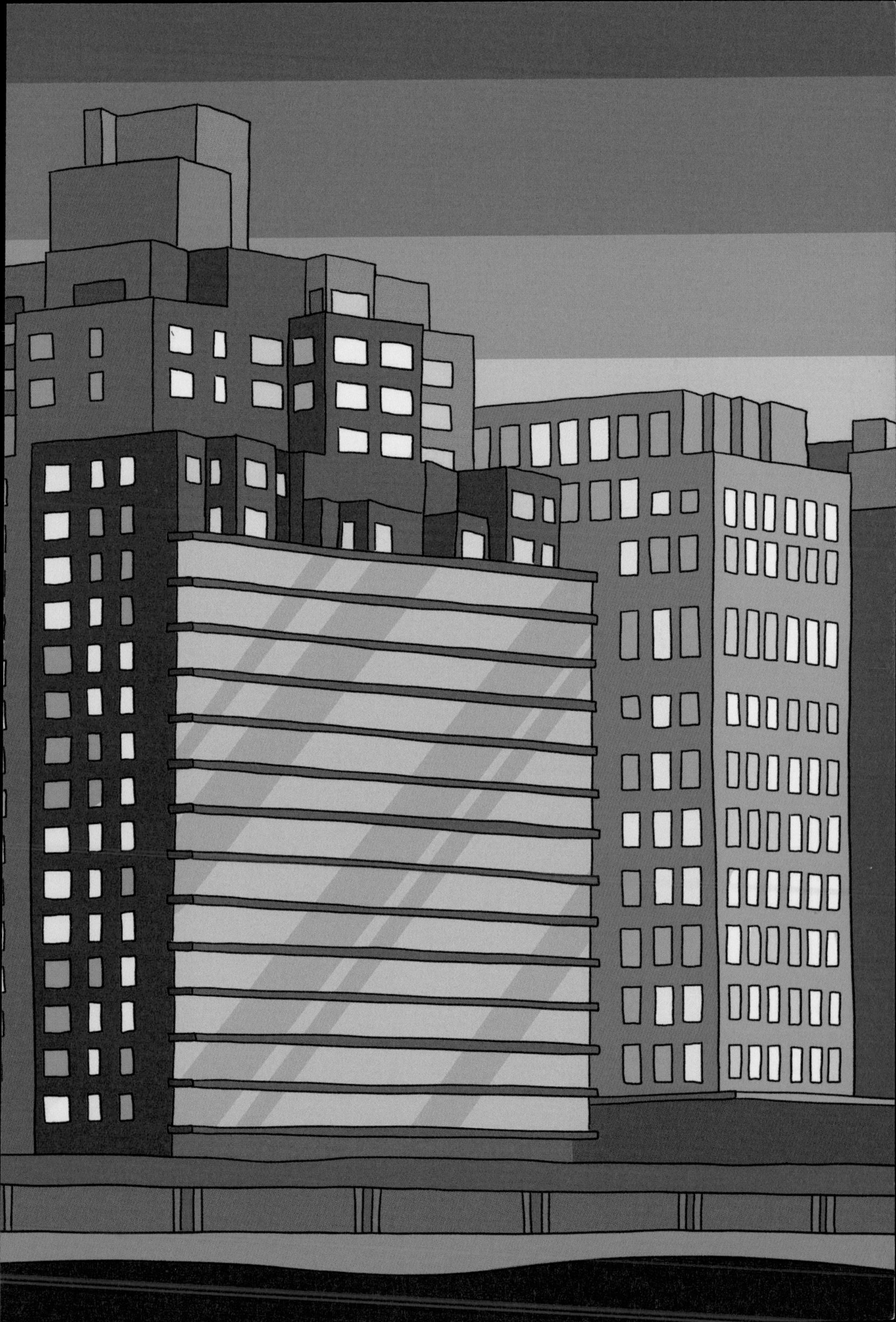

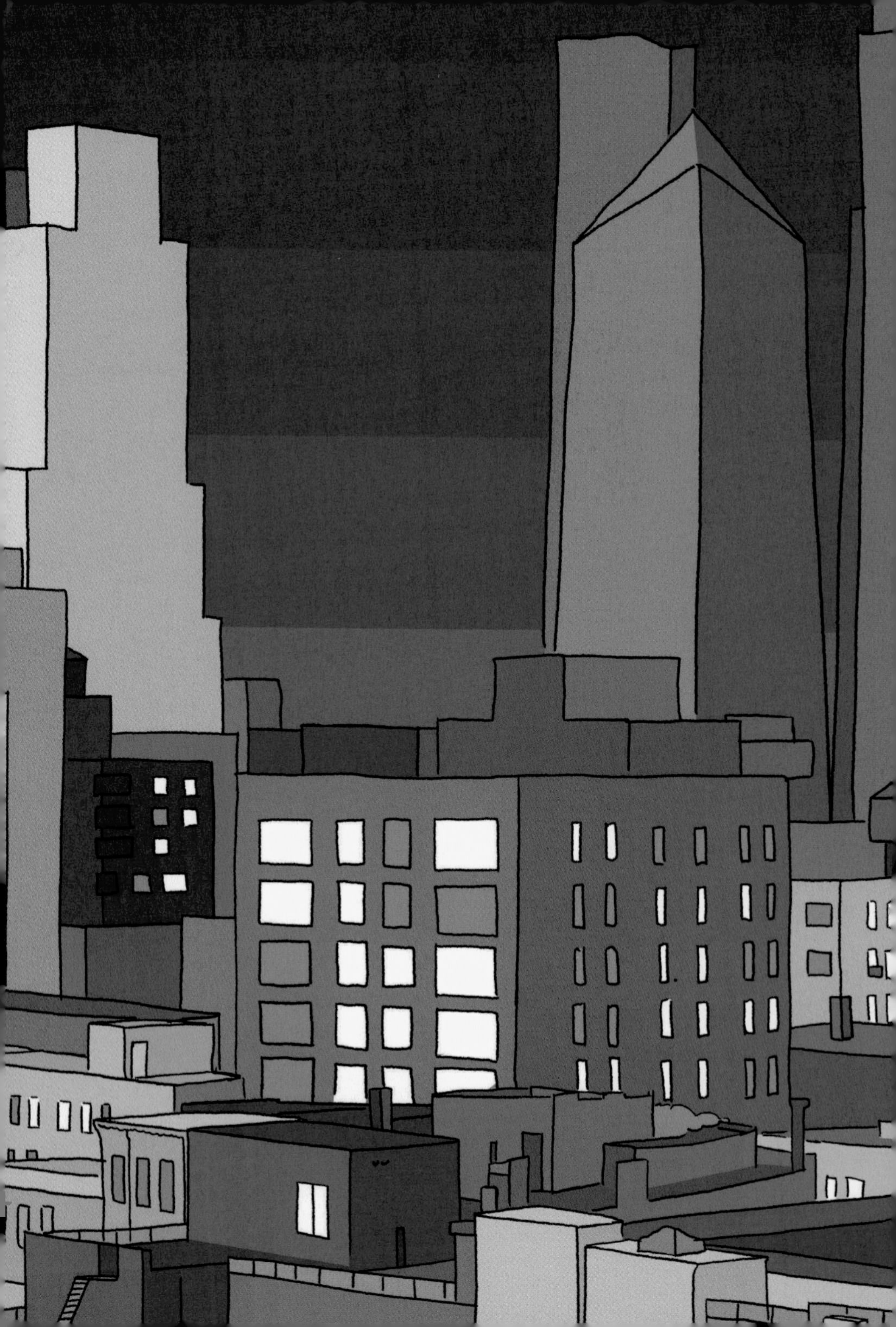

CHAPTER TWELVE
The lost Odd

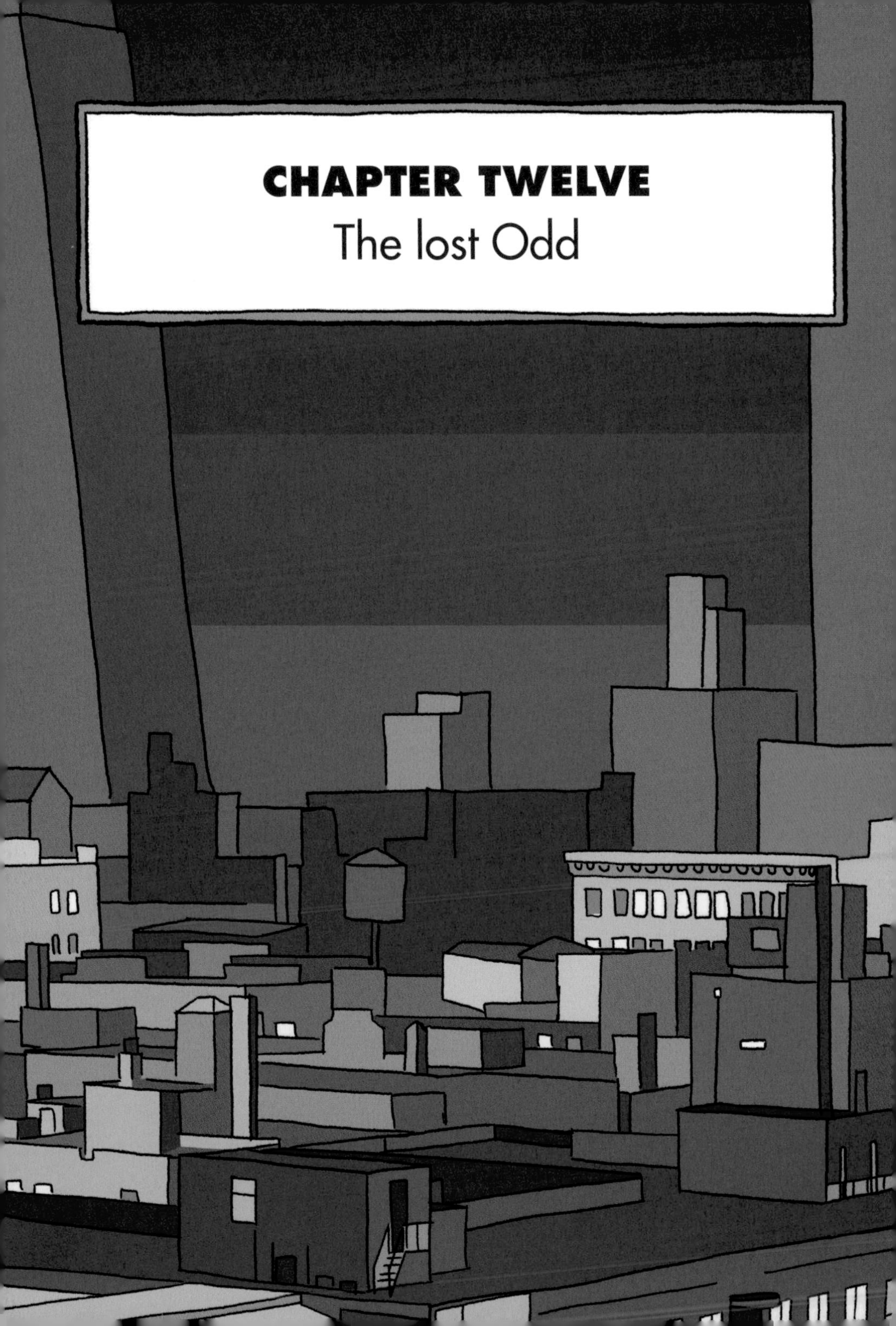

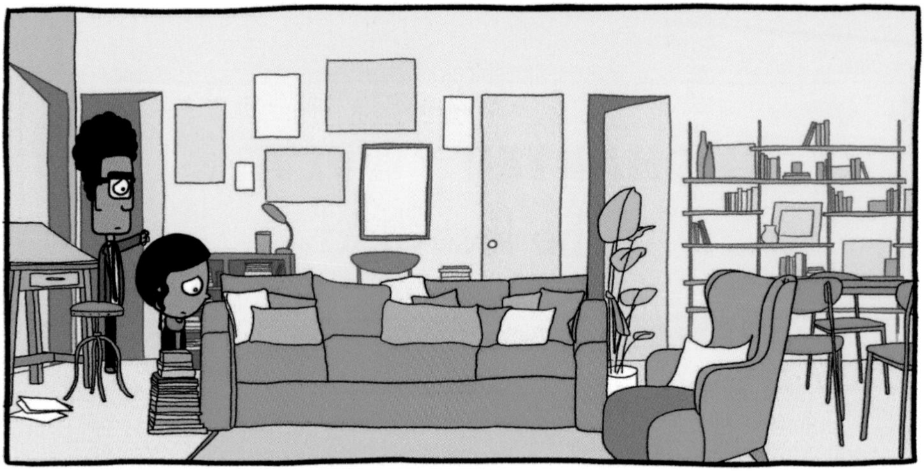

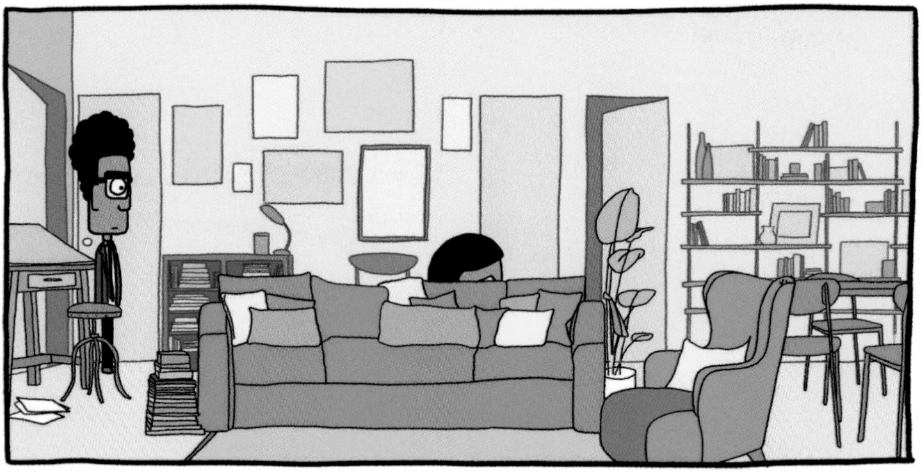

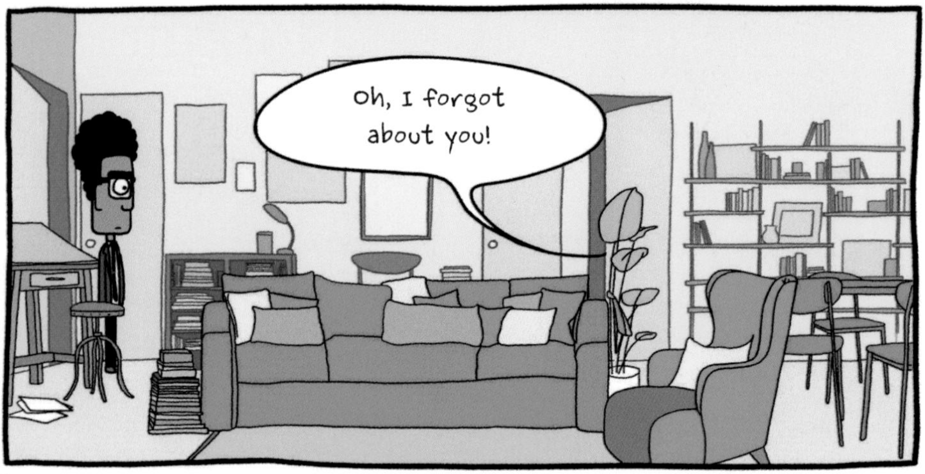
Oh, I forgot about you!

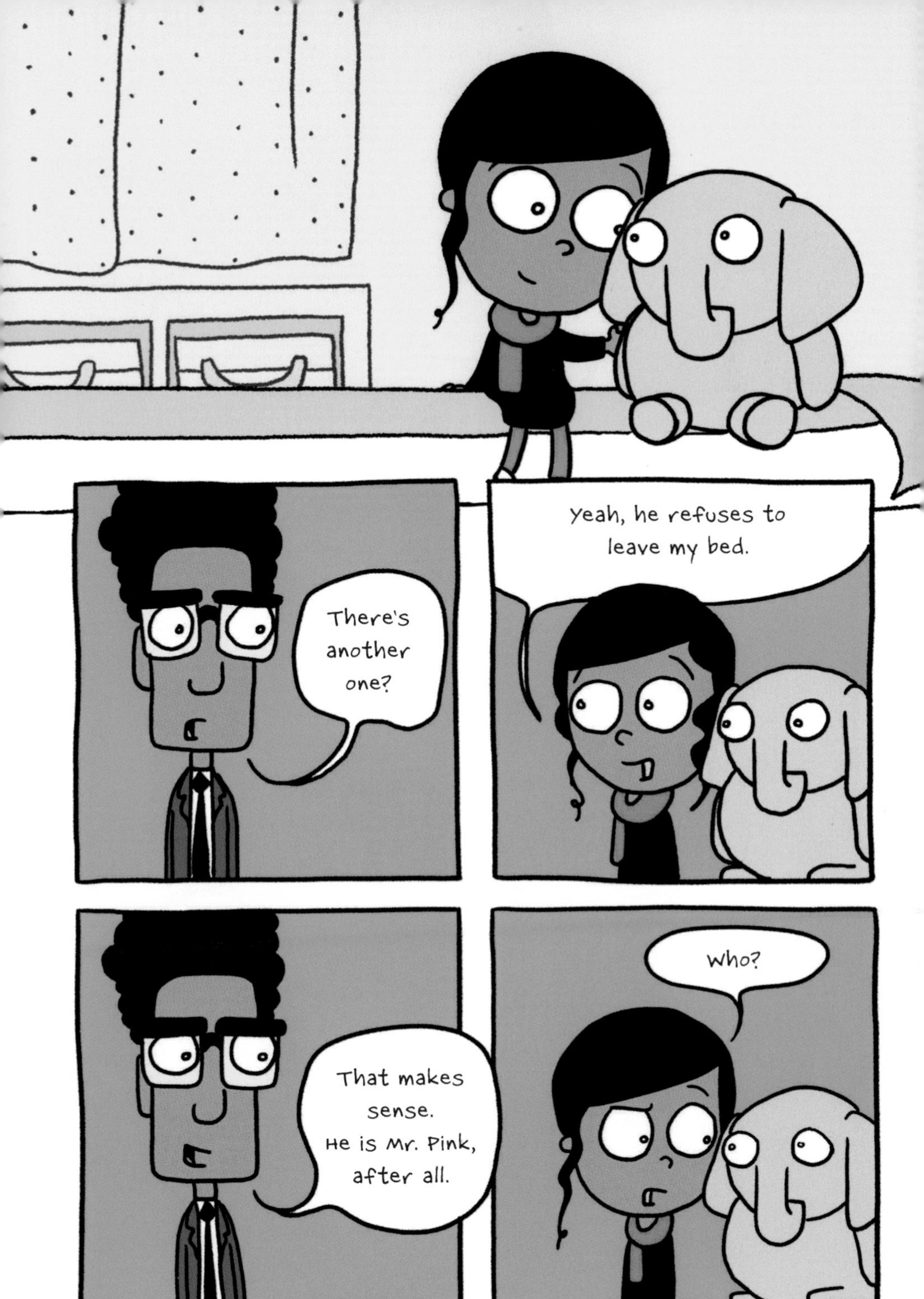
There's another one?
Yeah, he refuses to leave my bed.
That makes sense. He is Mr. Pink, after all.
Who?

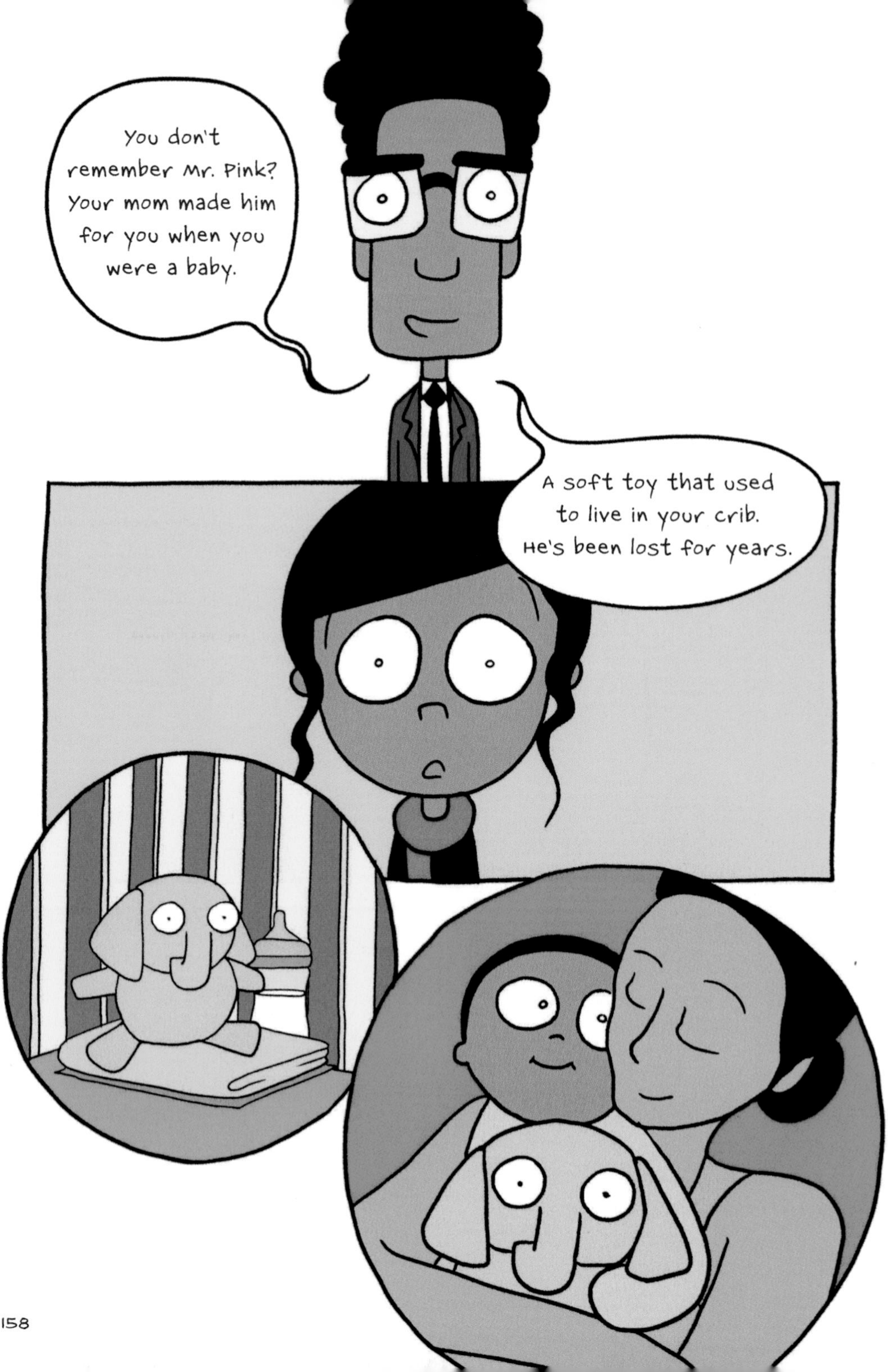
You don't remember Mr. Pink? Your mom made him for you when you were a baby.
A soft toy that used to live in your crib. He's been lost for years.

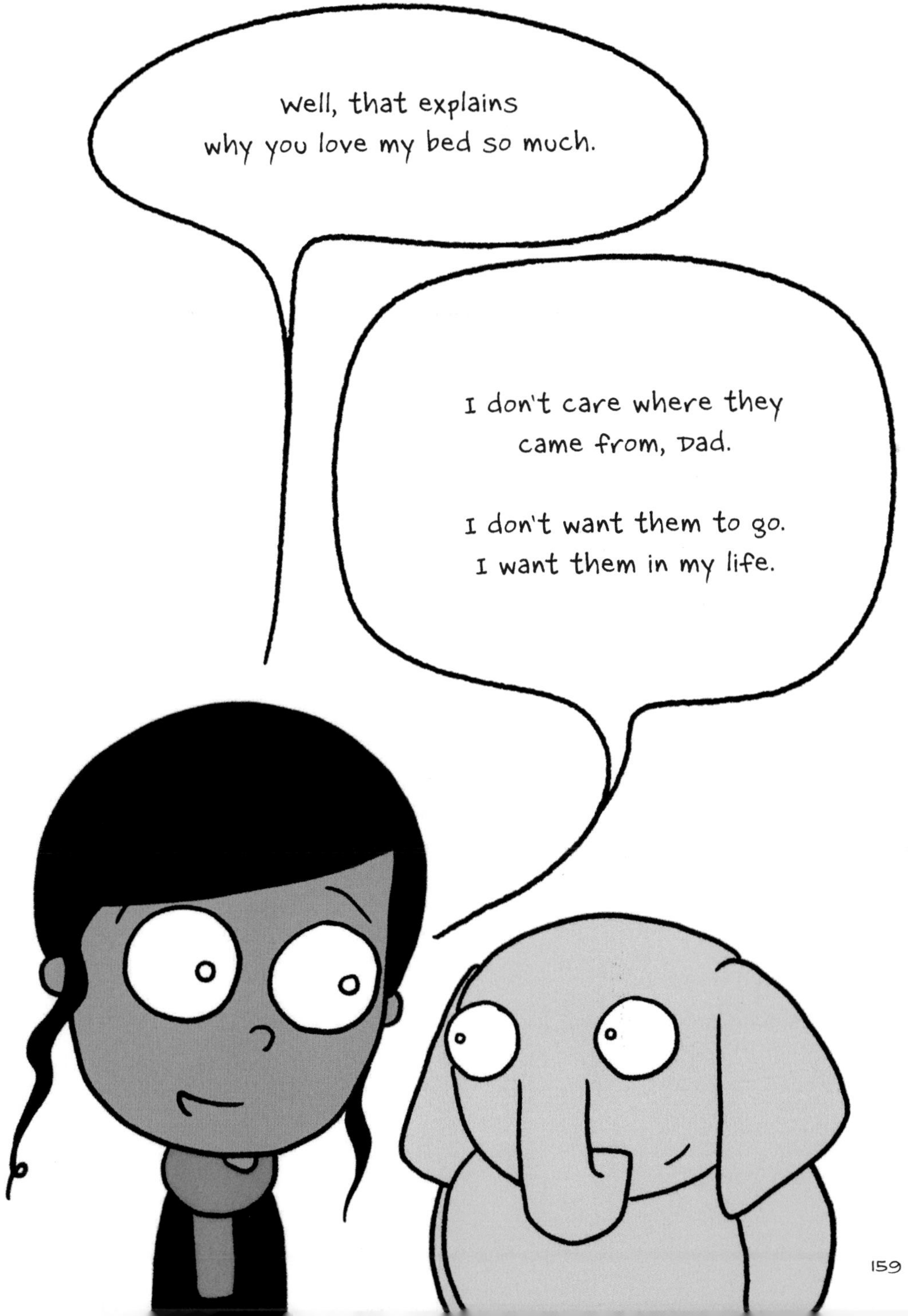
Well, that explains why you love my bed so much.
I don't care where they came from, Dad.
I don't want them to go. I want them in my life.

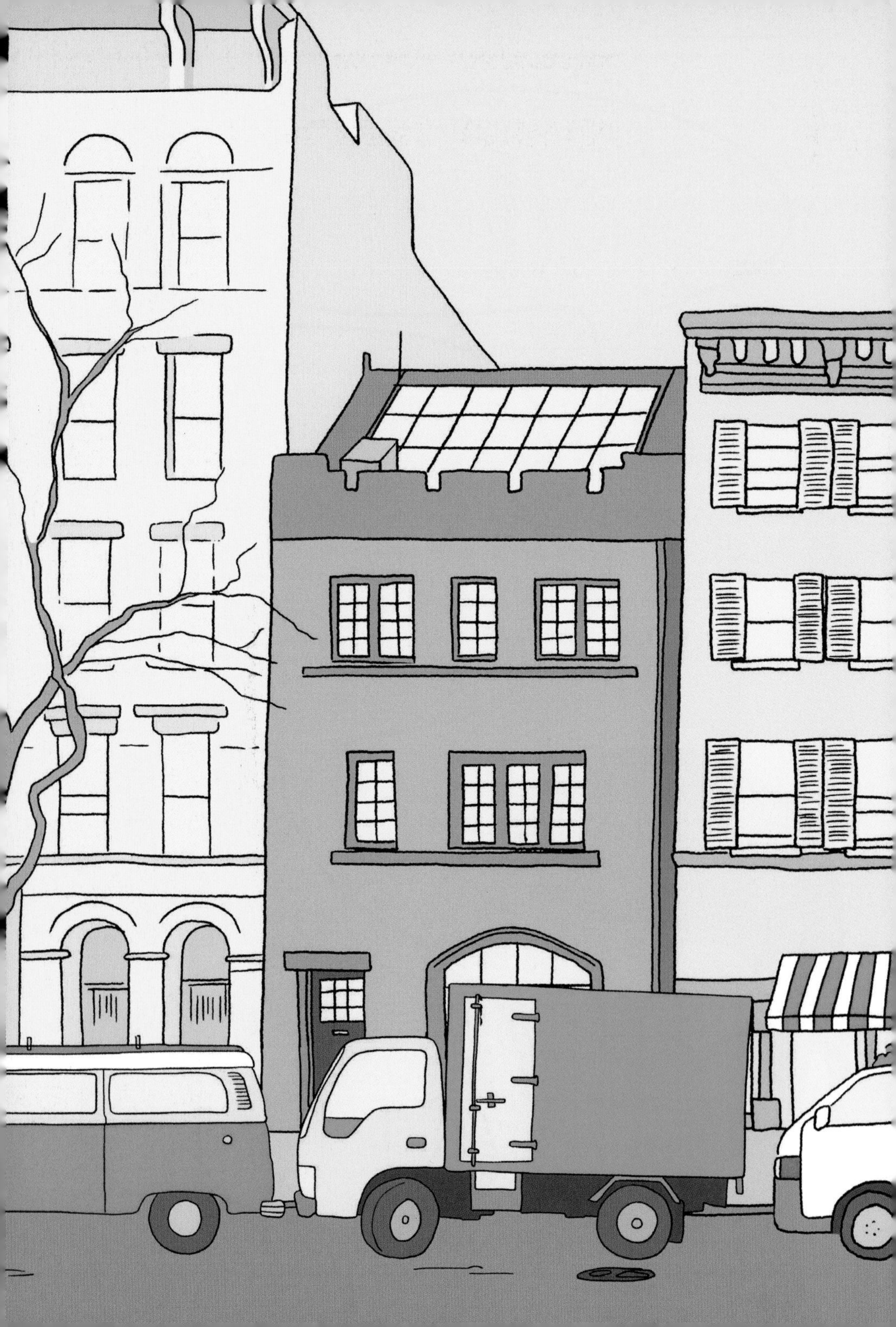

CHAPTER THIRTEEN

The Odds return

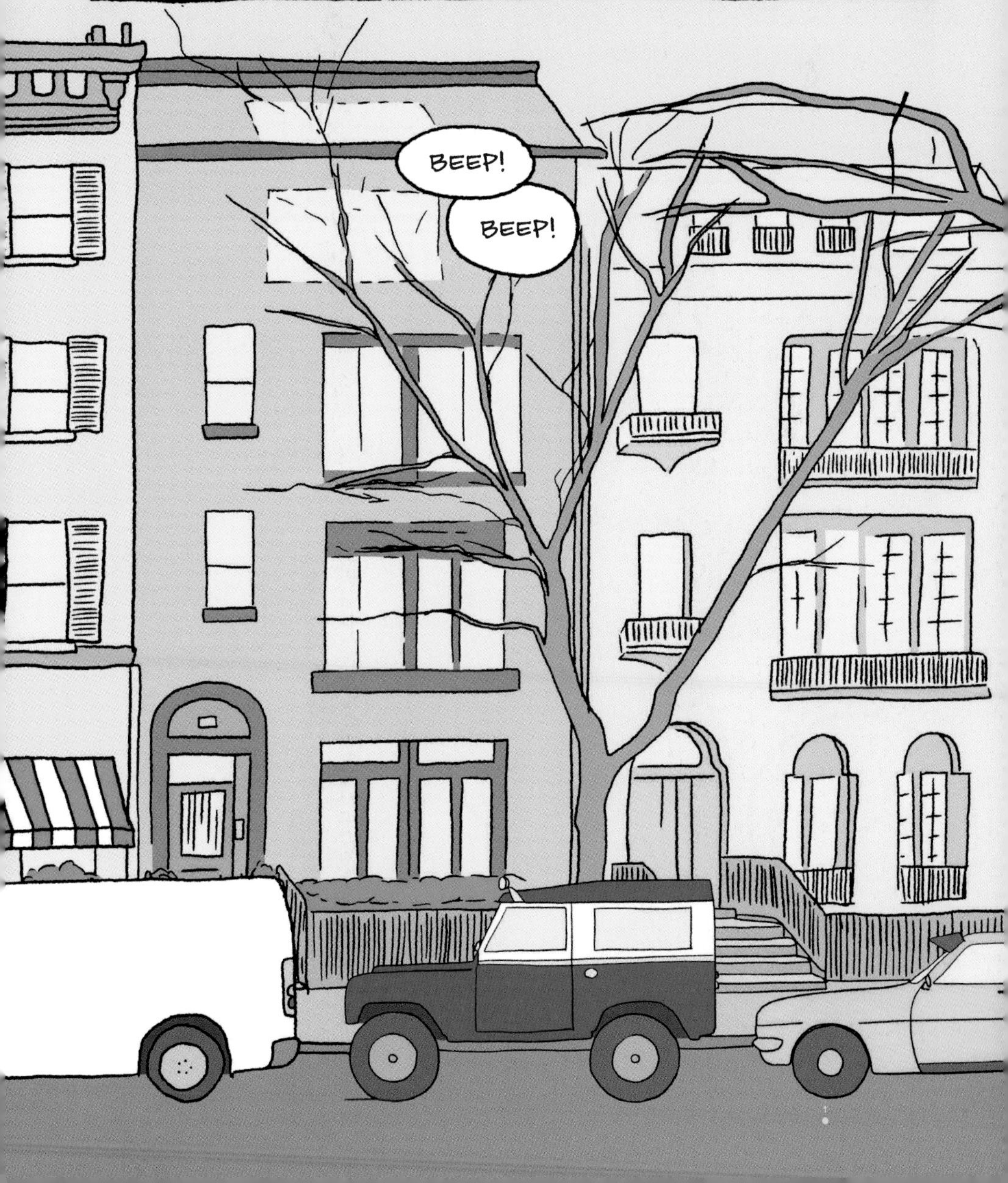
BEEP!
BEEP!

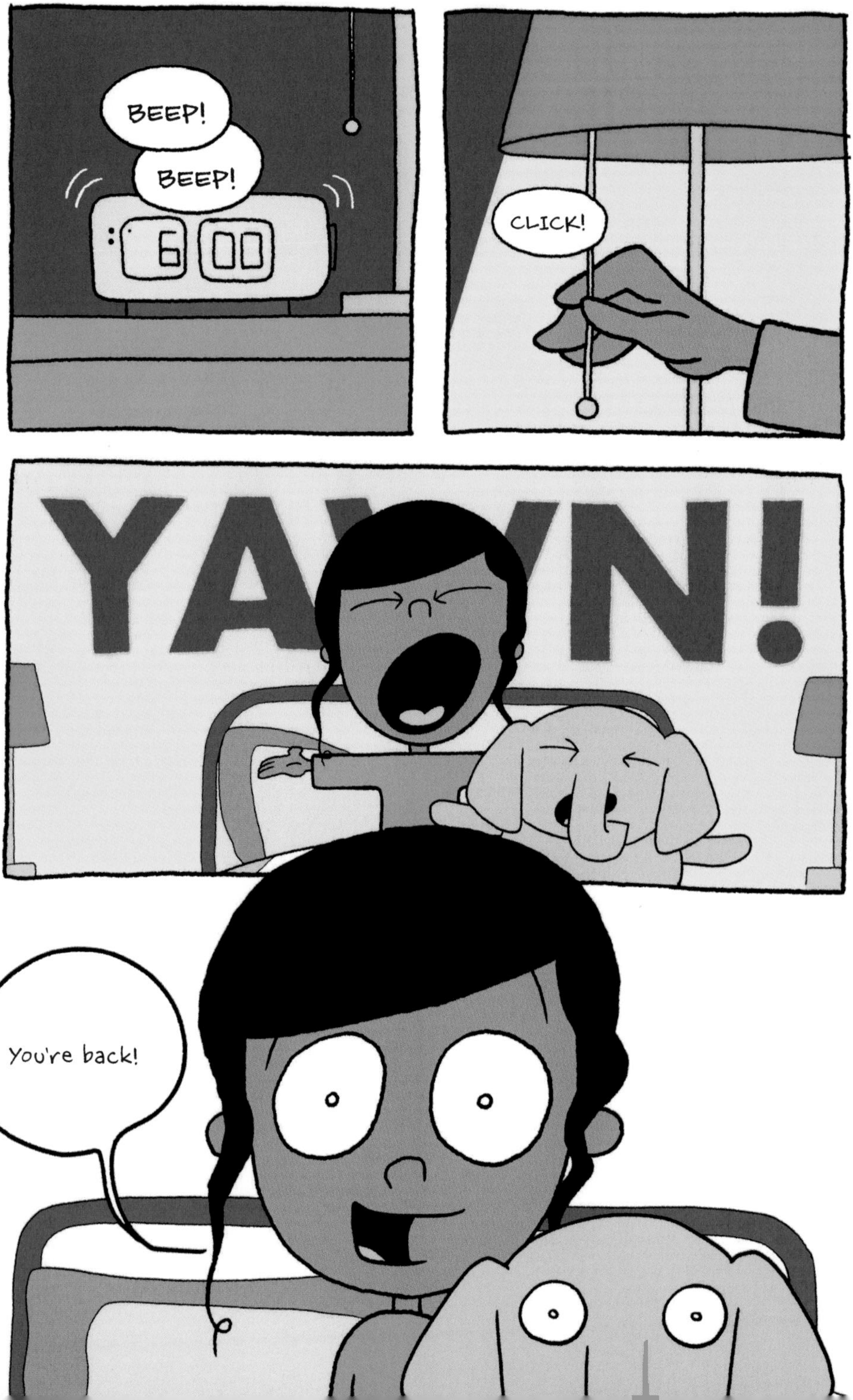
BEEP!
BEEP!
6:00
CLICK!
YAWN!
You're back!

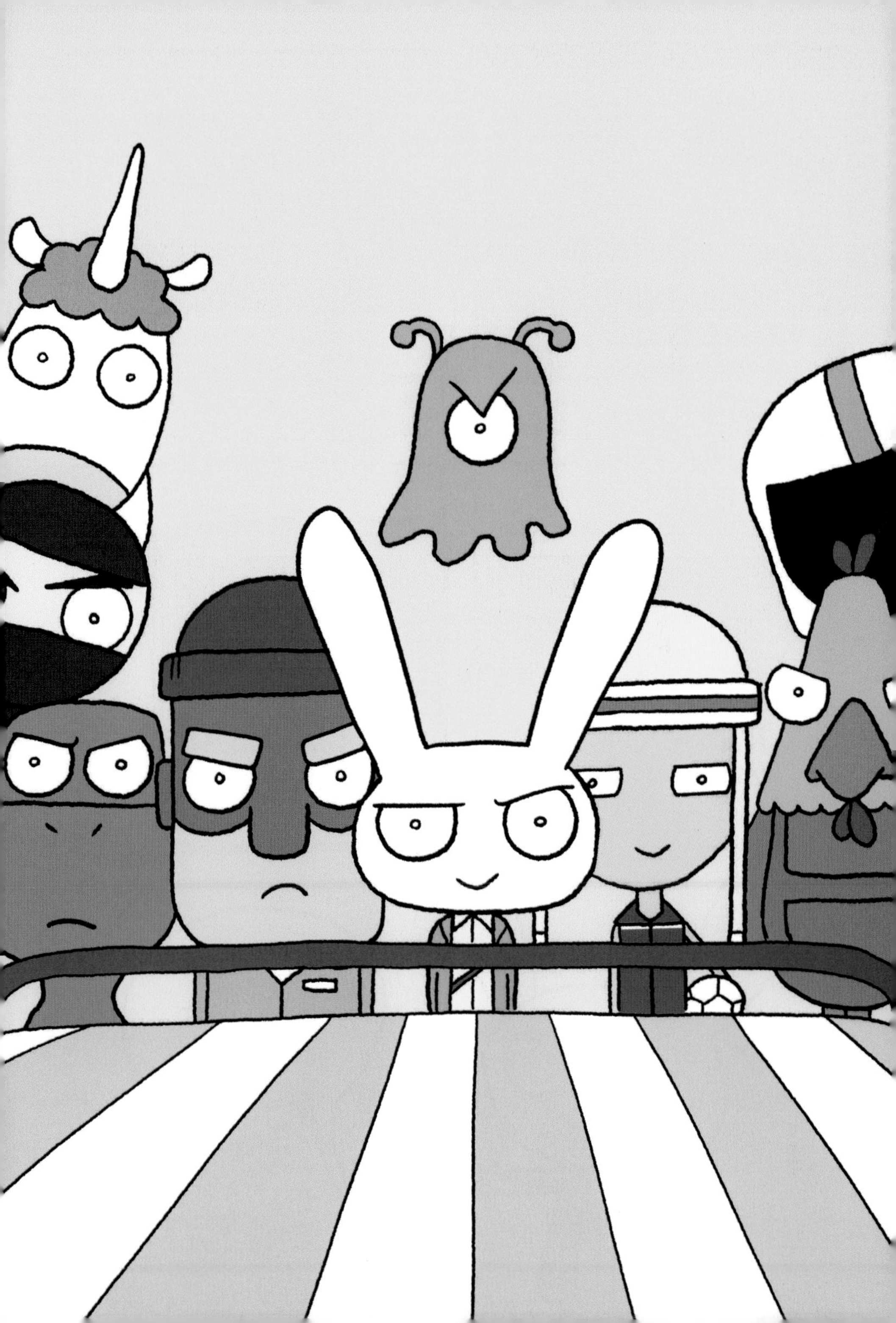

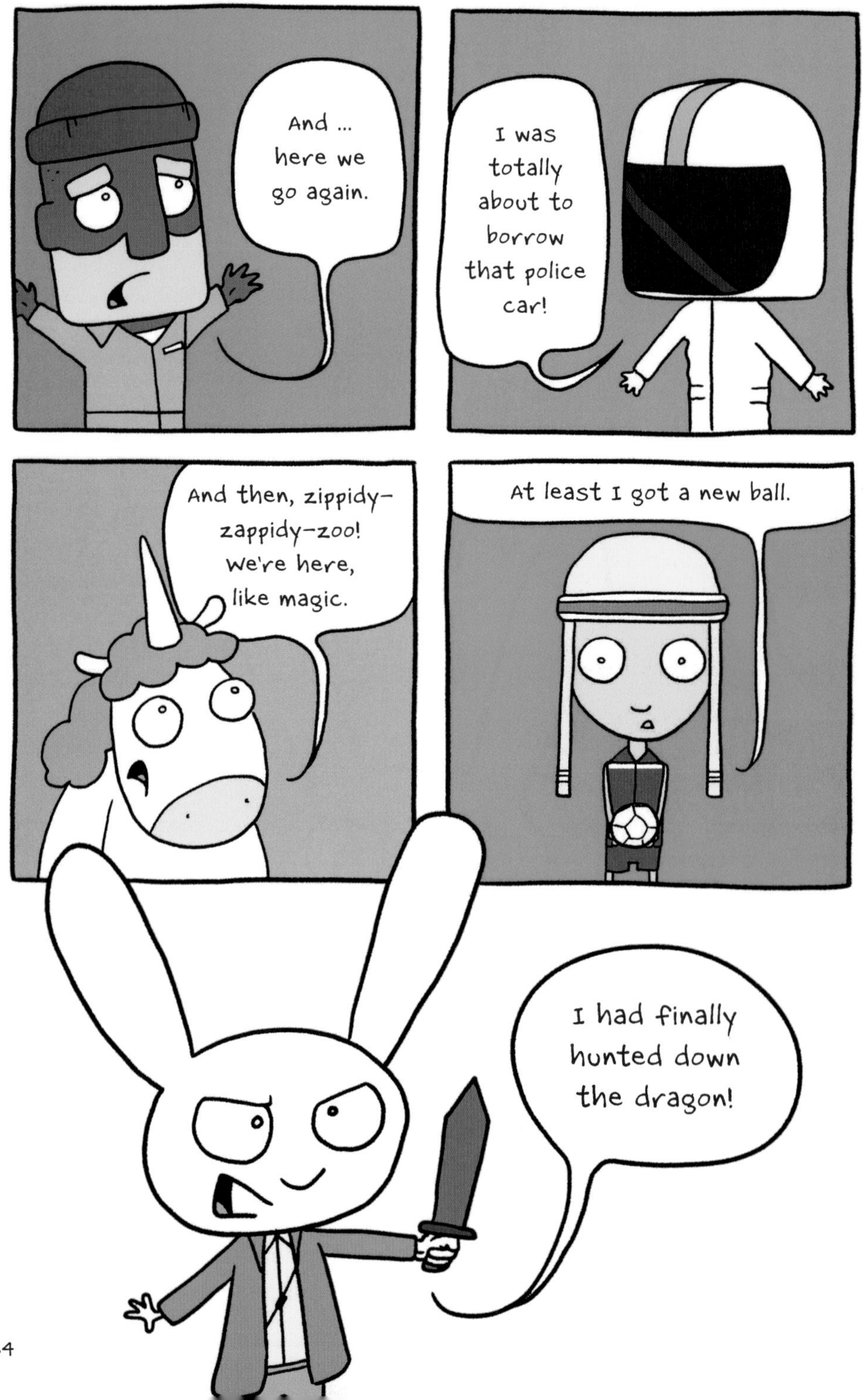
And ... here we go again.
I was totally about to borrow that police car!
And then, zippidy-zappidy-zoo! We're here, like magic.
At least I got a new ball.
I had finally hunted down the dragon!

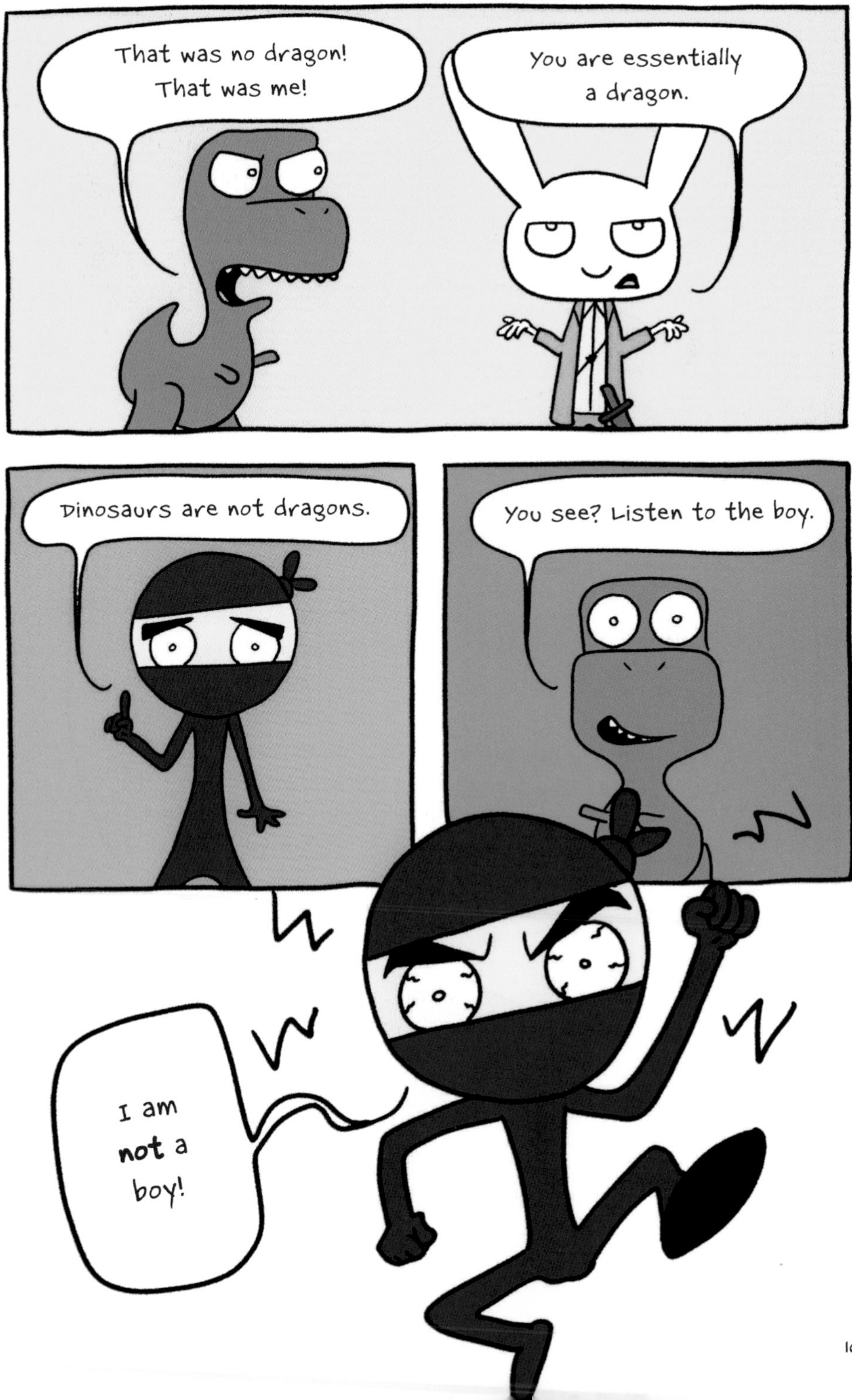
That was no dragon! That was me!
You are essentially a dragon.
Dinosaurs are not dragons.
You see? Listen to the boy.
I am **not** a boy!

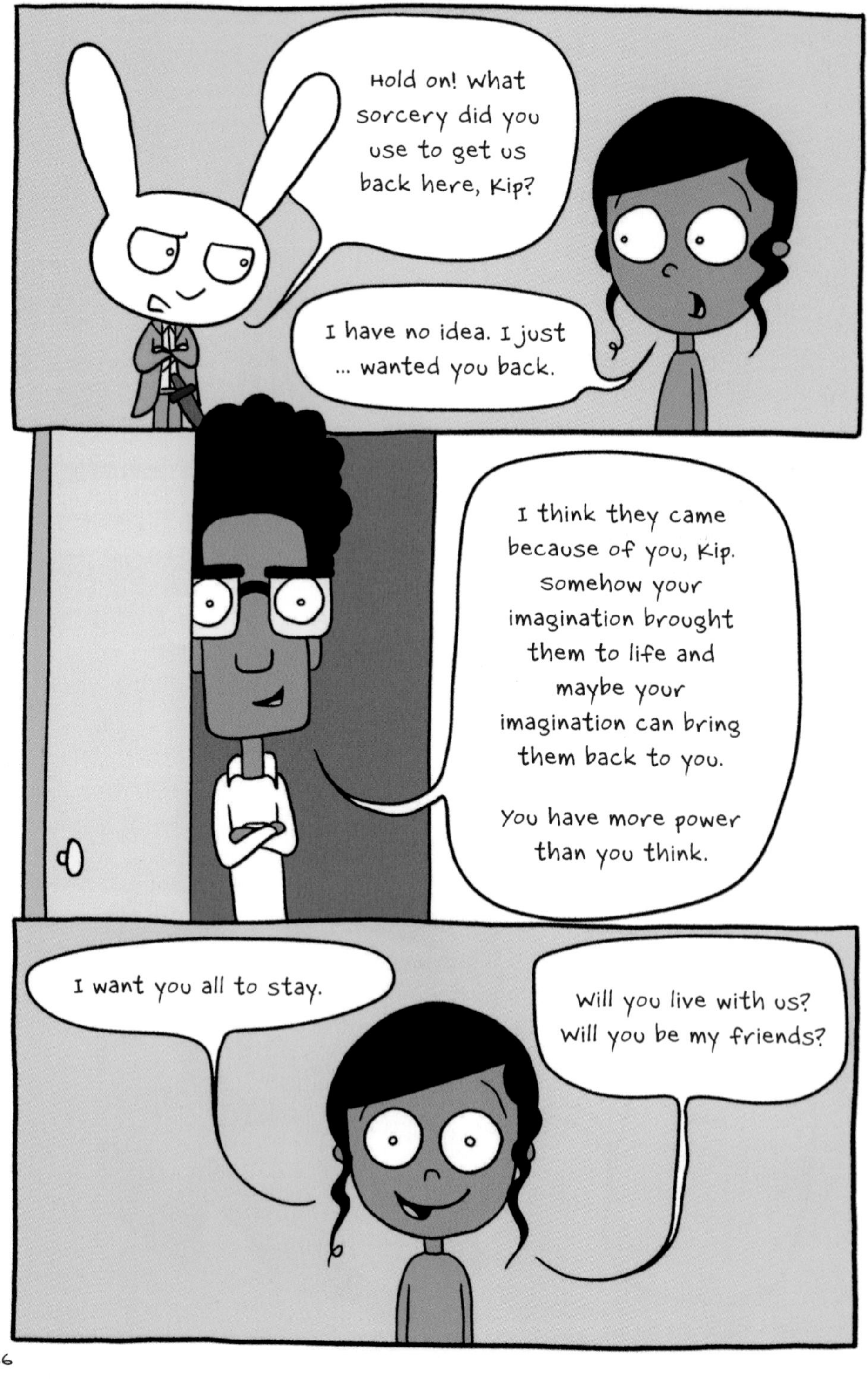
Hold on! What sorcery did you use to get us back here, Kip?
I have no idea. I just ... wanted you back.
I think they came because of you, Kip. Somehow your imagination brought them to life and maybe your imagination can bring them back to you.
You have more power than you think.
I want you all to stay.
Will you live with us? Will you be my friends?

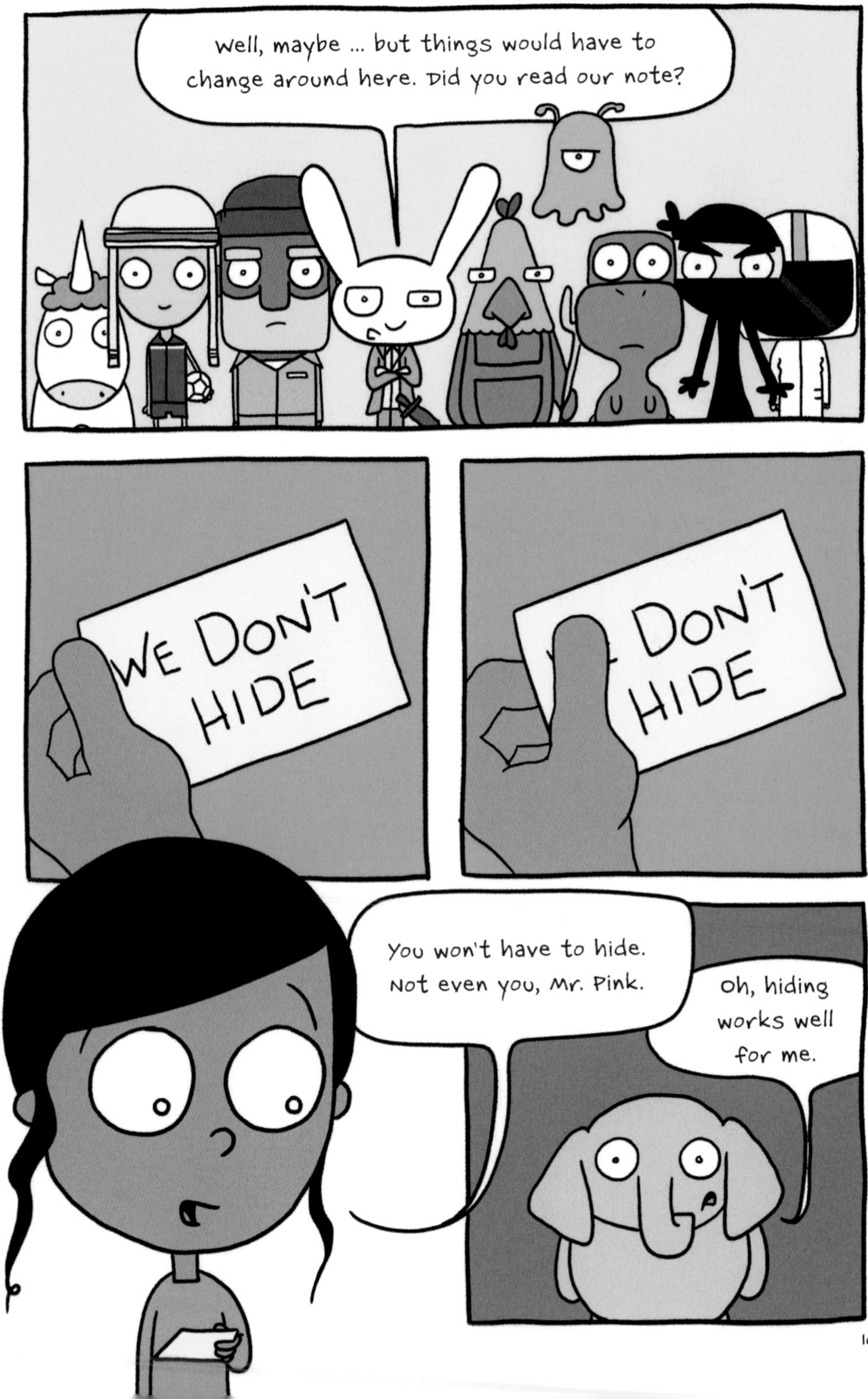
Well, maybe ... but things would have to change around here. Did you read our note?
WE DON'T HIDE
DON'T HIDE
You won't have to hide. Not even you, Mr. Pink.
Oh, hiding works well for me.

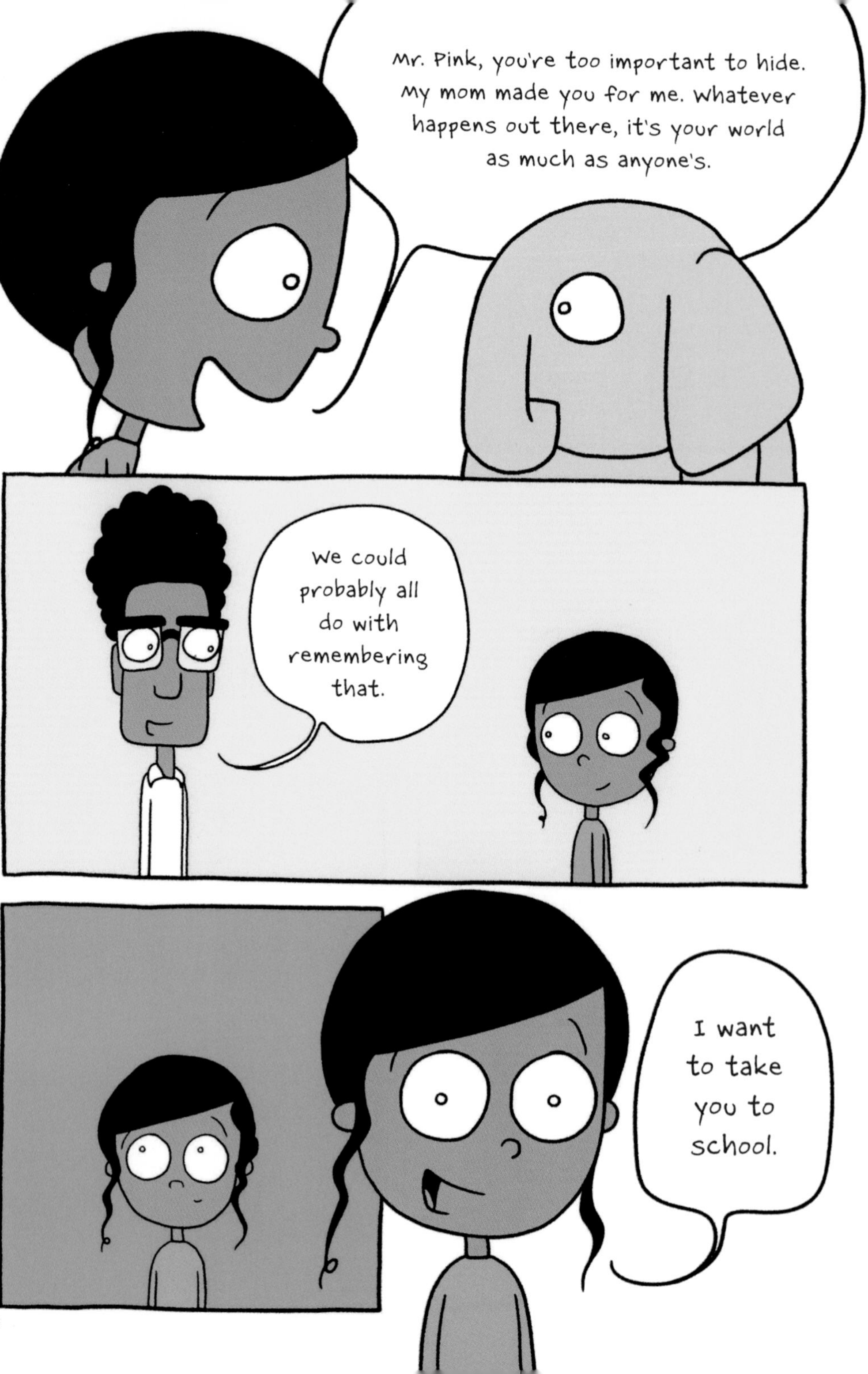
Mr. Pink, you're too important to hide. My mom made you for me. Whatever happens out there, it's your world as much as anyone's.
We could probably all do with remembering that.
I want to take you to school.

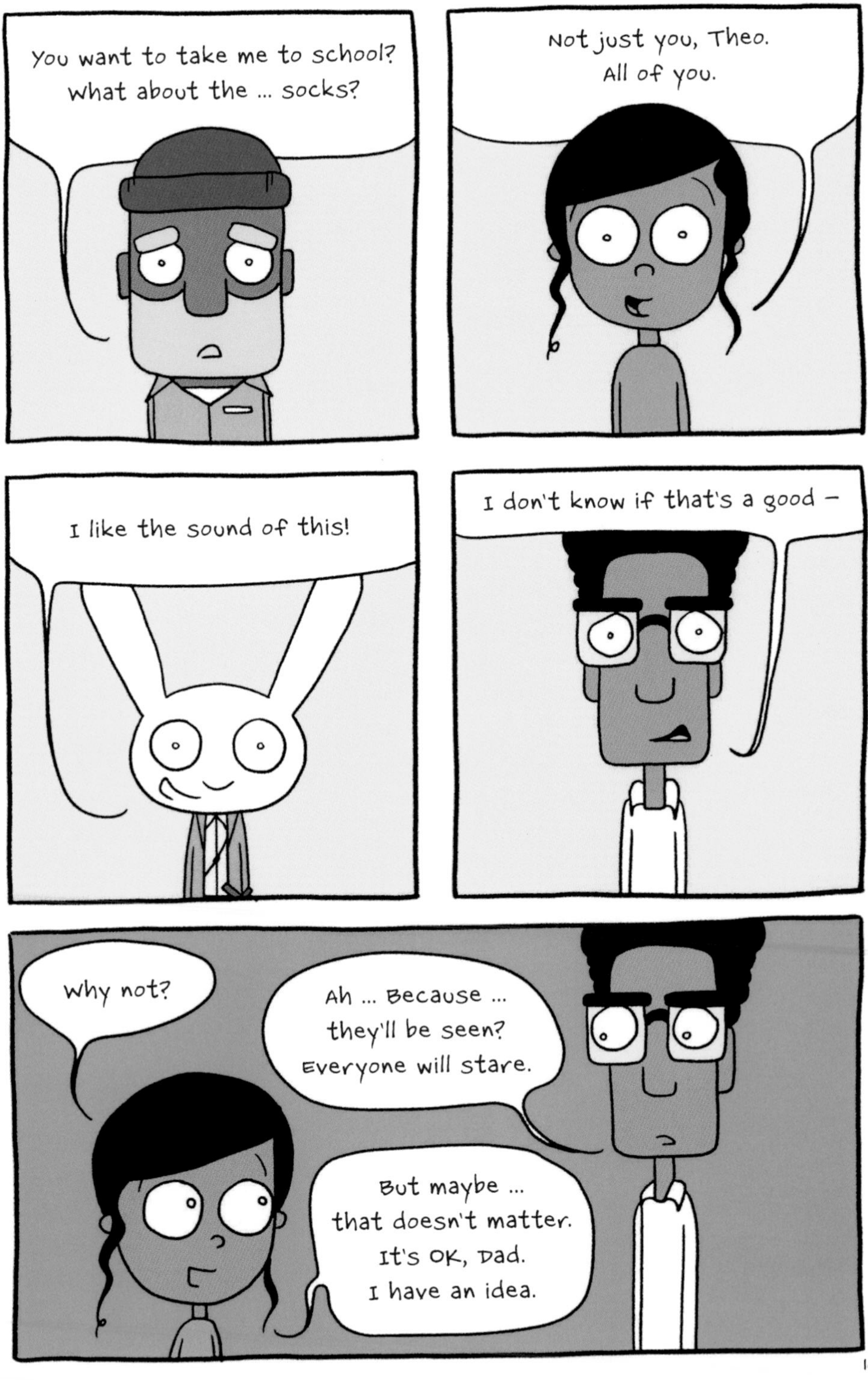
You want to take me to school? What about the ... socks?
Not just you, Theo. All of you.
I like the sound of this!
I don't know if that's a good –
Why not?
Ah ... Because ... they'll be seen? Everyone will stare.
But maybe ... that doesn't matter. It's OK, Dad. I have an idea.

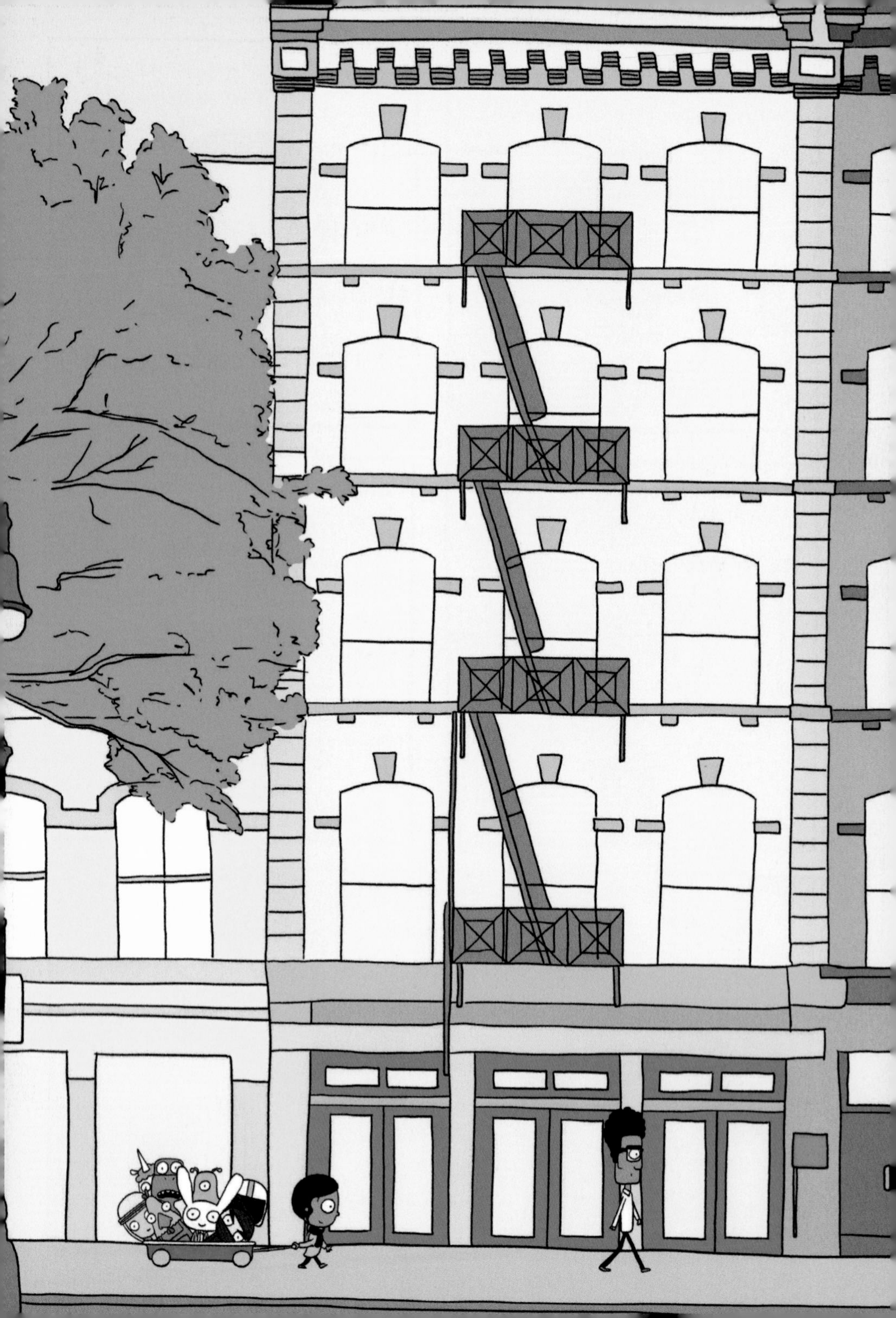

CHAPTER FOURTEEN
The Odds play make-believe

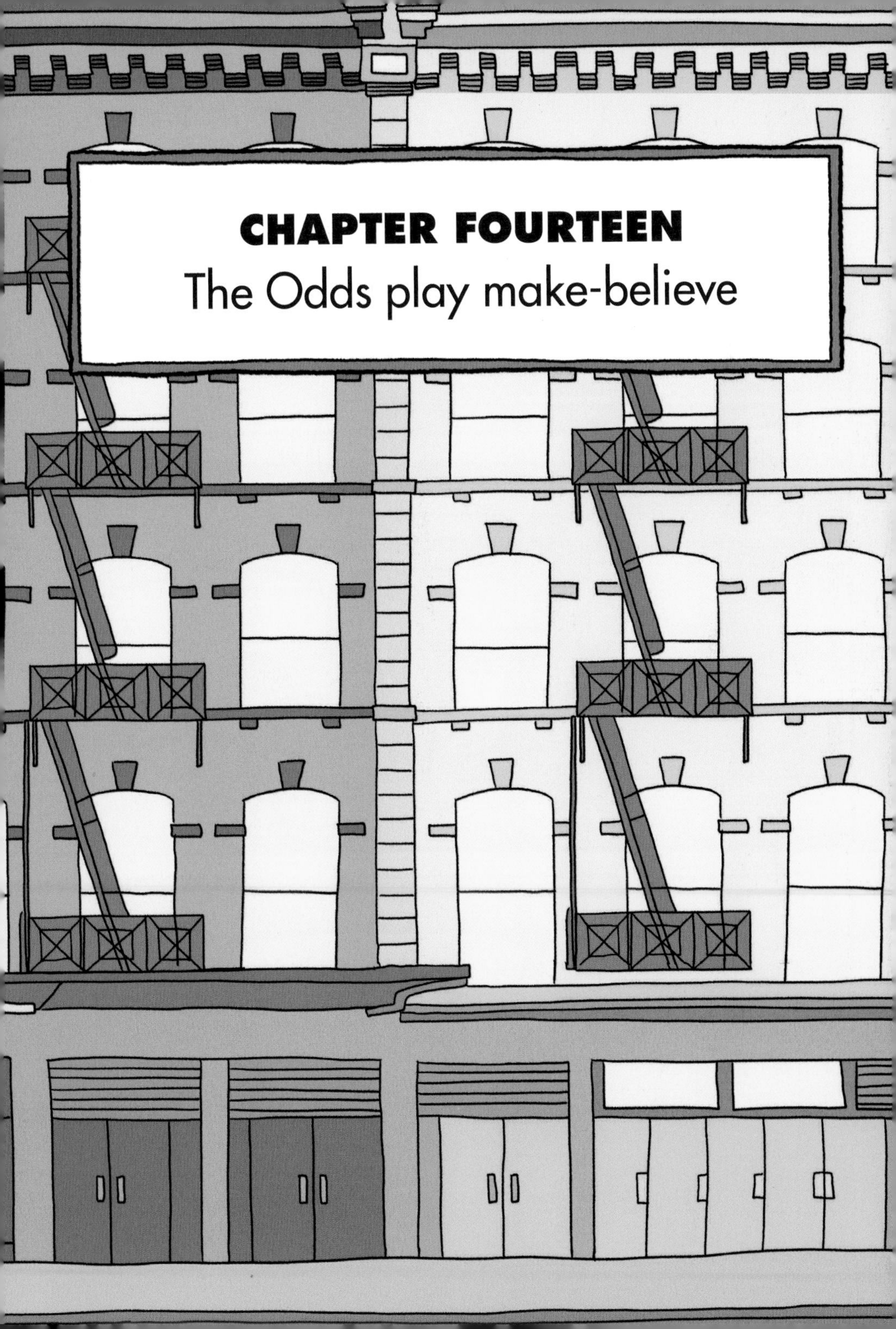

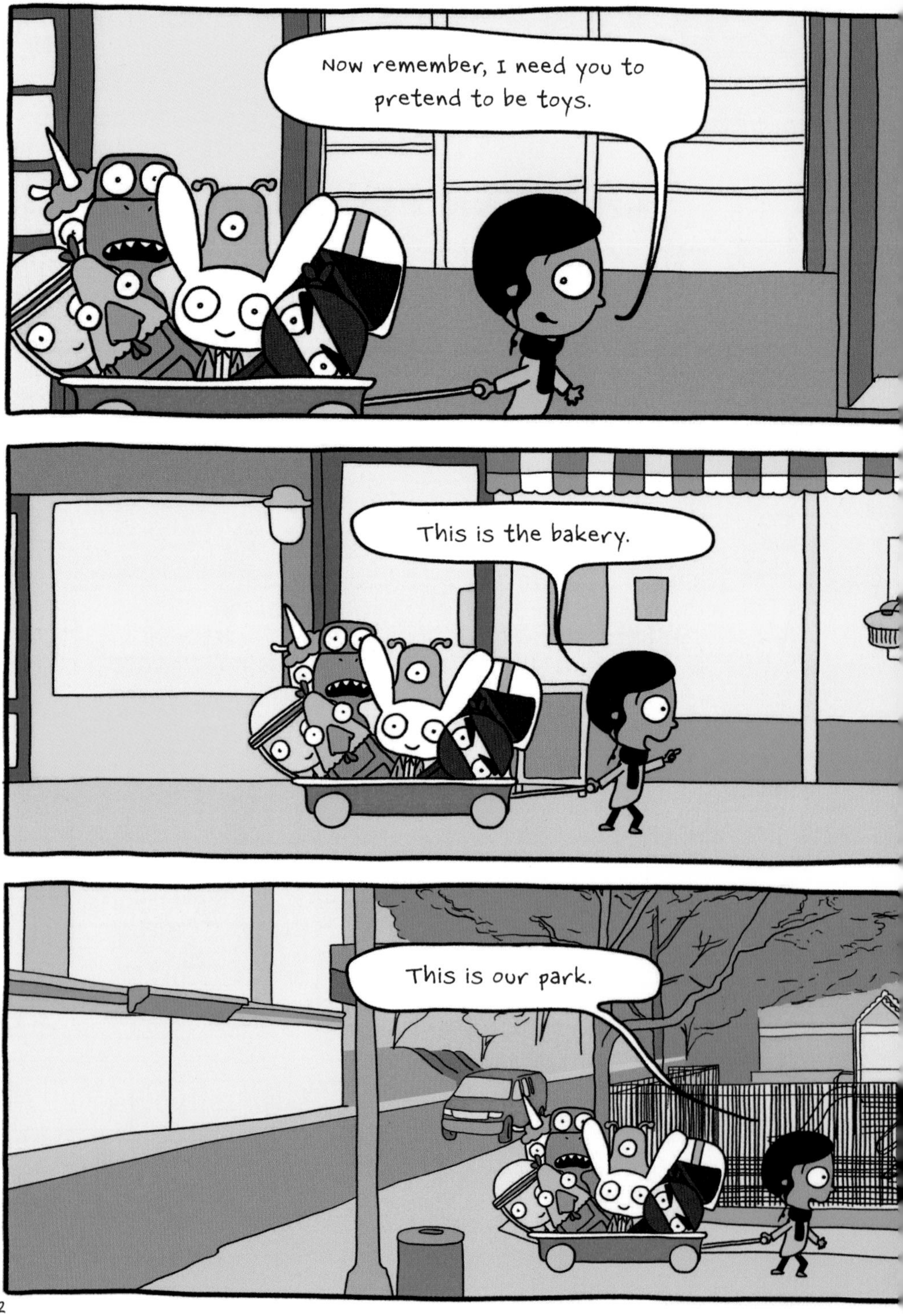
Now remember, I need you to pretend to be toys.
This is the bakery.
This is our park.

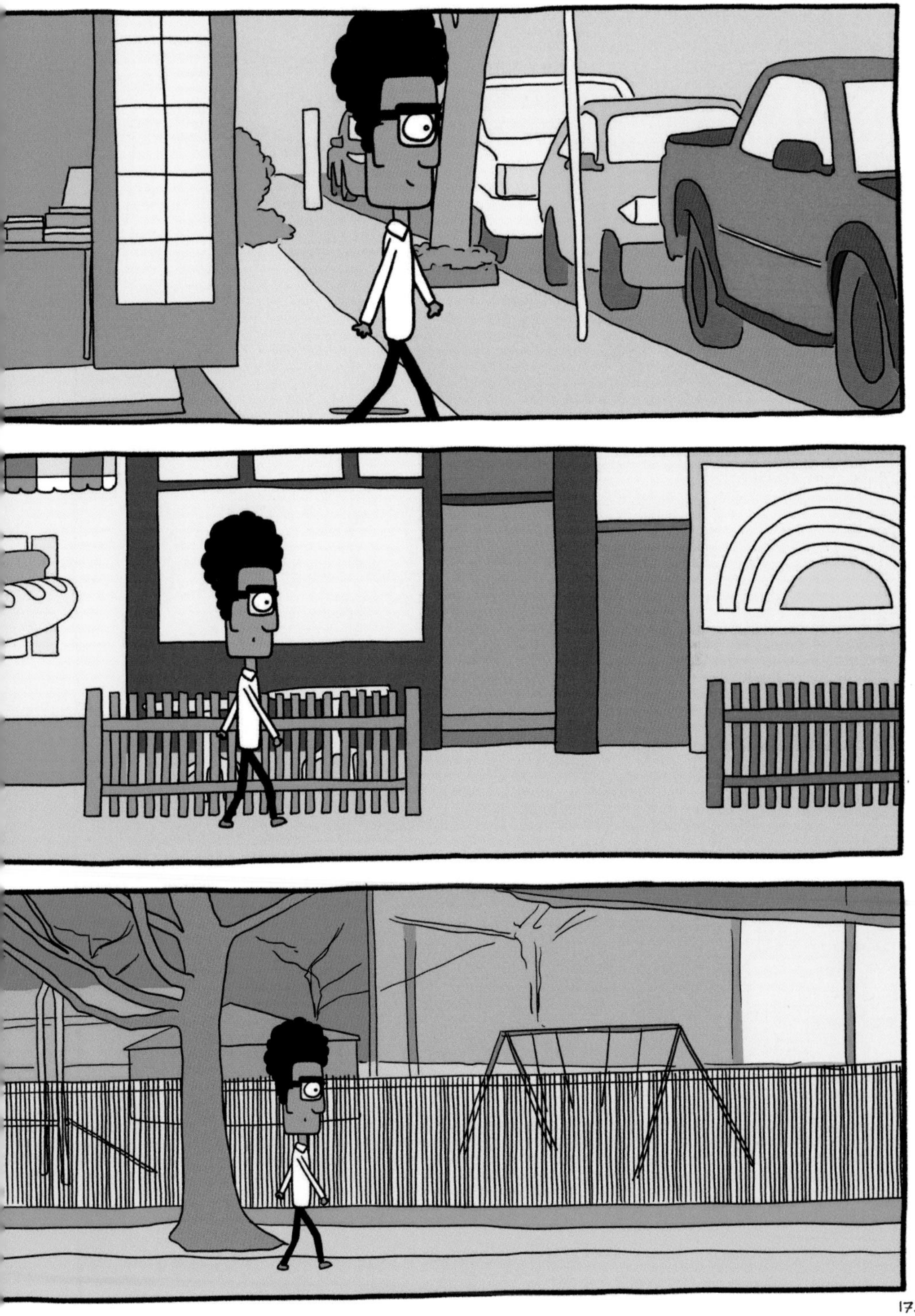

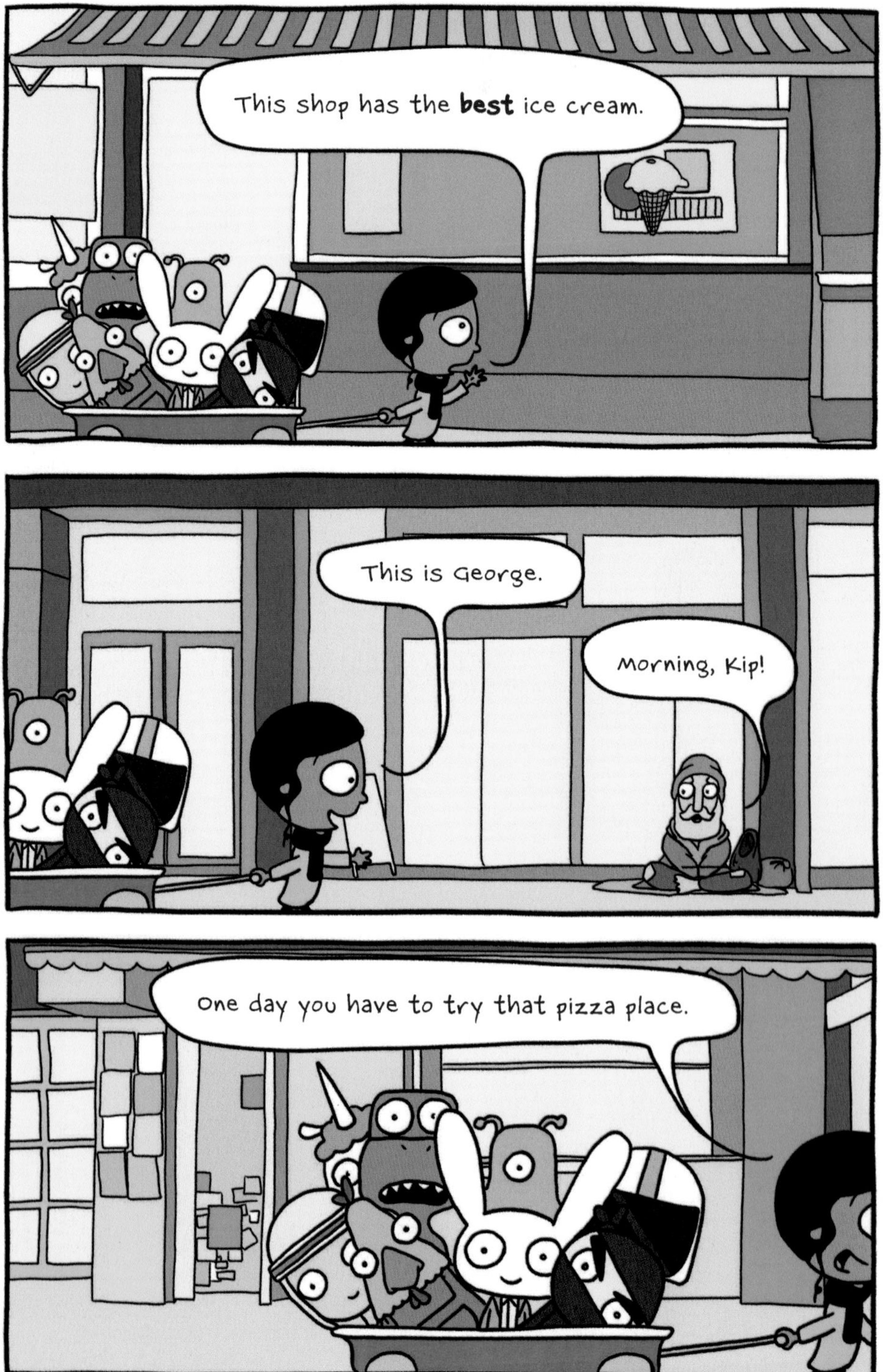
This shop has the **best** ice cream.
This is George.
Morning, Kip!
One day you have to try that pizza place.

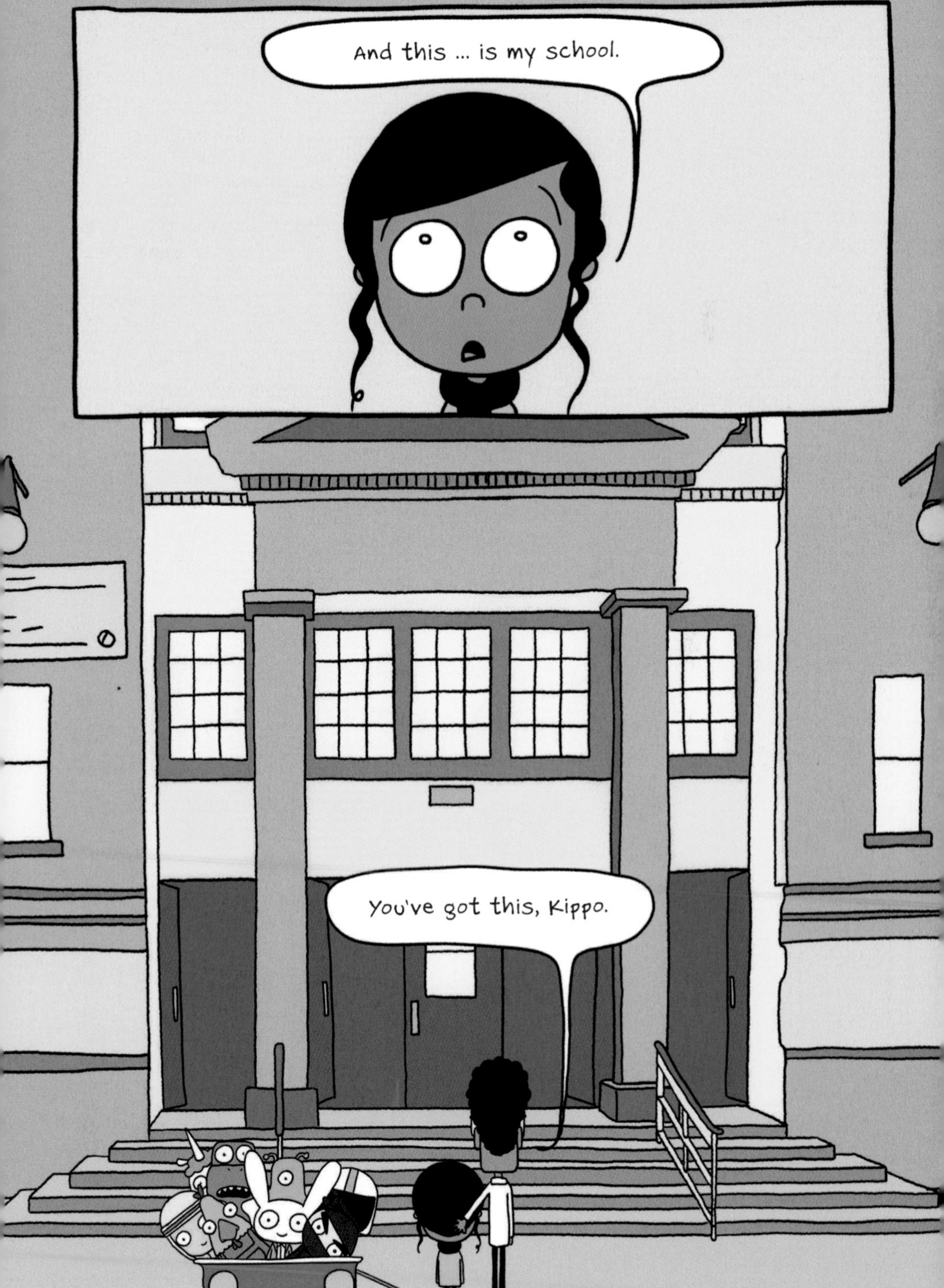
And this ... is my school.
You've got this, Kippo.

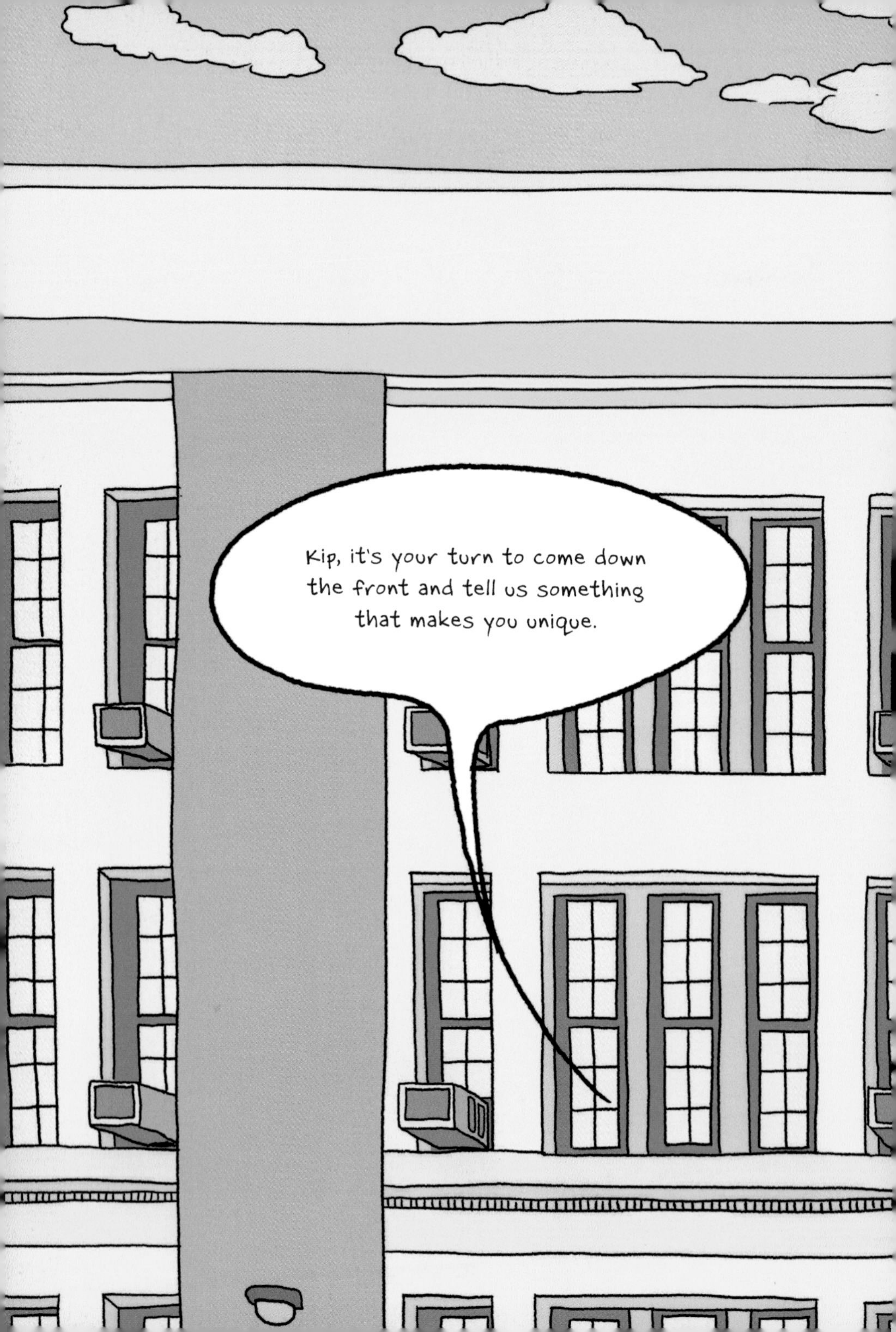
Kip, it's your turn to come down the front and tell us something that makes you unique.

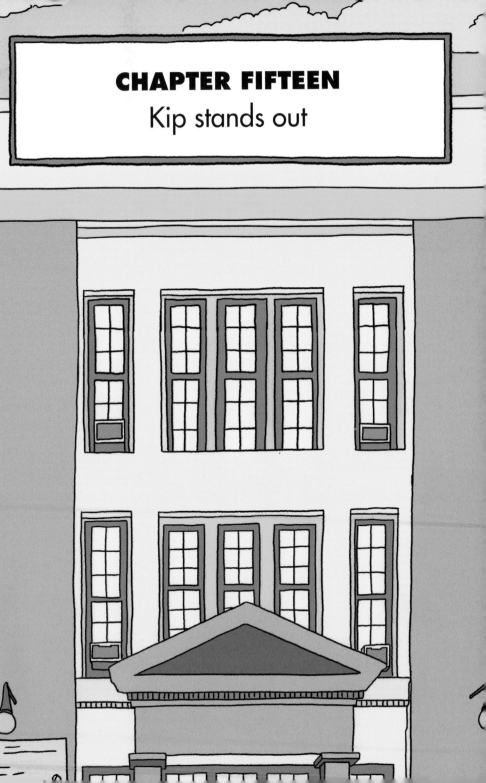

CHAPTER FIFTEEN
Kip stands out

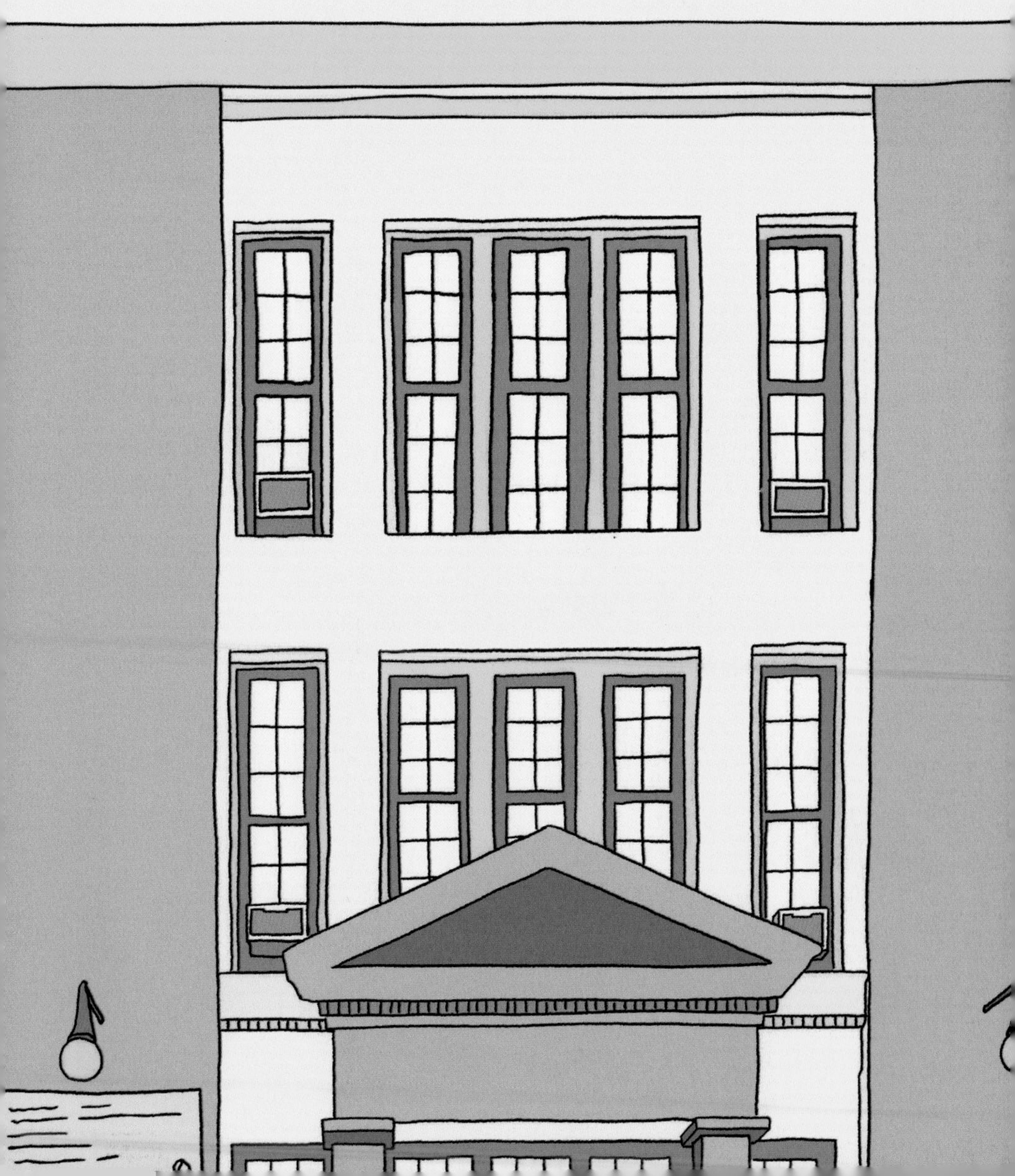

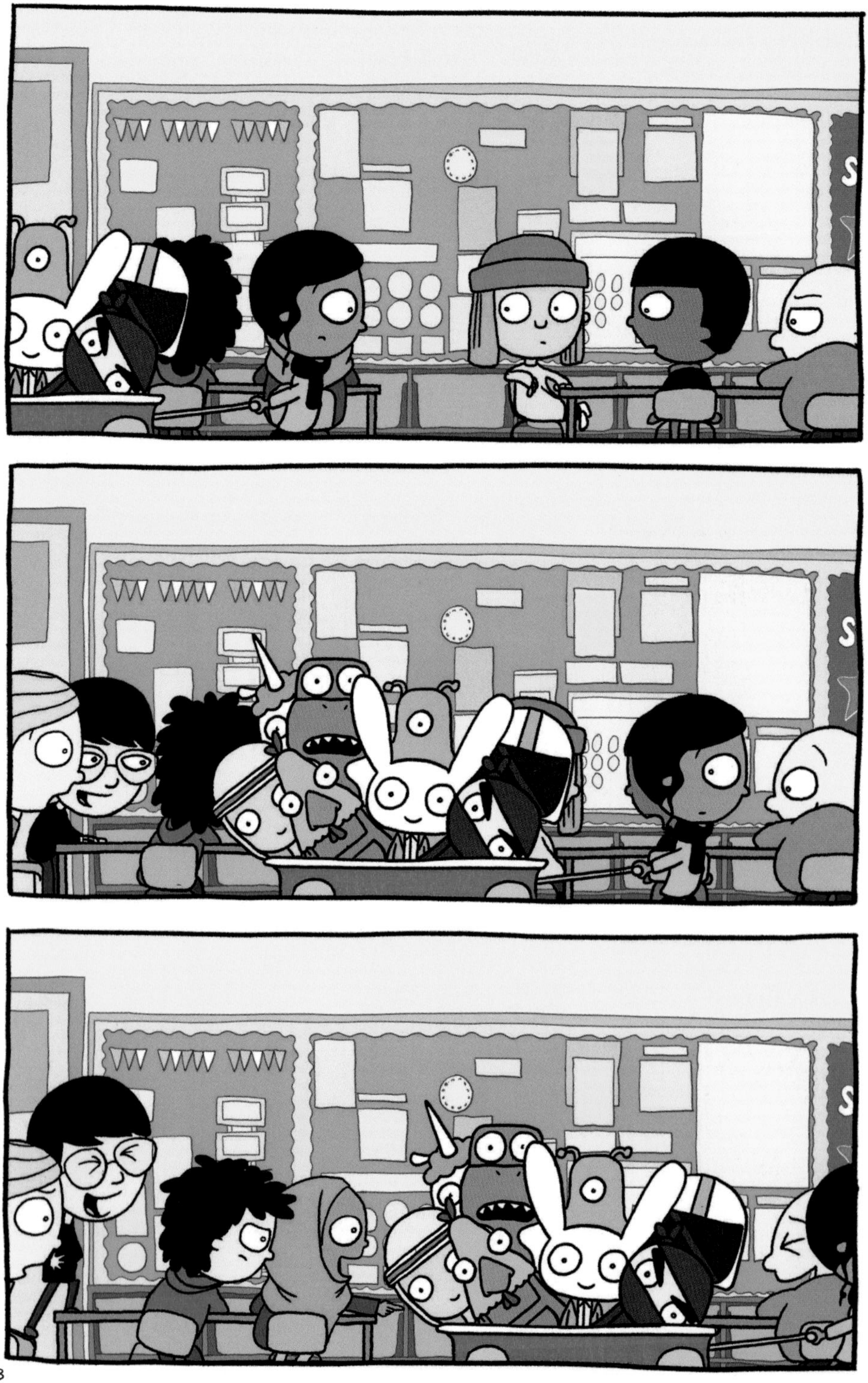

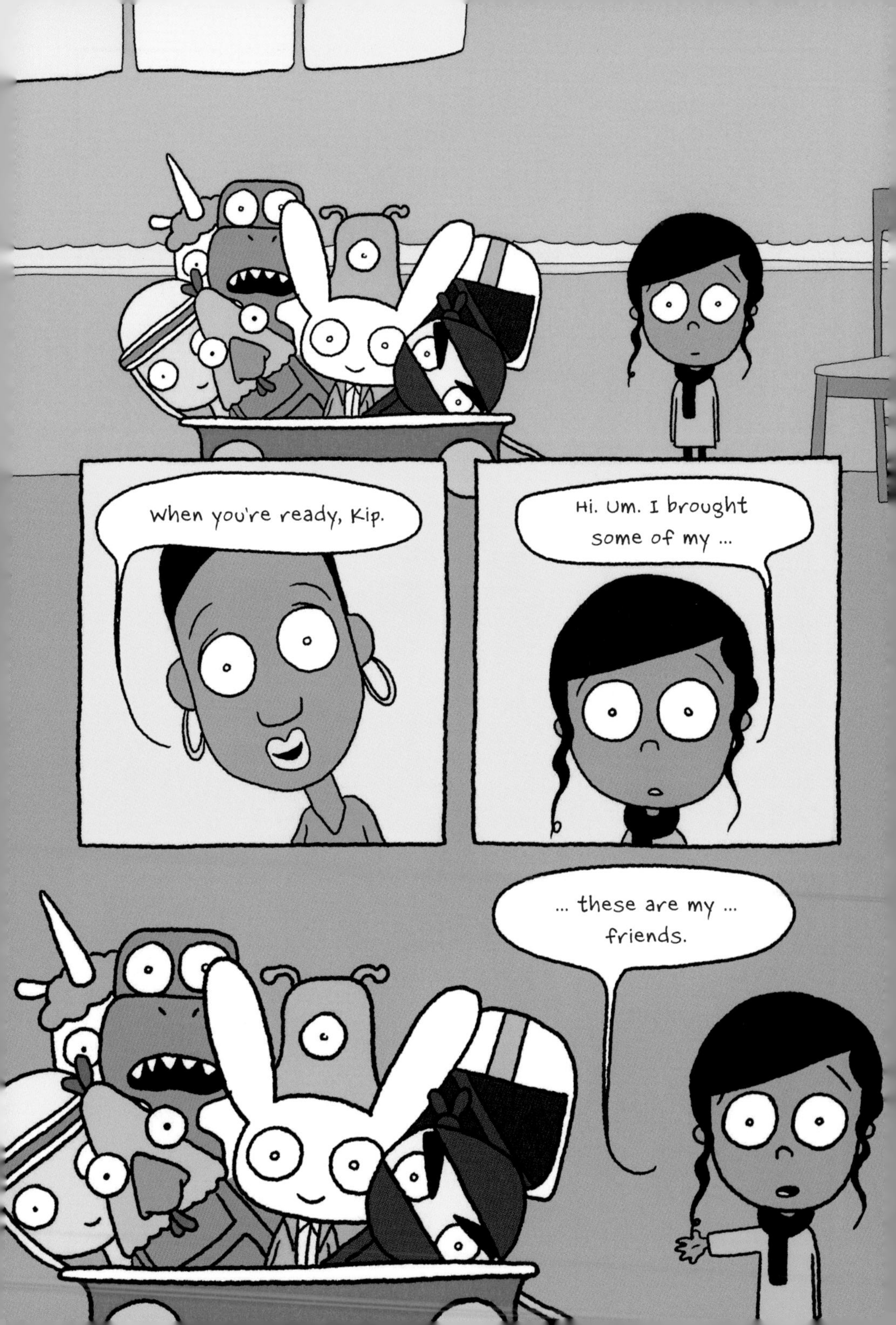
When you're ready, Kip.
Hi. Um. I brought some of my ...
... these are my ... friends.

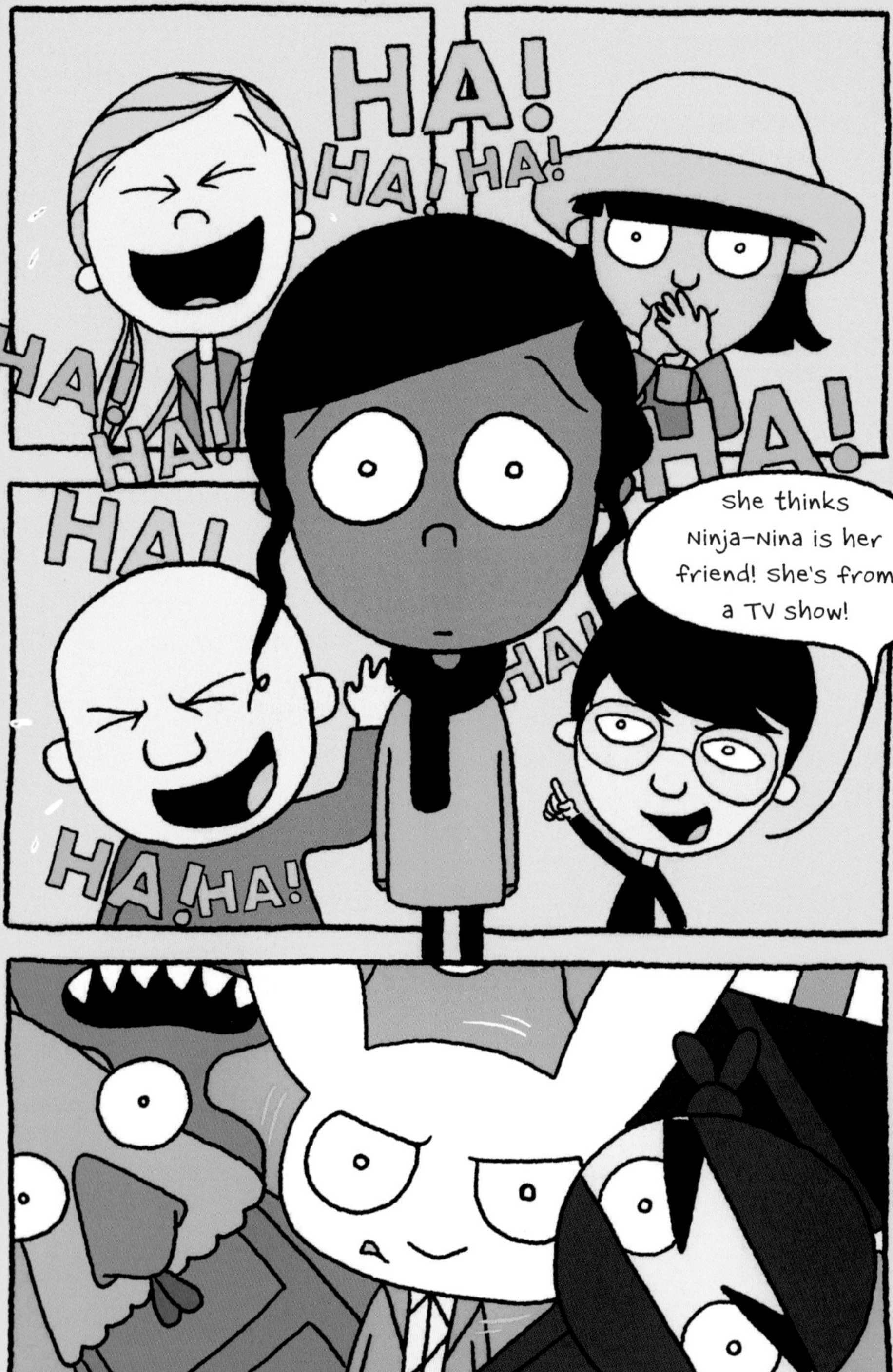
HA!
HA! HA!
HA!
HA!
HA!
HA!
HA!
she thinks Ninja-Nina is her friend! she's from a TV show!
HA!
HA! HA!

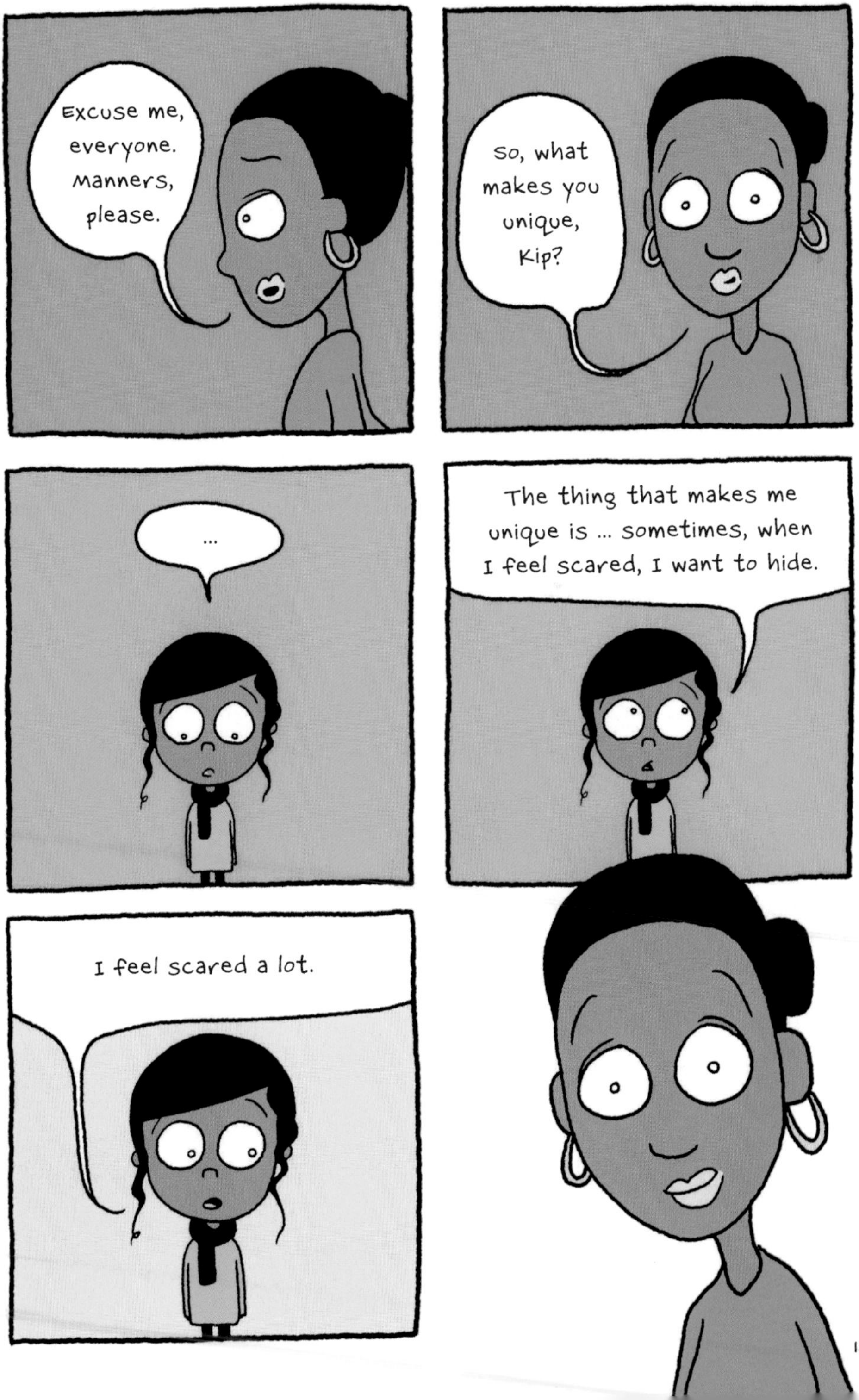
Excuse me, everyone. Manners, please.
So, what makes you unique, Kip?
...
The thing that makes me unique is ... sometimes, when I feel scared, I want to hide.
I feel scared a lot.

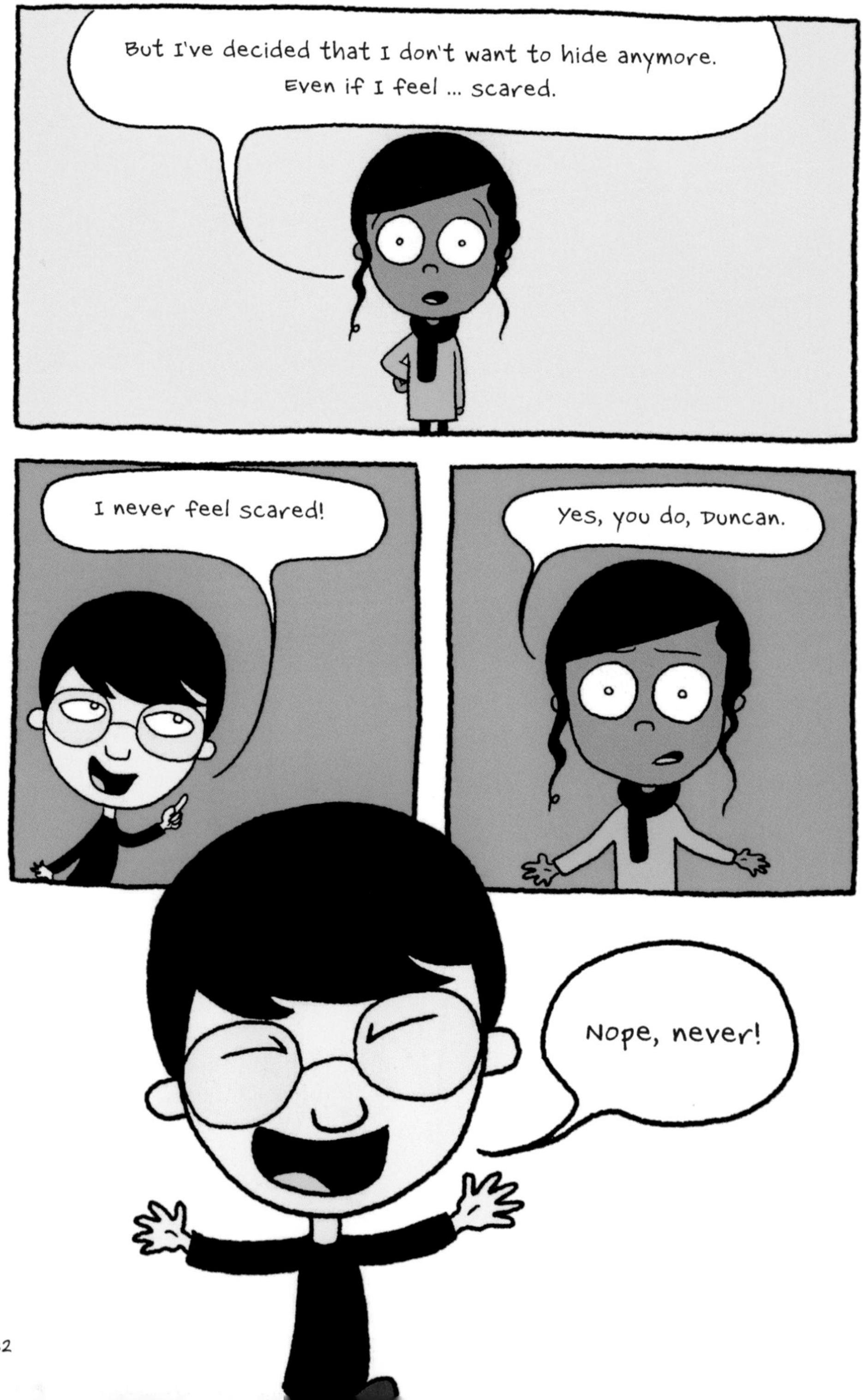
But I've decided that I don't want to hide anymore. Even if I feel ... scared.
I never feel scared!
Yes, you do, Duncan.
Nope, never!

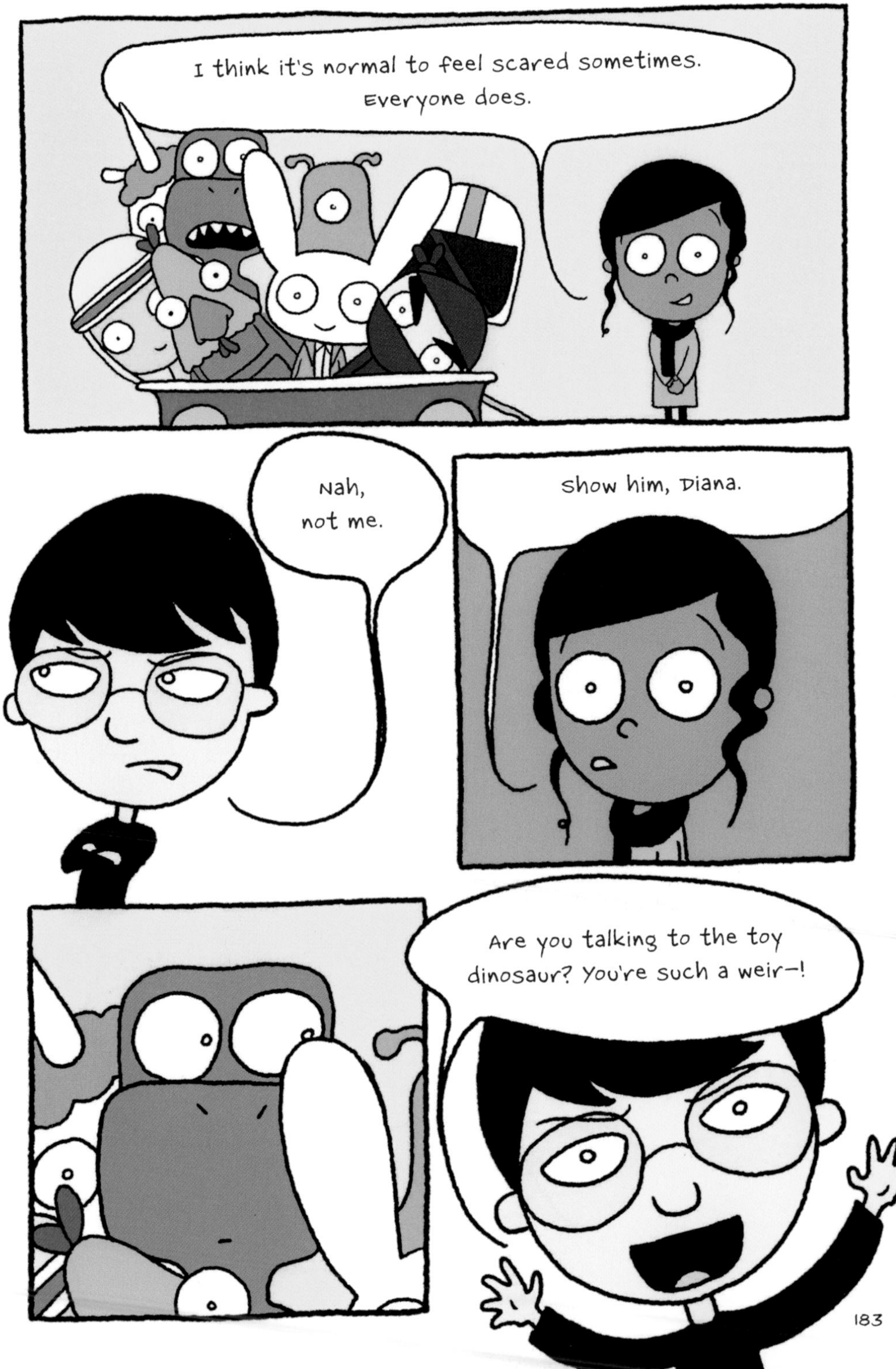
I think it's normal to feel scared sometimes. Everyone does.
Nah, not me.
Show him, Diana.
Are you talking to the toy dinosaur? You're such a weir—!

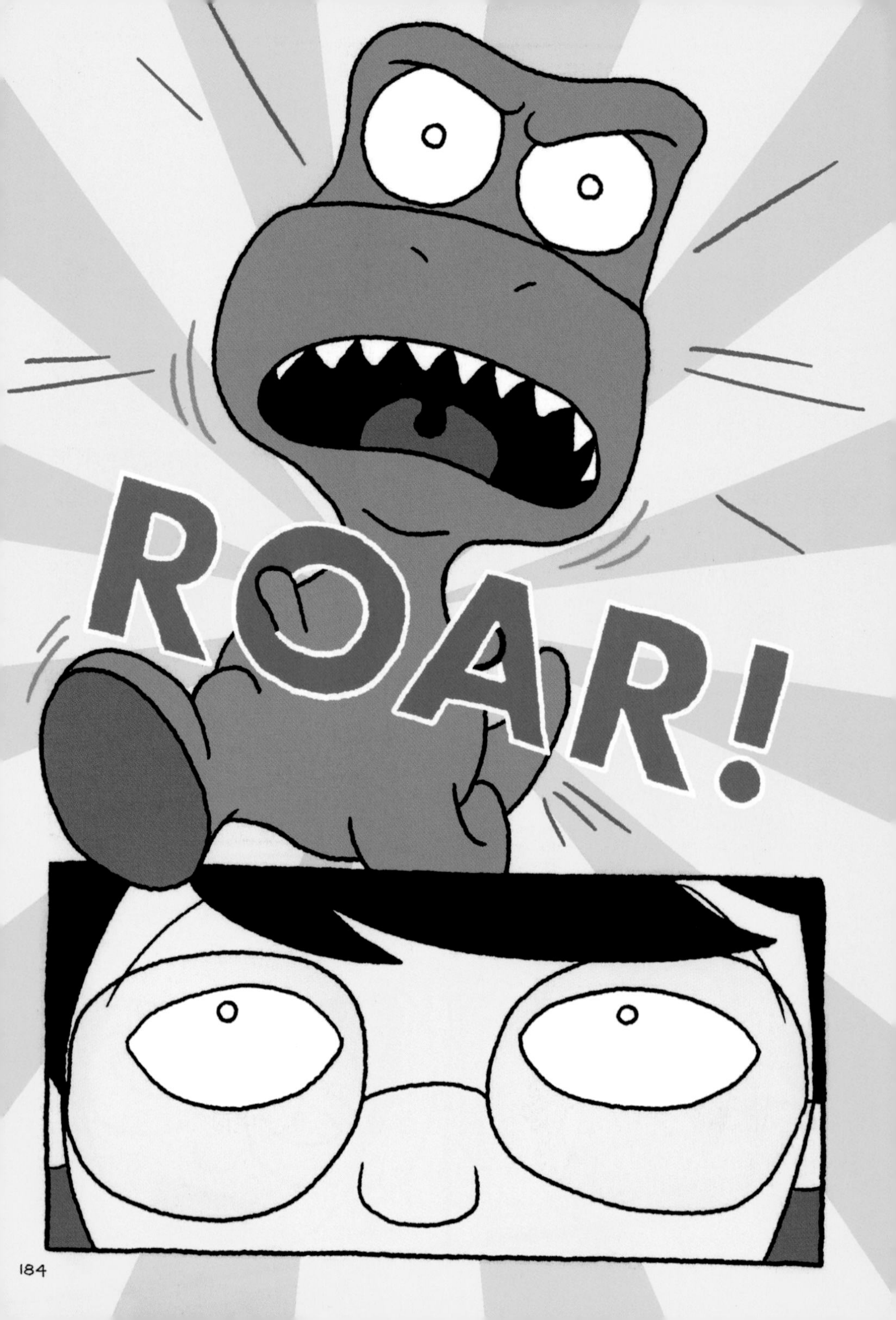
ROAR!

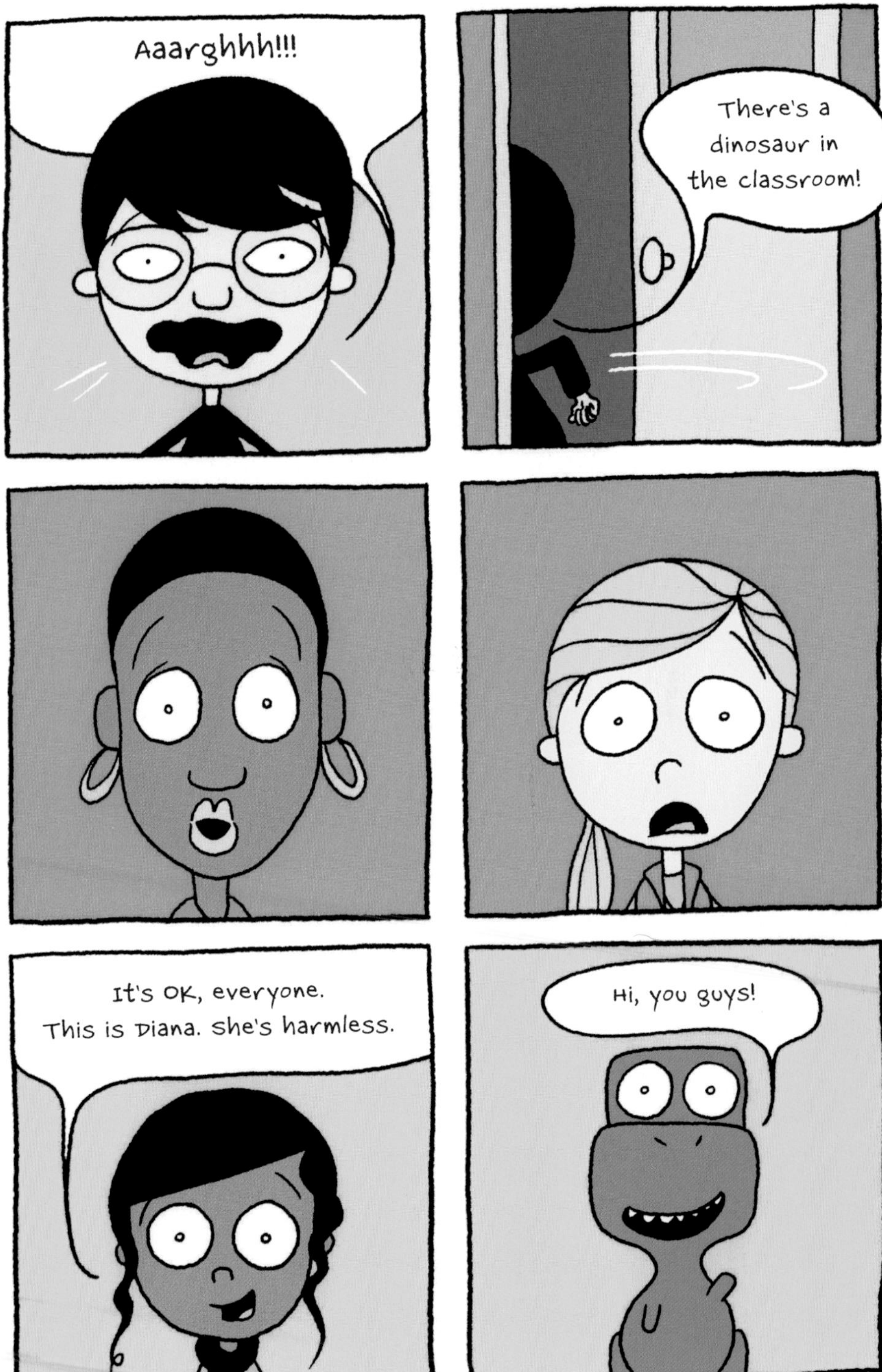
Aaarghhh!!!
There's a dinosaur in the classroom!
It's OK, everyone. This is Diana. She's harmless.
Hi, you guys!

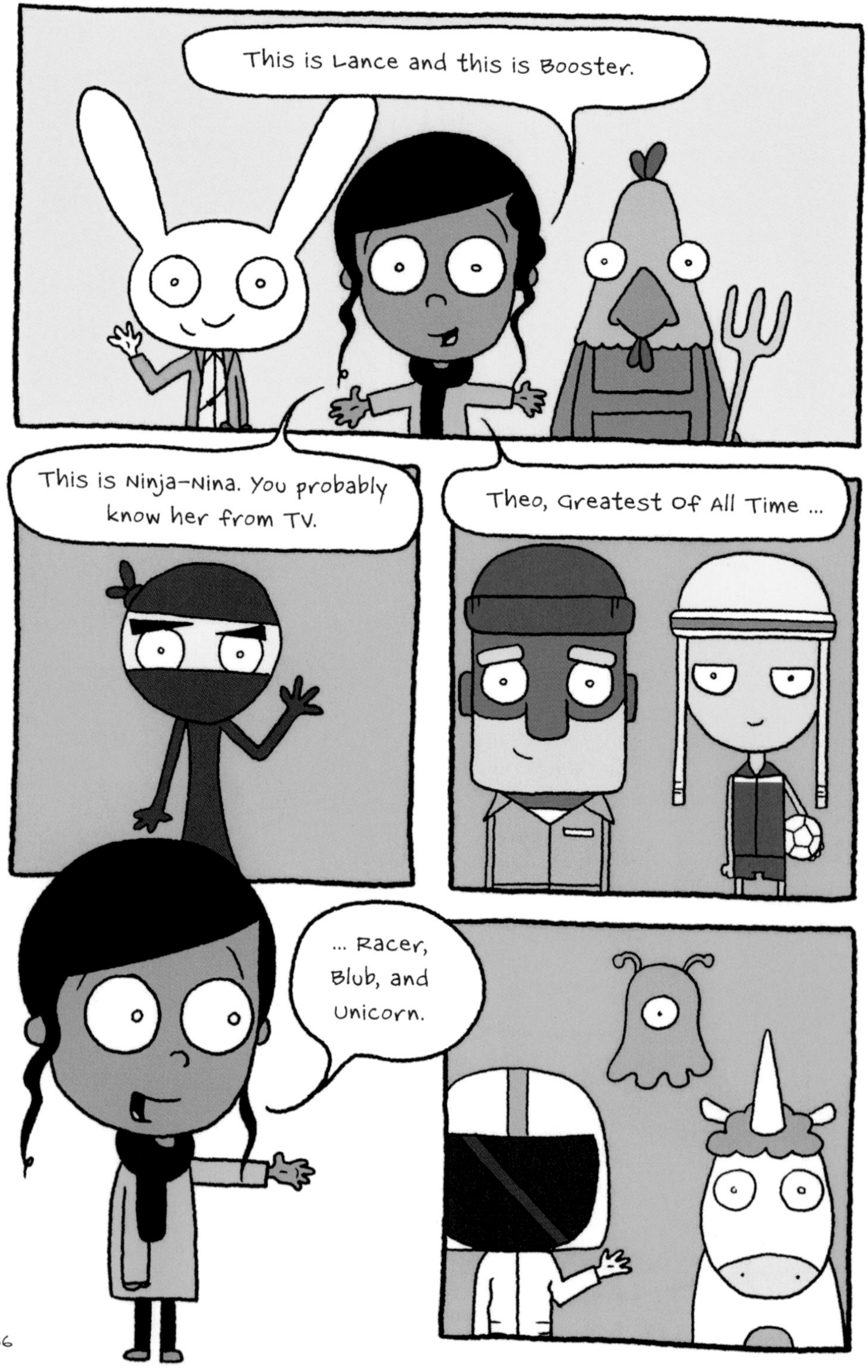

This is Lance and this is Booster.
This is Ninja-Nina. You probably know her from TV.
Theo, Greatest Of All Time ...
... Racer, Blub, and Unicorn.

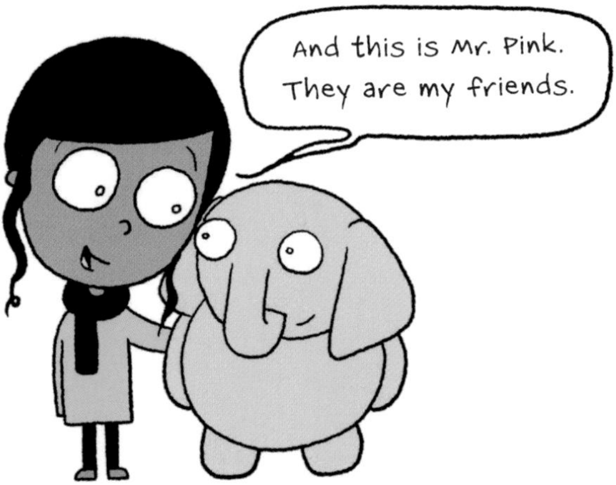
And this is Mr. Pink. They are my friends.

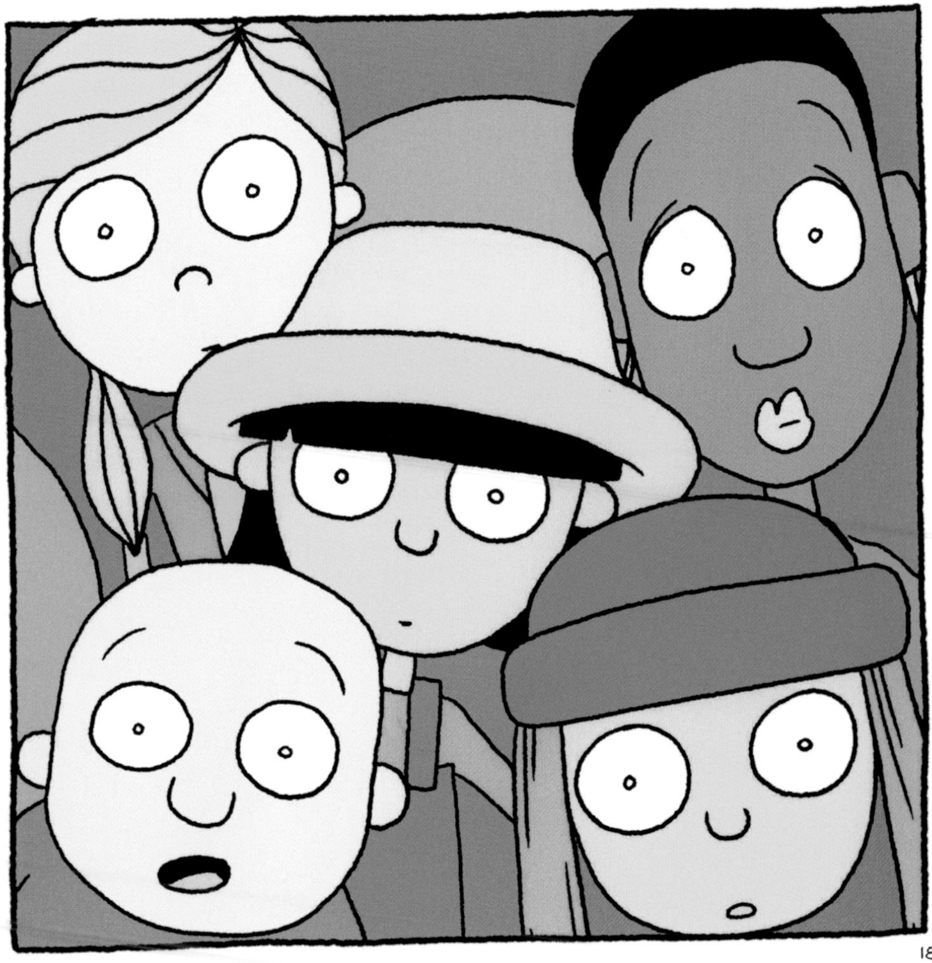

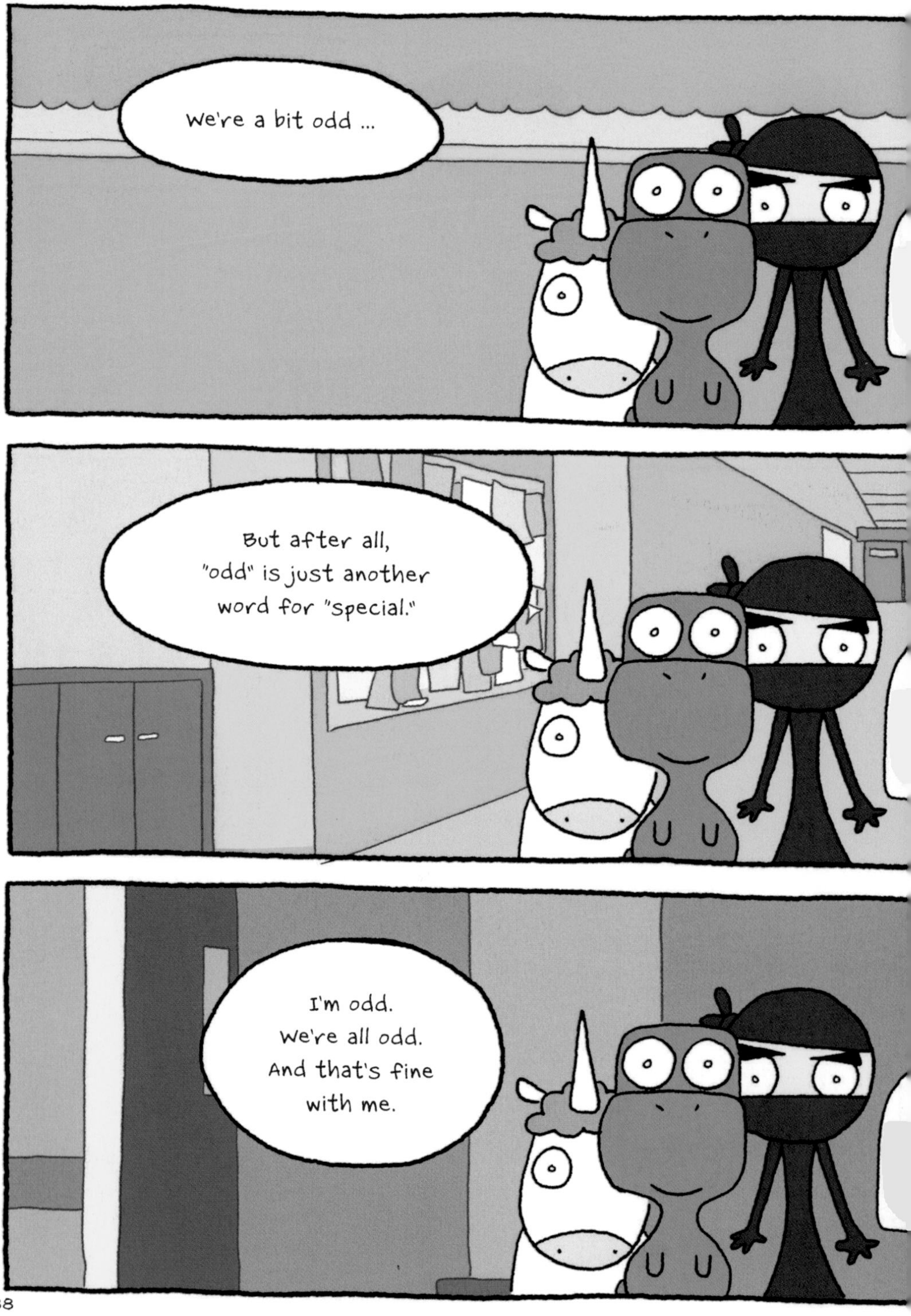
We're a bit odd ...
But after all, "odd" is just another word for "special."
I'm odd. We're all odd. And that's fine with me.

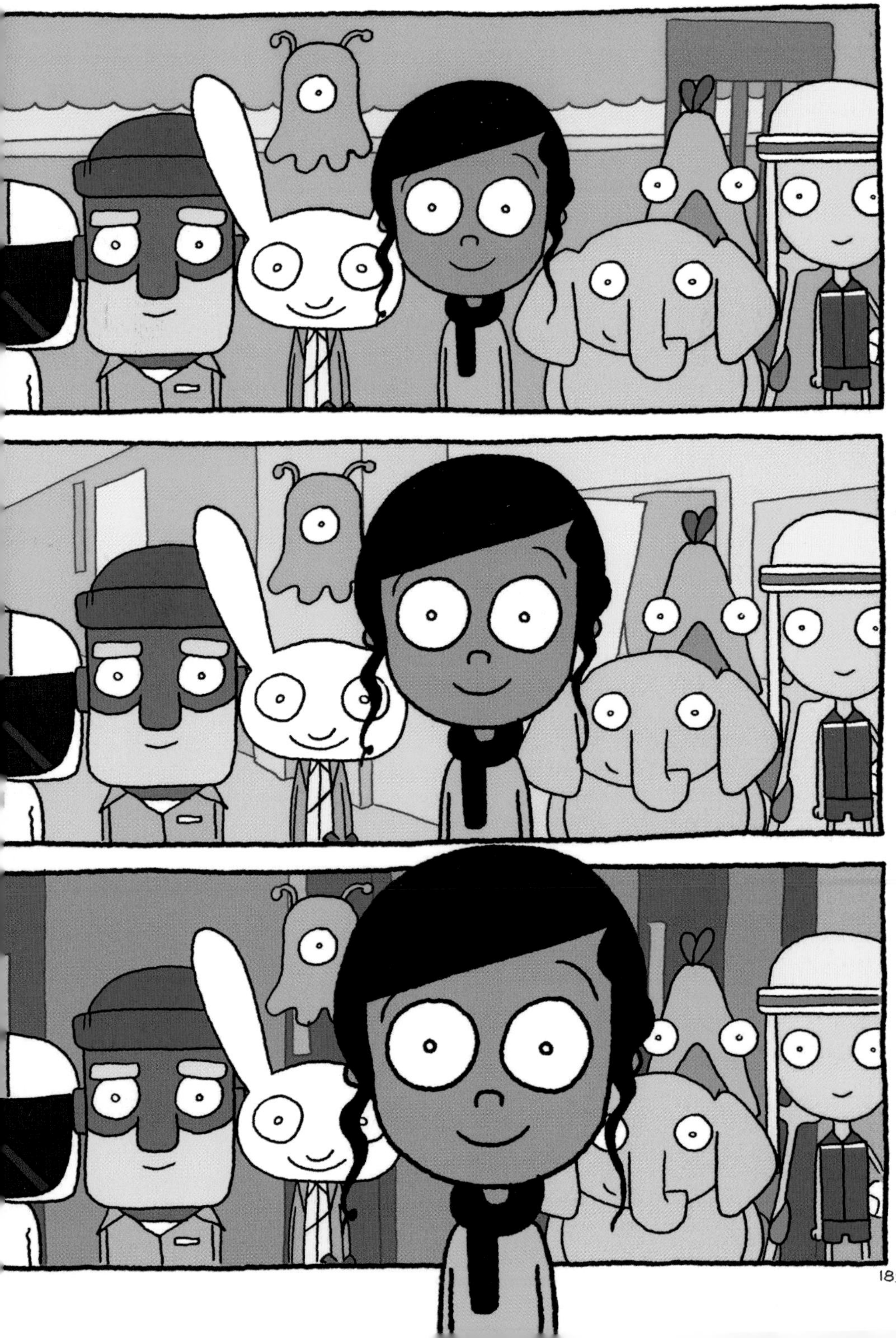

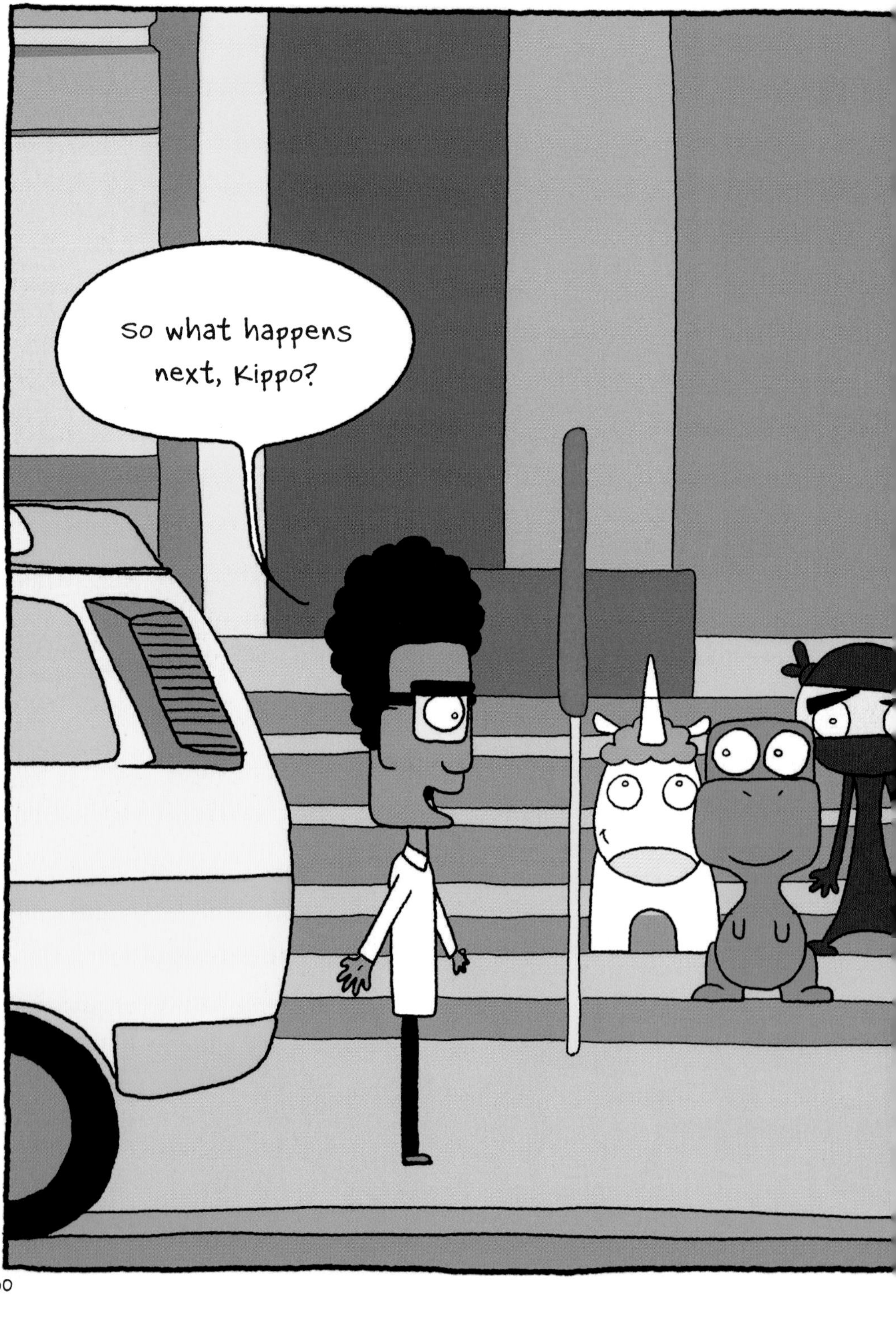
so what happens next, Kippo?

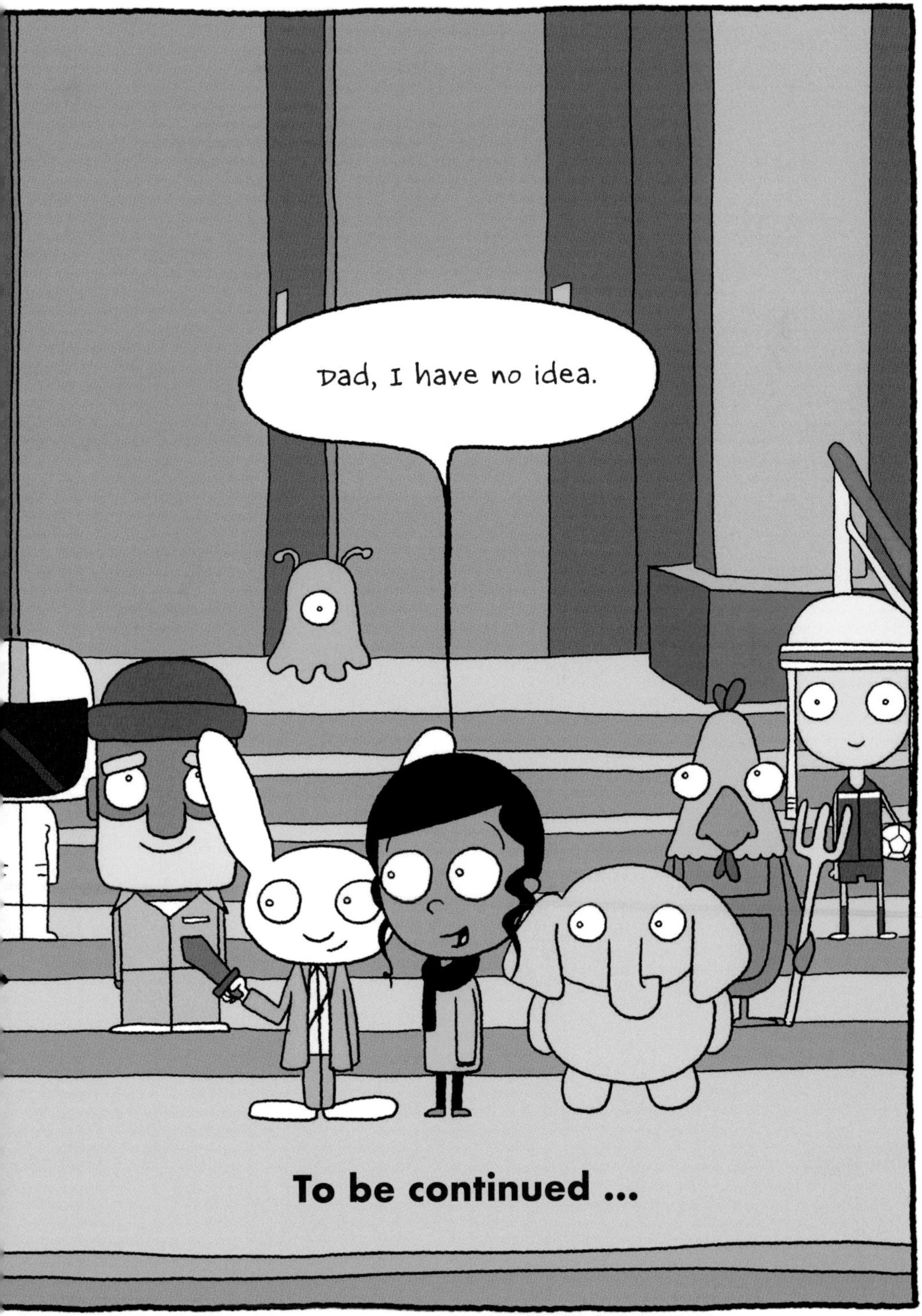
Dad, I have no idea.
To be continued ...

**Kids all over the world
are emailing Matt!**

**Who's your favorite Odd?
Tell Matt!**

matt.stanton@gmail.com

ACKNOWLEDGMENTS

This bit is like the credits at the end of a movie.

There are teams of people who work on getting this book from my imagination into your hands. They are some of the most wonderful people you could ever meet:

Chren Byng

David Linker

Emily Mannon

Anna Bernard

Andrea Vandergrift

Carolina Ortiz

Jessica Berg

Shannon Kelly

Kate Burnitt

Cristina Cappelluto

Jim Demetriou

Pauline O'Carolan

Elizabeth O'Donnell

Then there are teams at the printer, in the warehouse. There are fantastic people who talk to bookshops about *The Odds*. There are amazing humans working in bookstores, libraries, and schools all across the country who help make this book available for you to read.

To all of these people — thank you. You have made *The Odds* come to life.

To my publisher, Chren Byng. You helped me discover *The Odds* in one of my most difficult creative moments. From the bottom of my heart, thank you.

To my US editor, David Linker. I can't tell you how excited I am to see what you and your team have done with *The Odds*. Thank you.

To my wife and partner in all things, Beck Stanton. This book only exists because of you. You inspire me and compel me to create things that matter. Thank you.

To my kids, Bonnie, Boston, Miller, and Sully — you make my day, every day. Thank you.

And to you, the kids who have joined your imagination with mine in reading this book, you are so important, so creative, and you make the world a better place. Thank you.

Matt Stanton

Books by Matt Stanton

Funny Kid series

Funny Kid for President

Funny Kid Stand Up

Funny Kid Prank Wars

The Odds series

The Odds

Pea + Nut! picture books

Pea + Nut!

Pea + Nut Go for Gold!

Books That Drive Kids Crazy! picture books

with Beck Stanton:

This Is a Ball

Did You Take the B from My _ook?

The Red Book

Wait!

The Book That Never Ends

Self-Help for Babies picture books

with Beck Stanton:

Sleep 101

Whine Guide

Dummies for Suckers

One-Ingredient Cookbook

Fart Monster and Me series
with Tim Miller:

Fart Monster and Me: The Crash Landing
Fart Monster and Me: The New School
Fart Monster and Me: The Birthday Party
Fart Monster and Me: The Class Excursion

Fart Monster + Friends picture books
with Tim Miller:

There Is a Monster Under My Bed Who Farts
There Is a Monster Under My Christmas Tree Who Farts
There Is a Monster on My Holiday Who Farts
The Pirate Who Had to Pee
Dinosaur Dump
Don't Spew in Your Spacesuit
Burpzilla
Happy Farter's Day

Are you reading Funny Kid?

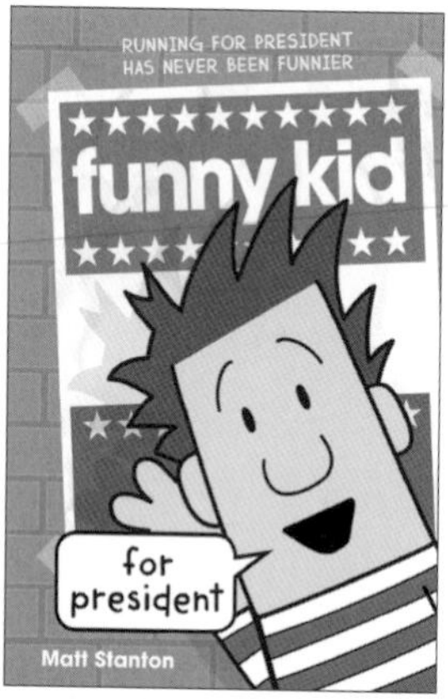
RUNNING FOR PRESIDENT
HAS NEVER BEEN FUNNIER
funny kid
for president
Matt Stanton

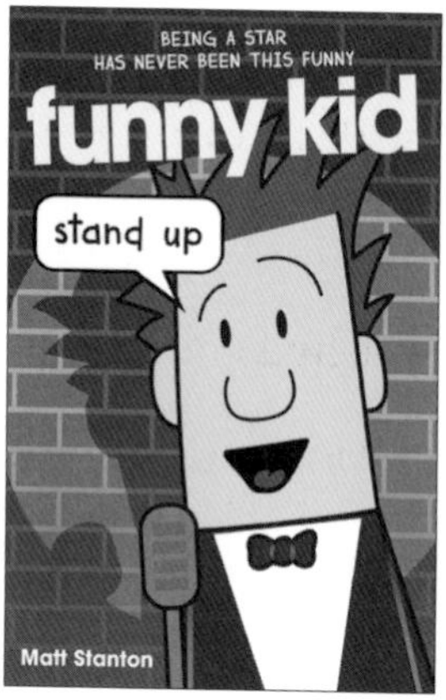
BEING A STAR
HAS NEVER BEEN THIS FUNNY
funny kid
stand up
Matt Stanton

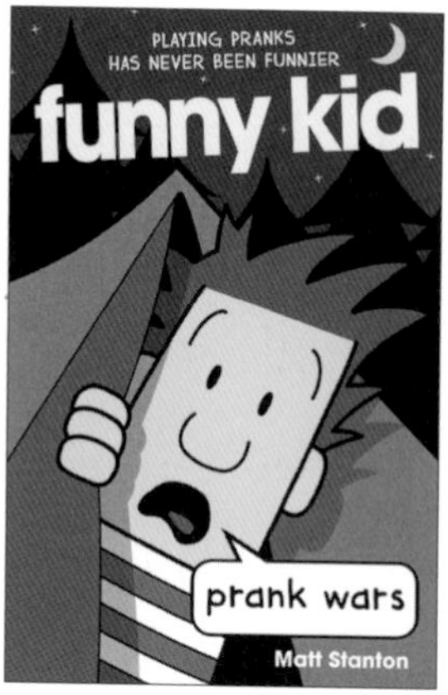
PLAYING PRANKS
HAS NEVER BEEN FUNNIER
funny kid
prank wars
Matt Stanton

Photo © Jennifer Blau

Matt Stanton is a bestselling children's author and illustrator who has sold more than one million books worldwide. His middle grade series Funny Kid debuted as the #1 Australian kids' book and has legions of fans across the globe. He has published such bestselling picture books as *There Is a Monster Under My Bed Who Farts*, *This Is a Ball*, and *Pea + Nut!*, and produces a daily YouTube show for kids. He lives and works in Sydney, Australia, with his wife, bestselling author Beck Stanton, and their children.

mattstanton.net

Come and subscribe to Matt's YouTube Channel!

Matt Stanton's
**funny
drawing
show**

We learn to draw funny stuff!

Talk about how to write funny stories!

funny kid

LIVE!

Now, that's
Book launch
what you call a

YEP! WE SHOT IT OUT OF A CANNON!

And sometimes we launch a book out of a cannon!

MattStantonTV
youtube.com/mattstanton